THE MIRACLE PRINCE

THE RAVEN'S VEIL

William Edmonds

FIRST EDITION: 2021

ISBN: 978-1-8383004-2-5

www.williamedmonds.com

Edited by Belle Manuel
Cover design by 100Covers
Formatted by BB eBooks

Harramore Glossary

Useful Terms

Basketball – The most popular sport among Nephilim and the origin of the Ordinary game with the same name. Fifteen points are awarded for a basket, five for handicapping an opponent with a Seela, and one penalty point is awarded for fouls.

Big Five – A term used to refer to the first five Guardians; they are all brothers. Generally considered the most powerful Guardians

Golden Pearl – An object owned by Marfin, allowing him to possess and live in the body of any creature he wishes. Often referred to as simply, 'The Pearl'

Guardians – A group of immortal beings responsible for managing the world; each is responsible for a different element of the planet (Guardian of Fire, Guardian of the Sea, etc.)

Harragram – Harramore's leading social network. A place to post photos, message friends, etc.

Harranet – Harramore's internal internet. Not connected to the Ordinaries' internet

Nephilim – The descendants of the Guardians, gifted with the power to use Seelas

Ordinary – A regular, non-Nephilim human without the ability to use Seelas

Seela – The powers that Nephilim inherit from their Guardian ancestor(s)

Seelastry – The study of and practice of using Seelas

The Guardians

The Big Five

Rei – The King Guardian; Alaric's father. The eldest of the Big Five brothers. Killed by Naidos prior to Alaric's birth.

Ceus – The Guardian of the Sky; the de facto King Guardian after Rei's death. The second oldest of the Big Five.

Solo – The Guardian of the Earth. The third oldest of the Big Five.

Marfin – The Guardian of the Sea; typically takes the form of a dolphin. The fourth of the Big Five brothers.

Naidos – The Guardian of Death and the youngest of the five brothers. Turned against Rei and his other brothers in search of power.

Other Guardians

Ar – The Guardian of Air

Bella – The Guardian of Love and Beauty

Cria – The Guardian of Creation

Forto – The Guardian of Strength

Fura – The Guardian of Fire

Guerris – The Guardian of War

Jeeline – The Guardian of Cats

Luna – The Guardian of the Moon

Master Ogden – Headmaster/Guardian of Oakwood

Orm – The Guardian of Snakes; Naidos' closest ally

Paz – The Guardian of the Mind

Seeba – The Guardian of Knowledge and Literature

Sol – The Guardian of the Sun

Sort – The Guardian of Happiness and Good Fortune

Wawet – The Guardian of Wolves

If you'd like to know more about William Edmonds and 'The Miracle Prince' series, please visit his website at williamedmonds.com. And if you'd like to receive exclusive content and updates on future releases, join the William Edmonds Readers Club!

CHAPTER 1

CEUS CHECKED HIS watch. It was two minutes to midnight, and they'd be here any moment.

He rarely had visitors into his office, for it was levitating thirty thousand feet in the air. But it was probably for the best anyway, as this place wasn't exactly the most welcoming.

It was lit only by a single candle on his otherwise bare desk, giving off the dimmest of dim lights. The stuffed bats and birds that cluttered his shelves made the atmosphere only spookier. If it hadn't been for the ceiling—an exact replica of the daytime sky—it would've taken the happiness out of even the jolliest man on Earth.

One minute to the hour. Ceus looked up towards the bronze door of his office. It remained shut but then again, what was he expecting? It was still only one minute to midnight, and he knew they were always exactly on time: not a minute early, not a minute late.

Gently, he fingered the large crystal orb he had on

his desk. He stared into it as though hoping to see something new amongst the smoke inside. But he wasn't that naïve. It had been stating the same thing now for thousands of years, nothing ever changing. As much as he wished it were wrong, everything that orb had ever told him had proven true. And he knew the moment was coming.

Ceus' watch beeped. It was midnight and sure enough, they were there. There was a thundering knock on the heavy metal door, and Ceus rose out of his throne to go and answer it. He must have been at least eight feet tall and was an incredibly intimidating figure. His breastplate made his chest seem even larger than it truly was, his crooked nose sitting conspicuously above his brown, bushy beard. However, his most prominent feature was his hands. They were the size of dinner plates and he'd no doubt be able to pick up a fully grown man with one hand and no trouble. It worked to his advantage of course, as when he opened the door, his hands were the only pair in existence large enough to turn the knob. That, combined with its elevation, was the office's entire security and he'd never had a break-in before.

As he pulled the door open slowly, the two men who greeted him could scarcely have looked more different. The one on the right was barely four feet tall and had the exact appearance of a garden gnome with his red cone-shaped hat, long white pointed beard, and knee-high wellingtons. The other man, however, looked about six feet tall. He was dark of face and his hair was short and perfectly groomed, in perfect harmony with his pin-striped suit and tie.

'Good evening, Solo,' Ceus said to the gnome in his extraordinarily deep voice. 'To you, Mr Iglehart, also. Please do enter.'

The man called Solo and the one called Mr Iglehart followed Ceus to his desk. They all walked in complete contrast to each other: Solo tiptoed like he was up to mischief; Iglehart strolled with a nonchalant swagger, while Ceus seemed to march around, aware of the kingly presence being the Guardian of the Sky gave him.

'Please, gentlemen, do sit down,' Ceus invited, gesturing towards the two chairs opposite his desk. The guests obliged, and Iglehart sat comfortably with his legs crossed while Solo shuffled on his seat nervously. After a few seconds, he decided to kneel on the chair, seemingly to at least come close to the height of the adjacent man, or perhaps to hide the fact that his feet didn't reach the floor.

'You two are probably wondering why I decided to summon you here at such an hour,' Ceus began. 'The reason is, I have some important news to tell you. I have already informed Marfin, but the nature of his condition rendered it impractical for him to attend tonight. I'm afraid this is some worrying business. I have reason to believe that what we feared has now happened.'

Iglehart stared at Ceus blankly as Solo shuffled uncomfortably in his seat, the corner of his mouth twitching as he spoke. 'Y-you m-mean,' he said in his squeaky voice, as if not saying it would stop it being true, 'that the-the Veil…'

'Has been torn, yes,' Ceus said, bowing his head solemnly. 'The prophecy has always said it would happen. I was hoping it wouldn't come to this. However, if its predictions continue to be correct, we need to be prepared.'

'That's what we're going on?' Iglehart asked incredulously. 'A prophecy? I mean, surely you must know, predicting the future, prognostication isn't the most exact science.'

'I am well aware of the pitfalls of prognostication, Hal, having studied it for thousands of years,' Ceus asserted. 'However, this prophecy has proven reliable thus far.'

'I'm sorry, but surely we can't rely exclusively on one prophecy,' Iglehart countered. 'If it was created thousands of years ago, it can't have predicted everything.'

'Well, of course not. It doesn't mention an incompetent governor, for starters,' Ceus said bitterly, making Iglehart look suddenly less comfortable.

'I've won the last three elections. I think we'll let the people decide on my competence,' Iglehart said through gritted teeth once he'd regained his composure.

'By lying to the people,' Solo snapped, 'telling them the disappearance of Naidos was some master plan of yours. You had nothing to do with it at all. It was a pure stroke of luck that Alaric was born when you happened to be Governor.'

'We digress, gentlemen,' Ceus said with a raised voice before Iglehart could open his mouth to retort. 'After the death of Rei, I was appointed to be in charge of the Guardians for the time being—'

'Yes, appointed by yourself,' Iglehart snarled.

'SILENCE!' Ceus thundered, hammering his fists down on the table so hard, the entire room seemed to tremor. Solo almost fell off his seat and Iglehart froze, his face expressionless with shock.

'We, the other Guardians, approved this measure,'

Solo said, his lips thin under his white beard.

'Thank you, Solo,' Ceus sighed before turning to Iglehart. '*Nothing*, I repeat, *nothing*, gives you the right to speak to a Guardian like that, Hal, even if you are the Governor of Harramore. Do you hear me?'

Iglehart shuddered and nodded, Solo smirking boyishly.

'Now,' Ceus went on, 'I needed to brief you on the matter. If the Veil is indeed torn, then that poses great threats not only to Harramore but to the Ordinaries as well. Already, reports of ghost sightings in the Main World have skyrocketed.'

'F-forgive me f-for interrupting,' Iglehart hesitated, 'but are Ordinaries not always reporting ghost sightings?'

'Yes, they are,' Ceus said. 'There's rarely any truth to them, but these ones seem too similar for it to be a coincidence. Always the same thing—fuzzy apparitions of deceased loved ones, voices in their heads. There's something to these reports. I wish it weren't true, but I had been expecting it. After that incident with Alaric and Rei at the Land of the Dead, I suspected the moment had come. And unfortunately, once there is a tear in something like this, it only gets bigger. Ideally, therefore, the best thing to do would be to fix it as soon as possible.'

There were a few moments of silence in the room as Solo and Iglehart took this in. Iglehart remained focused on Ceus as if expecting him to say more, while Solo stared down at the floor. He'd realised the truth.

'But we can't fix it,' Solo said weakly. 'No living Guardian can; not even Rei would've been able to. The one we need has been missing forever…lost,' he said.

'Indeed,' Ceus sighed. 'So, that means our only option is to prepare for the worst. Now, Solo, I need you to keep an eye on Alaric…from a distance. Keep him out of trouble; his safety is of the utmost importance. Hal, I cannot intervene with your governing of Harramore, but I suggest you increase security, especially around Oakwood. Be ready for another war. Is that understood?'

Solo nodded, Iglehart maintaining a neutral expression as if musing on what Ceus had told him. 'I'll consider the necessary measures in the morning,' he said.

Ceus stared into Iglehart's eyes. He knew perfectly well what Iglehart was thinking. He could just do nothing and pretend there was no problem. But what he'd learnt from fourteen years of working with him was that any efforts to persuade him otherwise would be futile.

'Very well, then,' Ceus said, at last, breaking the tension in the room. 'Solo, I trust you to do a good job and Hal, please consider these measures carefully. Your reputation in history is at stake.'

And from Iglehart's expression, it was evident that something about those last words had stuck with him. And it was a good job Ceus didn't realise how. For if he had, he may have wished he'd never said them.

CHAPTER 2

ALARIC STILL HEARD his father's voice every day and night. It had been several weeks, and it was still there, in his head.

No one else had ever noticed it. Even when Alaric heard the voice in a room full of other people, he was the only one who did so. On one occasion, he'd been watching a documentary about Ancient Egypt with his adoptive family, the Trolleys. He stared ahead at the image on the screen of the sphinx guarding the Great Pyramid, admiring how it cut out most of the horizon.

Been thousands of years since the sphinx has been called into action, he heard a deep, booming voice say inside his head.

'You mean, it comes to life?' Alaric said, assuming it was his adoptive father, Mr Trolley, who'd spoken. He knew it was not unusual for statues to spring into life, as he'd learnt last year. He remembered as if it had been yesterday, the moment when he'd first come to Harramore and spoken to the statue of Charles

Chattoway at his school, Oakwood.

'You're hearing it again, aren't you?' Mr Trolley said, his face sinking, his lips thinning behind his goatee. 'But yes, she does. They say she's guarding something; no one knows what.'

Alaric nodded slowly. 'I don't know why,' he said. 'But I keep hearing it.'

Mr Trolley gripped Alaric's shoulder firmly. Alaric shivered slightly. 'The doctor said it's normal. It'd happen to anyone after what happened at Giant's Causeway.'

Alaric stared down at the carpet. Thinking about that night always gave him the same, empty feeling, like his insides had disappeared: the way he'd gone to the Land of the Dead with his friends, Lucy and Laurence, to stop the evil Naidos being freed; the moment he found he'd been lured into a trap by Walkul Goblinsfoe, the very man who'd been so protective of them; the fact the barrier between life and death weakened, allowing his deceased father to save his life. Just the memory of looking into his dad's real face for the first time gave him that feeling of emptiness, like he just wanted to open up the ground and be swallowed. If someone had told him this time last year that he'd soon be with a family he loved, living with his best friend like a brother, enjoying a summer holiday like every other fourteen-year-old, he wouldn't have believed it. But now, he barely wanted to exist at all. He had had such a difficult summer that on the final night of the holidays, he was unsure whether or not he wanted to go back to Oakwood.

He went to the room he shared with Laurence for the evening. He needed to read alone, not wishing to be with anyone else. He picked up his copy of *Myths and Legends of Harramore* and started flicking through the pages. He glanced at the section on the Land of the Dead and considered momentarily whether to reread it. He decided against it. That would only make him feel worse; he knew it. He continued turning the pages, looking for a story to read, but to no avail. He'd already read each chapter multiple times, and now, none of them gave him any excitement.

'Alaric, have you got a moment?' Alaric stopped reading and looked towards the bedroom door. Mr and Mrs Trolley were standing there with Laurence. Alaric had never seen the parents look so serious, almost concerned. At the same time, Laurence seemed unsure how to feel, his expression changing every second as he scratched his mop of chestnut hair.

Alaric nodded, and they all entered and sat side-by-side on Laurence's bed, the three of them barely fitting.

'Now, Alaric, Laurence,' Mrs Trolley began, her eyes widening behind her glasses. 'The two of you are *not* to get involved in anything you shouldn't this year. Last year, you two nearly got yourselves killed, and besides anything else, it made things worse.'

'Why'd we do that?' Alaric said. 'I don't wanna die either.'

'We never suggested you did,' Mrs Trolley said calmly, 'but you didn't go into last year planning on it either.'

'The issue is,' Mr Trolley said, 'that last year, things would've been easier if you hadn't intervened. We know you didn't mean to cause trouble, but we just know that this year, you'll both be worried. So, we're not supposed to tell you this...it's top-secret government information, in fact.' He lowered his voice, apparently concerned one of the other three Trolley children may hear him. 'The Golden Pearl, as a physical object, was destroyed. It was difficult, but its powers are now part of Marfin; only he will ever be able to possess other creatures. That information is being kept secret to distract supporters of Naidos from other ways of bringing him back.'

Alaric's stomach cramped at those words. 'Other ways?' he said.

'We don't know for sure what the laws of the Land of the Dead dictate regarding Naidos,' Mr Trolley said. 'There are so many points associated with this, and it's even more complicated because of Naidos' situation. Then, when you throw all the family laws into the mix, it becomes a right nightmare to figure out.'

The four of them remained silent as Alaric and Laurence took in what the parents had just said. If they'd come to make them feel better, they certainly hadn't succeeded.

'Okay, so whatever, we'll stay out of trouble this year,' Laurence sighed eventually. 'Anything else?'

'No,' Mrs Trolley said, 'we'll let you both get to bed. Need to get back into the habit of early nights.'

'That we do,' Mr Trolley said brightly, and he rose from his chair and started towards the door. 'And staying out of trouble, especially important. Now, off to sleep, goodnight.'

Alaric and Laurence groaned and got ready for bed. It could've been half an hour before either of them finally slept, Laurence moaning to Alaric about how his parents must have thought they were stupid. Alaric didn't respond much, just giving a simple "yeah" every now and again. His mind was elsewhere, too many questions beginning to circulate. Why did he keep hearing Rei's voice? Had something happened at the Land of the Dead last year? Did Mr and Mrs Trolley's words mean Naidos could easily come back? He tried to brush the thoughts from his mind, to focus on happier things. Tomorrow, he'd be seeing his other best friend, Lucy. She'd understand. She always did. And as the image of her face came into his head, he finally dozed off.

ALARIC GLANCED UP at the sky. The city lights meant no stars were visible, despite the clearness of the night. He'd only been to this place a few times in real life but recognised it immediately. He was in London. The moonlight reflected off the Thames, giving it an almost alien glow. Several boats were scattered along the banks, none of them moving at this time of night. Then, across the water from him was one of the most magnificent buildings he'd ever seen: Westminster Palace, Victoria Tower rising up through the air, watching over the whole of London.

Then, it hit Alaric. Night-time in one of the biggest cities in the world. Where did he want to go most? He thought back to a school trip he'd been on once, the outing he'd enjoyed the most out of any he'd been on:

the Natural History Museum. He could see the place so clearly in his mind: the life-sized dinosaur models; the blue whale; Charles Darwin. And it was night. He could have the place to himself. He didn't know the way, but of course, he was dreaming. He thought back and remembered an extract he'd read about Big Ben in a book the Trolleys had given him.

If Big Ben ever strikes thirteen, the lions of Trafalgar Square will come to life and roam the streets of London.

He stood, thinking hard, and the bongs came, echoing off seemingly every building in sight, penetrating right through the night's air. Thirteen of them.

Then, as always happens in dreams, there was no delay between cause and consequence. Within a second, something furry was rubbing its head against his waist. He looked down and saw one of the lions of Trafalgar Square, who raised his head to the air, showing off his magnificent mane. Alaric ran a hand through its thick fur. He felt the creature's neck vibrate as it purred almost as loudly as Big Ben had chimed. Nervous about hurting the lion, he mounted its back, clutching its mane and then, they were bounding into the night. Through the streets of London, they went, along the Thames, past the walls of the Tower of London. They continued down several backstreets, and then Alaric saw the unmistakable building of the Natural History Museum, its doors and towers looking almost like a cathedral in the night.

But the lion did not stop bounding. Alaric tried to dismount, but he couldn't. His legs would not move, as if he and the lion had fused into one body. He opened his mouth to tell the lion to stop, but no sound came out, and they carried on through the streets of London. His stomach seemed to do a series of somersaults like he was looping the biggest rollercoaster he'd ever been on before the lion, after several minutes, finally skidded to a halt.

Alaric didn't even have to cling to the lion's mane now, still apparently fused to it. He scanned the vicinity and realised he didn't recognise where he was. They were in some sort of courtyard, and he could see a building ahead. Next to him was a lump of a statue, sitting on a box, kneeling, apparently thinking hard. And he and the lion were no longer alone.

On the steps to the doorway stood two men, seemingly oblivious to Alaric's presence. Alaric, even in the darkness, recognised the first one immediately. Smiling as serenely as ever, leaning on his walking stick, was the wizened figure of Walkul Goblinsfoe. His face tightened at the mere sight. Were he not fused to the lion, and were he not certain this was a dream, he would've charged at the man. He wanted, more than anything else in the world, to hurt him at that moment.

Alaric did not recognise the other man, for it was too dark. He was dressed from head-to-toe in black with his back to him, and Alaric only knew it was a man from his broad shoulders and deep voice when he spoke.

'Was it done?' he said.

Goblinsfoe's smile widened slightly, his mouth opening a crack. 'Indeed. We'll have you out in no time, my master.'

The other man bowed his head. 'Excellent. And Alaric, is he safe?' There was genuine concern in his voice, almost fatherly. Alaric questioned whether he was now seeing Rei in his sleep until the man continued to speak. 'And please, call me Naidos. First name terms and all that.'

Alaric froze to be completely still, paralysed with fear. Even in a dream, the sight of the man who'd killed his father, tried to destroy the world, turned his whole body to ice.

'Yes, Alaric is perfectly safe,' Goblinsfoe said. 'He's a remarkably bright boy, you know? Sometimes a bit slow on the uptake, but he really does seem to be something special.'

'Well, that's hardly surprising, is it?' Naidos said neutrally. 'Rei was a powerful being, and Alaric is his son. Plus, as I understand it, his mother is a remarkable woman.'

Alaric furrowed his brow and leaned in towards the conversation, unsure if he'd heard Naidos correctly. His mother *is* a remarkable woman? Solo had always told him his mother never wanted him, but that was all he knew. Did this mean she was out there somewhere? His thoughts were interrupted as he felt something grab his shoulder, and his body was shaking.

'Alaric, Alaric, get up.'

Now, Alaric could see only blackness, feeling his bed beneath him. He opened his eyes immediately, expecting to see the early morning and that he'd overslept for school. But the only light in the room was the moon shining through the gap between the curtains. Mrs Trolley's face was above him, glowing white under her hair which looked like a bird's nest from her time in bed.

'What's going on?' Alaric said groggily.

'We're going to Oakwood. Now,' she said. 'And keep your voice down. Don't worry about getting dressed. We'll bring your stuff later. We just need to get out of here.'

Alaric sat up in his bed, trying to take in what Mrs Trolley had just said. However, before he could do so, she grabbed his shirt and pulled him off the mattress. He started towards the bedroom door, bewildered by the whole affair. He could see it was still pitch-black outside. Why was Mrs Trolley telling them to leave? Had the traffic suddenly worsened? Surely something drastic hadn't just happened with Harramore's daylight hours? He scratched his head as he reached the doorway, only for Mrs Trolley to grab his shoulder so firmly, he almost fell over.

'You can use Ceus' Seela, right?' she said. 'Like last year at the crazy croquet, you reckon you could do it now?'

Alaric stared at Mrs Trolley speechlessly, utterly baffled. 'I think so. I've hardly really practised it, to be honest,' he said. 'Why?'

'I need you and Laurence to go out the window, not through the front door, please,' she said urgently, entirely serious. 'Please just do as I say. This is really important.'

'Why?' Alaric said. 'What do you mean? It's the middle of the night and—'

'Because,' Mrs Trolley said firmly, 'the house is under attack. We think they might still be downstairs.

Edward will drive you all to Oakwood now, and Master Ogden will be there to welcome you. Please, this is extremely important.'

Alaric looked around the room in silence. He could hear feet shuffling, voices he didn't recognise downstairs, and his whole body shuddered. 'Okay,' he said, his voice trembling. He turned to Laurence, who was sitting, his face even more colourless than his mother's, on the bed opposite. 'Let's go, mate.'

CHAPTER 3

ALARIC HADN'T FELT such a sense of urgency since Goblinsfoe had tried to kill him. He could hear several voices he didn't recognise downstairs, and it was hard to tell whether or not they were inside the house. Within a few moments, the sound of chatter had been drowned out by glass smashing. The whole place seemed to shake as something crashed to the floor downstairs. Then, Mr Trolley came hurrying up at a speed someone of his age and stocky build should never have been able to match. The remaining Trolleys-Grace, Hector and Jacob-followed. Each of them looked as shocked and dishevelled as each other, Hector and Grace's hair as messy as their mother's.

'We need to get out quickly,' Mr Trolley panted. 'They're smashing the house, throwing things at the windows. No chance of me fighting them off, I'm afraid.'

Alaric's heart was drumming against his chest as he approached his bedroom window. It'd been so long since he'd used Ceus' Seela. In fact, he'd never even done so knowingly. The bones in his legs seemed to vanish when he looked and saw the drop downwards. Without thinking, he grabbed his bedding and hurled it out the window, hoping it could cushion his fall if necessary. The Trolleys all seemed to understand as they hurried out the bedroom and returned quickly with duvets and pillows. Everyone was there now as Alaric, fighting his every instinct, put one leg out the window. He stared straight ahead, knowing there was no way he could do this if he looked down. He closed his eyes, took a deep breath, and jumped. He anticipated the fall, the moment where he'd land and break a bone. He covered his neck with his hands to make sure he didn't die. However, like at Giant's Causeway, like when he'd first come to Harramore, the crash never came. Instead, his falling slowed, and he gently touched the bedding on the ground. Then, he watched the other Trolleys land and clambered to his feet.

'To the car!' Alaric heard Mr Trolley shout.

Alaric sprinted towards the Trolleys' seven-seater, neither knowing nor caring whether the stampeding around him was the Trolleys or their attackers. Past the dodo bird pen, he was the first there. He tried the handle frantically, praying the door would open even though he knew it was locked.

Why can't the Nephilim just adopt Ordinary technology? He thought to himself as Mr Trolley arrived a few seconds later and turned the key in the driver seat door. All the Trolley children scrambled into the back on top of each other. Before they'd even arranged themselves into their own seats, they jerked backwards as Mr Trolley put the car into gear and drove.

Alaric glimpsed the figures outside the house. None of them was identifiable in the blackness of the night, all dressed from head to toe in such dark clothes. He didn't get time to count them. There were too many to tally in the split second they could see the house. Through the smashed windows into the kitchen, Alaric saw two people who didn't look tall enough to be adults. But as they looked up, he realised he recognised them immediately. Franco Sprott's podgy, pasty white face was unmistakable, and his friend, based on his muscular build, could only be Dwayne McGlompher. Hot rage coursed through his veins, and if they'd stopped driving for a second, he might've leapt out of the car and charged towards them. But they continued on at high speed, and no one spoke for a few moments until the house was out of sight, Alaric sitting in silent fury.

'Who were they, Dad?' Grace said, her voice higher-pitched than usual. Her face, like everyone else's, had drained of colour in shock at what had just happened.

'Descendants of Naidos, no doubt about it,' Mr Trolley said, his voice shaking with rage. Alaric had never seen his adoptive father angry before. To him, he'd always been a gentle, jovial character with no temper, but this seemed to have pushed him over the edge. 'They know Alaric lives here. They must do. I TOLD IGLEHART THIS WOULD HAPPEN!' He took a few breaths to calm himself down. 'Ever since last year, they've been so much more confident. They see real hope Naidos could return now.'

'Do you think it could happen?' Alaric said. 'Naidos coming back, I mean.'

'No, of course not,' Hector chimed in. 'Everyone knows we can't actually travel between the Lands of the Living and Dead. It's all speculation, nothing to it. Isn't that right, Dad?'

Mr Trolley seemed to think about his answer for far longer than usual as the whole car looked in his direction. 'The trouble is, Hector, as you know, Naidos isn't dead. And after what happened with Alaric and his dad, we know some form of the deceased can escape. If the same thing happened with a living person…well, we can't rule it out.'

Alaric gulped. It was precisely what he feared. Everyone in the car remained silent, too shocked to speak as Mr Trolley turned on the radio.

'Good evening,' said the gruff, clear voice Alaric recognised as Norman McNulty's. 'Tonight's top story is that the sale of Harramore's largest pharmaceuticals firm, Remy's Remarkable Remedies, to business tycoon, Peter Barrett, has been finalised. Negotiations had concluded a while ago before the legal paperwork was approved by Walkul Goblinsfoe. However, events with the Deputy Governor led to a delay in finalising the sale, which has now gone through. The firm accounts for over 90% of Harramore's pharmaceuticals market…'

'At least it looks like we're in the clear about the stuff with you and the Pearl,' Mr Trolley sighed, but the relief in his voice was hardly noticeable. 'You have no idea how difficult it was to deal with that. At least Iglehart should lose the next election, though. Just hope it's to Ali Chandyo and not Vido Sadaarm.'

'Who are they?' Alaric asked.

'Vido Sadaarm is one of the worst Nephilim still walking Harramore, a huge supporter of Naidos in the war,' Mr Trolley said. 'He's running for Governor next year, and I think he has a chance of winning. Chandyo's the best man for the job, but unfortunately, he's too old for most people.'

'He's Ora's grandpa,' Jacob said.

'Really?' Mr Trolley said uninterestedly. 'My word, if they catch those people in our house, they better get proper punishments'

'Any idea exactly who it could've been?' Jacob said.

'Not within a few minutes of the crime, Jacob, no,' said Mrs Trolley, as though to end the conversation.

'I saw Franco and Dwayne inside,' Alaric forced himself to say, his lips thin.

'Goblins,' Laurence said through gritted teeth.

Mr Trolley braked so suddenly, everyone in the car jerked forward, almost hitting their heads on the seats in front. Alaric felt a pain spread through his neck.

'Don't use *goblin* as an insult, Laurence,' Mr Trolley said firmly. 'Who are Franco and Wayne?' He turned around in his seat with his brows furrowed.

'Franco and Dwayne,' Alaric corrected. 'They're kids in our year. House of Naidos, absolute sprout-heads, both of them.' His rage was building up as he spoke, and now he couldn't refrain from full-on shouting. 'I'M GONNA KILL THEM WHEN WE GET TO OAKWOOD!'

'You do no such thing,' Mrs Trolley said sternly.

'We told you to stay out of trouble.'

'Iglehart, I am going to kill, though,' Mr Trolley seethed. 'Trust me, I'll make sure he pays for the damages to the house. And I don't mean with our taxes. I mean with his own money. Now Franco and Wayne, what are their surnames?'

'Franco Sprott and Dwayne McGlompher,' Alaric said, his tone almost gleeful. If Mr Trolley worked in government, maybe he could get them locked up.

'Hmm, makes sense,' Mr Trolley mused. 'I remember back when Naidos fell, and we gathered up his most prominent supporters. Captured a few Sprotts; there was at least one we had executed. No doubt he's related… that's hardly a common name. McGlumper, or whatever you said, doesn't ring a bell. But there were so many supporters of Naidos who weren't arrested in the end, like Vido Sadaarm.'

'Why?' Alaric said.

'It's a long story, Alaric,' Mr Trolley sighed, 'but you can't just arrest everyone. It was a war, sometimes with friends and families on different sides. It was much better to do away with the leaders and make peace. Shutting down an idea can be more dangerous than the idea itself.'

Alaric continued to stare out the window, unable to

see much in the night. He could only have had a few hours' sleep, but he wasn't feeling the slightest bit tired after what had happened. He kept thinking about what Mr Trolley had said: Franco's relative being executed. For a short moment, he felt a twang of guilt, almost sorry for Franco as he realised his birth had done that to his family. Then, he thought about seeing them inside the Trolley's house, what they'd done to it, and felt nothing but hatred boil inside him.

When they arrived, in the darkness, Alaric recognised Oakwood instantly. It was the thick, dense wood of oak trees around the edge of campus that gave the school its name, the way the moonlight reflected off them. The car park was unsurprisingly deserted, except for one man standing on the edge of the woods with a torch. Just enough light brushed his face to make him identifiable by the crescent-shaped scar running down his cheek. It was the school's head, Master Ogden. Alaric managed to chuckle as he saw he was wearing a combination of clothes that was peculiar even by his standards: his floral Hawaiian shirt inexplicably accompanied his tartan pyjama trousers and fluorescent yellow running shoes.

'Oh, Quentin, thank you so much for getting out of bed at this time,' Mrs Trolley said as Master Ogden came to greet them. 'They came in the night, you see. Oh, it was so worrying, they could've been armed, we didn't know what to do.'

'I understand completely, Victoria,' Master Ogden said calmly. 'Must've given you quite the shock. We'll get that house fixed in no time, don't worry. I assume you haven't got any luggage right now?'

'No, we left it at the house. Hopefully, it wasn't stolen,' Mr Trolley said, his eyes widening at the thought.

'Ah, well, it's not to worry for the time being,' Master Ogden said reassuringly. 'We have plenty of emergency supplies here. There are always students who forget something, you see. Will you want a coffee or anything?'

'No, thank you, Quentin,' said Mr Trolley. 'We really best get back to the house, talk to the police. Alaric already had two names, didn't you? Pupils at the school, in fact.'

Master Ogden turned his head towards Alaric, his face expressionless. He stared Alaric in the eyes for a few seconds as though trying to read his mind, unnerving him. 'Is that so?' he said softly. 'Who?'

'Franco and Dwayne,' Alaric said, unable to suppress a grin. Could he get them expelled?

'Well, we'll have to look into that,' Master Ogden said, seeming slightly taken aback.

'Will they get kicked out of the school?' Laurence said excitedly.

'I can't comment on that,' Master Ogden said, his voice shaking slightly. 'You all best come with me, hopefully get some sleep before daybreak.'

It started to get lighter as they followed Master Ogden through the woods and into the gardens of Oakwood. A few rays of dim sunlight found their way through the dense canopy of leaves overhead, lighting the way slightly. However, even with that and Master Ogden's torch, it was still too dark to see much. Once they'd arrived at their accommodation and Master Ogden had settled them down, neither Alaric nor Laurence went to sleep. Too much had happened as they sat awake, discussing the whole night's affair.

'Did you know?' Alaric asked Laurence. 'About the Sprotts?'

Laurence shook his head. 'It doesn't surprise me, though. There were quite a few Naidos supporters executed; a lot of them had kids and stuff. Some were bound to be at this school.'

Alaric got out of his bed and started to pace the length of the bedroom. He stared into the fireplace, musing. 'So, if there's Franco and Dwayne, d'you reckon there are many others?'

'Oh, for sure,' Laurence said. 'There's a whole society: The Mammoth Club. Basically, any of Naidos' descendants were on his side. The same goes for Orm because he was Naidos' closest ally. Descendants of Paz, they're divided.'

Laurence's words lodged themselves like pebbles in Alaric's throat. To him, Naidos' dream of wiping out the human race had always seemed so unfathomable, but Laurence was making it sound like a common, reasonable opinion.

'Why do so many Nephilim support Naidos?' Alaric said after a few moments of pensive silence.

'Because, Alaric,' Laurence said, sitting up straight in his bed, 'Naidos' ideas for a lot of people seem pretty good. You wouldn't understand, living in the Main World most of your life. But you know the history of the Nephilim, why most of them live in Harramore. You and Lucy came top of the class in Master Idoss' lessons last year.'

Alaric briefly considered what Laurence had said before speaking again. 'You mean they started out in Ancient Egypt, then got burnt for being witches? So, they fled here.'

'Exactly,' Laurence said, 'and—'

'They want revenge,' Alaric said. It was clicking now.

'Sort of. It's just always been a thing over time. Ordinaries have always killed people for being witches. Even now, some don't like magic. Look at what happened to Goblinsfoe's daughter.'

'It can't happen to many Nephilim these days, though?' Alaric said.

'No,' Laurence replied, 'but that's not the only reason. Naidos always said he wanted Ordinaries gone because of what they do to the world. And well, for a lot of Nephilim, that seems like a good idea. You know what Ordinaries did to dodo birds and quaggas, and stuff. Even a few descendants of Marfin joined Naidos because of the rubbish in the seas. Same with trees being cut down…he appealed to Solo's descendants over that whole thing.'

Alaric softly paced to the window, looking out over the grounds of Oakwood. The sun was rising over the sea now, the sky a sweet, pinkish-orange. He took in what Laurence had said, his stomach sinking. When he thought about it, it all made sense on some level. He tried to picture himself as a Nephilim who'd never lived in the Main World. What if his family had been killed by Ordinaries? But to him, something felt wrong. There was a nagging thought in his mind that told him it wasn't right, even if he couldn't identify it.

'But we can't just...kill,' he said weakly. He didn't know how to explain.

'I know,' Laurence said. 'The problem is, people don't care that much when they see Ordinaries destroying the world. It's hard.'

Alaric flopped down onto his bed. He lay his head against the soft, plush pillows, starting to feel tired. Yet, even when he let his eyes close, he still couldn't sleep, pondering everything Laurence had said and the events of the night.

He was still awake when Master Ogden returned at about nine o'clock in the morning with a car full of breakfast. He was not feeling even slightly tired as he and Laurence wandered into the lounge. Master Ogden was there, bouncing on the balls of his feet, already dressed in his violet suit and rainbow bow tie.

'Good morning,' he said genially as they entered. 'I thought we'd have a big breakfast today. I need to talk to you when the others join us, you see. We've got sausages, eggs, black pudding, caviar, fish and chips, chilli con Carne, and ice cream. I forgot to order the brownies to go with the ice cream but decided not to mention it.' He lowered his voice slightly. 'The chef didn't seem best pleased that I'd got her out of bed to make it. She was looking forward to her last morning off, I think. Oh well, here come the others.'

Grace, Hector and Jacob all came into the lounge area, dressed in their pyjamas, rubbing their eyes groggily. Clearly, they'd all slept, unlike Alaric and Laurence. They and Master Ogden all sat around the coffee table on the sofas, eating off plates on their laps.

'Good news,' Master Ogden said, shoving half a sausage into his mouth and gulping it down like a lion. 'Your parents sent a message early this morning; your belongings are all fine. In fact, it seems the attackers left shortly after you did. Once they thought you'd seen them, they appear to have fled. The damage to the house is fairly substantial, though. It's fixable, but you'll need to stay here for the next weekend or two, I'm afraid.'

'Did they arrest anyone?' Alaric asked hopefully, grinning at the thought of Franco and Dwayne behind bars.

'Afraid not,' Master Ogden said. 'Anyway, useful you saw your friends, Franco and Dwayne in there. Obviously, we can't arrest fourteen-year-olds, but if their parents were in on it as well, that's simpler. It gives us a lead.'

'What, so Franco and Dwayne get away with it? They get nothing?' Laurence said indignantly.

'Well, I expect Madame Sang and I will have a chat with them if needs be. We can give them a detention or two.' Master Ogden smiled as though this were reassuring and continued eating.

'Is that it?' Alaric said, the pitch of his voice rising. 'I've had worse from Madame Sang for coughing.'

'Well, I mean, I don't tend to expel students. Everyone deserves a second chance at their age,' Master Ogden said, now seeming more interested in his breakfast than he was in the teenagers.

'Franco and Dwayne don't,' Laurence muttered bitterly.

'They do just as much as anyone,' Master Ogden said suppressively. His tone became suddenly more upbeat. 'How was summer?'

Realising they weren't going to get any more information out of Master Ogden, they entertained the conversation. Grace and Jacob seemed too tired to speak, Hector making somewhat more effort for the duration of the meal. When Master Ogden left to prepare for the day, Alaric and Laurence—starting to feel tired—caught some sleep through the morning before the Trolleys dropped off their luggage. They hardly engaged in conversation, evidently just as tired as the children, large bags under their eyes. They then spent the afternoon watching the other students arrive through their window. Alaric glimpsed Trevor Bertrand from the House of Solo, as well as Felix, Jorge, Rodrigo, and Carlos from the House of Sort, who all seemed to have arrived together. A part of him wanted to go and greet them, but he was too exhausted to do so; he knew he'd see them in lessons tomorrow anyway.

The one person Alaric was truly hoping to see was Lucy, who did not arrive until the evening. He leapt up from his seat when he saw her approaching the cabin door and speed-walked to the lounge area. He arrived just as she lagged her cases through the door, accompanied by her mother, who seemed to have given Lucy her tall, slim build and ginger hair. Her mother did not greet them verbally. Rather, she stared fixedly at Alaric as if he were a zoo exhibit, making him uneasy.

'Oh, Alaric, how are you?' Lucy said in one breath. 'Master Ogden told me what happened. It must've been so scary. I'm so glad you're all okay.'

'I'm fine, bit tired, but it doesn't matter,' Alaric said, trying not to lock eyes with Lucy's mother.

'Urm, these are my friends, Mum,' Lucy said. Her mother nodded slowly, keeping her eyes fixed on Alaric.

'You know? Alaric and Laurence? I've told you all about them.' Lucy's tone had become hesitant, as though she were saying something that'd be difficult to take. Still, her mother did not respond verbally but nodded, maintaining her stare.

'Okay, well, we'll be off then,' Lucy said with bulging eyes. 'I'll see you later, Mum.'

'Nice to meet you,' Alaric said, trying to hide his unease, and they set off towards the canteen for supper.

'Sorry,' Lucy said awkwardly to Alaric, 'my mum's not normally like that. I don't know what was going on.'

'Don't worry about it. I've had weirder experiences,' Alaric said, unsure what else to say.

'How was your summer?' Lucy asked.

'Great,' Laurence replied. 'We've been to the beach loads of times. Shame about Alaric's voices, though.'

Lucy furrowed her eyebrows thoughtfully. 'Voices?'

'Yeah, didn't Alaric tell you he's been hearing these voices?' Laurence said. Alaric's throat closed up.

Lucy's expression changed from pensive to one that was halfway between curious and concerned. 'What kind of voices?'

Alaric's skin went cold despite the heat of the evening. He knew he had to tell Lucy about this but had no idea how. After a few moments of silence, he decided to come clean. 'It's been like it all summer. My dad, I keep hearing his voice. Sometimes it's at night, but then sometimes I think it's someone who's really there.'

'Dad says he's probably just reliving last year, at the Land of the Dead,' Laurence said.

'Hmm, I don't know,' Lucy muttered. Something seemed to prickle Alaric's skin, unsure whether to feel alarmed or relieved.

'What d'you mean?' Alaric said weakly.

Lucy sighed before answering. She spoke slowly, as if unsure what to say. 'Well, weird things have been going on in the Main World too. You have to look beyond the headlines, but I've been keeping a lookout in the papers my mum buys.'

Laurence stared at Lucy blankly while Alaric absorbed what she'd just said. 'So, are you saying that you think it could all be connected?' he asked.

'Hmm, well, perhaps,' Lucy said. 'It's difficult getting updates from Harramore in the Main World, but there have been reports in the papers. At first, they were just snippets, but now they're sometimes half a page or more. It's always the same thing.'

'And what are those stories?' Laurence said. Alaric was starting to shiver, feeling cold for the first time in months.

'Ghost sightings,' Lucy said simply. 'Sometimes it's voices like Alaric's been hearing. At first, I was sceptical—everyone in the Main World still is—but there seems to be something to them. It's a weird thing.'

Alaric's body slumped as the three of them continued strolling towards the canteen. 'So, it's not just me?'

Lucy sighed lightly. 'I don't think so, no. Everyone in the Main World thinks people are just grieving. Some are joking about an invasion of ghosts, but I'm not entirely convinced. After what happened at Giant's Causeway, there could be something to this. We know the barrier between life and death weakened when Rei escaped. What if it stayed weak?'

Alaric gulped.

'Hmm, Dad did say Naidos' support's getting stronger too. And that reminds me, we have some juicy stuff on Franco and Dwayne,' Laurence said, a smile surfacing on his face. He told her they'd seen them vandalising their house and recounted what Mr Trolley had said about Franco's family history.

'So, you reckon Franco and Dwayne's family are right in there with Naidos' supporters?' Lucy asked.

'Wouldn't be surprised,' Laurence said. 'We know how they are towards us, especially Alaric.'

'Exactly, and if they're descendants of Naidos as

well, they probably support him,' Alaric said.

'Almost certainly,' Laurence muttered.

Lucy looked like she was thinking hard for a moment before her face lit up. 'Hmm, d'you reckon Master Ogden will—'

'No,' Alaric said bitterly. 'He told us he wouldn't expel them. They get off with a couple of detentions.'

Lucy clenched her teeth. 'Unbelievable.'

They continued towards the canteen, and to Alaric, something seemed to be missing from campus. But he couldn't put his finger on precisely what. Christina the Courageous had still been guarding the lodgings, though was too engrossed in a sword fight with another suit of armour to notice them leave; all the statues Alaric remembered still seemed to be there. Charles Chattoway even gave them his customary disapproving glare as they strolled past. Even the gardens looked more or less the same, some of the plants changing colour as they walked past. But there was one thing missing, which Alaric realised as soon as he saw it.

As they reached the canteen, the seven-foot hedge around the field's perimeter was browning, withering. Alaric had never once seen a plant shed its petals or leaves on Harramore as this hedge was doing. They always looked perfect in Harramore's seemingly never-ending spring/summer season. In such a situation, Alaric would have expected numerous gnomes to be seeing to the emergency. However, only a single garden gnome was traipsing the length of the hedge. It watered the plants with the look of a man who'd lost everything that mattered to him at once. And then, Alaric realised this was the only gnome he'd seen on campus all day. *Where were they all?* Were they late back from the holidays? Did they even take summer holidays? He dismissed these thoughts from his mind as he, Lucy and Laurence entered the canteen, the smell of quiche wafting through the room.

'Hey, Alaric,' a cold, nasal voice said from behind them. Alaric turned around to see the pasty white face of Franco Sprott looking up at him. His friend, Dwayne, stood menacingly, fists clenched beside him. 'How's your house?'

Franco twisted his lips into a smirk as Alaric's whole body heated up with rage. Before he could stop himself, he lunged forward at Franco, flailing his fists wildly as he repeatedly struck his face. A hand grabbed Alaric by the hair, pulling him upwards, ripping strands from his scalp. He could hardly breathe now as Dwayne's thick, muscular arm tightened around his neck. Laurence, who'd floored Franco, and was repeatedly kicking his stomach, turned to them and threw a fist at Dwayne's face. Alaric felt Dwayne jerk back as he lost hold of him with the impact. He leant on the nearest table, regaining his breath, and sensed Dwayne approach him from behind. He threw a fist backwards, praying it'd be enough to stop him. But a strange, intense heat coursed through his hand, and it almost missed its target, ricocheting off Dwayne.

And now Dwayne was howling, whining like an injured puppy. Alaric turned on the spot, expecting to see Laurence holding him or something of the like. But he was wrong. Instead, Dwayne was rolling around on the ground, Franco, Laurence, and Lucy all standing in shock. His clothes were on fire. And as Alaric thought about the heat in his hand, he realised he'd probably done it. But it was impossible; that was Fura, the Guardian of Fire's Seela. The only ones he'd used since coming to Harramore were Solo's and Ceus'. Then, he thought back to the time he'd set a house on fire with the candles on his birthday cake. He had this Seela as well.

'RIGHT! WHAT ON EARTH?' a voice shrieked from across the hall. Alaric turned to see Madame Ettoga, the cryptozoology teacher striding towards the mêlée, her one large cyclops eye squinting with anger.

She hastily grabbed a jug of water from the nearest table and threw it over Dwayne. The flames on his clothes were extinguished immediately, and he lay there, his face expressionless with shock as he breathed irregularly.

'Alaric, Laurence. Explain yourselves,' Ettoga said, trembling with rage.

'Well,' Alaric began, then no more words came out. He had no idea what to say. 'They asked how our house was.' He knew it sounded ridiculous as soon as he said it.

'Yes, I heard the conversation,' Ettoga said, every wrinkle tightening on her livid face. 'Now, you will eat your dinner quickly and then I shall escort Mr Swift and Mr Trolley to see Master Ogden.' Her voice became softer, kinder as she turned to the others. 'Lucy, dear, I'm sorry you had to see that. Franco, I suggest you walk Dwayne to see the nurse.'

Alaric, Lucy and Laurence hardly spoke over their meal. Lucy seemed too subdued to speak as Alaric contemplated what Master Ogden might do. Would he phone up the Trolleys to come and collect him and Laurence? Surely not, he thought to himself. Franco and Dwayne were getting away with detentions for breaking into the Trolleys' house. But then, that hadn't happened in school, during term-time. He knew he was strongly forbidden from using Seelas against students outside of basketball. Then, he hadn't meant to do it. Would Master Ogden understand? Alaric pushed away most of his food untouched, his stomach churning. A part of him wanted to bite the bullet and see Master Ogden now, the other part of him desperate to delay the meeting as he and Laurence left the canteen.

The walk across the gardens of Oakwood with Madame Ettoga seemed to stretch for miles, Alaric was feeling so apprehensive. Neither he nor Laurence spoke as Ettoga marched them to see Master Ogden. She was muttering furiously about how she "never would have expected that of Alaric", and "Alaric could really have hurt Dwayne". When they reached the staircase down to the headmaster's office, Madame Ettoga almost lost her balance as they descended. Then, her lips as thin as her wrinkles, she knocked on the door and glared at Alaric and Laurence disapprovingly. The door swung open almost instantly, and Master Ogden stood there, his face lighting up at the sight of the three of them.

'Ah, good evening, Erica,' he said, 'and Alaric and Laurence, as well, how lovely. I haven't seen you since this morning. So, to what do I owe the pleasure today?'

'Quentin!' Ettoga snapped. 'These boys are in deep

trouble. They attacked Franco and Dwayne in the canteen. Alaric even used a Seela, and one for a fact that I know he's not allowed to use.'

'Oh, is that so?' Master Ogden said with a smile, which he forced himself to turn into a frown as Ettoga squinted hard and disapprovingly. 'You two best come in then.'

Alaric and Laurence followed Ogden into his office, the headmaster shutting the door behind them. He gestured to the sofa opposite him, and Alaric and Laurence sat on its edge. Alaric was feeling slightly better after seeing Master Ogden's smile but was not ready to relax just yet.

'So, what Seela was it?' Master Ogden said. 'Ceus'? Solo's is the one you use in basketball, right?'

'It was Fura's,' Alaric said monotonously.

'Crikey,' Master Ogden replied, his whole face rising. 'Very useful against enemies. Good grief, Madame Ettoga doesn't look happy, does she?' he glanced up through the ceiling, where they could see the grounds of Oakwood above them. Ettoga was marching through the gardens, scowling like a woman on a mission, coughing into her hands a few times.

'I don't understand, sir,' Alaric said. 'Are we not in trouble?'

'In the most literal definition of trouble, yes,' Master Ogden said. 'After what Franco and Dwayne did to your house, your actions were understandable, even if I can't endorse them. I have to put you both in detention, though, since I am supposed to deal with it, and Madame Ettoga wouldn't be impressed otherwise. It'll be with Master Idoss, however, so it won't be too bad.'

Alaric looked into Master Ogden's laid-back expression, feeling now much more relieved, then glanced at Laurence, who was eyeing the door as if keen to leave. He, however, seemed much more relaxed when Master Ogden dismissed them from his office, inviting them to leave through the ceiling.

'Oh, and I'll speak to Master Idoss about your detention,' he said as they prepared to jump. 'I think we'll try to arrange it for some evening this week. He'll be relatively soft on you. I wouldn't worry.'

Alaric and Laurence both nodded, Alaric's body slumping slightly. Then, he launched himself upwards, feeling the familiar suction as he was pulled through the ceiling and into the grounds above Master Ogden's office.

CHAPTER 4

THE FIRST LESSONS of term were the next day, and Alaric, to his relief, didn't hear Rei's voice overnight. He, Lucy and Laurence rose early and wandered straight from breakfast to cryptozoology with Madame Ettoga. She gave a slight smile as the class filed into the room, which seemed to fade as she saw Alaric and Laurence.

As they settled down, she coughed loudly, and the chatter died, all the students staring fixedly at her. Alaric knew from his first year at Oakwood that she wasn't a teacher to get on the wrong side of, especially after angering her the day before.

'Right, good morning, class and welcome back,' she said. She cleared her throat once again and continued to speak. 'I thought we'd do something a bit different today, so no need to get your books out. I'd been thinking over the summer that we spend a lot of time studying these animals, but we never get to see and observe them. So, I've brought to Oakwood, with special permission from Master Ogden, a real woppanine.'

Alaric stared blankly around the room. Half the class, including Laurence, was murmuring in excitement, while the others looked just as blank as he did.

'What's a woppanine?' he said to Laurence so quietly, he was almost mouthing.

'You'll find out in a minute,' Madame Ettoga said. Alaric jumped as she spoke, having forgotten how acute her sense of hearing was. 'Now shortly, I shall lead you to see the woppanine, but first, I must ask you to be very careful.' She coughed a couple of times, clearing her throat, before continuing to speak. 'Woppanines can be particularly temperamental, unpredictable creatures. So, no one is to approach the animal other than me unless I say so. While this one is a rare captive-bred, and therefore tamer, it will still have a bit of a wild side, so you must be careful. Is that understood?'

There was a murmur of "yes" around the class, as some nodded.

'Good,' Madame Ettoga said tonelessly. 'In that case, if you could all follow me, please.'

The class stood up, and the sound of chairs scraping and being tucked in filled the room. The excitement among the students was unmistakable as they followed

Madame Ettoga out of the classroom and into the grounds of Oakwood. They walked for about fifteen minutes, Ettoga leading them into the woods and through the oak trees to a part of campus Alaric had never visited before. There were all sorts of plants he didn't recognise: some had bright, rainbow blossoms, which seemed almost artificial; one tree had roots that were just visible above the ground and had coiled themselves around a rabbit. The animal now looked crushed and half-dissolved, making Alaric shudder.

'Need to be careful with some of these plants,' Ettoga said. 'Most of these are only young, but the larger ones will eat humans if you're not careful. Still, best not to step on the roots. They might trip you up.'

Alaric wasn't entirely sure what to think. A part of him thought man-eating plants sounded incredible, while the rest of him squirmed at the idea. He looked down as he walked, careful not to tread on any of the roots. Though, by the sounds of things, someone had already done so as he heard a crash and a scream. He turned his head towards the source of the noise and saw the round-faced Trevor Bertrand on the ground, one of the trees' roots coiled around his ankle.

'Oh, for goodness' sake, I told you to be careful, Trevor,' Ettoga sighed, rolling her one eye. 'At least you have Solo's Seela. You'll be able to ask the tree to release you.'

'I can't. I'm not that good at Seelastry,' Trevor said with a hint of a whimper.

'Just clear your mind and try,' Ettoga said curtly. Miraculously, the tree uncoiled itself from around Trevor's ankle, Trevor leaping up and limping from the pain in his leg.

'I did it!' he exclaimed, grinning as if he'd come top of the class in a test.

'Yes, well done,' Ettoga said, forcing an unconvincing smile. The whole class looked at each other, all apparently aware Ettoga had done it, not Trevor. 'And also, everyone, while we're on the topic of trip hazards, remember to be careful around here. All the foliage is very overgrown. A lot of the gnomes got sick over the summer, and unfortunately, well, many of them died.'

'So that's why there are no gnomes around,' Alaric murmured.

'Indeed. We'll be looking at ordering some more from the garden centre, but until then, the grounds won't be looking quite as good as normal, I'm afraid,' Ettoga said.

Alaric looked around. Everyone appeared as perplexed as one another, for nobody seemed to have heard him except Madame Ettoga. They continued to wander through the woods, the footpath narrowing, before disappearing under the foliage entirely. Alaric was hoping there wouldn't be much further to go. Walking through the woods in his school shoes was much harder than when he had trainers on for basketball.

'Ah, here we are,' Madame Ettoga said.

The trees thinned, and they reached a perfectly circular, grass clearing. Ettoga stood in the centre, holding on a leash, one of the most peculiar animals Alaric had ever seen. Its head looked like it belonged to a deformed dog; its large, brown eyes and fur almost appeared adorable. However, the curved horns protruding from its ears, almost meeting in the middle to make an arch, undid this effect. Moreover, the head seemed far too small to fit onto the creature's body. Its grey, leathery stomach almost scraped the floor, concealing its legs and giving the impression that it must have weighed hundreds of pounds. Then, as it turned, Alaric could see a brown, bushy tail, more in keeping with the head than the rest of the animal. The class looked on in awe as it stared at each one of them intently, a curiosity in its eyes, before grazing.

'Voilà,' Ettoga said, visibly struggling to keep the

creature controlled on its leash. 'This is a woppanine. I imagine this is the first time any of you have ever seen one for real, as it is one of the most curious creatures known to Nephilim. Copy this down, please.'

'You didn't tell us to bring our stuff,' Georgia Beautang said indignantly.

'I thought that might have been obvious,' Ettoga said sourly. 'Those of you who didn't bring it are going to struggle very much with today's lesson.'

Alaric looked around and saw that while he and Lucy had their equipment, Laurence and most of the class did not. They began to moan to each other.

'Silence!' Ettoga snapped. 'Now, those of you who remembered to bring your equipment, it is worth noting that the woppanine is one of the rarest creatures in the world. Only a few dozen are thought to exist, predominantly in the Main World in Eastern Africa. Despite living so close to them, Ordinaries are unaware of their existence for three reasons: firstly, their rarity; secondly, anyone who dares get too close is trampled to death. The third is something I best show you.'

Alaric jotted all this down as Ettoga spoke, remaining focussed as she described the creature's anatomy.

'Now, today's task should explain a lot,' she went on. 'Please all gather round, and in your books, I would like you to do your best sketch of this woppanine. Those of you without your books, gather 'round someone who remembered and watch. All will become clear.'

Alaric, Lucy and Laurence found their place in the circle around the woppanine as the class chattered, rather upbeat for the first lesson of the term. Alaric had been expecting a far more demanding exercise, and clearly, so had the rest of the class as they wittered, working in groups. Laurence, Trevor, and several other people watched over Alaric's shoulder as he attempted to draw the woppanine. He felt awfully self-conscious, well aware his drawing was no good. He had to start again thrice before the head even slightly resembled the woppanine's.

'My drawing's gone!' the frizzy-haired Florence Le Guin from the House of Sort called. Her eyebrows were furrowed, red-faced as she flicked through her note-book like she'd accidentally turned the page and forgotten.

'Perfect!' Madame Ettoga called, much to everyone's surprise. 'Everyone, continue drawing, and you'll see the same happen to yours once your image starts to look like the woppanine. You see, this is one of the most remarkable beings in existence. Not only are they the sole creature known to be resistant to the lethal farafig poison, but they also can only be looked at directly. That's to say, they do not appear in mirrors, through cameras, in photographs, and even when you try to draw them, the sketch will disappear. So, while their existence is known to Nephilim, few have ever seen one.'

Alaric noted everything down, listening interestedly. As much as he enjoyed this class, never before had he encountered an animal he'd not heard of. He continued sketching, and by the end of the lesson, he was beaming in amazement; his drawing had vanished from the paper.

'Well, I hope you enjoyed that lesson,' Madame Ettoga said. She gave a cough before continuing to speak. 'For your homework, please write a three-hundred-word summary of the section on woppanines in your textbooks.'

The class filed out of the clearing and back through the woods, into the school grounds. There was an excited whisper among the students as they headed to their next lesson. Alaric doubted Ettoga had ever enthralled an entire class like that before.

'Just wish we didn't have Madame Sang next,' Laurence said, disgruntled. Alaric's heart sank. After such a great first lesson, Madame Sang was the last teacher he wanted to see. Every class with her last year had been guaranteed to mean detention, even if he'd done nothing wrong. His shoulders slumped as the classroom came into sight, looking as derelict as ever. Even though every teaching space in the school was identical, this one somehow always looked worst. Perhaps it was the lack of light in its clearing; maybe it was the dustiness of the windows; or it could've been the tight, always livid-looking face of the woman standing outside it.

'Hurry up! Class starts in one minute,' Madame Sang snapped as the students ambled towards her classroom. 'We have a lot to do today.'

Not daring to push Sang's temper, the class picked up a brisk pace. Alaric led the way. He still went into every lesson hoping to avoid detention, even if in vain.

'Ah, Swift,' Madame Sang said, her mouth twisting into a menacing smile. 'You'll enjoy today's lesson. In fact, I recall you doing so well on the exam last year, I think I'll put you in a pair with Trevor. He needs some help after coming last. And I should hope for your sake you make the best medicine. Otherwise, I might have to put you in detention.'

Alaric pursed his lips. He hadn't even done anything yet, and he was already on the threat of punishment. Still, working with Trevor had to be better than being paired with Franco and Dwayne like he usually was.

'Right, children,' Madame Sang said, causing most of the class to roll their eyes. 'Today, there is no time to waste. As you may have noticed, there aren't many gnomes on campus at the moment because a lot of them decided to get sick and die. So, today you'll be doing something useful and making some medicine for the few we have left. If anyone gets stuck, ask Alaric. He has plenty of experience caring for gnomes, don't you?' She gave Alaric a sick smile as the class watched, bemused. Alaric's face became hot as he remembered Sang making him care for an ill gnome last year.

He tried to dismiss the thought from his mind and read through the instructions on his desk with Trevor. It felt vaguely familiar to him. He remembered watching on, perplexed as Madame Sang stirred her concoction, seemingly randomly. To Alaric's great relief, she hardly bothered him at all that lesson, apparently too focused on making her own batch of medicine. The last thing Alaric needed after Trevor burned their Kraken skin was Madame Sang criticising him over his shoulder.

'Alaric, could we have a hand, please? Madame Sang

said we should ask you,' said an annoyingly familiar voice from behind him. He turned to see Franco sneering, leaning nonchalantly against his desk. Dwayne was sitting next to him, flicking through a magazine. Their dish was empty, all the ingredients untouched, and Alaric clenched his teeth.

'You haven't even done anything,' he said contemptuously, turning to continue stirring his concoction.

'Alaric, give Franco a hand, or I'll put the whole class in detention,' Sang said tonelessly. She didn't even look up as she poured her vat of medicine into a flask.

Alaric screwed up his face and stormed over to Franco and Dwayne's desk. 'Trevor, carry on stirring,' he said, dreading to think what the mixture would be like when he came back. The whole class watched as he arrived at Franco and Dwayne's desk. 'What's difficult for you?' he asked, trying to sound civil.

'Well, we've got a bit behind, you see,' Franco said as if it were an unfortunate accident. 'We could do with a little help.'

'You've done nothing,' Alaric said through gritted teeth.

'Well, yes, that's what I said. We're a bit behind.' Franco contorted his face into a horrible grin, which disappeared as Alaric roughly measured his Kraken skin, threw it into the saucepan and turned on the heat.

'There you go. I need to help Trevor,' Alaric said, wandering off before Franco could retort. He snuck a glance back at him and Dwayne, smirking, as their Kraken skin stuck to the pan, almost caramelised. He turned his spoon upside down and started stirring his own mixture with the handle and watched, relieved as the gloopy liquid miraculously became transparent.

'Alaric, it smells like Franco and Dwayne need help again,' Madame Sang said. An acrid odour had begun to emanate from their desk.

Alaric clenched his fist and continued stirring. 'I'm busy,' he said.

Madame Sang tightened the lid on her flask of medicine and rose from her chair for the first time all lesson. 'Well, well, well,' she said. 'Apparently, Alaric is so selfish and lazy that he won't help his struggling friend. In fact, he'd rather put the whole class in detention for his own benefit.'

'That's not true!' Alaric protested. 'It's your job to help them, not mine.'

Madame Sang's face stiffened, and Alaric knew he'd gone too far. He regretted what he'd said immediately.

'You've just bought yourself an entire week's detention,' Sang sneered. 'The rest of the class, eight o'clock this evening, in here.'

'THAT GOBLIN,' LAURENCE said as they left Madame Sang's classroom after the lesson.

'I'm convinced she looks for reasons to give detention,' Alaric grumbled. 'First day back, I already have a week's worth with Madame Sang, plus that one with Master Idoss.'

Laurence sighed. 'I'd forgotten about that one,' he said dejectedly.

Alaric's day—after starting out so well—had turned miserable. He stared at the ground as he thought of the week ahead with all his detentions, as well as the fact he'd landed the entire class into one. He could think of nothing to say as he, Lucy and Laurence started towards the canteen for lunch.

'No one blames you, Alaric,' Lucy said. 'Everyone knows Sang is just like that. Whatever you did, you'd have lost.'

'I know,' Alaric said. 'I was being stupid, though. The whole class didn't need the trouble. I just didn't want to give Franco and Dwayne the satisfaction.'

'I don't blame you,' Lucy said. 'I almost don't care that we have detention if Franco and Dwayne have it as well.'

Alaric chuckled, feeling slightly better at the

thought. He knew whatever Madame Sang inflicted on them in detention, it'd be hardest on Franco and Dwayne, who could barely spell their own names.

'Still, weird about those gnomes, right?' Lucy said.

'What d'you mean?' Alaric asked.

'Well, gnomes are meant to live for hundreds of years. They don't normally just all drop off at once like that,' Lucy said.

Alaric pondered the thought as the canteen came into sight. 'I dunno, I remember that gnome Sang made me care for last year was really sick. Like, clearly they can get ill.'

'But they normally survive,' Laurence said.

'Exactly,' Lucy agreed. 'To have killed off so many gnomes so quickly, it'd have to be something pretty serious.'

Alaric mused as they entered the dining area and collected their lunch. Lucy and Laurence did the same, all helping themselves to generous portions of falafel.

'The thing is,' Alaric said, 'none of the gnomes exactly look young, do they? Like they've all got white beards and everything, probably due to die soon.'

Lucy and Laurence burst out guffawing, a falafel falling off Laurence's plate, he was laughing so hard. Alaric stared at them like they'd just declared themselves to be purple flying pigs.

'Alaric,' Laurence said, snorting with laughter. 'Did you really think gnomes ever looked young?' The last words of his sentence almost got lost in his throat among his hysterics. Lucy and Laurence's faces were as red as tomatoes. They seemed to have given up containing their laughter now.

'Had you not noticed all the gnomes are also men?' Lucy managed to say in-between laughs. 'Like, did you honestly think they ever had kids, took them to school and everything?'

Alaric considered the matter for a few moments. Lucy was right; he couldn't recall ever once seeing a female gnome or a child. 'I hadn't really thought about it,' he said, now feeling rather daft.

'They're born that way,' Laurence explained, his laughter having calmed down a bit. 'They clone and then garden.'

'You mean, they don't learn how or anything?' Alaric said.

'No, it's an instinct, like breathing. Gnomes are born, and they start gardening. After all, Solo, created them and he's a Guardian,' Lucy said, now cutting a falafel.

'Right, so if some of the gnomes are actually young,

and they're all starting to die,' Alaric said, 'then—'

'Something's up for sure,' Lucy said. 'And they're very similar to humans. They can survive a cold or flu with no trouble, so there's got to be something weird going around.'

'Like some sickness or something?' Alaric said.

Lucy pursed her lips, concentrating hard, as Laurence shoved an entire falafel into his mouth.

'The thing is,' Lucy said, 'if it were like a disease, humans are too similar to gnomes for it not to have jumped over to us by now. I think someone has it in for them.'

'Why?' Alaric said, the idea seeming far-fetched to him. 'They do nothing wrong.'

'Precisely,' Lucy said. 'They're weak, so they'd be an easy target if you were just looking to hurt someone for fun.'

'That's horrible!' Alaric exclaimed. 'They garden for us and everything. What would they gain?'

'Nothing,' Lucy said. 'But people are the same with animals sometimes. Say someone had attacked the gnomes and disguised it as a sickness—'

'They couldn't do that,' Alaric said. 'If you wanted to attack them, you'd just do it quickly. Disguising it like that…how'd you even do it?'

Lucy took a mouthful and chewed while thinking. 'Well, we don't know what the sickness killing them all was like, so it's hard to say. Though you have to admit, Madame Sang seemed slightly off today. Sure, she gave detentions as usual, but sitting down, making her own batch of medicine, not shouting at people during the lesson. She seemed worried.'

Alaric continued eating, digesting what Lucy had just said. Even by Madame Sang's standards, the way he'd been treated in her lesson was strange. But none of the other teachers had seemed worried at all. Master Ogden had been his usual, wacky self; Madame Ettoga hadn't come across as especially perturbed when she mentioned the gnomes.

It was only when Hector, who captained the basketball team, led them to training later in the week that Alaric realised just how dense and overgrown the grounds were. When he'd arrived at Oakwood, he'd been too preoccupied absorbing what had just happened at the Trolleys' house to notice. Even when Madame Ettoga had pointed it out, he'd assumed it had just been in the more remote parts of campus. But in fact, the pathways in the woods had now almost completely vanished, and it was nearly impossible not to snag clothing on the brambles.

'So, Forto won their match against Sort in the first round,' Hector said as he led them to the stadium. He was the only one who was seemingly unperturbed by the thick, dense growth around. 'This means we'll be against them in our first match. That's a tough game. It's winnable for sure, but we can't get complacent.'

Alaric continued to struggle his way through the foliage. Travis the Tree was coming into sight now, his tall, thick trunk protruding from the ground and towards the sky, ready to spring into life in a few moments. And within seconds, the familiar sound of metal grinding against metal filled the air around them as Travis the Tree sprouted his branch-like limbs, stomping to block the campus exit. Laurence visibly shuddered, Alaric half-smiling. Of course, Laurence's reaction was more than understandable. The last time they'd been faced with this tree, it had nearly hurled him to his death, only for Lucy's quick thinking to save him.

'Leaving campus?' Travis croaked through the high-up crease that was his mouth.

'We are indeed,' Hector said, handing him a note from his pocket, which Travis read, furrowing his leafy eyebrows.

'How are you doing, Travis?' Alaric piped up. Travis

turned his focus to him and Laurence, whose face seemed to have been drained of all its blood.

'I am not allowed to disclose information, as you know,' Travis replied tersely. Alaric looked at the ground, his ears hot. He'd been hoping to break the tension and had hardly thought that information was especially sensitive, certainly not more so than his name.

'So, it's basketball training, is it?' Travis said.

Hector nodded, the only one not seeming slightly unnerved by the way Travis had put Alaric down.

'Well, have a lovely time then,' Travis said with the closest thing to a smile his mouth could produce. 'It's a nice day for it.'

Alaric, Laurence, Jacob, Grace and Hector wandered past the tree and into town, all looking slightly perplexed except Alaric.

'That was weird,' Jacob said. 'The tree's normally way ruder.'

'His name's Travis,' Alaric said. 'Use it, and he actually becomes kind of helpful...almost a nice guy at times.'

'He tried to kill me last year,' Laurence said. His voice was trembling slightly, the colour returning to his face.

'Really? When, why?' Grace said.

'When we went to Giant's Causeway,' Laurence said. 'He didn't like us leaving campus, so he grabbed me and tried to kill me.'

Hector's expression became pensive, as though Laurence had just told him a particularly fascinating fact. 'Well, you shouldn't have broken school rules then, should you?' he said with a smile.

Alaric gave a slight laugh, Laurence looking somewhat flustered as they climbed the slope up to the basketball stadium. As soon as they started practising, Alaric realised how much he'd missed playing basketball in this ground. With the first match against Forto still several weeks away, the team spent the session going through basic drills, which Alaric thought was for the best. It was the worst they'd ever played as a team. Hector blocked all of their attempted Seelas, Alaric missed almost every shot he took, and Jacob and Laurence kept dropping the ball, their passes wayward.

'Right guys,' Hector said at the end of training, looking like he was trying to hide how unimpressed he was. 'Not our best session, but that's normal after such a long break. We do, however, have a lot of work to do. Does it work for everyone if I put in an extra practice session each week?'

The four other team members looked at each other, apparently unsure how to answer. Still, before they could, Hector cried out 'Excellent!' and they were on their way back to the grounds of Oakwood, all red-faced. Alaric clenched his fists, knowing how much Madame Sang liked to make her longer homework pieces coincide with basketball.

'Look, I know I schedule a lot of training,' Hector said, 'but it's for the good of the team. It worked last year, didn't it? We reached the final, and I'm sure we would've won if it hadn't been for...well, circumstances.'

Alaric shivered, his skin seeming to turn to ice despite the heat of the day. Even months on, the memory of forfeiting the final to Naidos lodged painfully in his mind. They were approaching Travis now, and the same familiar sound of metal grinding against metal surrounded them as he stomped to block the exit.

'Hey, Travis,' Alaric said. He stepped forward confidently, ready to answer the question that would allow him back onto campus. Then, he slowed his walk as Travis stood motionless, his mouth unmoving, and he eventually slowed to a halt. He waited for a few seconds, but Travis' question did not come. Instead, he raised one of his arms and gestured to Alaric with his twig-like finger to approach. He did so hesitantly, his stomach knotting. Was Travis really going to just let him in like that, unchecked? He continued walking towards him, almost past him when the tree snapped, 'stop!' Alaric did as ordered, knowing Travis' power. The next thing he knew, the tree's long, spindly fingers grabbed his hair and yanked. Alaric yelped in pain, putting his hand to the burning spot on his scalp where Travis had torn out some hairs. He looked up and saw the tree putting the hairs into his mouth, chewing them as if they were a particularly succulent steak.

'That's great, thank you,' Travis croaked. 'You may go.'

'What was that for?' Alaric said indignantly.

'Security has been raised. DNA sampling is the new procedure,' Travis said simply.

'Why?' Alaric said.

'I am not allowed to disclose information,' Travis replied.

Alaric rolled his eyes, shook his head and stormed off. 'Can still disclose that security has been raised,' he muttered to himself. He waited a few yards down the pathway for the others as he heard them give yelps of varying volumes, and they joined him, rubbing their heads in pain.

'What d'you reckon that's about?' Grace said. 'DNA testing, just why?'

'He said they've increased security,' Alaric grumbled.

'I know, I heard,' Grace said. She was still rubbing her head, traces of blood appearing on her fingers. 'But why? And what does that even achieve, ripping out our hair?'

Alaric shook his head, sucking in the air through his teeth. Laurence, who'd given the loudest yelp of all, plucked up the strength to speak. 'He's not allowed to—'

'Disclose information,' Alaric said with a roll of his eyes. 'We know that. But why so sudden d'you reckon with the security?'

The trees were thinning now, and their question was soon answered. Master Ogden stood waiting for them by the edge of the woods, looking as solemn as Alaric had ever seen him.

'Ah, excellent. I've been looking for you five,' Ogden said. 'You need to go back to your accommodation immediately, please.'

The five basketball players all stared at Ogden, their brows furrowed, confused by this instruction. It was barely four o'clock in the afternoon, and lights-out was still hours away.

'Is everything all right, Master Ogden?' Hector asked.

Ogden shook his head, frowning. 'Madame Ettoga has been taken to hospital. It seems to be the same sickness the gnomes had. We need to get everyone into their accommodation for safety. It's just a precaution for the moment, but we don't want things to get any worse.'

CHAPTER 5

THERE WAS A strange atmosphere in the House of Rei's accommodation that evening. As soon as the five basketball players arrived back to greet Lucy, she leapt up immediately and hurried over to greet Alaric and Laurence.

'We have to go to my bedroom. Now!' she said.

'W-what why?' Alaric said. 'We haven't even showered yet.'

'Well, you can do that after,' she said. 'This is important.'

Alaric sighed and shook his head. He was still too worn out from basketball training. 'What even is it?' he said.

'You heard what happened to Madame Ettoga?' Lucy asked. Alaric and Laurence both nodded, prompting her to continue speaking. 'It's brilliant, isn't it?'

Alaric raised his eyebrow so high it was invisible under his hair. 'Are you nuts, Lucy? She's in hospital.'

'Yes, I know that,' Lucy sighed. 'But I mean, let's

look on the bright side.'

'Which is what, precisely?' Alaric said.

Lucy glowered at Alaric, Laurence looking just as puzzled as he did. 'Come into my room, and we'll discuss,' she said.

'Fine,' Alaric sighed, 'make it quick, though.'

Both red-faced and looking rather tired, Alaric and Laurence followed Lucy to her bedroom. Alaric had never been in her room before but noticed straight away how much better it looked than the one he shared with Laurence. Her four-poster bed was positioned centrally against the back wall, decorated with elaborate patterns that could've been created with real gold leaf. Her fireplace and mullioned windows were as grand as those in the boys' bedroom, and it was far tidier. There was not a single item of clothing on the floor, her books all neatly stacked on her mahogany desk. Alaric would never have thought he could be jealous of someone else's room with the one he had, but now he felt a slight, envious itch.

'Right,' Lucy said before she'd even shut the door and sat down, 'you remember this whole thing about the gnomes?'

'Yes,' Alaric said, not seeing where she was going at all.

'As I was saying, gnomes are kind of seen as sub-human, and they got this sickness. Now, the first non-gnome to catch it is Madame Ettoga, a cyclops. Does it not seem strange to you that it had to be her, of all people, to be attacked?'

'Attacked?' Laurence said with a furrowed brow. 'She's ill, Lucy. You don't attack people like that.'

'Gosh, Laurence, you're so ignorant!' Lucy said, her pitch rising as she rolled her eyes. 'Have you never heard of biological weapons?'

'No,' Laurence said.

'It's this idea of infecting something, then giving it to someone…attacking with a sickness,' Alaric interjected before Lucy could speak. 'I remember it cropping up in a history lesson at school in the Main World, but Lucy, I think you're making stuff up here. She was coughing when she told me and Laurence off, and in class. She was clearly just ill.'

'What? So, it just happens that no one else has this?' Lucy said fervently. 'Does it not seem like too much of a coincidence to you?'

The room fell dead silent as Alaric tried to take in what Lucy had just said. Laurence looked too lost for words to say anything as Alaric composed himself to speak. 'It's a disease. It might not infect humans,' he said, restraining himself from ridiculing Lucy.

Lucy looked up at the ceiling, her eyes popping out their sockets like she wanted to hit Alaric. 'Do you not see this? So, last year, there was all that stuff with the Pearl. Then, next thing we know, voices in Alaric's head, loads of people in the Main World having the same thing. The attack on your house comes at the end of summer, and now this. Everything's happening.'

Alaric shook his head, completely lost for words. 'Lucy, I get a lot of stuff has happened, but it's not all automatically linked,' he said.

Lucy let out a frustrated scream, tightening her hands. 'Alaric, I'm not stupid. I beat you in a lot of classes last year. You don't need to talk down to me like that. You're just not seeing this.'

'There's nothing to see, Lucy,' Alaric said, his voice rising as he struggled to contain his frustration. 'The voices—that could be because the barrier to the Land of the Dead was weakened; the attack on the house—that's because of Iglehart; the gnomes—well, they're sick because they're sick.'

'To be fair, Alaric,' Laurence said, 'gnomes don't get sick that often. And a lot of weird stuff has happened since you came to Harramore.'

'Great, so it's my fault, is it?' Alaric said hotly.

'No, Alaric, no one's saying that,' Lucy sighed. 'It's just that....'

'That what?' Alaric snapped.

Lucy took a deep breath as if trying to compose herself before speaking. 'Well, we all know your connections with Naidos. And everything that went down with the Pearl last year...it was about using you to bring him back. Then, ever since, things have got worse. Like that attack on your house would've been unthinkable last year. You said the barrier between the Lands of the Living and the Dead weakened. What if Naidos is trying to use that in some way?'

'To make gnomes and cyclops sick?' Alaric scoffed. 'Yeah, really likely story.'

He huffed, shook his head and strode to the shower, too enraged to speak to Laurence or Lucy anymore. What they were saying was perfectly clear. It was all his fault: it was because of him they were in trouble with the Governor of Harramore last year; it was because he lived with the Trolleys that their house was attacked; and now, somehow, he had made the gnomes and Madame Ettoga ill. He turned the shower to its coldest setting and washed himself. He was too hot from basketball, from his confrontation with Lucy for anything else. He'd never felt so numb to such icy water in his life, not even shivering as he got out, dried himself, and changed into a fresh set of clothes. He sighed with rage, the same rage that had been there before he showered as he started towards the lounge.

Alaric, calm down.

He looked around the corridor, hoping, praying to see someone there. But he was alone. The voice that had spoken was now all too familiar to him. Rei's voice was sounding in his head again. Exasperated anger boiled up inside him, and now he was feeling worse than he had when he stormed out on Laurence and Lucy. He grabbed his hair in his fists, stifling a furious scream. He was still a freak.

Go to your room. Take five minutes to breathe, calm yourself and go and speak to Lucy and Laurence. Rei's voice now had a sense of fatherly authority for the first time Alaric could remember. Even though he knew Rei wasn't physically present, it was not a tone he could disobey, and he set off towards his room.

The bedroom was empty and eerily quiet without Laurence there. Alaric sat on the end of his bed, looking down at the floor, breathing heavily. The voice had come back into his head. He thought it had been over. Eventually, his breathing slowed to normal. He got up and started towards the lounge area, almost dreading seeing Lucy again now. When he got there, she was sitting on the sofa, reading her prognostication textbook. She looked up as soon as Alaric entered the room, then looking back at her book, more concentrated than before.

'I'm sorry,' Alaric said.

Lucy sighed, shut her textbook and put it on the coffee table. 'What was that about?' she said. 'I know we didn't agree, but it's only me.'

'I know,' Alaric said. 'Do you mind if I sit down?'

Lucy gestured to the empty space next to her on the sofa, and Alaric took a seat.

'I heard my dad's voice again,' he said.

Lucy shuffled towards Alaric and put a warm arm around his shoulders. 'Just now?' she asked.

Alaric nodded, and Lucy tightened her grip around him.

'I don't get how,' Alaric said, 'but it's like he knows what I'm doing sometimes. It's as if he's watching me. I know it sounds crazy, but it's true. And it's too real to be my imagination.'

Lucy nodded. 'I believe you,' she said. 'This is what I mean, though, about everything being strange.'

Alaric sighed and leaned forward, not wanting to repeat the conversation they'd just had. 'I know, Lucy. Things are weird at the moment, but I just don't want to think about it right now.'

'It's okay,' Lucy said. 'We'll leave it.'

BAR THE USUAL rush of colds that came with the start of the school year, no one at Oakwood became ill over the next few weeks. There was hardly any news on Madame Ettoga, who was staying in hospital for the time being. Every time they passed her classroom, it was almost abandoned, her woppanine, whom the school nurse was looking after, grazing outside the front door. Lucy quietened down about her theories regarding the sickness, and basketball training became more intensive as the game against the House of Forto approached.

Laurence became his usual nervous self in the days leading up to the match, seldom talking unless spoken to. A black market for betting developed around the school, with many students from all houses keeping a close eye on this game.

'Five nuggets I have on you to score at least three baskets,' Carlos Belmonte, a tanned, skinny boy from the House of Sort, told Alaric in Master Idoss' lesson. 'I'll be at the game tomorrow; I'm rooting for you. I have another bet with Felix. He doesn't reckon you'll win.'

'Thanks, Carlos,' Alaric said, sneaking a glance at Laurence. He was staring down at his textbook, though it didn't look like he was reading it. Master Idoss had split them into groups to make posters on the cyclops' rights movement. Alaric was reading the textbook and making notes as Laurence remained silent. Carlos, meanwhile, was giving a monologue about the basketball, which didn't seem to be helping Laurence's nerves at all.

'You see,' Carlos went on, 'Felix thinks you relied quite a lot on luck to get to the final last year.'

'Does he?' Alaric said, trying to ignore what he was saying, not letting it get to him as he read the textbook.

Historians have long debated the importance of the factors contributing to discrimination against cyclops. It is generally agreed that the widespread prejudice stems from a natural wariness of difference.

The cyclops' singular eye has led them to be often portrayed as monsters in Ordinary folklore. Early prejudice against cyclops among Nephilim was only recorded after such portrayals in Ordinary literature, leading some to suggest this was imported from their culture.

'You see, the thing is, last year, you only beat Ceus in the semi-final because they didn't turn up for the first quarter of the game. You had a massive head start. Without it, you'd have been thumped,' Carlos said.

Alaric's insides squirmed as he looked up at Carlos, resisting the urge to slap him. When he looked across at Lucy's group, they'd already started making the poster. Carlos was doing nothing to help them, only making Alaric feel worse about the game tomorrow, Laurence busy daydreaming as if in a trance. 'I think we deserved the win,' he said defiantly, returning his attention to his textbook.

Some have argued that the discovery of cyclops flu in the 1800s fuelled such prejudice. While the disease did not originate in cyclops, the first human to die from it was a cyclops.

Alaric re-read the last sentence of that paragraph, checking he'd read it right. Something about it was nagging his mind: "the first human to die from it was a cyclops." *What clumsy English,* he thought to himself. He stared into space, screwing up his face with disapproving bewilderment. He seemed to have attracted Master Idoss' attention as the blue and bushy-haired teacher came strolling towards him.

'Gosh, you three ought to get a move on,' he said with a slight smile. 'You haven't even started writing yet. Is everything okay? Something confusing you, Alaric?'

'No, it's all right,' Alaric grumbled with a slight shake of the head. 'Just a sentence in there, kind of annoying. Shouldn't that say, "the first death from it was a cyclops"?'

'Well, I mean it could do,' Idoss replied, 'but that wording works too. Cyclops are also humans.'

Alaric stared up at Idoss with a similar expression to the one he'd made after reading the textbook. 'In what way?'

'In the same way as you or me, Alaric,' Idoss said. He looked somewhat shocked like Alaric had said something offensive. 'You ought to be careful, actually. I know you were raised in the Main World, so you don't know all this, but cyclops and humans are the same species. Sure, cyclops have better hearing, and, for some reason, diseases affect them differently, but otherwise, they're the same. Neither of Madame Ettoga's parents was a cyclops, in fact. They look different; that's all it is.'

'What, so that's it?' Alaric said indignantly. 'They have different rights because they have one eye?'

Master Idoss' body slumped. 'Regretfully, yes,' he said. 'Unfortunately, with many people, no matter how valid your opinion is, if you're not like everyone else, it's meaningless.' He strolled away to look at Franco and Trevor's work, which from where Alaric was sitting, looked just as non-existent as his own group's.

'I wonder if a cyclops has ever played basketball,' Carlos said.

Alaric sighed and returned his focus to the textbook.

'Can you at least start writing a title?' he said to Laurence and Carlos, slightly miffed.

Laurence picked up a pen absentmindedly, removed the lid and started scribbling, Alaric unsure whether to comment.

'What do we write?' Carlos said.

Alaric looked up from his textbook, giving Carlos a glower. 'I told you, just the title. Cyclops' Rights or whatever. I've been sitting here trying to read the textbook, and you've just been ranting about basketball.'

Carlos blushed furiously and started writing. Alaric was sure the finished poster would be the lowest mark he'd ever received in one of Master Idoss' lessons. He ended up instructing Carlos and Laurence on what to write, most of what was being produced barely legible. He knew he would not be voluntarily working with Carlos on a group project again.

The rest of the day seemed to drag on as Fridays always did. They spent the whole dinner that evening at the Trolleys' house discussing the game. Mr Trolley explained in great detail how Hector, Jacob and Laurence having the same Seela as Forto could be an advantage or a disadvantage.

By morning, Alaric, for the first time all year, started to feel slightly nervous about the game ahead of him. The usual thoughts he always had before a match began to circulate in his mind. What if they really had been lucky when they won their last three games? From what he'd heard about the House of Forto, he knew they could beat them, but he was dreading the thought of another nail-biting contest. It was no help to anyone's nerves that they were also the away team, meaning the stadium was packed with thousands of opposing fans.

'Okay, everyone,' Hector said to the team before they wandered out onto the pitch, 'don't worry about not having the crowd on our side. In all honesty, while we need to guard against complacency, I think that's Forto's only advantage. Their shooting stats haven't looked great recently, so if we can limit the use of their Seelas, we can win this. Just stick to the game plan.'

Hector gave each player a bracing whack on the shoulders, and then, they stood side-by-side with the Forto players in the tunnel. Each of them, dressed in their gold and scarlet kit, was of the same muscly build as the Trolley brothers. Alaric knew for sure he'd be able to outdo them for pace but couldn't help feeling that alone wouldn't be enough. They shook hands, Jacob striking up a conversation with one of the Forto players he knew from his year.

'Not now,' Hector hissed, pulling him away. 'Stick to our own team. It's more professional.'

The Forto players snuck looks at each other, appearing slightly amused. Alaric felt himself blush somewhat as they jogged out onto the field to be greeted by a sea of scarlet scarves. He started to feel the pressure of the occasion even more as he found himself marked not only by the Forto keeper but also by their two defenders. In fact, as he looked up the field, he noticed that their entire formation seemed further back than normal. Their midfielder was standing where Alaric thought the defenders normally would, the forward, who was the only girl on the team too far back to seem a threat. Did this mean they were going to sit and defend for the whole game? Alaric remembered football teams doing that in the Main World, as though playing for a draw, but surely that couldn't work in basketball? It was too quick, too high-scoring a game for that tactic to be effective.

Alaric's thoughts were interrupted as the tall, pony-

Alaric felt someone dive into him as he fell to the ground, the ball now rolling away from his grip. The referee blew her whistle to award Rei a point, and Alaric tensed his hands in frustration. He took a deep breath to calm himself; he'd had a chance now and knew another would come. He looked up at the scoreboard. Forto: 8—Rei: 2. One basket would change the outlook of the game for sure.

Still, Forto persisted in slowing the play down, searching for fouls. But Hector had become more prudent to the tactic now. He was stronger than even any of the Forto players, taking to mowing them down when he dribbled along the field, no foul given. He'd started giving them a dose of their own medicine.

Now, the contest was purely physical as Hector, Jacob, or Laurence would collide with the Forto players, always being anyone's guess as to who'd come off worse. Any attempted Seela by Alaric or Grace was blocked with ease, the game becoming one of the ugliest Alaric had ever played in. Every now and again, one of the Forto players would succeed at using their Seela, only for Jacob, Laurence or Hector to do so at the same time, meaning no points were awarded to either team. With one minute to the end of the second quarter, the score was nine points for Forto and four for Rei.

And finally, Alaric had broken free from the Forto keeper and had the ball in his hands. An expectant roar from the small section of Rei fans in the stands. He looked up at the clock. Forty-five seconds to go. He was running, increasing his distance from the keeper. He knew Forto's Seela too well. Their strength was useless if he could outrun them, as he continued to do, closing in on the basket. Thirty seconds till halftime. He looked up to the basket, poised himself, ready to shoot. He was there now, in the ideal position to score. Perfect shot. The ball was on course to land in the net.

Then, something happened that Alaric had never seen before. The basket pole was falling downwards, collapsing. Dozens of supporters scrambled to get out of their seats as it landed somewhere among them, the ball hitting the ground. The Forto keeper had used his strength to knock over the basket pole. And the referee blew her whistle for halftime. Was that even allowed? Forty thousand pairs of eyes in the ground were all on the referee, who remained silent, looking as perplexed as the supporters. Clearly, she'd never seen such a tactic before either. She jogged over to the touchline, the players all remaining where they were, not even huddling for their customary team talk.

'What do I do about that?' she said to her assistant,

sitting on a bench among some physios on the sideline.

'Well,' he said, stroking his bushy beard pensively, 'as far as I can see, they handicapped an opponent with their Seela…it's five points to Forto.'

The referee stared back at her assistant dubiously. 'But that's something you're supposed to use on your opponents, not vandalise the pitch. We can't fix that before the end of the game. Are there even regulations about this?'

'I can't say I've ever come across anything of the kind,' the assistant replied. 'Though about your first doubt, I'd say a Seela creating holes in the ground is a similar thing. As in, it's damage to the pitch rather than your opponent, so that's five points to Forto. Your second doubt, I have no idea.'

The referee stared silently, blankly into space for a few seconds. Then, she started towards the tunnel, looking almost in shock.

'Five points to Forto,' she said, almost muttering as the fans applauded their approval. The Forto players all grinned, starting to celebrate, as the Rei team just stood in stunned silence. Forto: 14—Rei: 4. Alaric tried not to be too concerned at the sight of the scoreboard. He'd been in losing positions at halftime before and had always won. He knew one basket would flip the result, but it just hadn't happened so far.

'I can't believe that's allowed,' Hector said as the team took drinks. 'Never seen that trick before. There's no way they'll be able to get that basket back in place for the rest of the game.'

'What'll happen then?' Jacob said.

Hector sucked in air through his front teeth, shaking his head. 'I don't know. I can't see a way they could end the game and award it to Forto. Though, it may be paused and resumed at another point. We'll see what the referee says. In any case, don't be concerned yet. They're slowing the game down; we need to come at them fast and get the ball to Alaric. That way, it'll only be a matter of time before we score a basket. It'll be a while before we resume play, so take a breather. I'm going to speak to the referee.' His voice turned to a furious mumble. 'I mean, really, we can't give teams points for wrecking the pitch.'

'You reckon the ref will take those points back off Forto?' Laurence said to Alaric.

Alaric shook his head. 'Not a chance. No one really knew what was going on, did they?'

Laurence took a gulp of water. The rest of the Rei team sat in a deflated silence, cooling down from the heat as Hector fruitlessly waited for and argued with the referee about Forto's points.

'Whatever you say, the decision is made now. I can't reverse it. Otherwise, we could go back all game and look at this stuff,' the ref said firmly.

Hector huffed, his face tightening at the realisation he wouldn't get his way. 'And what about the basket? Will you pause the game?'

The referee looked at Hector, then the rest of the Rei team, almost regretfully as she prepared to answer the question. 'That's what I've just been looking up. There are no provisions for a scenario like this. We can't easily re-erect the net, so we have to play with it like that.'

Hector's jaw sunk, his eyes widening in shock. He seemed too lost for words to express his indignance at this.

'You'll have one quarter each shooting in the bad basket,' the referee said sympathetically before strolling into the centre of the field. Then, she blew her whistle to start the third quarter of the game.

Alaric took a deep breath as the ball travelled among the Forto players. Ten points behind, and they were shooting into the basket that was still standing. He knew, surely, if he were to score a basket, it had to be in this quarter. There was no way of getting the ball into a toppled net.

Predictably, Forto seemed to be continuing their strategy of slowing the game down, not letting Rei have possession, blocking attempted Seelas. They seemed to know as well that as long as Alaric didn't score a basket in this quarter, they'd surely be on course for victory. Alaric controlled his breathing, watching as each tackle Laurence or Jacob attempted to make was evaded. But the plan was working. As they had their challenges dodged, they pressed Forto, pushing them further down the field towards Alaric. They were surrounding the Forto players, caging them in tightly. Alaric had his opportunity now. He watched as the Forto midfielder tossed the ball to the defender, diving in for the interception. And he had the ball, pivoted, shot.

A thunderous roar from one corner of the stadium shook the ground. The ball was netted in the basket, and at last, Rei had the points they needed. Five minutes into the third quarter: Forto: 14—Rei: 19. Forto would have to change their strategy now.

And they, too, seemed to have sensed the problem. They couldn't score in the toppled basket, and if Alaric netted another one, they were in trouble. They carried on trying to retain possession as though waiting for the final quarter to launch their onslaught. And once again, Grace, Laurence and Jacob pushed them towards their own basket, pressing hard. Now, Alaric had the ball again. He tried the same move, pivoting, shooting. But the ball hit the ring of the basket and bounced back onto the field. He gave a wry smile as he looked up at the clock. They were almost halfway through the quarter now, meaning only a couple of minutes had passed since he scored. He'd get more chances. He knew it.

As the third quarter of the match went on, Forto persisted with their frustrating style of play. Alaric forced himself to remain patient as the game went through its next cycle: Grace, Jacob and Laurence closing Forto down, pushing them back. He stamped the ground as Laurence mistimed a tackle, sending the Forto midfielder toppling to concede a point, and more importantly, reset the play. Six minutes left in the quarter. And Alaric needed another basket.

He watched as the game resumed its cycle. Rei pressed Forto backwards, closing them down. And now Grace had intercepted the ball, tossed it up to Alaric. He pivoted around the keeper, almost there now, ready to shoot. Then, he lost his footing as he felt the Forto keeper grab his shirt, and he fell to the ground. Another point, but still, the game was in the balance. Forto: 15—Rei: 20.

Five minutes until the end of the quarter. The same cycle. Forto desperately trying to keep the ball, slowing the game down more and more. The defender to the midfielder, back to the defender. And now, Jacob had intercepted it. They all scrambled towards Alaric. But they were too slow as it landed in his hands. He turned, shot. Another thunderous cheer shook the ground as the ball landed in the net. Rei were twenty points up.

Alaric grinned and looked up at the clock as play resumed. Three and a half, three, two and a half minutes left in the quarter. Forto: 15—Rei: 35. Another basket would do it, surely, put the game beyond doubt in Rei's favour. Alaric had the ball once more, two minutes left on the clock now. He shot…missed. And the Forto keeper was charging towards the ball, which had landed on the ground. He was several metres ahead of Alaric, with no chance of being caught. Alaric cleared his mind, hoping no one would see what he was trying to do. His heart jumped as the grass grew, wrapping itself around the keeper's legs, and he fell to the ground. Five more points to Rei, and he had a clear path to the ball. A chance to score another basket. He was closing in on it. But the keeper tripped him up yet again, inching towards the ball, which he pushed out of play. It wasn't the basket he wanted. But as he looked up at the scoreboard at the end of the third quarter, he realised Rei were in a solid position to win the match. They led by forty-one to fifteen.

'Right guys, that was a great quarter for us,' Hector said during the interval. 'It's not over yet, though. Obviously, now we're shooting in the basket that's fallen over, we won't score that way again. We need to keep tight defensively; two baskets, they lead, one, and they're back in it. They'll really come at us in these last fifteen. Try to win a few fouls and use our Seela to get our points tally up a bit, and we should be all right, but please, please don't get complacent.'

Everything Hector said proved to be true as the final quarter of the game got underway. Forto were pushing forward like they never had at any point in the game. They got two shots off in the first three minutes, thankfully both ricocheting off the outside of the basket's ring and onto the ground. By the halfway point in the quarter, Hector had been forced into two fouls, Alaric finding himself slightly on edge. It seemed like only a matter of time before Forto netted a basket. With seven minutes remaining in the match, the score was, Forto: 17—Rei: 41. Two baskets for Forto would put them in the lead. And Alaric shuddered as he remembered the semi-final against Ceus last year when they'd conceded two baskets in the last two minutes. He couldn't have a repeat of that now, especially as there was no way they'd score a basket themselves. Rei took to the same strategy as Forto had been throughout the game, keeping possession, slowing the game's pace down as far as possible. Six minutes, five minutes to go and still Forto hadn't had another chance. But Rei were being closed down, pegged back into their own half.

And now the Forto forward had the ball again. An expectant roar from the sea of scarlet in the crowd. He sprinted down the field, twirled around Hector, dodging his tackle. Alaric tried it once more, clearing his mind. And he breathed a sigh of relief as the hole he'd pictured formed under the forward's feet. Four and a half minutes to go. Forto: 17—Rei: 46. But still, two baskets would be enough for Forto to steal the lead.

'Yes, get in there, Alaric!' Hector shouted, applauding with delight. 'Keep it going, guys!'

The referee blew her whistle to resume play. The game's cyclical nature continued, Forto pushing Rei back once more. But Rei still had the ball, four minutes to go. As long as they could run down the clock, it surely wouldn't matter. Three and a half, three minutes left. Grace lobbed it over the Forto keeper's head to Alaric. He ran, taking it to the other end of the field.

Two and a half minutes now. They could win a game comfortably for once, Alaric thought.

'Okay, don't do what we did against Ceus,' Alaric muttered to himself as the Forto keeper chased him down. They were all coming. He was surrounded. He didn't want to concede five points to a Seela, so he lobbed the ball back to Grace. Last two minutes now. One and a half, one minute. And finally, Forto had possession again. Straight to the forward. Fouled by Hector. The entirety of the Forto team seemed to stamp the ground in frustration, knowing that must have been the game lost for them. Forty-five seconds remained, and they were twenty-eight points behind. All Rei had to do was keep the ball.

The referee blew for play to resume, and Rei nonchalantly passed the ball among themselves. The game was theirs now as even Alaric joined the passing circle. Thirty, twenty seconds. It wouldn't matter now if Forto got the ball. Grace passed to Jacob, to Laurence, to Alaric. Thirteen, twelve seconds as Alaric caught the ball. He sensed the charging Forto player, passed to Grace again. And he felt the Forto player send him to the ground in frustration. Ten seconds to go, and the referee blew her whistle to award Rei one more point.

And there was no time for the restart. Full time.

Forto: 18—Rei: 47. For a change, they'd won a game by a clear margin.

'That was a good match,' Laurence said to Alaric as they climbed into the Trolleys' car to go home for the rest of the weekend. 'Dad, can we have Lucy round for tea?'

'I'm afraid not,' Mr Trolley replied.

'Why?' Laurence said instantly.

Mr Trolley took a deep breath. 'Madame Cassandra up at the school, she's been admitted to hospital. It's the same thing as Madame Ettoga and the gnomes, it seems. Master Ogden doesn't want too much interaction between students this weekend. That way…well, they can decide what to do about the school.'

Alaric and Laurence exchanged urgent glares. Madame Cassandra had not seemed ill at all at any point during the week. Alaric realised it. Lucy had been right all along. This was no sickness; it was a poison. And someone had a reason to want Cassandra dead.

CHAPTER 6

'SO, DO THEY think this gnome disease can infect humans as well?' Hector said as Mr Trolley started the car.

'They're not sure,' Mr Trolley replied. 'The thing with Madame Ettoga was, being a cyclops, she is slightly different to most humans, so they were less worried. But Madame Cassandra, she's well—'

'She's a seer,' Laurence said.

Alaric saw Mr Trolley furrow his brow in the mirror, not speaking for a few moments, struggling to digest what Laurence had said. 'Yes, but what's that got to do with anything?' Mr Trolley asked. 'Seers, fortune tellers, whatever you want to call them...they're still human, even if often a trifle eccentric.'

'A lot of people don't like them,' Laurence said.

Alaric kicked Laurence in the shin, not willing to let him say too much. He remembered what had happened last year when he told Master Idoss everything they knew about the Golden Pearl. 'Don't go on about that,' he hissed.

'It's true,' Mr Trolley agreed. 'I doubt that's why she got ill, though. I don't think diseases have preferences like humans.' He gave a laugh that came right down from his belly. He was the only one who did so, though, the rest of the car remaining silent, worried.

'What does it look like they're going to do?' Grace asked.

'No idea, I'm afraid,' Mr Trolley said. 'Master Ogden's meeting Peter Barrett, you know, owner of Remy's Remarkable Remedies to discuss. They're going to look into a cure for this thing, work out what's causing it. Might shut the school in the meantime. If this killed gnomes, it could do the same to humans.'

'I hope they do shut the school,' Jacob said. 'I haven't even started my essay for Madame Sang yet; it would save me doing it.'

'You would make up for any lost time in the holidays,' Mr Trolley said firmly. 'Don't get too excited.'

Jacob sighed and looked out the window, clearly disappointed by this news.

'But, if it can kill humans, should we not be worried?' Grace asked.

'Hmmm, maybe. Though Ettoga's in a stable condition. It doesn't seem as dangerous to humans as gnomes, even if it isn't fun. Just got to monitor the trends, see who gets ill next,' Mr Trolley said.

'And if one of us goes to hospital?' Grace said.

Mr Trolley's face visibly twitched at these words, and it took several moments for him to gain control of his expressions. 'W-well, I'm sure it'll be fine. You're young and healthy; you'll be able to fight it, I'm sure.'

No one in the car seemed even slightly convinced as Mr Trolley drove them through the Harramore countryside and back to the house. All the children were sitting in nervous silence. They'd been barred from seeing Lucy this weekend; Master Ogden was considering closing the school; something was going on. As soon as they arrived back at the Trolleys' house, Alaric and Laurence headed straight to their room, not even greeting Mrs Trolley on their way in. Laurence sat on his bed, Alaric tightly shutting the door.

'Seems odd, doesn't it?' Alaric said. 'This whole thing. Madame Ettoga had been coughing a fair bit when we last saw her, but Madame Cassandra, not at all. I could believe Ettoga was ill—'

'But not Cassandra!' Laurence said.

'No, she was fine in our last lesson. This just suddenly happened with her,' Alaric said.

'So, do you think Lucy was right then?' Laurence asked.

Alaric nodded. 'It definitely could be a poison, but that leaves so many more questions.'

'What do you mean?' Laurence said.

Alaric got up from his bed and started slowly pacing up and down the small amount of floor space in their bedroom. 'Well,' he said, 'there's firstly the issue of why anyone would want to poison the gnomes and these people. What connects them exactly?'

'I thought we figured that out already,' Laurence said. 'The gnomes are an easy target, Ettoga is a cyclops, and Cassandra is a seer. None of those is popular.'

Alaric tightened his face as though suddenly feeling a sharp ache. 'The trouble is, it's difficult with a poison. You have to really plan it. It'd be easier just to blatantly kill these people. Plus, we've seen with Cassandra and Ettoga that they may not even want them dead. The motive must be stronger than a bit of fun, but what could it be? Then, how are they even getting the poison into these people without noticing? And who's doing it?'

Laurence ran his fingers through his mop of hair, shaking his head pensively. 'That's a lot of questions, Alaric, but the *who* is obvious, isn't it?'

Alaric looked at Laurence blankly. 'Who?' he said weakly.

'Madame Sang,' Laurence replied.

'Excuse me!' Alaric exclaimed. He knew how much of a grudge they had against Madame Sang, but to him, this seemed crazily far-fetched.

'Well, it'd have to be a teacher since no one else was at school over summer to harm the gnomes. And name another teacher who'd do something like that,' Laurence said triumphantly.

Alaric mused for a few moments. He couldn't deny that Laurence had a point. Practically, it was very likely that the culprit would've had to have been at the school to do the crime. So, that meant a teacher or student would need to be involved. But Madame Sang? It seemed too obvious, almost too good in a way to be true. She was too close to Master Ogden; she'd stuck up for them when they were accused of stealing the Pearl last year.

'I don't know. Does Sang have any beef with Ettoga or Cassandra?' Alaric said.

Laurence's face lit up like he'd had an idea. 'Jacob!' he called.

'I'm watching TV!' Jacob shouted back from downstairs.

'We need to talk to you!' Laurence yelled.

'Come down here then!' Jacob replied.

'Lazy git,' Laurence sighed, rising from his bed and starting towards the door. Alaric followed him downstairs into the living room. Jacob was lying comfortably on the sofa, watching two men have a particularly gruesome sword fight on the TV. He glanced up as Alaric and Laurence came in and sat down on the adjacent settee but did not verbally acknowledge their presence.

'So, Jacob,' Laurence said. Jacob remained focussed on the TV, Alaric wincing at how graphic the fight was. 'You know how Ettoga and Cassandra are both in hospital?'

Jacob grunted as Alaric glared at Laurence, dreading what would come out of his mouth next. Alaric couldn't let Laurence get them into trouble like last year, so thinking quickly, he said, 'what does that mean for our classes? If there are no teachers, who will take them?'

'I dunno,' Jacob said, 'I'm not the headmaster; maybe they'll bring in subs. Was that all?' He sounded both annoyed and amused at the same time. When Alaric gave it some thought, it did seem a strange thing to ask Jacob of all people.

'No,' Laurence said. 'Did any teachers have anything especially against Cassandra or Ettoga? Like Madame Sang, maybe?'

'What's that got to do with anything?' Jacob said, still looking at the TV. 'I don't think Sang exactly likes many people. Though, Clarissa always said Cassandra was into Sang's husband.'

'Madame Sang has a husband?' Alaric exclaimed, unable to imagine how anyone could voluntarily commit to a lifetime with her.

'Yeah, I know, right, poor guy,' Jacob said with a snigger. 'Still, it gets better.' He sat up on the sofa, paused the TV, and turned his attention to Alaric. 'You know who Sang's married to?'

Alaric shook his head, leaning forward towards Jacob, Laurence also staring fixedly at him.

'Master Ogden's brother,' Jacob said, grinning smugly.

'What?' Alaric said with bulging eyes.

'Yep,' Jacob said, 'not many people know that; she doesn't exactly scream it from the rooftops. Clarissa and I reckon that's why she didn't take Ogden's name, doesn't want people to know about it.'

'How did you find out?' Laurence asked, sounding half annoyed he hadn't been told sooner, half sceptical.

Jacob burst out into uncontrollable laughter, trying to speak but unable to do so, his face a deep shade of scarlet. 'So, at the start of last year, I had this week of detentions...asked Sang if this anti-anger antidote was for her to use herself,' he managed to say.

'Oh yeah,' Alaric said, grinning as he remembered.

'So, I was in my first detention with her, and Clarissa and Ora were there too for laughing at what I said, and we were crushing vampire fangs—'

'Hey, she made us do that once too,' Alaric said.

'Shut up, let him speak!' Laurence snapped. Alaric shuffled in his seat, tightening his lips.

Jacob took a deep breath before continuing to talk. 'So, yeah, it was getting late in the night, and we heard the door open. This guy came in who looked like Master Ogden without the scar and wearing normal clothes. He didn't notice us to start with and called Sang "darling", telling her they needed to get home. Sang just said she'd be there soon, but her voice was shaking; I don't think I'd ever seen her so white. Then, this guy came up to us and shook our hands and told us his name was Levi Ogden, married to Sang. She cancelled the rest of our detentions if we agreed not to tell anyone. She said if we did, she'd put us in detention for the rest of our time at Oakwood. So, yeah, you cannot tell anyone about that, not even Hector or Grace...crikey, I'd been dying to get that off my chest like you wouldn't believe.'

Alaric and Laurence both sat silently, grinning, as they processed all this information. He remembered Mr Trolley telling him Sang had been bitter for years over Master Ogden being a Guardian instead of her. His eyes widened as he imagined the friction there must be between them if Sang was also married to Ogden's brother. Did the siblings even get on? Or were the three of them actually very close? The only piece of information missing was—

'How do you know Cassandra's into Levi, though?' Laurence said.

'Oh yeah,' Jacob said, 'well, apparently Levi works in government too, in the education department. He came into one of our lessons a couple of months later, working as an inspector. You should've seen Cassandra then; I'd never seen her keep her eyes open for so long.'

Alaric and Laurence looked at each other with open-mouthed grins. Alaric had almost forgotten why they'd questioned Jacob about this before he spoke again.

'Why did you ask anyway?' Jacob said.

'Ah, w-well, it-it was just that we thought Madame Sang might be in a better mood if her least favourite teachers weren't there anymore,' Alaric said. His palms sweated as he realised how unconvincing he must've sounded.

'Wouldn't bank on it,' Jacob said with a chuckle, much to Alaric's relief. 'Still, promise not to tell anyone.'

'What about Lucy?' Laurence said. 'She only talks to us anyway.'

Jacob concentrated hard before speaking. 'I'm not sure,' he said. 'I wasn't really supposed to tell you.'

'Come on, it's not like she's high-risk,' Alaric said. If he were honest, he thought she'd definitely keep a secret better than Laurence.

'Urrrmmm...all right then, but no one else,' Jacob said firmly. He shaped his mouth into a mischievous smile. 'My plan for my last week at Oakwood is to spread that around the whole school.'

Alaric and Laurence chuckled.

'Thanks, Jacob,' Alaric said, 'we'll leave you to it.'

He and Laurence rose from the sofa and headed back towards their bedroom in excited silence.

'We have to tell Lucy all of this, right now; this is golden,' Laurence said gleefully as soon as Alaric had shut the door behind them.

Alaric shook his head. 'We don't want to be overheard by someone. Jacob just did us a massive favour telling us all of that. We owe him the secrecy at least.' He spoke in a hushed voice to avoid one of the other

Trolleys overhearing him.

'But what if school closes and we're not back on Monday?' Laurence argued.

'We'll consider that if it happens,' Alaric said firmly. 'To be honest, the worst thing that can happen right now would be your dad hearing us. We don't want him to think we're up to no good again.'

Laurence sighed and sat down on his bed, accepting Alaric was probably right. Besides, Alaric knew he'd need the rest of the weekend to work out what all this information could mean, if anything. Madame Sang certainly seemed to have a motive for wanting to attack Cassandra, but Ettoga was another issue. To him, being a cyclops alone didn't seem a strong enough reason. He spent the whole of Sunday distracted from his home-work, instead thinking hard about Madame Ettoga. Had she or Sang ever said anything even slightly spiteful about each other? Not that he could remember. And in the case of Madame Cassandra, would that really be strong enough a motive for Sang? Cassandra's crush on Sang's husband was all a theory anyway. Plus, would Sang really do something like that? He knew she was a vile woman, but enough so for this? There were too many doubts in his mind now to be convinced. He needed to talk to Lucy.

CHAPTER 7

'IS THIS FOR sure, all the stuff about Sang, Ogden and Cassandra?' Lucy said as she, Alaric and Laurence sat down for coffee on Monday morning.

'Yeah, they were definitely married last year; that's what Jacob told us?' Alaric said.

'Assuming he was telling the truth,' Laurence said bitterly.

Lucy shook her head, blowing on her cup of coffee. 'It'd be too far-fetched to make up. So, we know for sure Sang is married to Ogden's brother. But then does Cassandra definitely come into it?'

'That's the thing,' Alaric said. 'Cassandra and Levi feel like a long shot, even if it seems to fit.'

Lucy sipped her coffee, staring hard into space. 'It'd make sense. If it's anyone on campus, Sang would be my bet. But why Ettoga? Just because she's a cyclops?'

'I guess,' Alaric said. 'I'm not sure that's strong enough on its own, though. Did we definitely rule out that this was just a disease?'

'I spent the whole of yesterday looking it up,' Lucy said. 'Could not find a single illness that infects cyclops, gnomes and humans. Even if the three are similar, they're different enough for that to never happen.'

'So, it *is* a poison,' Laurence said, almost triumphantly.

Alaric nodded and checked his watch to see they had fifteen minutes until their lesson with Madame Sang. He rose from the sofa and commenced his usual pacing ritual when thinking. 'It's definitely likely,' he said. 'Now the two questions are, firstly, what is the poison, and secondly, how is Sang getting it into the school?'

'The good news is we have Madame Sang's class next,' Lucy said.

'How's that going to help?' Alaric said. 'You're not really going to ask her about it, are you?'

Lucy sighed and stared at Alaric with thin lips. 'What else do you suggest?'

Alaric shrugged, staring wide-eyed at Lucy. 'I know that's not a good idea for sure. Imagine Sang's reaction when you say, "Hey miss, you know this thing that's made the gnomes sick? Well, we think it might actually be you poisoning them; how are you doing it?" We'll get detention for the rest of the year.'

Lucy huffed, picked up the nearest cushion and threw it at Alaric's head.

'Hey!' Alaric exclaimed, putting his hand to his cheek where the cushion had hit him, which was stinging slightly.

'That's for being so stupid,' Lucy said. 'I'll be subtle. I've just got to make the questions seem innocent—'

'Yeah, because Madame Sang's always one for a nice, friendly chat,' Alaric said sarcastically. Lucy picked up another cushion and threw it at him, this time narrowly missing and landing on the floor.

'Do you think I'm an idiot?' Lucy said, unamused. 'I'm not going to have a "nice, friendly chat". I'm going to ask questions I may actually be concerned about. Sure, Sang may think I'm nosy, but really all she'll do is shout at me and put me in detention, just the usual.'

'Or she could make us our next target,' Alaric muttered.

Alaric braced himself as he saw Lucy reach for another cushion, but she seemed to have second thoughts as she put her hands on her lap. 'If she were going to go for you, she'd have done it first, before anyone else,' she said. 'So, the plan of action is as follows: I'll do the talking; you two can keep quiet.'

Alaric nodded. He was perfectly happy to let Lucy

take care of this task. He had no idea how to extract information from Madame Sang. Meanwhile, Laurence, whose red face looked mildly affronted, would have been the worst person for the mission.

It was five minutes to the hour when the three of them decided to pack their bags and start making their way over to Madame Sang's classroom. Alaric's stomach was already twisting at the thought of the lesson that lay ahead. These classes were difficult enough at the best of times. If Lucy put a foot even slightly wrong, disturbing Sang's fragile temper just the littlest bit, he knew this could be the worst hour of term.

The journey to the classroom was short, but Alaric's legs felt leaden as reached its clearing, already filled with the other students in the class. There was, as always, a muted, downbeat chatter as they waited to be called into the classroom. After a few moments in which Alaric, Lucy and Laurence stood together in silence, the door swung open, and Madame Sang stepped out. She looked no happier than usual, but her expression carried a different kind of misery. It was almost tired as bags visibly formed under her dark eyes.

'Enter,' she said, her lips thinning. Alaric shuddered once more, strongly feeling that now would not be a good lesson for Lucy to irk Sang. The class shuffled into the room, not a single smile in sight as they took their seats. Alaric sat in his usual place with Franco and Dwayne. He was sullenly unpacking his books from his bag when he looked up and saw Madame Sang was not alone at the front of the room.

Standing with her was a man Alaric recognised. It was only after he'd read the writing on the board that he realised where from: Remy's Remarkable Remedies. His heavily gelled, slicked-back hair, his ostentatious suit was all the same as when he'd seen him on the news. It was the famous Peter Barrett.

The whole class stared on in anticipation. No one dared to speak, but the excitement was still obvious. No teacher, let alone Madame Sang, had ever invited a guest speaker in.

'Hurry up, books out!' Madame Sang snapped at the few people still unpacking, and they emptied their bags onto their desks. 'As you have probably noticed,' she said coldly, 'we are joined by Mr Peter Barrett. Today, he is here to talk to you about recent events with the gnomes and your teachers. Mr Barrett is the owner of Remy's Remarkable Remedies, one of the most noteworthy medicine companies in the whole of Harramore. He will be talking to you today about the situation and what's being done about it. He will then brief you on career opportunities at his company for those who are interested.'

A few people sniggered at the thought of working in medicine, including Laurence. Alaric restrained himself from expressing his feelings as Madame Sang gave the class a silent, furious stare. She'd hardly been the best advert for such a career path.

'Questions?' she said in a tone with such aggression, you'd have been brave to respond. However, Lucy's hand shot up into the air at lightning speed, causing Sang's lips to turn somehow even thinner. 'What, Lucy?' she said through gritted teeth.

'What'll happen with our cryptozoology and prognostication lessons? We've already missed weeks of Ettoga's classes and—'

'We will sort it,' Sang interrupted, scowling at Lucy. 'Any other questions?'

Lucy's hand shot back up into the air, and Sang rolled her eyes.

'What?' Madame Sang said so violently, spit visibly sprayed out of her mouth.

'What's wrong with Ettoga and Cassandra?' Lucy said. Alaric clenched his fists in frustration. There was no way this was going to get them anywhere.

'The same as with the gnomes,' Sang said, her voice

rising to the point where she was almost shouting. 'Seems like a cold to start with, then gets serious. We don't know exactly what it is, which is why Mr Barrett is here today. Is that all?'

Alaric braced himself for an outpouring of rage as Lucy shot her hand into the air for the third time, Sang visibly tightening her hands. Alaric thought that had Peter Barrett not been there, she'd have surely screamed at Lucy by now.

'Are the teachers missing Ettoga and Cassandra?' Lucy blurted out.

'They're both colleagues to us, and we get on well, so yes,' Sang said curtly. 'Now, if you don't mind, I'll allow Mr Barrett to start speaking. He's a very busy man and hasn't got all day to listen to us discussing our social lives.'

Peter Barrett shuffled awkwardly to stand by Madame Sang's whiteboard. Several of his facial muscles twitched as if the prospect of speaking to a room of fourteen-year-olds made him nervous. He stood with his body tight, wringing his hands as he started to talk. 'W-well, urrrmmm, h-hello everybody,' he said, forcing a smile as awkward as his posture. 'Th-thank you for s-such a w-warm w-welcome, M-Madame Sang.'

The class looked around at each other, some smiling

slightly in amusement. As far as Alaric was concerned, Sang's welcome could scarcely have been less warm.

'N-now, I-I'm P-Peter Barrett, and I am i-in charge of R-Remy's R-Remarkable R-Remedies, a m-medicine company h-here in Harramore.'

Alaric looked down at his desk. Barrett hardly projected his voice, speaking with such an air of nervousness, Alaric thought it a miracle he'd ever become so successful. He doubted the people at the back of the classroom would've been able to hear him at all.

'N-now, I know a lot of you m-might be concerned a-about r-recent events, s-seeing two of your teachers in hospital. A-a lot of you are p-probably w-worried. I-I would be in your s-situations,' Barrett went on. He slapped one of his hands away from the other as if it were a bee, then stood with his arms rigidly by his sides. 'So, I wanted to assure you that there is no need for you to worry. Whatever this sickness is, it is contained, and your teachers are in a stable condition. We are working on a cure and now expect to have one available by winter. Plus, we will provide it to the school, free of charge.'

His voice had suddenly become more composed, louder and almost booming, echoing off the walls. It was still as monotonous as before, earning him several strange looks from around the classroom. Madame Sang looked particularly unimpressed, and Alaric thought Barrett would be in several detentions were he a student. A few class members looked like they were struggling to stay awake and were only kicked back into focus when Sang gave them a glare. Alaric noted what Barrett said absentmindedly, doubting he'd be able to even read any of it. Lucy seemed to be the only genuinely focused person, her hand shooting straight into the air when Barrett asked if there were any questions.

'Now, I looked up diseases this weekend, and there were none I could find that infect gnomes, cyclops and humans,' she said. 'Does this mean this would have to be a new sickness?'

Apparently not expecting such a question, Peter Barrett gave a start before answering, his stutter returning. 'Ah, w-well, I mean there are all-all sorts of s-sicknesses that w-we don't know a-about, s-so I w-wouldn't worry too much.'

Alaric and Lucy exchanged perplexed looks. When they were let out of their first detention-free lesson with Madame Sang, Alaric asked Lucy and Laurence what they thought. Laurence seemed as nonplussed as Alaric was, Lucy as confident as ever in her response.

'It's obvious, isn't it? Barrett hasn't got a clue,' she said.

'What d'you mean?' Laurence asked.

'Well, he never really seemed to know what he was talking about, did he?' Lucy said. 'Plus, his answer to my question…what even was that?'

'You can tell he's a businessman, not a doctor, can't you?' Alaric said, recalling Norman McNulty's news report where he'd been called a "tycoon".

'Hmmm, I think he's concerned, to be honest,' Lucy said. 'They have no idea what's causing it, and the number of times he said not to worry…you only say that if you're actually worried yourself.'

'He's got no idea it's a poison. We should tell him, shouldn't we? Or we could go to the nurse, tell her how to treat it?' Laurence suggested.

Alaric scoffed as Lucy looked pensive, Alaric unable to see how this could be a good idea.

'We have no evidence of any of this,' he said. 'They'll think we're mad, and besides, we can't go shouting the stuff about Sang and Ogden's brother everywhere.'

'I think, Alaric, we have a good lead,' Lucy claimed. 'The two people infected and the gnomes have an obvious link. Plus, all that stuff with Cassandra,

Ogden's brother and Sang fits our theory. We know this is a poison, and whoever's doing it would have had to have been at Oakwood over the summer. So, it's a member of staff who's behind this and who else could it be?'

'But have any of us ever even been to the nurse?' Alaric countered. 'She hardly knows us and would just think we're mad students.'

'Oh, for sure,' Lucy agreed. 'I'm not saying we should go to the nurse. She'd think we're crazy. Laurence, I'd suggest going to your dad. He's in government—'

'No, he doesn't want us looking for trouble this year,' Alaric interjected.

'I know,' Lucy said, 'which leaves Master Ogden. Last year, he didn't exactly approve of us getting involved with the affair with the Pearl, so we need to build up harder proof first.'

Alaric, Lucy and Laurence continued sauntering towards the canteen for lunch in a few moments of pensive silence as they considered the matter. Alaric had no clear idea as to how they could build up such evidence. To him, the only obvious answer was to wait and see how events unfolded, to spot the patterns in who became sick next. None of it was ideal, but it seemed inevitable.

'We'll just watch,' Alaric said, 'I guarantee you the next person to get ill will be someone Sang hates. Hopefully, it won't be one of us. I'm watching what I'm eating for now.' He lowered his voice as he helped himself to some salmon and boiled potatoes, not wanting to risk being overheard by the students around them.

'Alaric, it won't be in the school food,' Lucy said. 'Everyone would get ill if it were that; we all eat it.'

Alaric furrowed his brow and glanced out of the window into the overgrown field. Still, just a single gnome was dejectedly traipsing around the fence, trimming the hedge's leaves with a pair of shears nearly as large as himself.

'Do we even know who feeds the gnomes?' Alaric asked.

'Probably no one. Gnomes always kind of go off and do their own thing,' Laurence said. 'You buy a few, they garden for you then shelter in underground houses. I'm pretty sure they cook for themselves.'

'With what though?' Lucy said. 'I've never seen a gnome in a supermarket. Someone must give them the ingredients.'

'Well, I guess so,' Laurence said. 'I dunno, we never

had gnomes. My parents said it took the joy out of gardening.'

Alaric cut a potato in half as Lucy sat chewing, musing. 'Where we are at the moment,' Alaric said, blowing on a forkful of food, 'we're pretty sure it's a poison. Madame Sang is our top suspect, even if that's just because she's our only one. So, for now, all we can do is research poisons, see who gets sick next and figure out how she's doing it.'

'Agreed,' Lucy nodded. 'I'm pretty sure our textbook talks about venoms and antivenoms, so I expect it'd probably have a bit about poisons as well. I could even look it up now.'

She took the most enormous mouthful Alaric had ever seen and returned her plate to the counter. She then came back and withdrew her medicine textbook from her bag. She flicked through it and read in concentrated silence. She didn't speak for the rest of the lunch hour as Alaric and Laurence finished eating, not even looking at them as she frustratedly flicked through the pages.

'I can't find anything in here,' she said at last as Alaric and Laurence finished eating. 'I think one of us needs to go and see the nurse at the end of the day…or at least at some point.'

Alaric sighed. 'I thought we agreed telling her all this was a waste of time.'

'Yes, it would be. That's why we're going to get information, not give it,' Lucy said as if the matter were already settled.

'What d'you mean?' Alaric said. 'What's the nurse going to tell us?'

'I guess we'll find out,' Lucy replied. 'The thing is, I expect Ettoga and Cassandra would've been to see the nurse before they were admitted to hospital. We can find out how quickly it developed; one of us can pretend to have a cold, see how worried she is.'

Alaric raised his eyebrows in pleasant surprise. 'You know, I reckon that's a good idea. I can pretend to have a cold; I've got a bit of a cough anyway, so that should be easy,' he lied, not wanting to let Lucy and Laurence loose without him there to intervene.

'That works,' Lucy said. 'I'll come and do the talking since I know what needs to be said. Laurence, it'd look weird if all three of us go, so best you stay here.'

'So you're side-lining me?' Laurence said indignantly, 'thanks.'

'Laurence, it's not personal,' Alaric lied. 'Remember last year when we went to the Land of the Dead, you and I left Lucy at the lake. You'll be in action next time.'

'Right,' Laurence said, though Alaric could tell from his tone he wasn't entirely happy about the situation. The Ancient Egyptian classroom had come into sight now, and people were already filing inside for their lesson with Madame Moyglot.

'We'll go there tonight,' Alaric muttered to Lucy.

ALARIC AND LUCY went to see the nurse straight after dinner that evening, Laurence heading back to the House of Rei's lodgings. Alaric had spent the afternoon practising his fake cough to fool the nurse, Lucy planning precisely what she was going to say. Alaric's skin was starting to tingle with a mixture of nerves and excitement as they strode through the gardens of Oakwood, the blood-red sunset glowing down onto the surrounding trees. Neither of them had ever been to see the nurse before, and having to guess where it was based on what they knew, they set off into the forest, winding down a pathway right into its heart.

When they arrived, the office reminded Alaric more of a witch's house than a health centre. Not only was it in the middle of a forest, but its thatched roof seemed sunken down by years of neglect, numerous bizarre plants growing out the front door. There were spotted toadstools that reached Alaric's waist and daisies which were even taller, seeming to lean in and stare at them as they approached. Alaric, forcing himself not to spend too long observing the setting, walked towards the wooden door with Lucy and read the sign that was nailed to it:

PLEASE KNOCK AND WAIT TO BE CALLED IN

Alaric clenched his fist and raised his hand to knock on the door but stopped suddenly when he heard voices on the other side. Lucy furrowed her brow in response and raised her arm as though to knock, Alaric slapping it down and indicating at her to listen.

'How many students are in hospital, Beatrice?' Madame Sang asked, her voice lower than usual.

'Five,' Beatrice replied.

'And all in one day?' Sang asked, her pitch rising inquisitively.

'Indeed,' said Beatrice. 'All came in with a cold a few hours ago, then started throwing up and losing their breath. They're in hospital now.'

'Good,' Madame Sang said indifferently. Alaric and Lucy exchanged urgent glares as she continued to speak. 'And which students?'

'A young lad, about fourteen, Felix Bell…Ora

Chandyo, three others,' the nurse said.

Alaric looked at Lucy with a puzzled expression. He tried to think about why anyone would want to attack Felix or Ora. Lucy, however, was still listening, concentrating hard on what was being said.

'And the medicine, is it working?' Sang said.

'Well, it's kept them all alive. The gnomes were all dead without it,' Beatrice said simply.

'Look, Beatrice,' Madame Sang replied, 'I really do feel that if you allowed me to make the medicine rather than sourcing this stuff from Barrett's company—'

'No, never,' Beatrice interrupted. 'This remedy works very well, and Mr Barrett is kindly providing it for free. The students, they're not dead, are they? This has saved their lives, for goodness' sake.' She let out a chuckle which was impossible to interpret, sounding like something between a cackle and a chortle. Alaric looked at Lucy, who appeared just as perplexed.

'I'm the expert on this,' Sang snarled, 'and I say you should withdraw the medicine.'

'And you don't make the decisions,' Beatrice said firmly. 'Now, I suggest you leave since I sense I have students waiting on the other side of the door.'

CHAPTER 8

THE DOOR SWUNG open from the other side straight away. Madame Sang exited the health centre immediately, staring rigidly at Alaric and then Lucy as she sidled past. Alaric desperately kept his expression neutral and innocent as she did so but wasn't convinced he'd fooled her as she strode off into the distance. He shuddered and turned his attention to the nurse, who was standing, smiling with bright red lips that matched her thick, spiked-up hair.

'How can I help you two today?' she said gently.

Alaric gave a start. For a moment, he'd forgotten the plan. 'I have a slight cold,' he said. 'Been coughing a lot.'

'Of course,' said the nurse, 'do come in. Your friend can come in too; you don't want to leave her outside. I think it's going to rain soon.'

Alaric and Lucy followed the nurse in. She led them into a room with six beds, all stripped except one. The room's white walls and floor made it well-lit, despite the darkness of the woods outside.

'Please, take a seat,' said the nurse, pointing to the one bed that was still made. 'I don't believe we've met, have we? What are your names?'

Alaric and Lucy introduced themselves, the nurse heading over to a cupboard in the corner of the room.

'Ah yes, I've heard about you both,' the nurse said. 'Of course, who hasn't?' she gave a small chuckle. 'I'm Madame Bork, but call me Beatrice. Had you been waiting long then?'

Alaric and Lucy exchanged worried looks, unsure what to say. She'd clearly known they'd been outside, but they couldn't let her know they'd overheard the conversation between her and Madame Sang.

'It's fine. I know you were listening in,' she said with a reassuring smile. 'I saw you coming through the window, just best you don't tell anyone. Sang's really not happy about this new medicine we've been using, always bitter about these things. The one we've sourced from Mr Barrett has kept all these students and your teachers alive. The one she made for the gnomes didn't save a single one. Honestly, you'd think she wanted them dead.'

She gave another laugh, and Alaric and Lucy exchanged puzzled looks again. Beatrice seemed to have a sense of humour that was at best strange and at worst morbid. Alaric watched on as she rummaged through her medicine cabinet and brought him two small pills and a glass of water on a tray, which Alaric took.

'That should clear up the cold in a couple of hours,' Beatrice said sweetly. 'Anything else I can help you with?'

'No, that's all, thank you,' Alaric said, forcing a smile, and he and Lucy headed off back towards the House of Rei's accommodation.

'SANG'S ONTO US,' Alaric said to Laurence once they'd arrived back, seated around the fireplace in their bedroom. Alaric and Lucy had told Laurence what they'd heard between Madame Sang and Beatrice at the health centre, Laurence looking alarmed and white of face.

'How d'you know?' Laurence said.

'When we were at the health centre, and Madame Sang came out, the way she looked at me and Lucy…she knows we're up to something.'

Lucy said very seriously, 'What about these students, though? We know Felix is half-Ordinary—'

'What?' Alaric asked. 'He never told me.'

'Well, you probably never asked, did you?' Lucy said

tersely. 'You really ought to take an interest in people other than me and Laurence.'

Alaric shuffled in his seat, mildly affronted, even though he knew she was probably right. 'But what about Ora?' he said.

'Well, I was getting to that before you interrupted,' Lucy said with raised eyebrows. 'The nurse said her surname is Chandyo. Now, I'm just guessing, but I know from the news that Ali Chandyo is competing against Iglehart in the election. Are they related?'

'Yes, I remember Jacob saying Ora's his granddaughter once,' Alaric said.

'So, whoever is behind all this, they've got to also want Iglehart in government. That rules out most people,' Alaric said bitterly.

'Not really,' Laurence replied. 'Dad always said Naidos supporters would vote for Iglehart. He does a lot of stuff they like, and because he's useless, they get away with stuff like that attack on our house.'

'And Sang is a descendant of Naidos. Who's to say she doesn't secretly support him?' Lucy said.

'It certainly seems plausible,' Alaric muttered.

The night had now fallen outside, the full moon glowing down onto the sea, rain ominously lashing down against the windows. When he got to bed, Alaric hardly slept with the noise, his mind also too riddled with thoughts about what Madame Sang and Beatrice had said. He thought especially about one sentence: *You'd think she wanted them dead.* Was this why Madame Sang was so keen to make the medicine? So she knew the sick people wouldn't be cured? How could someone like that get into a school to teach? As the night went on, he became more dubious about the idea of Sang being behind the poisonings. After all, she'd been approved to work at the school; Mr Trolley had even said she'd been his favourite teacher at school. Surely, she couldn't have changed that much? And if she was behind these attacks, why had she suddenly decided to do it now?

When he finally fell asleep, it was for such a short time that he awoke feeling incredibly groggy, far too tired to express his doubts to Lucy and Laurence. They helped themselves to toast and cereal before sitting down, eyeing the TV in the corner of the canteen. Norman McNulty was presenting the morning's news, looking somehow even more sullen than usual. His normally pin-striped jacket was replaced by a plain black one, which still looked on the brink of splitting.

'Good morning,' he said. As usual in the canteen, he was muted, the words he mouthed subtitled at the bottom of the screen. 'This morning's top story is that the leading candidate for Governor of Harramore, Ali Chandyo, has been found dead in his home. The Harramore Police have assumed this is a murder—'

'Someone definitely has it in for the Chandyos then,' Lucy said.

'Hmm,' Alaric agreed, now feeling more awake. 'This couldn't have been Madame Sang, though. There's just no way she'd have done that overnight.'

'Oh no, this is something much bigger,' Lucy said. 'Sang or whoever's doing this is part of an organised group.'

'I was thinking last night, though, I'm not sure if it is Sang. It's just that now seems like a weird time to suddenly start doing this to everyone,' Alaric said.

'No, it's really not,' Lucy asserted. 'With everything that's been going on, this is the perfect time.'

'It's just none of it makes sense,' Alaric said. 'Why Felix specifically? Surely, they'd go for Lucy before, and why have they not gone for me yet?' Alaric's last sentence lodged itself in his throat like a sharp stone, and he lost his appetite instantly.

'It could be like last year?' Laurence suggested, his face colourless. 'Maybe they need you for something?' Alaric shuddered, and what little was left of his appetite was now gone for sure.

'There are a lot of mysteries, no two ways about it,' Lucy sighed. 'I think we, or rather, you, have some investigating to do.'

'What d'you mean?' Laurence asked.

'This weekend, you two are going home, right?' Lucy replied.

'Yeah,' Laurence said, perplexed.

'So, you're going to get some information from your dad. He works in government, so he should have some answers about Ali Chandyo. Just ask innocent questions, find out what's going on,' Lucy said.

'But Lucy, my parents don't want us getting into trouble this year,' Laurence argued.

'And? Do you really think he'd have wanted us going to the Land of the Dead last year? Be subtle about it, pretend you're worried,' Lucy said.

'She's right,' Alaric said, his shoulders slumping. 'Don't think I'll need to *pretend* to be worried, though.'

THE REST OF the week seemed to drag on. Alaric, Lucy and Laurence spent their time trying to distract themselves from the sickness around the school, in a sense waiting for something more to happen. Whenever the topic came up in conversation, the same points were repeated, and the exchange was cut short. Then, no further developments in the saga unfolded before the end of the week. Alaric had spent the whole of Friday drawing up what he could say to Mr Trolley in his mind, but as they sat down for dinner, it became clear he needn't have done so.

'Very worrying times indeed,' Mr Trolley said in response to the news. Norman McNulty had given a pessimistic account of the hospitalisations at Oakwood and Ali Chandyo's death, claiming Harramore was on the brink of another war.

'D'you think McNulty could be right about another war?' Alaric asked.

'I think a lot of what's been happening lately is concerning: the affair with the Pearl last year; the tensions with Naidos' descendants; the infections at Oakwood; and now this with Ali Chandyo. Indeed, there seems to be something very fishy going on,' Mr Trolley said.

'But at Oakwood, that's a sickness,' Hector pointed out. 'You're not saying it's all connected, are you?'

'Well, we never quite know,' Mr Trolley said.

'But the people of Harramore don't want another war,' Mrs Trolley said reassuringly. 'We all remember what the last one was like. People would try to avoid that.'

'I certainly hope so,' Mr Trolley sighed. 'With Ali Chandyo dead, unless someone else stands, Iglehart will stay in power. The only alternative would be Vido Sadaarm, a huge supporter of Naidos.'

As they took this in, there was a short silence; Alaric's throat seemed to close up, and he couldn't speak for a few moments.

'Is there any lead on who killed Ali Chandyo yet?' he asked eventually.

'None at all,' Mr Trolley sighed. 'It's a complete mystery. I reckon Vido Sadaarm is behind it, a large-scale, secret plot. We have to look at this logically—supporters of Naidos are the one group who'll benefit from this; they're bound to be in on it.'

Alaric and Laurence exchanged urgent glares, and they ate the rest of the meal in a downbeat silence. When it was over, they headed straight to their room to discuss what Mr Trolley had said, their suspicions compounded. Lucy was onto something.

CHAPTER 9

'I'M CALLING LUCY now,' Alaric said as soon as Laurence had shut their bedroom door behind them. He pulled his phone out of his pocket and started dialling. He scratched the palm of his free hand with his thumb, agitated as he heard the familiar ringing tone, his heart seeming to stop as Lucy picked up.

'Hey, what's up?' she said.

'We've got a lot to tell you,' Alaric replied.

'Is Laurence there?' Lucy said. 'Turn on video.'

Alaric babbled incoherently, unsure what to do. He'd called Lucy several times before from Harramore but had no idea if a video call would work on the island; none of the phones for sale even had screens. He took his own smartphone away from his ear and, not sure what to expect, touched the video icon. He watched the loading screen for a few seconds, almost jumping when he saw Lucy's face appear.

'What the...is that Lucy?' Laurence exclaimed.

Alaric and Lucy burst out laughing, Alaric realising

this was probably the first time he'd ever spoken to a face on-screen.

'Yes, Laurence,' Lucy said between her laughs, 'what's up?'

'It's like talking to a TV,' Laurence said, his mouth hanging open with astonishment.

'Yes, and you have 3D TVs over there, so this shouldn't be that weird for you,' Lucy said. 'Now, what's the news?'

Alaric recounted to Lucy everything that Mr Trolley had said. Lucy sat in silence for a few seconds as she absorbed all of the information, musing on what it meant.

'Well, your dad's mainly right, I think,' she said.

'How d'you mean?' Laurence asked.

'Well, of course, this is good for Naidos' supporters. So, maybe Sang is behind it, maybe some of the students like Franco and Dwayne as well...you never know. Then again, Iglehart and the people close to him will also benefit,' Lucy said.

'So, you think Iglehart could be behind it?' Laurence asked.

'We can't rule it out, but I doubt it,' Lucy said.

Alaric nodded in agreement. 'Iglehart may love his power, but I reckon he's too much of a coward to risk that. The obvious suspect is Peter Barrett, based on what we heard. He's close to Iglehart and has the money to pay an assassin.'

'Hmm, he could definitely be at the helm of it or part of this network. He's only been to the school once, though, so he couldn't have poisoned everyone,' Lucy said.

'But he'd benefit, right? People getting sick means more people buying his medicine?' Laurence suggested.

'Not enough people have been sick though for it to make that much of a difference, and he's giving us the medicine for free,' Alaric pointed out.

'It's not a bad idea, though,' Lucy said. 'Say this is a network behind all of this; there's got to be an agent stationed at Oakwood—'

'Madame Sang,' Laurence said.

'Most likely,' Lucy agreed. 'Just the question is, where's all of this going?'

The three of them mused silently for a moment. It would only be so long before someone else became sick, Alaric thought. That could provide them with more information, but it seemed like only a matter of time before too many people were in hospital.

'Lucy, dinner!' called a voice on Lucy's end of the call. Her mother poked her head around her bedroom door. She then shuffled towards Lucy, her eyes fixated on her phone screen. Alaric started to feel uneasy, sensing she was staring at him again, just like she had when Alaric last saw her.

'Okay, I've got to go,' Lucy said awkwardly, also appearing to have sensed her mother staring at Alaric. 'I'll speak to you on Monday, all right?'

'Okay, see you,' Alaric and Laurence mumbled, and Lucy's face vanished from Alaric's screen. He turned to Laurence. 'Why does her mum always stare at me like that?'

Laurence shrugged. 'Weird woman, I guess.'

Alaric gave a start as there was a knock on their own door, and he felt a twang of guilt, realising he and Laurence hadn't helped clear up after dinner. He pulled the door open, expecting to see Mr or Mrs Trolley standing there, ready to moan, but instead, Hector greeted them on the other side.

'Hey, you two. I've got some bad news, I'm afraid. I've just received the news of our quarter-final draw, and we're against Naidos. Obviously, they won the cup last year, so they're a difficult team in any case, but against us, they'll also play dirty,' Hector said.

Alaric's body became hot at the thought of it. He was full of peculiar energy; on the one hand, he was relishing the opportunity to give them a beating but at the same time apprehensive. He couldn't think of anything worse than losing that match. 'We better beat them,' he said bitterly.

'I think we can,' Hector said. 'The thing is, we're away. If we were at home with the crowd behind us, I'd make us the favourites. Away, I'm less sure. So, even though the match isn't until after the winter break, I still want to start training this weekend. The next session is tomorrow evening, okay?'

He marched off to inform Jacob and Grace, Alaric slumping. Even with three classes cancelled, he still had a large pile of homework to get through that weekend, and the forecast was for heavy rain. That didn't dissuade Hector from forcing the team to practice passing routines in the garden. Alaric's clothes became stuck to his skin as the weather drenched them and they all returned indoors worn out, Alaric's legs sore from the rain. He and Laurence then spent most of Sunday working through their essays, giving them little time to discuss the affair surrounding Ali Chandyo and the infections at Oakwood. Any hopes of talking about the matter with Lucy in their free cryptozoology lesson were then dashed. The hour was no longer open as Master Ogden announced he'd be taking the class. They arrived to see Beatrice Bork tending to the woppanine's teeth outside the classroom. She gave Alaric and Lucy a reassuring smile as they approached before tickling the woppanine behind its ear.

Upon entering the room, Alaric's spine started to shiver immediately. There was a chilling atmosphere in the room. It was evident it hadn't been used in weeks, dust having visibly gathered on the furniture. Even though only Felix was missing from the regular group, the absence of Madame Ettoga made the place feel a lot emptier than it ever had. The class waited, the atmosphere muted, no one looking forward to an hour-long lesson when Master Ogden entered a few minutes later. He was wearing a dark suit as if he'd tried to tone down the usual boldness in his look, an effect that was undermined by his red shirt and rainbow bow tie.

'Good morning all,' he boomed with a smile as he entered the classroom. 'Is everyone here? Looks like it. The late stragglers can catch up if not.'

There was a rustling sound around the classroom as all the students opened their books to start note-taking. However, just like the last time they'd been in this classroom all those weeks ago, they were told to put them away.

'Now, obviously, you haven't had any proper cryptozoology classes for quite a long time at this point,' Master Ogden said. 'I am also well aware that teaching yourself, reading the textbook, is not a very good way of learning. So, I wanted to use this opportunity to talk to you all about the status of your education as a whole. I'm sure you all know that several teachers and students have been admitted to hospital with what seems to be the same illness that killed many of our poor gnomes. This is equally alarming for us as staff because this gives us a significant safety problem. We don't know what's causing this sickness to spread, and today, things have worsened. I regret to inform you that another one of your classmates, Georgia Beautang, was admitted to hospital over the weekend.'

There was an outbreak of panicked muttering around the classroom. Georgia's friend, Chloe Alkoff, burst into tears; Carlos looked too stunned to speak. Alaric, Lucy, and Laurence eyed each other. Why had Georgia now been targeted? Alaric remained silent, refusing to talk about it in front of Master Ogden, not wanting him to know that they were up to something again.

'I want to assure you,' Master Ogden went on, 'that Georgia, the other students and your teachers are in a stable condition. The medicine Mr Barrett has provided from Remy's is working well, keeping them alive, and they don't look like dying as the gnomes did. However, I must warn you that if more students or staff fall ill with this, I will have no choice but to close the school as a precaution.'

There was no collective groan around the class like Alaric would've expected. Rather, everyone looked as shell-shocked as each other. First Felix, now Georgia. Two students in their year already. The class watched on, only half-listening in subdued silence as Master Ogden detailed how they'd compensate for missed classes. Alaric doubted he had many people's full attention for the hour. It was, therefore, not a surprise to him when no one had any questions when Ogden asked, most of the class relieved to have been freed from the room.

'Well, we know Georgia's half-Siren,' Lucy said as they left the classroom to wander to Madame Sang's lesson. 'Though, I didn't know people had it in for them so much.'

'Oh yeah, they do. I'd imagine so anyway,' Laurence said. 'Anything people call sub-human.'

'Makes sense in a way, I guess,' Lucy said. 'Though, why'd supporters of Naidos target them?'

Alaric thought hard, remembering a cryptozoology

class with Madame Ettoga the previous year. It had been the only lesson where Ettoga hadn't shouted at Georgia. Her knowledge of Sirens had unsurprisingly been better than any other students'. He remembered Ettoga saying Sirens only ever attacked Ordinaries, so surely Naidos supporters would be quite fond of them? Something wasn't adding up.

'Maybe this is a decoy?' Alaric suggested. 'Trying to throw suspicions off-course. Really, there's no reason for supporters of Naidos to target Sirens when you think about it?'

'That's what I mean,' Lucy said. 'Unless there's another reason they'd attack Georgia, whoever's behind it isn't doing things the way we'd expect.'

'We'll have to see what happens next,' Alaric said. 'Now Ogden's threatened to close the school, I think the culprit might change their tactic.'

Lucy pursed her lips and nodded, Madame Sang's classroom coming into view. 'I think you might be right,' she said.

Indeed, as Alaric had predicted, the rest of the week passed without another student going to hospital. This gave Alaric, Lucy and Laurence little more information to go on as they tried to find evidence of who was behind the infections. They decided that whoever was responsible must've wanted the school to stay open unless they knew Alaric, Lucy, and Laurence were onto them. Ogden, meanwhile, still seemed to think it was a sickness.

'Well, Madame Sang hardly seems to love her job, does she?' Laurence said over a study session one evening. 'I don't know why she'd be so desperate to keep the school open.'

Alaric and Lucy chuckled and turned their attention back to their cryptozoology textbooks. They'd read the section on Sirens several times a day for the last week but could still make no sense of it. As fruitless as it was, they continued reading just in case they'd missed a crucial detail, but it was no use. Lucy sighed and shut her book, seeming to have given up.

'I think we need to abandon this for now; come back to it with fresh eyes,' she said.

Alaric followed suit and shut his book, struggling to disagree. 'We can research poisons or something in the meantime. What would give you a really bad cold?'

He, Lucy and Laurence thought hard. Alaric rose from his seat and started pacing the lounge area, no one saying a word. Many poisons and venoms had come up in Madame Sang's classes and homework, but none had even slightly matched the symptoms.

'Also, Alaric, my mum wants you to come for Christmas,' Lucy said, changing the subject suddenly. Alaric stared at Lucy, unsure how to react, while Laurence looked rather offended. The only encounters he'd had with Lucy's mother had been extremely uncomfortable, and he wasn't partial to the idea of spending one day with her, let alone several.

'W-well, I think I'm with Laurence's family for the holidays,' he said awkwardly.

'Yes, for New Year's,' Lucy said, 'you'd only come for Christmas. What d'you think? It'll be great. You don't celebrate Christmas here anyway.'

'Urrrmmm, okay,' Alaric said, reluctantly realising there was no polite excuse to say no. 'I'll check with Laurence's parents.'

'Great, and don't worry, I'll talk to her about her staring,' Lucy said, then turning to Laurence, noticing his offended expression. 'I asked if you could come, but she said she wasn't sure about having people she didn't know in the house for Christmas.'

'She doesn't know me any more than Laurence,' Alaric blurted out.

'Well, she spends so long looking at you, she probably wouldn't recognise me,' Laurence laughed. Alaric chuckled in response, Laurence looking more relieved than offended now.

'Stop, that's my mum you're talking about,' Lucy said with a smile, but her tone was still firm.

Alaric sat back down on the squashy settee, wringing his hands. As much as he liked Lucy, he struggled to imagine spending several days in her house with her and her mother. As accustomed as he was to awkward small talk with his previous foster families, none had stared at him and put him on edge as much as Lucy's mother did. Even John and Sue had been better before they'd tried to eat him.

AFTER NO DEVELOPMENTS or progress in the sickness affair over the next week, the winter break arrived, and any talk of the school being closed seemed to have virtually died down. Ettoga, Cassandra and the students were still in hospital as term ended, Master Ogden assuring the school they were in a stable condition and likely to be back after the holidays.

'Must've been a powerful poison, keeping them in hospital for that long,' Alaric said as he, Lucy and Laurence headed to the car park to be picked up.

'Hmm, none fitted the symptoms that we could find, though,' Lucy said. 'I think we're going to have to raid Madame Sang's office after the holidays.'

'How?' Laurence asked. 'Imagine if we got caught. Plus, when would we even do it? She's always there, and I bet she locks it.'

'Well, we've got plenty of time to plan. It's not like Sang can attack anyone while no one's at the school,' Lucy said.

'Well, yeah, the worst outcome is she gives us detentions, which'd hardly be anything new,' Alaric grumbled.

There was a murmur of agreement from Lucy and Laurence as they reached the car park, where Mr and Mrs Trolley were waiting patiently. They greeted the three of them, Laurence bidding goodbye to Alaric and Lucy as he got into the Trolleys' car. His parents checked Alaric had everything for his stay with Lucy over the next week before driving off. Alaric's stomach started to cramp as it now dawned on him that he was alone with Lucy and her family. Together, they waited as Lucy's taxi pulled into the car park and ground to a halt. Alaric recognised it instantly; it was the same bright orange one that had taken them to the Guardians' Palace. The size, number plate, everything was the same, and the woman who stepped out of the cab seemed to recognise them as much as they recognised her.

'Ah, it's you two again,' said the silky-haired woman in her Southern American accent, wearing the same, perfect smile as last time. 'Not trottin' off to the Guardians' Palace again, are we?' She gave them another smile, which, while evidently supposed to be friendly, was more annoying than anything else.

'No, we're going to the port. You know that,' Lucy said curtly, and the driver shuffled backwards like a child who'd just been told off, Alaric's ears going hot.

'Ah yes, well, in you get then,' she said with a smile that was much more forced than the last one.

Alaric followed Lucy into the cab, far less comfortable than he would've normally been with the room to stretch his legs right out. He was still feeling the slight embarrassment of Lucy's confrontation. The driver appeared to be feeling it too, as she drove in silence, even more violently than she had done last time. She turned so sharply around bends, Alaric may have thought he'd woken up in a movie car chase. He didn't dare open his mouth to speak out of fear of throwing up, even though he hadn't eaten in hours. Even looking out the window didn't help as the fields and houses of Harramore zoomed past in a blur, making his head spin even more. This made the journey drag on, and by the time the taxi ground to a sharp halt, Alaric's whole head was burning, his vision blurred. They climbed out of the cab, Alaric's legs almost giving as the driver handed back their suitcases, forcing a small smile. Lucy paid the driver as Alaric caught his breath and took a sip of water, his head slowly clearing.

He took a deep breath and examined his surroundings. The vast, clear blue sea was before him, stretching right out to the horizon. Behind him were stone walls, like those of a castle, which seemed to reach the sky. They were perfectly preserved like they'd been plucked straight out of the medieval era and placed in the present day. Even the man at the top of the tallest tower stood watching, a bow and arrow in hand, all the windows glassless. It was like the wall of an ancient city; only, bizarrely, Harramore didn't seem to have such defences on any other stretch of its coastline.

'They try to protect Harramore from invasion,' Lucy said in response to Alaric's perplexed expression. 'Makes no sense, really, since no one could invade Harramore.'

'What d'you mean?' Alaric asked.

'Well, most Nephilim live on Harramore; it's their land, so no Nephilim would build an army and invade. That leaves no one left to attack,' Lucy replied.

'So, can Ordinaries not get onto the island? I mean your mum—'

'Yes, she could, but only because I was with her. Solo gave her an exemption. The thing is, if any Ordinary ship started to get close to the island, a storm would start and carry on until the boat had been blown far enough away. Apparently, a lot of Nephilim don't even know that,' Lucy explained.

'But, if say, you had a massive cruise ship with one Nephilim on board and loads of Ordinaries—'

'It'd still be blown off-course. No Ordinary can get onto Harramore without formal permission from one of the Guardians,' Lucy said.

They were strolling down a pier now towards a docking station. There were only a few small boats there, most of which seemed to be for fishing, far too small to hold passengers. The only one that seemed large enough to be a form of public transport resembled a small pirate ship, and Alaric would've been surprised if even that could hold more than a score of passengers. Its wooden exterior was exactly like Alaric had seen in films, the mast at least thirty feet high. In fact, the only difference from a pirate ship seemed to be the lack of skull and crossbones that would be on the mainsail. Instead, there was the distinctive five-striped flag of Harramore: the purple, chartreuse, white, black and blue stripe each represented one of the Big Five

Guardians.

'How long is the journey?' Alaric asked.

'It depends,' Lucy said. 'Obviously, if someone wants to go to Australia or somewhere, the ship has to re-route, and it can take a few hours longer to get to England from there.'

'A few hours from Australia to England?' Alaric asked incredulously as they mounted the stairway onto the boat. He knew even flying took a whole day; a ship would have to take weeks, at least.

'It's a fast ship,' Lucy said simply. 'Should be in England before midnight, though.'

'That's eight hours,' Alaric exclaimed as Lucy showed two tickets to a woman on the deck dressed in a sailor's uniform.

'Just be grateful you don't have to do it every week,' Lucy muttered as they descended the staircase into the passenger cabin. When they reached the bottom, Alaric actually audibly gasped at what he saw for the first time in many months.

'Yes, it's bigger on the inside,' Lucy said indifferently. 'I was kind of impressed when I first saw it, but it's like the most used trick in the book.'

Alaric nodded as he tried to take in his surroundings. He had, of course, come across bigger insides many times in novels he'd read, but never had he expected to experience it. In fact, the passenger cabin was so spacious that even though there were already a few dozen people on board, it didn't feel crowded in the slightest, almost empty. What was more was that one look around the place told him being stuck on this ship for days would be no problem as he'd never get bored. They were standing in the centre of one of the highest marble halls he had ever seen. The hanging chandeliers gave off the air of being on a cruise ship, a couple of staircases leading up to a balcony overlooking the scene. The circular entrance hall then had several corridors shooting off it, each with hanging signs pointing to different places which looked as interesting as each other: there was a cinema, a library, a theatre, a restaurant, a café, a crazy croquet course, a shopping mall, a museum, an art gallery and even a swimming pool. However, Lucy led him to none of those places, but instead down a separate corridor signed "Observation Area".

'You'll want to see this, trust me,' she said.

Alaric followed her down the corridor, his body starting to tingle with excitement. The prospect of being on this ship for a few hours had made him almost forget about the week that lay ahead with Lucy's mother. They speed-walked down a well-lit, carpeted corridor lined with pictures of various fish, seashells, and mermaids before they arrived at a room with three glass walls. The lighting would've given the room an almost romantic glow were it not packed with dozens of parents and young children gazing at what was outside.

They were underwater, and hundreds of fish, spanning the colour spectrum from black to burgundy to bright blue, swam serenely in their tight shoals, around the coral reefs, which were all bright shades of fuchsia.

'It gets better as well,' Lucy said with a smile in response to Alaric's slightly open mouth.

As she said that, the ship sounded its ear-splitting horn and started to sail through the sea, the shoals of fish dispersing as the boat drove through them. As they progressed and the water got deeper, the small fish became dolphins, sharks and whales. Then, there was nothing but blackness, and Alaric started towards the room's exit, the only person who did so as Lucy grabbed his shirt to stop him.

'Wait,' she said.

Alaric did so, deciding to trust Lucy's judgement on the matter. After a few minutes of pitch black, a distant light shone, barely visible, like an underwater lighthouse. Then, as they got nearer, the single light split into dozens, then hundreds of white lights. Alaric's initial thought was that they'd be the type of fish he'd seen on TV once that could glow in the dark, but he could hardly have been further from the truth.

They were approaching an underwater city, exactly like those the legends had spoken about. All the stone houses and walls were perfectly preserved, like new. They glided over the city centre, scores of mermaids and mermen swimming past them, looking completely carefree. Some of them were going about their business in the city, gliding along the ocean floor, browsing the market stalls. A few of them were walking their pets like any human would have done, only all their dogs had gills, their webbed paws enabling them to swim.

'These cities…they're real?' Alaric said.

Lucy nodded. 'We're at the bottom of one of the deepest parts of the ocean. Not many humans see this place. Ordinary submarines don't work this far down.'

As they sailed over the city, Alaric questioned for the first time since he'd arrived at Harramore whether he was dreaming. Each mermaid and merman looked as different from one another as any humans. Some men had beards, others didn't; the hair colours varied from bright red to jet-black, and some were even bald, and the body shapes varied as much. It was a human city underwater. A few of the merpeople waved as the ship passed them, and some children waved back, jumping up and down excitedly.

'Do Nephilim and mermaids get on?' Alaric asked Lucy.

'Mostly,' Lucy replied. 'Although, apparently, it depends where you go. In places where Ordinaries have polluted the sea more, they can be hostile.'

Now, the city had passed, and they were plunged into complete darkness once more. The parents and their children started to file out of the room, Alaric about to follow suit when Lucy grabbed his shirt once more to stop him from leaving.

'There's still more,' she said.

'Why are they all leaving then?' Alaric asked.

'You'll see,' Lucy said with a smile that told Alaric she'd say no more.

It took a while for Alaric's eyes to adjust to the return to darkness, but when they did, still all he could see was sediment floating through the water. He took a seat on one of the now free benches and rested his head in his hands, bored, waiting for something to happen. The room was incredibly stuffy, Alaric feeling his shirt sticking to his back, and he thought he could do with a drink, but still, Lucy wouldn't let them leave.

'We'll see it any moment now,' Lucy assured Alaric. The whole boat jarred as if it had hit an enormous rock, Alaric giving a start. 'This'll be it.'

The boat started to move again. Only, it did so very slowly, as if there were many obstacles in this part of the ocean that Alaric couldn't see. Then, he shuddered, falling backwards off the bench at what he saw, Lucy's face turning scarlet with laughter.

What could have been hundreds of long, ropy tentacles were dangling down from above the window, stretching far below the boat. Alaric's first thought was that this was going to be some sort of giant octopus. But as the ship collided with one of these tentacles, they all impetuously coiled themselves around the boat like a hundred long pythons. Then, the body of the creature came floating down into Alaric and Lucy's view. It was translucent, almost the ghost of a Kraken and Alaric realised at once what he was looking at: the largest jellyfish he'd ever seen. Its body seemed as big as the ship itself, and Alaric was sure it could feed on prey at least as large as people.

'Parents don't like their kids seeing this,' Lucy said. 'This jellyfish eats humans, and it's just the start.'

'What d'you mean? This journey isn't dangerous, is it?' Alaric asked.

'Well, no, not with a boat of this size,' Lucy said, grinning like she was enjoying Alaric's nervousness. The giant jellyfish was now uncoiling its tentacles from the boat. It had clearly decided it was too large a piece of prey to handle, and the vessel advanced slowly through the murky water.

'How much more is there to see?' Alaric said, his mouth stickily dry. 'I really need a drink.'

Lucy chuckled. 'We'll get you one after this.'

As soon as she finished the sentence, the boat shook again as a giant, muscular tentacle struck the window so hard it seemed a miracle that the glass didn't crack. And Alaric felt his heart speed up dramatically as he saw this creature's body.

It could easily have been the size of a whale. Its tentacles were so long and muscular, Alaric wouldn't have been surprised if this creature *could* coil its arms around the boat and crush it. But it didn't do so. Instead, it fluttered its tentacles and sank lower, spreading them as if about to grab the boat and eat it. Alaric's stomach backflipped as the ship dived lower, dodging the creature's appendages, and Alaric caught his first glimpse at the creature's face. Its features were almost human: the pupils in the eyes, the chiselled nose and the mouth. Its horrible, ghastly mouth. As the creature opened it to reveal its sharp, dagger-like, slimy teeth, Alaric felt all of a sudden like his insides had melted. It let out a high-pitched, ear-splitting scream like a thousand vultures all being set on fire at once. Alaric knew exactly what this creature was. It was a Kraken.

'How do they get the skin off that for medicine?' he forced himself to say, amazed he didn't vomit.

'It sheds apparently,' Lucy replied, her face also white as though seeing this beast never became any less frightening. 'Still, to get the skin, they have to distract it. When people on Harramore are sentenced to death, they're fed to the Kraken.'

'That's barbaric,' Alaric said, rising from his seat and starting towards the door. He couldn't stand to see any more of this, no matter what Lucy said, but she seemed to agree as she followed him down the corridor.

'Well, they're always dead before they're used as food,' Lucy said, panting, seemingly just as horrified as Alaric was. 'I looked this all up when I first saw the Kraken. It was one of Goblinsfoe's reforms actually when he first got into government. He made sure criminals were killed...well, in a nicer way before they were fed to the Kraken.'

'That's still horrible,' Alaric said.

'Well, I agree that we shouldn't kill criminals at all, but we don't make the laws,' Lucy said.

Alaric felt sick at everything he'd just seen and heard and needed a drink now more than ever. He and Lucy headed back down the corridor and sat at a table for two in a restaurant, both ordering lemonades. They agreed they ought to order some pizza as it'd still be a few hours before the ship pulled into the English docks and hardly spoke after that. Alaric was too busy taking in everything he'd just seen and heard. How could humans be so cruel as to feed each other to that beast? He tried to dismiss the image from his mind as the waitress brought them their pizzas. He desperately wanted to eat, but he still wasn't the slightest bit hungry.

'I'm glad you decided to come for Christmas,' Lucy said as she started to cut up her vegetarian pizza, 'especially this year since my cousins aren't coming. It would've been lonely with just me and my parents.'

'It's a pleasure,' Alaric lied, though seeing Lucy made him sound far more convincing, perhaps because she made it truer.

'My mum will come off the whole staring thing, don't worry,' she said with a small laugh, taking a mouthful of food.

'It's okay. I enjoy being with you,' Alaric said. 'Us two never get time alone since Laurence and I live together.'

Lucy giggled. 'Do you not like Laurence?'

'No, no, of course, I do,' Alaric said with a smile. 'It's just different with him, you know? He's like my brother whereas you're…' The rest of his sentence got lost in his head. In truth, he had no idea what he was trying to express.

'I'm what?' Lucy laughed.

'A friend?' Alaric guessed. It seemed the safest thing to say.

'Right,' Lucy said, somewhat confused as she took another mouthful of her pizza. Alaric felt his head go hot, blushing furiously. He looked down at his food and cut off another chunk of his pizza, trying to seem natural. They both chewed their mouthfuls in awkward silence, Alaric gulping his down so quickly he almost choked.

'Do you not agree?' he said in an attempt to break the tension, then deciding it would have been better if he'd said nothing.

'No, I do,' Lucy replied. 'I've never had anyone actually give me a run for my money in classes. My connection with you is different than with Laurence.

You just didn't sound very sure, that's all.'

'I'm certain,' Alaric said, possibly a tad too firmly. Lucy gave him a strange look, and Alaric started to think that she was probably getting the wrong idea. 'It's nothing more than friends; I don't fancy you,' he blurted out, then looking back down at his food. Once again, he thought it would've been better if he'd stayed silent.

'Well, good,' Lucy laughed. 'You can rest assured that the feeling's mutual.'

Alaric wasn't sure how to react, feeling a mix between affronted, embarrassed and relieved. Lucy had honestly never given him romantic feelings, but he was sure he'd made it seem otherwise. Keen to divert the focus, he changed the topic of the conversation to Christmas, something that, much to his relief, made the awkwardness disappear almost instantly.

It was another couple of hours before they pulled into the docks at Southampton. By that time, both Alaric and Lucy were feeling immensely tired. Together, they disembarked the boat and greeted Lucy's mother in an almost deserted car park. Somehow in the dark, the similarities between her and her daughter were even more noticeable. Their silhouettes were virtually indistinguishable, their heights and slim figures a near-exact replica of each other's as they loaded their bags into the car boot. This time, Lucy's mother didn't acknowledge Alaric. She didn't even look at him as if avoiding his eyes, which was somehow even more unnerving than when she'd stared at him.

'Thanks for having me, Mrs Ray,' Alaric said as he got into the car.

'That's no problem,' she said distractedly as she started up the engine and reversed out of the car park.

'How was the drive here, Mum?' Lucy said.

'Fine,' her mother replied.

Lucy looked at Alaric with a shrug. He could see that her cheeks were reddening even in the darkness of the night.

'How long's the drive back then?' Alaric asked.

Lucy's mother didn't respond at all this time, leaving a few moments of hanging silence, which Lucy broke. 'About half an hour,' she said.

Alaric looked out the window at the nearly empty road, watching the few cars around pass by. His stomach tightened. If this exchange was anything to go by, this week would be even more awkward than he was expecting.

'What do you do for a living then, Mrs Ray?' Alaric said, deliberately specifying her name so she couldn't dodge the question.

'Teacher,' Mrs Ray said.

Alaric clenched his fists in frustration. 'And do you enjoy that?' he asked.

'Yes.'

Alaric sighed as lightly and quietly as he could, realising he was flogging a dead horse. He glanced at Lucy, whose cheeks were now even darker.

'Mum, why don't you tell Alaric what we've got planned for this weekend?' she said.

'We're going to the British Museum in London.'

Alaric waited for a few seconds just in case there was any hope of Mrs Ray elaborating.

'That sounds nice. Have you been before?' he said.

'No.'

Lucy sighed loudly. 'Mum, what's going on? Every time you're around Alaric, you act so weirdly, and it makes us both uncomfortable. You're never like this around anyone else.' She was almost shouting, struggling to stifle her exasperation.

Mrs Ray did not respond to Lucy verbally, instead slowing the car and stopping in a lay-by at the side of the road. She took a deep breath and then spoke. 'There's something I was going to tell you while Alaric was here. To be honest, I was going to wait, but I think it'd be easier just to do it now, rip off the plaster.' She sniffled like she was on the brink of tears, Alaric crossing his legs in the little space he had. His palms began to sweat.

'What is it, Mum?' Lucy asked. Her tone was shaking, almost worried.

'I-I didn't think I'd ever see him again,' Mrs Ray said, almost sobbing now.

'See whom?' Lucy asked.

'Alaric,' Mrs Ray replied.

'What do you mean, "see him again"?' Lucy asked. Alaric leaned forward, apprehensive, unsure what to expect.

But whatever he thought Mrs Ray was going to say, it was not what she actually did.

'Alaric, I'm your mum.'

CHAPTER 10

THE THREE OF them sat in silence for several minutes. It couldn't be true. Alaric just did not believe the woman driving this car was the same woman who hadn't wanted him as a son. This woman was the reason he'd never had a stable family before the Trolleys. His mind was too full of thoughts; he had too much to say to be able to speak. How did she recognise him? Was she sure about this? Why had she given him up? And this must have meant that all this time, Lucy had been his sister? Had she even known? He had no idea which question to ask first, and it was probably for the best when Lucy spoke before him.

'Are you sure about this, Mum?'

'Positive,' Mrs Ray said. 'I knew the moment I saw Alaric that it was true. He looks so much like me and you: the tall, slim build, and he has his face.'

'Whose face?' Lucy asked.

'His father's. The hair, the jawline, it's everything,' Mrs Ray sniffled.

A strange numbness overcame Alaric. He'd gone from having a terrible stomachache to feeling like he had no stomach at all. To him, it seemed perfectly plausible that Lucy was his sister. They had so much in common. Yet, one thing still wasn't making sense.

'He has a different surname though,' Lucy pointed out.

'I know. I can't explain that,' Mrs Ray said quietly, 'but I know I'm right about this. As soon as that Mr Solomon man showed up, I knew it was true.'

'Knew what was true?' Lucy asked.

'Everything he said. I had my suspicions when you were doing these strange things, Lucy. Still, I always dismissed it as my imagination, assumed there'd be some other explanation, but no. Alaric's my son, and I never thought I'd see him again, but here he is.' Mrs Ray's last words almost got lost, stifled by a strong sob.

'What do you mean, Mum? Who said what?' Lucy asked, her voice shaking. Alaric chanced a look at her for the first time since this conversation had started. He could tell she was no longer blushing, and all colour had drained from her face.

Mrs Ray took another deep breath, composing herself to speak. 'Alaric was only two days old. He woke up crying in the night, so your father and I got up to see what was wrong. Then, there he was, standing by the doorway, as tall as the ceiling, a shield propped against the wall. At first, I thought it was Alaric's father, but I knew it couldn't be. He was dead. Then, I saw his nose was different. He told me he was Alaric's uncle, and I couldn't keep the baby. He said it was too dangerous, told me all about Guardians and descendants and unending war. He claimed Alaric was special, that people would be after him, and it wasn't safe for me to keep him.

'I refused to hand him over, but he insisted. Still, I said no. Then, he lunged forward, tried to snatch Alaric. My husband lashed out and tried to stop him, told him to get away from me, but this man threw him against the wall so hard I thought he'd killed him. I didn't know what to do. I hurried over to him, but then there you were, Alaric, lying in the cot. This man grabbed you, picked up his shield and fled. I tried to chase him, but he was too quick. Even when I called the police, they said no man was seen on CCTV cameras at all that night. I spent months looking for you, but there was no sign anywhere.

'I had Lucy just over a year later, hoping that would fill the void. It helped, but the regret never went away, and I don't think it ever will. I'm sorry we never told you that you had a half-brother, Lucy. Your father and I thought you'd be better off not knowing since we didn't think we'd ever find him. But then Mr Solomon turned up as our gardener. I always thought he was a strange man, knew something was off from the moment I saw him.

'When he told me about you having these powers, Lucy, everything made sense. Then, when you came home from Harramore one weekend, told me about Alaric, I was hopeful. I had to come with you to meet him when term started. And I knew straight away.'

Alaric's throat started to feel very dry, as if he may choke. It all fitted too well not to be true. Everything she'd said about the man who came being Alaric's uncle, the description, it was all too accurate.

'So, you never gave me up?' Alaric just about managed to say. 'Mr Solomon, Solo, he said you never wanted me?'

Mrs Ray's bottom lip, which Alaric could see quivering in the mirror, froze as her face became stiff, now more raging than sad. 'Well, that man is never setting foot near our house again,' she said as if bottling up her anger, which sounded like it could explode at any moment.

Alaric's whole head became just as hot as his mother's seemed to. All that time, throughout all those years moving between families, Solo had been lying to him. Why? How could he do this? He cramped up his hands as he thought of him, trying to dismiss the thought from his mind. He knew even a mental image of that man's face for much longer would make him scream.

He tried to think of the positives: finally, he had a family. A wide grin surfaced on his face at the thought of it. He looked at Lucy and realised precisely the words he'd been looking for over dinner on the boat. He felt no differently about her now he knew the truth. To him, she'd always been like a sister and the same happiness coursed through him as when he'd first met the Trolleys.

Now, his mind turned to the Trolley family. Another kind of emptiness filled him as he thought about how happy he'd been there, how welcome they'd made him feel when he first arrived. Would he still live with them? After all they'd done for him, he couldn't just leave.

Everyone in the car was silent as Mrs Ray started the car up again and drove. Each of them was too deep in thought, too busy trying to process everything to be able to speak. Alaric had lost any perspective on the amount of time that was passing and had no idea how long the journey had been when they pulled up into

Lucy's driveway. It was a much smaller house than the Trolleys', a thatched cottage in the middle of a village. They were greeted inside by a carpeted floor and a ceiling barely high enough for Alaric not to have to stoop. He stood awkwardly in the small hallway, waiting until someone spoke.

'I'll show you to your room,' Lucy said.

'No, it's fine, I'll do it,' Mrs Ray said.

Alaric followed his mother upstairs, no one speaking. The steps creaked like the house had been well-loved, the landing doing the same as they walked its length, and Mrs Ray gestured towards the room at the end.

'Here we are,' she said.

Alaric turned the wooden knob and was greeted on the other side by the nicest bedroom he'd ever had in a house. A large double bed stood against the centre of the back wall, already made up with several plush-looking pillows and a navy, spotted duvet cover. A set of cupboards stood fixed against one wall, a desk and leather chair next to the window. He even had a small bookshelf by his bed, filled with novels of varying genres and sizes, several tasteful paintings hanging on the walls.

'We always tried to keep this room tidy, in case you

ever came back,' Mrs Ray said softly, a hint of emotion in her voice.

'It's great.' It was all Alaric could muster up the strength to say.

'You know,' Mrs Ray said as Alaric put his suitcase by his bed, 'you're always welcome here. I understand if you'd rather stay with the Trolleys, but if you ever need a home, this will always be your bedroom.'

Alaric nodded, unable to speak, his eyes filling with tears he was holding back. He didn't look at his mother, knowing doing so would make him cry there and then. They stood, not speaking for a few moments before Mrs Ray slipped out of the bedroom.

Alaric changed into his pyjamas straight away and went to bed but didn't sleep. Instead, he just lay there, trying to reflect on everything that had happened that day, hot tears running down his cheeks as he thought about it all. The boat journey, seeing those mermaids and mermen, the man-eating jellyfish, the Kraken all seemed a distant memory at this stage. He didn't want to be alone. He needed someone he knew well, whom he trusted, who'd understand. He needed to be with Lucy.

He wiped the tears from his face and sat up in his bed, contemplating going over to see her. Then, he realised he didn't know which bedroom was hers, and she'd probably be asleep now anyway. However, as he thought about this, he heard a knock on the other side of the door, giving a start as it happened.

'Come in,' he said.

The door opened slowly, and Lucy came creeping into the room in her fluffy dressing gown. She switched on the lamp by the wall, giving the room a pleasant glow and came to sit on the bed next to Alaric.

'I'm glad you're up. I can't sleep,' she said.

'Me neither,' Alaric replied.

'I feel we need to talk alone about this,' Lucy said.

Alaric nodded. 'I just can't believe Solo lied to me all that time, then didn't even tell us we were half-siblings. What was he going to do? Just let us get along as friends and never know? Hope by some miracle that we never found out?' His tone was bitter, and he couldn't remember hating someone as much as he loathed Solo at that moment.

'Maybe he meant for us to find out eventually,' Lucy shrugged. 'It'd be impressive for us not to. He can't be that stupid.'

'Yeah, well, he's a git,' Alaric grumbled.

'I know,' Lucy agreed. 'How could he send Ceus to treat my mum like that and attack my dad? I want nothing to do with him anymore.'

Alaric stared down at his knees, unsure what to say. He and Lucy sat thinking for a few moments before Alaric spoke.

'Your mum, our mum…said I could live here…if I wanted,' he said.

Lucy grinned, showing all her teeth. 'That'd be great,' she said excitedly. 'Do you think you will?'

'I don't know,' Alaric said truthfully. 'It's complicated.'

'I understand,' Lucy said, though the disappointment in her tone was unmistakable. 'For me, it's hard enough getting my head 'round the fact that I actually have a brother.'

Alaric gave a slight smile at the thought. They spent most of the night chatting about how life could be if they lived together. As much as Alaric enjoyed it, he couldn't make the nagging thought in the back of his mind about Laurence and the Trolleys go away.

They finally went to sleep in the early hours of the morning, waking up soon after, and Alaric felt not even slightly tired as he went down for breakfast. Lucy and Mrs Ray were already downstairs, Lucy sitting at the table as her mother prepared a cafetière. She offered Alaric coffee and invited him to take a seat when Lucy's father entered. He was a tall, lean man with thinning grey hair and round glasses sitting high up on his nose.

'Morning all,' he said cheerily. 'You must be Alaric?'

Alaric nodded, triggering Mr Ray to speak again.

'Pleasure to meet you. I'm Roy,' Mr Ray said, shaking Alaric's hand firmly.

'I've told him about…everything,' Mrs Ray told her husband.

'Ah right, okay,' Mr Ray said, looking somewhat relieved. He froze in awkward silence for a few seconds before changing the subject. 'I'll tell you, I've had a tough week at the hospital. Seventeen patients came in with this weird thing. It seems to really be taking off now. It's bizarre.'

Alaric and Lucy looked at each other, and it was apparent they were both thinking the same thing.

'What is it, Dad?' Lucy asked.

'Same thing every time, I'm afraid. It starts off as a normal cold. They think nothing of it. Then, it gets worse suddenly. They start throwing up and develop these sorts of greenish bumps on their chest. They come to the hospital, and we try to reassure them, but every single one who comes in dies in a few days,' Mr Ray said solemnly.

'Gosh,' Mrs Ray said, 'and is there no idea what's causing it?'

Mr Ray shook his head. 'Nothing. They find no signs of infection at all. It's as if…I don't even know.'

Lucy and Alaric looked at each other again, both sets of eyes bulging so much, you'd have no idea neither of them had slept. There was no doubting this was a poison now. And it had reached the Main World. They were both desperate to hurry through breakfast, unable to do so as Mr and Mrs Ray made what felt like endless small talk with Alaric. He tried to respond as fully and openly as possible, but his mind was too absent for him to do so. When they finally escaped, they headed straight to Alaric's bedroom, talking immediately.

'So, they're targeting Ordinaries now?' Lucy said.

'Apparently,' Alaric said, 'and if there's no sign of infection, it's certain this thing is a poison, that it's intentional.'

Lucy nodded. 'And now we know it causes green bumps on the chest, this should be easy to find. We just need to look for a poison.'

'Hmm, does the Harranet work out here?' Alaric mused, opening his laptop and logging on. He clenched his fist in frustration as the dreaded message appeared on his screen: "No Signal".

'There's no way of contacting Laurence privately either,' Lucy sighed. 'They don't have proper phones in

Harramore, do they?'

Alaric snorted with laughter. 'They do, just only old-fashioned ones. The Trolleys have a family phone, but you're right; he couldn't speak to us without being overheard. We ought to call them anyway, though.'

'My mum's already on it,' Lucy said. 'She called this morning but said she'd talk to you about everything before me.'

Alaric shuddered at the thought. 'No, I want you to be there,' he said. He knew he couldn't stand such a conversation without Lucy by his side, and when Mrs Ray did come and knock on his bedroom door, he insisted she be there. Mrs Ray reluctantly agreed, and the three of them sat in the bedroom as Alaric's mother began to speak.

'So, I phoned Mr and Mrs Trolley this morning,' she said. 'I explained the situation, and they said they won't be offended whatever you want to do. Of course, they like having you, but fully understand if you want to live here, as do I if you want to live with the Trolleys. It's just that I'd love to make up for all that time we lost together.'

Alaric sucked in the air through his teeth, considering the matter. He was once again lost for words, clueless as to what to say.

'You don't have to decide now,' Mrs Ray said. 'I'll let you think about it. You could always spend time in both places.'

Alaric nodded. 'I think I need a few days,' he said.

'Of course,' Mrs Ray said gently. 'It's a big decision. Just know that you'll always be welcome here, no matter what you decide.'

Alaric nodded, and Mrs Ray slipped quietly out of the room. Alaric and Lucy ended up doing very little that day, the whole house too tired to go out. They spent much of the day playing cards as a family, something Alaric was particularly poor at having never played, not winning a single game. It was approaching dusk when the doorbell rang, Mr Ray leaping up to go and answer it, and Alaric recognised the man at the door's voice instantly.

'Good evening,' Master Ogden said.

'Hello,' Alaric heard Mr Ray respond, 'can I help you?'

'Yes, I'm just here to speak to Alaric and Lucy. Probably not a bad idea if your wife joins me as well. As for you, well, you do what you like,' Master Ogden said. Alaric, Lucy and Mrs Ray rose from their seats and headed into the hall. Master Ogden was forcing his way past Mr Ray, a baffled look on the latter's face, apparently unsure who this was.

'Urm, do you mind?' Mr Ray protested. 'You don't just barge into people's houses unannounced.'

'I'm not unannounced; I announced myself at the door,' Master Ogden said as if Mr Ray had said something particularly absurd. 'Now, please, I have an important conversation to have with the other three.'

Mr Ray stood, open-mouthed in shock as Master Ogden sidled past everyone into the living room, where a game of cards was still set up messily on the table. Alaric and Lucy—both looking rather amused—followed him in. Mrs Ray did the same, seeming somewhat uncertain as Master Ogden made himself comfortable, sitting in an armchair and crossing his legs. He was today dressed in a tweed suit, a look he hadn't quite mastered as he combined it with a pair of trainers and a lime green shirt, which clashed horribly with his jacket.

'Right, now Mrs Ray, I'm not sure we've met,' Master Ogden said.

'No, we haven't,' Mrs Ray replied, taken aback. 'Who are you?'

'Master Quentin Ogden, Guardian of Oakwood. I've been on the phone to Mr Trolley, thought we could all do with a chat.'

'About what, precisely?' Mrs Ray asked.

'Alaric, you, Lucy, the general state of the world,' Master Ogden said, almost musing.

'And you say you're a Guardian?' Mrs Ray asked, a pronounced bitterness in her tone. 'Does this mean you're friends with that Mr Solomon?'

Master Ogden exhaled audibly as if trying to solve a complicated puzzle. 'I wouldn't call him my friend, more an acquaintance, colleague, man I tolerate…any of those terms would work really. We have all sorts of disagreements, you see. He enslaved the entire gnome race, which I don't approve of; a lot of stuff he did with you three really didn't sit comfortably with me either.'

Mrs Ray said nothing, instead just staring at Master Ogden like he'd transformed into a scarlet sphinx. Alaric and Lucy exchanged amused looks, Alaric imagining this must've been more or less his reaction when he'd first met Master Ogden.

'Shall we begin then?' Master Ogden said like a teacher announcing storytime to his children.

'Sure,' Mrs Ray said, seeming to have resigned herself to going with the flow.

'So, as I say, Mr Trolley called me earlier, told me about your little…*situation*. I thought it was best I weighed in on the issue from a Guardian's perspective, explain why everything's happened this way. I thought it'd be better coming from me. I appreciate Solo is probably the last person any of you want to see now,' Master Ogden began.

'Right,' Mrs Ray said weakly, 'well, I think we're all still coming to terms with everything. I really would've preferred it if you'd called in advance.'

Master Ogden looked at Mrs Ray as if she'd said something particularly daft. 'Would you have let me come if I had?'

Mrs Ray's eyes widened. 'I don't think I would, no.'

'Exactly,' Master Ogden said. 'Now, I need to explain to you why everything that happened between you three did. Naturally, after Alaric's birth and Naidos' disappearance, Harramore was a dangerous place for some years. So, we needed to keep Alaric away from there, but also safe, where he'd never be found. The Guardians decided to have him live in the Main World, shielded from the instability.'

'And what exactly meant that was your decision to make?' Mrs Ray snapped.

'Well, he's important not just to Harramore, but also your world, which, remember, Naidos wanted to destroy. I should add, though, that I didn't exactly have a say myself,' Master Ogden said in response to Mrs

Ray's livid glare.

'But you went along with it anyway?' Mrs Ray said.

'I don't have as much control over these things as you think I do,' Master Ogden sighed. 'But yes, they never thought he'd be safe, and neither would you, hence why we changed his name so no one could trace him back to you.'

'They never came looking,' Mrs Ray said sourly.

'They did find him, though,' Master Ogden said. 'Over time, supporters of Naidos were tracked down by the Harramore Government. The most fervent were to be either executed or given very lengthy prison sentences, so they fled to the Main World. Last year, in fact, a set of Alaric's parents turned out to be Naidos-supporting vampires. Harramore became safer than the Main World.'

'Are you saying I should stay with the Trolleys?' Alaric asked, unsure how to feel. This would, at least, make the decision an easier one to make.

'We have a duty to keep you safe, Alaric; I trust you know that,' Master Ogden said. 'However, as I'm sure you've noticed, Harramore is having a lot of problems at the moment as well. Nowhere is completely safe right now, and unfortunately, as you get older, things are likely to get worse—'

'What do you mean?' Alaric interjected. Master Ogden's face whitened slightly like he'd said something he shouldn't have.

'Just that there are certain responsibilities you'll have as an adult,' Master Ogden said, almost shrugging off the question. 'Ultimately, though, you are old enough to make that decision yourself over where you want to live. However, I do suggest joining the Trolleys for New Year's as planned would be best.'

'But why was everything kept from me?' Alaric asked, his voice rising. 'Solo and the Guardians, for years, they left me in the dark, thinking my mum didn't want me, not knowing I was a Nephilim; I had no idea who my parents even were.'

'Now, Alaric,' Master Ogden said gently, 'I understand your frustration, but please don't take it out on me. Solo and Ceus made the executive decision that it would be safer like that. If I'd had my way, things would've been different. However, we are where we are now, and no amount of hindsight will ever change anything.'

Alaric stared at Master Ogden, scowling like a bulldog. He needed someone to be angry at, and right then, the headmaster was his best option.

'Now, moving onto Lucy, you have all probably

wondered why she has Nephilim powers unlike any other person with exclusively Ordinary ancestors?' Master Ogden went on.

At this, Alaric dropped his glower and, as Lucy and Mrs Ray both did, shuffled in his seat and leaned forward, listening attentively.

'Well, the reason is that Lucy was born only just over a year after Alaric. Having been born from and grown in the same mother as him, she inherited some of his powers. Being the King Guardian's immediate son, Alaric left his mark on you, Mrs Ray. This meant that a future child of yours would have Nephilim powers,' Master Ogden explained.

Alaric sat there, gaping as he processed this. Everything was clicking into place now. It made perfect sense how Lucy could have Ordinary parents.

'And were you ever going to tell us?' Lucy asked. 'Let us know that Alaric was my half-brother, that my mum was his mum? Or were you just going to let us find out for ourselves, maybe hope we never did?'

'I couldn't tell you anything unless the more senior Guardians authorised me to do so,' Master Ogden sighed. 'What Solo and Ceus had in mind, I don't know. Now, as for the present situation with Alaric, I'll leave that for you all to discuss with the Trolleys, but ultimately, Alaric should have the final say.'

Mrs Ray nodded, Alaric feeling a weight drop on his shoulders as he thought about the decision he was faced with. He didn't want to leave either family. On the one hand, the Trolleys were the first people to make him feel genuinely at home, but then again, Mrs Ray was his real mother; she and Lucy were his real family. He tried to dismiss the thought from his mind as Mrs Ray spoke.

'Is that it then?' she asked Master Ogden.

'Indeed, it is,' Master Ogden answered. 'Sorry for having disturbed your evening, but this conversation needed to be had. I'll see myself out.'

CHAPTER 11

THE WINTER BREAK was the most up-and-down period of Alaric's life. As much as he enjoyed his time with the Ray family, he felt a strange pang of guilt every time he remembered or thought of the Trolleys.

He then spent much of New Year far more downbeat than he had the previous year, feeling all of a sudden like he didn't belong, an outsider in the family. Just like over the summer, even basketball gave him little joy, his performance far below its usual standard.

The arrival of the new term at Oakwood cheered him up slightly, being able to be with Lucy and Laurence together for the first time in weeks. Still, none of those admitted to hospital in the first term was back at school, meaning they were left to teach themselves again in their cryptozoology lessons. Only now, Master Ogden had decided they needed supervision. Alaric, Lucy and Laurence found themselves a table at the back of the classroom, Madame Moyglot sitting at Ettoga's desk correcting students' translations. They kept their cryptozoology books open as if studying, quietly discussing what Alaric and Lucy had found out over the holidays.

'So, this poison thing is in the Main World now?' Laurence asked.

'Seems like it,' Alaric said. 'So, when Master Ogden threatened to close the school, whoever's behind this didn't lay off; they just found new targets.'

'And we now know the poison leads to green bumps on the chest,' Lucy said. 'We need to look this all up.'

Alaric eyed Madame Moyglot and, seeing she was looking down, concentrating hard on her marking, reached into his bag for his laptop. He paused, realising if he got caught using it, it'd likely be confiscated, instead pulling out his medicine textbook.

'It's not been useful so far, but it's the best we can do for now,' he said to the others.

Lucy and Laurence nodded as Alaric opened the book, putting it inside the textbook so Madame Moyglot wouldn't suspect anything if she looked up. They peered over his shoulder as he turned to the section on poisons and venoms. It was incredibly dense with text as they scanned the pages on different toxins, struggling to find those two key words: green bumps.

'Crikey, I wish Harramore would introduce ebooks,' Lucy groaned.

'What?' Laurence asked.

'Books on digital screens,' Lucy said exasperatedly. 'You can search for words in them, and they're way lighter.'

Laurence raised his eyebrows, apparently impressed by the concept, as Alaric sighed and turned to the subsection on venoms.

'We can skip that bit,' Lucy said.

'Why?' Alaric asked.

'Don't tell me you don't know the difference between a poison and a venom,' Lucy huffed. 'Venoms only work if a creature bites you. So, unless Madame Sang is sending in spiders and snakes to attacks these people, this section won't be any use.'

'Just trying to keep our options open,' Alaric said, his cheeks hot. 'We don't want to rule anything out.'

'We don't want to waste our time either,' Lucy said with her lips pursed as she grabbed the book from Alaric. 'From now on, I'm controlling the book. We will read the most likely sections first, then we'll revisit your ridiculous venom idea if that comes to nothing. Best way to save time.'

'Wouldn't the best way to save time be for us all to read different sections?' Alaric said with a smug grin,

Laurence trying to stifle a laugh.

Lucy flushed bright pink and gave Alaric his book back without speaking and reached for her own from her bag. Laurence did the same. They spent the rest of the hour reading in silence, Alaric hoping his research on venoms would come in useful to get his own back on Lucy. However, the only venom listed that caused green bumps was that of the medusa (apparently the name of the giant jellyfish he and Lucy had seen).

By the end of the hour, Alaric had therefore yielded no results of use, Laurence was yet to turn the page, while Lucy was flicking back through what she'd read, just as frustrated as Alaric.

'The trouble is that so many poisons cause green bumps as a symptom and then death if untreated,' Lucy said as they made their way to Madame Sang's lesson. 'I looked so many times, but none of them seemed to cause a cold first.'

Alaric sighed heavily. 'I found nothing either.'

'Hmm,' Lucy said. 'What about you, Laurence?'

'Nah, nothing,' Laurence mumbled.

'Did you even read any of the book?' Lucy said.

'Of course, I did,' Laurence said defensively. 'Just wasn't useful or interesting.'

Lucy sighed. 'Right,' she said, unconvinced, now

approaching Sang's classroom. 'We'll try the Harranet over lunch.'

Alaric nodded in agreement, his body slumping as he thought of the hour he had ahead with his least favourite teacher. Even the sight of her face was enough to suck all the life out of him as he unpacked to Madame Sang's usual shouts of "hurry up".

'Now you're all finally ready, we shall get started,' Madame Sang began. 'Due to the continued absences of Madame Ettoga and Madame Cassandra, the headmaster has decided other classes should overlap with their subjects. Since a discipline like medicine has little in common with something as speculative as prognostication, we'll be having a lesson today on the medicinal properties of animals. I've put a different set of ingredients on each of your tables. All include an extract from a particular creature alongside some instructions. The task is simple: do as directed. Go.'

Alaric picked up the recipe, Franco and Dwayne staring at him menacingly. He read through it carefully, well-aware that he'd get the blame for anything that went wrong.

'Right, it looks like we're doing a shrinking ointment,' Alaric said as diplomatically as possible.

'Oh great, we can make you normal size,' Franco

sneered. Alaric glowered at him, deciding not to respond.

'So, we have gnome extract, seems to be the key ingredient,' Alaric went on. 'What we really need to do first is cut up the yew tree bark.'

Franco and Dwayne both sighed and lethargically rose from their seats, picking up a knife each. Alaric followed suit, opening the packet labelled as bark and emptied out the reddish shavings. They cut up the ingredients in silence, which suited Alaric. The less Franco and Dwayne said, the better as far as he was concerned. He forced himself to ignore their occasional snide remarks about his height or the upcoming basketball match against Naidos.

He composed himself as Sang started her usual tour of the classroom. Her shoulders were hunched as she paced softly, hands behind her back with a malicious smile on her face. He turned the heat right down on their saucepan, leaving the ointment to cool. They were well ahead of schedule now. In fact, they'd finished their work with twenty minutes left in the lesson just for the cream to set. She visited each desk, finding something to criticise, giving several people detentions as usual.

'You can join my detention this evening, Mr Swift,' Sang said softly before she'd even reached his desk.

'What, why?' Alaric exclaimed, his voice high-pitched with indignance.

'Your bag is a trip hazard,' Sang said, her glabella narrowing.

Franco smirked at Dwayne as Alaric pursed his lips and looked down at the floor. He could've sworn he'd put his bag under his desk, which he had, yet the strap was sticking out ever-so-slightly. But Sang had noticed.

'I swear she looks for reasons to give me detention,' Alaric grumbled to Lucy and Laurence after the lesson, traipsing towards the canteen for lunch. 'Our ointment was literally perfect, but no. My bag is a small trip hazard. Seriously, she could've just told me to tuck it under, but of course, it had to be detention.'

'It's the same with everyone, mate,' Laurence said.

'You got away with it this time,' Alaric said bitterly.

'Barely,' Lucy chuckled. 'If Trevor hadn't set his desk on fire and distracted her, we were doomed.'

Alaric smiled slightly at the thought. As sorry as he'd felt for Trevor when Sang had issued him a month's worth of detentions, at least he hadn't been that unfortunate himself. His thoughts were interrupted, and the three of them were dispersed as Madame Sang barged through them. Alaric and Laurence stumbled backwards as Lucy almost fell over. Sang marched on towards the woods before coming to a sudden stop, turning sharply to speak to them.

'What might you three be doing?' she asked accusatorily.

'Going to the canteen,' Lucy said, a look of disgust on her face.

'Well, go quickly then,' Sang ordered. Her expression bordered on disappointment as she realised there was no reason to criticise them.

She continued on into the woods, Alaric, Lucy, and Laurence still heading towards the canteen. Alaric kept an eye on Madame Sang as they did so; she reached the edge of the woods before stopping again and looking over her shoulder, scanning the entire horizon. Alaric considered the matter momentarily as Sang continued into the trees before making his mind up. He turned sharply, marching in Sang's footsteps, for the first time in his life, desperate to get close to her.

'What are you doing, Alaric?' Lucy asked.

'Come on,' Alaric said urgently. Sang was getting deeper into the woods now, the foliage thicker, and soon she'd be out of sight. 'I dunno if it's just me, but Sang really doesn't seem like she wants to be followed.'

Lucy pursued him without hesitation, Laurence sighing.

'But it's Monday,' Laurence protested as he caught up with Alaric and Lucy. 'They always have brownies on Mondays.'

Lucy backhanded Laurence on his forehead. 'Sure, we'll go and ask Sang to wait till we've had our brownies so we can spy on her,' she said sarcastically. 'Honestly, Laurence, sort your priorities out.'

Laurence sighed, blushing as the three of them strode into the woods, gaining ground on Madame Sang very quickly. Soon, they were just a few paces away from her, hurrying between trees to hide behind in case she turned and saw them. They carried on further into the woods silently. Alaric's pulse was speeding up so much he could feel the blood being pumped in his body, even hear his heart beating.

'She's going to the nurse's office,' Lucy whispered.

Alaric nodded. He recognised this route. He cleared his mind and imagined what he needed: a tunnel to the nurse's office. There was no way Sang would be able to see them if they were underground. Alaric froze as the sound of leaves rustling filled the air. He even heard Sang's footsteps stop for a moment, and he could only breathe again when he heard her walk on.

'Let's go,' Alaric whispered, jumping down into the newly formed hole in the ground.

'You know?' Lucy said, coughing as she opened her mouth to speak and breathed in the air around her. 'As much as I hate Solo, his Seela does come in useful.'

Alaric nodded. He could taste the humidity in the air, and he didn't want to open his mouth and breathe in the soil, or worse, swallow one of the creepy crawlies around him. They wandered the length of the tunnel in silence, Alaric breathing only very shallowly as the weight of what was happening tightened around his chest.

The top window of the office was open, and Alaric could see Beatrice Bork inside, still tending to Trevor's burnt hand. She didn't seem to notice them and finished bandaging him up and gave him the all-clear to head off. Then, Beatrice turned towards them, and they ducked instinctively. Alaric froze, praying they hadn't been seen. If they had, there was no way they could claim they had reason to be there. He exhaled after several seconds, realising Beatrice hadn't noticed them. There were then a few moments of silence as they waited for Sang to arrive.

'Do you think she's already been here?' Laurence said softly. Lucy shushed him as they heard a door creak open, which could only mean one thing.

'I know why you're here, Saskia,' they heard Beatrice

say, 'and the answer is still no. I will change nothing. It's working.'

'It's the wrong poison, Beatrice, and you know it,' Madame Sang said as if she were speaking to Alaric. 'It's not strong enough.'

'If the poison were any stronger, the kids would be dead already, as you're aware,' Beatrice said through gritted teeth. 'That'd be completely pointless.'

'I don't deny that,' Sang said stiffly, 'but the students, Ettoga, Cassandra...they've been in hospital for months. It must end now.'

'It can't end now, but it will soon,' Beatrice replied. 'I believe you have a class to get to.'

They heard a shuffling sound as Sang headed towards the door. 'And when is *soon*?' she pressed.

'That's not for me to say. But I make the medical decisions in this school and what I say goes. Goodbye.'

'Ramp it up!' Sang snapped, and the nurse's door creaked open. Then, the whole building seemed to tremble as she slammed it shut.

Alaric, Lucy and Laurence all looked at each other at once, wearing the same dumbfounded expression.

CHAPTER 12

ALARIC GESTURED BACK towards the tunnel he'd made. They both followed him without questioning, hurrying there as quietly as they could. They jumped back down into it, making sure they'd walked a distance before speaking to ensure they wouldn't be heard.

'Okay, now we *have* to talk to Master Ogden,' Laurence said. 'We could get Sang sacked, or better, arrested. She'd get the death penalty, wouldn't she?' His voice rose with glee as he said this. Although he didn't want to admit it, Alaric couldn't say he was exactly averse to the idea.

'We need to get the evidence first,' he pointed out. While he had no doubt Master Ogden would believe them, the word of three fourteen-year-olds would still not be enough to convince the police.

'Yes, we do,' Lucy agreed, 'which is where your detention tonight comes in useful.'

'W-what do you mean?' Alaric asked, coughing as

he took too deep a breath of musty air.

'You're going to search Sang's classroom. Raid her drawers, cupboards, desk…as much as you can,' Lucy said.

Alaric scoffed. 'How am I going to do that unnoticed with Sang in the room? Have you even thought this through, Lucy?'

'Of course, I have, you idiot,' Lucy snapped. 'Laurence and I will create a diversion from outside the classroom, Sang will come looking, and boom, there's your chance.'

'And what exactly will you do?' Alaric asked incredulously.

'Throw something at the window, I don't know,' Lucy said with a shrug. 'It doesn't have to be anything difficult, just enough to lure Sang out of the room.'

'Right, well, be careful,' Alaric said. 'I don't want you getting into trouble as well.'

Laurence snorted a laugh. 'I'm not worried about that, mate. Once we have this evidence and Sang's sacked, she won't be here to put us in trouble.'

Alaric grinned, showing all his teeth as he climbed out the tunnel at the other end. As Lucy and Laurence followed him, he noticed how heavily stained with dirt their white shirts were. They'd definitely need to stay away from Sang for the rest of the day if they were to avoid another detention for scruffy uniform. That wasn't to mention the fact they'd not been keeping track of time at all this lunchbreak, and Alaric was certain they were late for their next lesson. They headed there at a run, all arriving red-faced and drenched in sweat, their clothes still muddy.

'Where have you been?' Master Idoss asked as they got in. 'You're nearly ten minutes late.'

'We got lost,' Laurence said. Alaric and Lucy rolled their eyes.

'You've been here for a year,' Master Idoss said, furrowing a blue, bushy brow.

'Lost track of time…that's what he meant,' Alaric said. He knew there was no chance of that being an acceptable excuse, but it had to be better than the truth.

'Right,' Idoss said, 'what have you been doing, though? You all look a mess.'

Alaric, Lucy and Laurence all opened their mouths a few times, no sound coming out except a few incoherent babbles. Alaric's body felt even hotter as he could feel every pair of eyes in the room staring at them.

'Sit down quickly,' Idoss sighed. 'I'll speak to you after the lesson.'

Alaric, Lucy and Laurence slumped into their seats

at their usual table. Alaric unpacked with haste and looked up at the board, scribbling down the lesson title: The History of Paz and his Descendants.

'Now, for the latecomers' benefit, could someone please recap what we've been discussing so far?' Idoss said, his usual gentleness back in his tone. The room was still for a few moments, some people glancing around the place as no one put their hands up. 'No one at all?' Master Idoss asked. 'How about you, Trevor? You mentioned Paz in one of your recent essays, I think.'

All eyes in the room turned to Trevor, whose round face whitened as he started to speak. 'Y-yes, he's the Guardian of the Mind.'

'Very good,' Master Idoss said, ignoring Chloe Alkoff and Olivier LeBeau as they giggled. 'And why's he so important that I'm doing a whole lesson about him today?'

'He kept changing sides,' Trevor mumbled, his hand in front of his mouth like he didn't want anyone to hear him.

'Indeed,' Master Idoss said encouragingly, 'excellent, Trevor. Yes, Paz is one of the most interesting Guardians outside the so-called Big Five.' He stopped speaking and turned his focus to Chloe and Olivier, both of whom were still giggling behind their hands. 'Something you two wish to share with the class?'

Chloe and Olivier stopped laughing instantly, looking down at their desk and shaking their heads.

'Right, please be quiet while others are speaking. That was very disrespectful to me and Trevor,' Idoss said firmly. 'Anyway, as Trevor rightly said, Paz was the most...with want of a better word, *indecisive* of the Guardians during the war. He switched sides between Naidos and Rei no fewer than one-hundred-and-eleven times before eventually settling down as a neutral. Thus, his descendants are the most divided among any of the Guardians'. It's estimated that those who aren't neutral are almost evenly split between the two sides.'

Alaric listened attentively to everything Master Idoss said. He remembered that Walkul Goblinsfoe had told him that he was a descendant of Paz last year. Then again, the first time he'd met Master Ogden, he'd used Paz's Seela and made himself invisible.

Idoss continued, 'Paz is the most fascinating of all Guardians, except perhaps Cria. However, given her existence is not confirmed, we, as historians, cannot study her as part of the curriculum. Now, for today's lesson, kindly read page two-hundred-and-thirty-three of your textbooks and answer the questions at the bottom of the page.'

There was a rustling of paper around the room as everyone turned to the correct place in the book. Alaric inhaled deeply and started reading a textbox at the edge of the page: Characteristics of his Descendants.

Each of Paz's descendants is known for having one key characteristic: their powerful mind. Used well, Paz's Seela can be more powerful than even those of the Big Five Guardians. Ceus' ability to fly and Marfin's ability to control water are easily eclipsed by the effective execution of Paz's Seela.

The mind is the most powerful weapon on Earth. As such, should a descendant of Paz concentrate hard enough when using his Seela, they can achieve almost anything. Some of the most advanced users of his Seela can even turn themselves invisible, control objects without touching them and fly like a descendant of Ceus. Consequently, many would say mastering Paz's Seela is equivalent to having the Seela of every other Guardian.

In fact, the House of Paz's mastery of the mind is often considered the reason as to why his descendants are so divided. Upon careful consideration, many of Paz's descendants supported Naidos, claiming there was a convincing case to wipe Ordinaries from the planet for the good of the world's ecosystems. Yet, despite the division among descendants, they all had one thing in common: letting their minds speak over their hearts.

'Sir!' Alaric called to Master Idoss across the room.

'Yes, Alaric?' Idoss replied with a smile, strolling over to his table.

'Are all descendants of Paz like this? Do they all have their heads speak over their hearts?' Alaric asked.

'Hmmm, to say *all* is a bit of a generalisation, but they do have a reputation for it,' Idoss replied. He shuffled behind Alaric to read over his shoulder. 'Paz's descendants are deep thinkers a lot of the time, and many try to remove emotion from their decisions.'

'Walkul Goblinsfoe was a descendant of Paz,' Alaric said. 'He wasn't like that. He supported Naidos because Ordinaries killed his daughter.'

Master Idoss took a deep breath and smiled down at Alaric admiringly. 'You do make good points, Alaric,' he said. 'Though, as much as some may try, I'd argue it's impossible to remove emotion from decisions. The human heart is just too strong, and even descendants of Paz can fall victim to it sometimes. You know Master Ogden; he's not exactly got a heart of stone now, has he?'

Alaric considered the matter for a few moments before asking the other question on his mind. 'Do a lot of Nephilim share these descendants' opinions? About Ordinaries, I mean?'

Master Idoss sighed with a wry smile. 'Alas, you ask a question that'd require years of lessons, and even then, I probably still wouldn't be able to answer it. What I would say, however, is that for a lot of Nephilim, this issue is not as black-and-white as you may think. Many have been confined to this island, unable to practice their powers outside of it for all of history. They see what Ordinaires do to the world, especially recently, and it's understandable why some of them may want their planet back. Others, of course, are categorically against the idea of wiping out an entire race but do have some sympathies…they try to be pragmatic, one could say. And to be honest, that's most Nephilim to varying degrees, including those who support Ceus and Solo.'

'But, Ordinaries, they're such a big part of the world they created. Why would the Guardians want it destroyed?' Lucy asked.

'The world that *they* created?' Master Idoss said, his eyebrows disappearing under his fringe. 'I don't think so. Remember, the Guardians we know of didn't create this world; they just manage it. The real creator of the world is unknown to even the Guardians nowadays.

That's why it's life's greatest mystery. No one can prove Cria's existence after all.'

'Cria? As in the Guardian of Creation?' Lucy asked.

Idoss nodded. 'Legends speak of a Guardian who existed before the others—one who created the moon and the stars and the Earth. A Guardian who knows all the laws of everything in existence. They say that the amount of energy it took to do this destroyed her. However, Guardians are immortal, so that's impossible. She is said to be weak, an empty shell of a body, existing somewhere no one would ever go. Yet, in the many millions of years this planet has existed, no such place has been found.'

Alaric, Lucy and Laurence listened attentively to what Idoss was saying. As the whole class tuned in, even Chloe and Olivier were focused, just as engaged as Alaric.

'What do you believe, sir?' Carlos piped up.

'Me? This is one of those things that are pure speculation, so what one chooses to think should not be subject to judgement. However, this is purely oral history we're talking about. The stories are bound to have been distorted to some extent over the years. Although, there may be some truth in them,' Idoss replied. 'Fascinating stuff. Gosh, I love this class.

Anyway, we're getting side-tracked. Back to work, please, just ten minutes of concentration before the end of the lesson.'

There was a collective groan as the class returned their attention to their textbooks. As gentle a character as Idoss was, his instructions carried enough authority that no one spoke for the rest of the lesson, no one having completed their work by the end.

'Alaric, Lucy, Laurence, don't forget I need to see you,' he said as the rest of the class headed towards the door.

Alaric tensed up. He had no idea how this talking-to was going to go. The closest he'd ever come to a telling-off from Idoss had been when he'd kept the three of them back for interfering with the Pearl affair. They packed their books away and waited until the other students had all left the room, at which point Idoss pulled up a chair and sat at their table with them.

'Now, I can't say I was impressed by your lateness today,' he began. 'Very uncharacteristic of you three. However, I am perfectly capable of putting two and two together. The state of your clothes and everything, the only explanation is you've been in the woods and perhaps underground as well. Alaric used Solo's Seela, did he?'

Alaric hesitated for a few moments, then nodded, realising there was no point in lying to Master Idoss.

'Right, now I don't know what you were all up to, and I won't ask. It's probably for the best that way. However, I suggest you be careful after what happened last year. Don't interfere with things out of your remit. If you're concerned, go and speak to someone trustworthy. I'll let you go and get cleaned up and changed before your next lesson. We don't want you attracting any more unwanted attention.' Idoss stood up and opened the classroom door for them, Alaric, Lucy and Laurence exiting through it.

'That went better than I thought,' Lucy said brightly.

'Yeah,' Laurence agreed, 'and we will see Master Ogden, won't we?'

'For sure, once Alaric's raided Sang's classroom,' Lucy said. Alaric shuddered as he remembered the idea.

'Have you figured out a plan for that yet?' he asked.

Lucy looked downwards, telling Alaric the answer was not the one he wanted.

'Can't you just go and tell Sang that Ogden wants to see her or something?' Laurence suggested.

'No,' Alaric said decisively. 'It's all very well getting Sang away, but I can't just go and rummage through her stuff in front of Trevor and everyone else in the detention.'

'It's not a bad idea, though,' Lucy said. 'Ogden's office is basically on the other side of campus. It'd take her about twenty minutes to get there and back. That should buy you some time for sure. Who else is in that detention?'

Alaric hesitated before answering. He really couldn't see where this was going, but in any case, he was sure the plan seemed reckless. 'Trevor, Carlos, Chloe, Olivier...they're definite, might be a few others.'

'Hmmm, well, with Sang gone, I reckon you can persuade Carlos, Chloe and Olivier to leave. Trevor would be more problematic—'

'Lucy, these people aren't stupid. If Sang gets back and finds they're not there, they'll get even more detentions, and they know that,' Alaric pointed out.

'For goodness' sake, Alaric, what do you take me for?' Lucy said exasperatedly. 'Your detention's at eight this evening, right? As standard, they're an hour long, so if I turn up at like five-to-nine, the others will leave at nine without trouble. Sang can't exactly say they should've stayed beyond the end, so you'll have plenty of time to search Sang's classroom.'

Alaric sucked in some air through his front teeth, still dubious about the plan. 'It's just a lot could go wrong, and this is Sang. She'd love an excuse to give them more detentions,' he said.

'You got anything better?' Lucy asked. 'And besides, once you're finished, there'll be no Madame Sang at the school to hand out detentions.'

Alaric sighed, realising he had no counterarguments. When he thought about it, the plan seemed sound enough, but there was one major caveat: what if he didn't find the evidence he needed? He tried to dismiss that thought from his mind, spending the rest of the afternoon focusing on nothing other than success. As evening approached and dinner passed, he'd convinced himself he was going to succeed, and by the time he set off for his detention, his skin was tingling. He must have been the first person ever to be excited for an hour being punished by Madame Sang.

When he arrived at the classroom, the door was propped open. Trevor was already there alone with Madame Sang, who wore a wicked smile as he entered the room and sat down. As the other students arrived, the silent tension in the room made the minutes seem like hours, the heat disappearing until goosebumps formed right down Alaric's arms.

'Right, children,' Madame Sang said at last as Chloe and Olivier arrived. Alaric clenched his fists under his desk. Somehow, being addressed thus was even more patronising when Sang said it. 'I recently received a box of mixed feathers. Trouble is, I need them separated and sorted according to the bird. Otherwise, it's useless. I have dodo, pexaro and gryphon feathers. Everyone grab a handful and sort them into piles. There shall be no need to talk.'

Each student in the detention traipsed to the front of the classroom and picked up two fistfuls of feathers. Somehow, the anticipation and excitement for what Alaric knew would happen at the end of this hour made it feel even longer than usual. The task was also exceptionally dull. While he'd never seen a real gryphon feather before, the novelty of doing so wore off very quickly, especially given its resemblance to a simple, large eagle feather. Examining a pexaro feather was mildly more interesting. He'd come across the creature in his cryptozoology textbook: it was a type of fish that escaped predators by jumping out of the water, its fins stretching out like wings as it did so. Its texture was unusual, almost scaly like a fish, though Sang snapped at him as soon as she saw him pausing to admire it. Alaric returned his focus to the task at hand immediately, almost shrugging off Sang's wrath, safe in the knowledge that this would be his last detention with her. He kept one eye on the clock at all times, counting down the minutes to when Lucy or Laurence would arrive at the classroom door. Then, at last, after what seemed like multiple hours, five-to-nine arrived, and the echoing knock on the door followed.

'What?' Sang shouted.

The door creaked open, and Lucy was on the other side, looking remarkably composed given the circumstances.

'Do you talk to the other teachers like that as well?' Lucy said.

Alaric held his breath as Sang's face tightened. *Please don't get complacent, Lucy,* he thought to himself. Sang didn't respond, just staring at Lucy as if about to break her neck, blinking a slow, furious blink.

'What is it?' Sang hissed, emphasising every single syllable.

'Master Ogden wishes to see you,' Lucy said calmly. 'He says it's extremely important, can't wait.'

Sang stood up and stepped out from behind her desk. Then, she paced softly towards Lucy, each student watching the scene unfold as if it were a play.

'And why did he send *you*?' Sang asked. Alaric shuddered. He felt the menace of Sang's stare even when she had her back to him like she had a second face.

'Why don't you ask him that?' Lucy said with a daring smirk. 'I didn't ask what it was about. I wouldn't want to be too nosy.'

Sang turned on her heel, striding towards her chair. Alaric waited with bated breath, praying she'd believed Lucy. He exhaled deeply but as quietly as he could as Sang picked up her coat and strode out of the classroom without saying a word.

'Does this mean we can just go?' Alaric said once he was sure Madame Sang was out of earshot. 'I mean, it's five minutes until the end anyway, and who knows how long she'll be with Master Ogden?'

Chloe and Olivier took little persuading as they shrugged and left immediately. Carlos and Trevor seemed slightly more hesitant, though, which Alaric had fully expected.

'What if Madame Sang gets back and we're not here?' Trevor said. 'Won't we get into even more trouble?'

'She could be a while though,' Alaric countered, 'and she never told us to stay, did she?'

'I'm going,' Carlos declared, rising from his seat and putting on his dark, corduroy jacket. 'If you wanna stay here all night, Trevor, you can, but I'm done.' He grinned, and the whiteness of his teeth was noticeable against his tanned complexion. Trevor glanced at the door, then back at his pile of feathers and back to the door again.

'Detentions are an hour long, Trevor. She can't expect us to stay any longer,' Alaric said. 'I'm leaving myself.' He got up and started putting on his jacket as if about to take off, Trevor eventually doing the same.

'You going back to the dorms, Alaric?' Carlos asked.

'Urm, I will be,' Alaric replied. 'You go on without me, though. I've just got something I need to sort out.'

To his relief, Carlos asked no further questions, and he and Trevor left the room. Alaric followed them to the doorway and waited, watching them disappear out of sight before he took off his jacket and marched over to Madame Sang's desk. He almost coughed as he picked up the first pile of papers on top of it from the dust that rose up. The table gave off the impression that it was never cleaned, the dirt visible on his fingers as he touched it. His breathing became heavier as he flicked through the first pile of papers, his heart sinking as he realised it was just students' homework.

'Hi, Alaric.'

Alaric jumped back so suddenly he nearly fell over, the papers he was holding flying around the room as he dropped them. He breathed the biggest sigh of relief possible as he looked towards the doorway to see Lucy giggling at his reaction.

'It's only me,' she said. '*You* should be more alert, you realise? I figured you might appreciate some help looking. Plus, better we both get caught than just you.'

'Yeah, that's great, thanks,' Alaric said, feeling slightly less nervous now.

Lucy laughed as she joined Alaric behind the desk, kneeling down and opening the bottom drawer. She pulled out all the papers in one go, placing them on the table with a thud, bringing up yet more dust to tickle Alaric's throat.

As it turned out, they needn't have spent much time searching. As Lucy opened the first folder from Madame Sang's drawer, she immediately punched the air in celebration.

'Take a look at this, Alaric,' she said triumphantly.

Alaric, his heart starting to race, peered over Lucy's shoulder. Straight away, his whole body shivered like he'd just jumped into icy water as he saw what was written on the top document. The heading, in large capitals: POSSIBLE POISONS. Alaric and Lucy remained speechless as they perused the page together.

Ordinary Poisons: Cyanide; Deadly Nightshade; Hemlock. Next to each of them was a prominent red cross along with scrawling reading "too easy", "too obvious", or "too weak". Alaric seemed to have lost the need to breathe or blink as he scanned the page, no longer reading all the annotations, just glancing at the cross. Lucy flicked the page over onto the next part of the list. The poisons became more obscure, and soon enough, Alaric had heard of none of them. Still, each of them was marked with a red 'X'. Then, at the bottom of the page, there it was.

Circled, underlined, highlighted, marked in every possible way to make it stand out was one singular word in capital letters: RUMIS. Then, underneath it was one simple phrase: *The perfect poison.*

Alaric and Lucy looked at each other and locked eyes, their expressions identical. Neither of them was able to speak, but there was no need. Their faces said everything.

CHAPTER 13

ALARIC MARCHED OUT of the room immediately, and there was no need to instruct Lucy to follow him. They didn't bother removing the evidence they'd been snooping. Alaric was too busy giggling at the thought of Sang returning to see her desk a mess. His face lit up even more at the idea of her reaction when she realised which document was missing.

'As soon as we get back, we look up this rumis thing, yeah?' Alaric said, almost panting they were walking at such a speed back to the lodgings.

'For sure,' Lucy replied. She said no more. The two of them were too filled with adrenaline to speak.

Their walks accelerated to a run, both impatient to get back into the House of Rei's accommodation and speak to Laurence. They arrived within minutes, rushing through the door to see him lying on the sofa watching TV, Jacob relaxing on the other settee.

'Laurence,' Alaric puffed, 'we need to talk in our room. Now.'

Laurence rolled off the sofa unquestioningly. He followed Alaric and Lucy to the bedroom, Jacob looking slightly startled but not saying anything.

'We've found out which poison Madame Sang's using,' Alaric stated, Lucy barely having shut the door.

'Great!' Laurence exclaimed delightedly. 'What is it?'

'Nothing we've ever heard of,' Lucy replied. 'Rumis. We're going to look it up now to confirm.'

Alaric—already logging onto his laptop—waved his hand at Lucy and Laurence in a "come hither" way. He kept his eyes locked on the screen as they joined him on the bed, watching over his shoulder as he typed the one word into the search engine. Rumis.

Rumis is a highly uncommon poison, taken from the leaf of the even rarer blue buttercup. It was often used by Nephilim in the earlier stages of the war, before falling out of fashion in the sixteenth century, read the first result. Alaric clicked on the link immediately. He needed to see more.

Rumis was considered too inefficient a weapon to be used due to the several weeks it takes to become lethal. The victim of rumis poisoning first develops cold-like symptoms, including a cough and runny nose. However, if large amounts of the substance are consumed, things tend to suddenly take a drastic turn for the worse after a few days. The unlucky victim develops green bumps on the chest and starts vomiting. Without treatment, its administration can be fatal.

'This is it,' Alaric said. 'It fits perfectly.'

Lucy nodded. Both she and Laurence were grinning so widely it was hard to say who looked more delighted.

'That's Sang done for then,' she beamed.

'Right, I'll print this off, and we'll take this paper from Sang's desk to Master Ogden tomorrow. She'll be out of the school before the end of the week,' Alaric said.

'Let's plan a party,' Laurence suggested. 'Goodbye, Madame Sang.'

As Laurence said this, there was a knock on the other side of the door. Alaric, Lucy and Laurence all froze.

Please don't be Madame Sang, Alaric thought to himself. She'd probably realised by now Lucy had lied to her and got back to an empty, messy classroom.

'Hello?' asked the person on the other side when no one responded. Alaric's body slumped as he realised the voice belonged to Hector.

'Come in,' he called back.

The door swung open, and Hector stood there, his

lips thinner than even Madame Sang's. 'I have some bad news,' he said. 'The match against Naidos has been moved.'

'When is it?' Laurence asked.

'Tomorrow evening,' Hector said, visibly clenching his fists.

'What?' Alaric shouted. 'Why? When did this happen? We haven't trained for a week.'

'The Naidos captain asked for the match to be moved,' Hector sighed. 'And given the adjudicator just happens to be the captain's dad, the request was granted.'

Alaric's mouth hung open, his eyes bulging as he looked at Laurence, then back at Hector.

'Why were we not consulted?' Alaric demanded.

'We should've been,' Hector seethed. 'But we can't appeal the decision because the match is tomorrow. Anyway, first thing in the morning before lessons, we need a light training session, I'm afraid. We'll go through the tactics over supper. My word, I am going to kill Titus McGlompher.' He stomped off, baring his teeth like a rabid dog, his head shaking.

'We have that massive translation for Madame Moyglot due in as well,' Alaric groaned. 'That'll take at least an hour. How can this even be allowed? What about the fans who'd bought tickets?'

Laurence shook his head in disgust. 'Reckon that Titus is related to Dwayne too. If he's playing, I'm going to ruin him.'

'I bet you anything this is just to throw us off too,' Alaric said bitterly.

'It doesn't matter,' Lucy said with a smile as she stood up, 'because you're going to beat them. You're a better team. I know it.' She patted Alaric and Laurence on the shoulder comfortingly. 'Goodnight, best let you rest now by the sound of things.' She gave them one more smile before leaving the room, shutting the door behind her.

'I don't wanna play this match tomorrow,' Laurence grumbled as they started to get changed for bed.

'We don't have a choice, it seems,' Alaric sighed.

THEY BARELY SEEMED to have got to sleep when Hector came knocking on their bedroom door again to tell them it was time for training. Alaric and Laurence both groaned and rolled out of bed, Alaric's eyelids feeling particularly heavy as he opened the curtains. It was still almost dark outside, rain lashing down like pebbles against the windows. He would've given anything to have been able to get back into bed at that moment for another couple of hours, but deep down, he knew he couldn't. They had to beat Naidos, whatever it took.

The five team members traipsed across the grounds of Oakwood and to their basketball stadium in silence, each of them looking as tired as each other. The whole training session seemed to drag on as the rain drenched them, and they communicated monosyllabically.

The bad weather continued throughout the day. Alaric started to hope the match would be called off, but he knew better than to be so optimistic. He hadn't ever felt so nervous in the lead-up to a basketball game. He knew if they lost this one, he'd never hear the end of it from the House of Naidos. It didn't help anyone's nerves that the game seemed to be the only topic of discussion around the school that day. People eagerly placed bets with Jorge Romero on the game's outcome, and Naidos seemed to have been made the favourites to win. And Alaric was starting to agree by the time Hector took the team through the game plan over supper.

'I'm hoping this strategy works,' Hector said. 'Sorry, I've only had twenty-four hours to devise it, but I've studied Naidos' style of play and looked at how we can beat them. They seem to be a very physical team, not scared to play dirty if they need to. They'll do whatever it takes to win. There's no doubt about that. Luckily, we have the strength to counter this, too, give them a dose of their own medicine. Alaric, Grace, you two best keep out of the physical battles as far as possible, rely more on your agility. Then, that leaves my biggest concern: their Seela.'

'We can block Seelas, no problem,' Jacob said confidently.

'That's not my concern, Jacob,' Hector replied with a shake of the head. 'The trouble is one or two will inevitably slip through. Then, we're left to deal with the power of the Seela because, as you may already know, it's the worst of all of them. Best-case scenario, it turns you blind for a few seconds; worst-case scenario, you see things.'

'What kind of things?' Alaric forced himself to say, already shivering at the thought of the answer.

Hector gulped as though forcing down a particularly large stone. 'Visions of your friends and family dead, hallucinations essentially. Sometimes, you may even see your deceased loved ones appearing to be alive. This is why so many people saw a lot of logic in Iglehart banning the Seela. Dad always said it was a nasty weapon in the war. The images were so vivid that it turned people mad and drove some to take their own lives.'

'That's horrible,' Alaric said weakly. He remembered how often he'd heard his father's voice over the holidays, how he'd felt then. He didn't think he could handle actually seeing him again.

'This is what I mean. Everyone needs to be constantly alert. Physical battles we can deal with losing, but the Seelas will be worse than just conceding five points. It'll affect us for the whole game,' Hector said.

Alaric looked down at his food, feeling sick at the mere sight of it now. His stomach rumbled painfully, and he pushed his meal away untouched. He knew nothing could prepare him adequately for this. He could practice blocking Seelas, producing them, shooting. But still, mentally, he was far too underprepared for the thought of actually getting hit by Naidos' Seela. He quietly watched the rest of the team finish eating as Master Ogden came strolling over to their table, dressed in all purple to show his support for Rei.

'Good evening,' he said jauntily. 'Your guard is here when you're ready.'

'Excuse me?' Hector said.

'Well, yes. There have been a few clashes between supporters in town, so we decided it'd be best if you were escorted to the stadium by an armed guard. Just a precaution. The fans are getting a trifle over-excited, you see,' Ogden said with a smile that couldn't have contrasted the expressions of the five team members more.

'What kind of clashes?' Grace asked, eyeing Master Ogden with a kind of concern that could easily have been interpreted as suspicion.

'Bit of a brawl outside the stadium,' Ogden said dismissively. 'Iglehart sent the police in, and it seems to have settled down. They're ushering everyone straight to their seats. Anyway, is that okay?'

Hector nodded, glancing at each of the four other team members, each of whom looked as nonplussed as the next. Alaric had no idea whether or not to be reassured by Ogden's unconcerned manner.

'Excellent,' Ogden said with a smile so wide, the scar on his cheek seemed to shrivel. 'Crikey, this is going to be a spicy match, I sense.' His grin became somehow wider still as he strolled into the distance.

'Ugly is probably more the word,' Grace grumbled, Alaric feeling like he could be sick at any moment.

The five of them rose from their table and headed outside the canteen, where their guard was unmissable. Each heavily armoured with silver steel helmets, ten men and women held large shields and swords as long as their legs. They stood waiting in silence, their faces intimidatingly expressionless.

'Rei basketball team?' the shortest and stoutest of the guards asked.

The five of them nodded, triggering the ten guards into action as they formed a circle around the team. Alaric started to sweat a cold sweat as they marched through the woods and into the town without saying anything. This whole experience was too alien for any of them to be able to speak. It was as if they had too much to say to be able to say anything at all.

It was only once they'd passed Travis and reached the basketball town that Alaric's legs started to feel like they were about to cave in under the weight of his body. His view of what was happening was heavily obscured by the guards encircling them, but he needn't have seen. The sound of it was unnerving enough, an army of Naidos supporters chanting their chant like a battalion preparing for combat.

'WE ARE NAIDOS! WE ARE NAIDOS!'

Whether it was the rhythm, the lack of notes, or its sheer volume, there was something about their song that made it seem like it was meant to scare. Alaric took deep breaths to calm himself. Laurence started to wheeze as they made their way towards the stadium to a cacophony of unpleasant sounds.

Alaric fought to keep his composure as they approached the ground, almost collapsing in a heap on the benches once they reached the changing rooms. They changed into their sports kit in an unsettling silence, making the chants from the Naidos supporters inside the bowl even more unnerving, the whole stadium seeming to quake.

This, combined with the return of the pouring rain, meant the warm-up seemed to suck any remaining warmth out of Alaric. He returned to the changing rooms for their final team talk, his teeth chattering, his whole stomach aching. Even as Hector tried to brace the team for the contest ahead, Alaric had never felt more like he wanted to avoid a match.

As the two teams stood in the tunnel, Alaric sized up each of the Naidos players. Franco and Dwayne were both on the team, sneering at the lot of them. The other three were even larger and broader-shouldered, all staring intently at the pitch ahead of them, their faces as rigid as Madame Sang's when she was in a foul mood. Then, the moment came.

They jogged onto the field, Alaric's freezing cold legs feeling heavier than ever as sixty thousand Naidos supporters screamed at once, applauding, stamping like a herd of wildebeest. Alaric tried looking at the small section of Rei supporters for comfort, but any little noise they were making was being drowned out. In fact, the way they were all sitting suggested they didn't want to be noticed at all, many making themselves look as discreet as possible.

The ball went straight to Franco, who charged down the field with three of the other team members as one. They were past Alaric within seconds, who resisted the temptation to dive in and floor Franco. Then, Dwayne had it. Past Grace, back to the widest player on the team. Now, Franco had it once more. One on one with Hector.

Tumultuous applause shook the ground as Naidos scored their first point. Alaric couldn't not grin as Hector slammed Franco to the floor, almost feeling the impact of the fall himself as Franco rubbed his head groggily.

Now, Rei had possession. Hector tossed the ball to Jacob, to Laurence, to Grace. Alaric scanned his surroundings, looked for some space as he prepared to receive the ball. He watched as Grace threw it towards him, readied himself to receive the pass.

SMACK. Before the ball had even reached him, the

colossal mass of the Naidos keeper came diving into him. He fell to the ground, the entire side of his body where he'd landed sore. Naidos: 1—Rei: 1.

As the game progressed, things only became more physical, and Alaric may have thought he was playing rugby by the end of the first quarter. Early attempts to use their Seelas were all blocked. By the halfway point, that element of the game seemed to have been entirely forgotten as it became the ugliest match Alaric had ever played in. He had to brace himself for each attack as it nearly always ended in him being thrown to the ground hard.

Hector had retaliated by adopting the same approach at the other end. Before long, fouls were being performed off the ball as well as on it. The rain had now also got so heavy that Alaric could no longer see the basket, meaning any chance he got to shoot came to nothing. The only upside was that Naidos' aggression meant Rei led at the end of the first quarter by fourteen points to ten, every single score arising from a foul.

'Right, guys, needless to say, that I'm pleased we're winning,' Hector said to his team during the interval. 'But there's also still a long way to go, and the game really hasn't got going properly yet. I imagine their captain will be saying the same thing to them, but we need to stop this fouling and giving away cheap points. It won't help us in the long run as they'll add up. It looks like tough conditions for you to score baskets, Alaric, but we need to try anyway and really start using our Seelas. I don't think we can win this game on fouls alone.'

Hector was right in one sense but wrong in another. In the second quarter, Naidos did not cut down on their fouls as every member of the Rei team continued to collect bruises. Naidos had, nevertheless, started to use their Seela, catching Laurence off-guard straight from the restart as he dropped the ball, having lost his sight. He then collided head-to-head with Jacob, a deafening celebratory cry shaking the stadium, giving Naidos the lead.

Newfound energy coursed through Alaric at the mere sight of the scoreboard, just seconds later charging forward past the keeper and getting a shot off, missing the basket by millimetres. He chased after the ball, knowing surely, he'd outrun the weight of the Naidos keeper but was pulled back, falling face-flat on the ground. He spat out a mouthful of muddy grass, wiping the dirt from his face as he stood back up. Scores level again. Alaric rolled his eyes at Franco's taunts and forced himself to ignore him, a plan brewing in his mind.

He watched, waiting as the ball moved back up the field towards Franco. He was barely visible in the rain, but Alaric could see his back was turned. Just what he needed. And the weather conditions were perfect. He concentrated hard, then punched the air with joy as it happened.

First, Franco's ankles fell beneath the surface of the ground. Then, his knees. Next, as if a set of hands were pulling him from below, he was stuck shoulders-down in the mud. He was unable to move, the ball tantalisingly in front of his face. And, for the first time in the game, the Rei fans cheered at the sight of the scene. Naidos: 15—Rei: 20.

Now, the game was opening up. The fouls kept coming, but less frequently now. On one occasion, Hector even managed to mask his foul with his Seela. Alaric laughed the biggest laugh he could muster as Hector picked Franco up and hurled him across the field. He then winced as he saw him stirring on the ground, finally finding the strength to stand back up after a timeout. But still, at the end of the quarter, not a single basket had been scored. This didn't matter to Alaric, though as he looked at the scoreboard: Naidos: 26—Rei: 28.

'Okay, great stuff, team, we're still winning, but it's

too close to call,' Hector said at halftime. 'Alaric, I know the conditions are tough, but it really would help if you could get us a basket or two. This game will only get more demanding, especially when they have the crowd on their side.'

As usual, Hector was not wrong. Both sides seemed desperate to score a basket or gain points through a Seela, neither succeeding in the first few minutes of the quarter. It was only when they reached the fifth minute of the fifteen that Franco finally made a breakthrough. Hector was forced to rugby-tackle him to the ground, reducing Rei's lead down to one point. Then, it was Alaric's turn.

The ball was coming down the field. Hector, straight to Grace, over the top of Alaric and the keeper. They were chasing each other to it, but Alaric was too fast. And the keeper knew it as he slid in and tripped him up. Naidos: 27—Rei: 29. Alaric ignored the pain in his legs as he got back to his feet, ready to chase the ball again. The rain was lightening now, and Alaric could see the basket again. If only he could score just once, give Rei the fifteen points they needed.

Now, his mind was drifting, his head emptying like he was dreaming. But it felt too real. The fans in the stadium all stood applauding Alaric. Why? What had he done?

He took his focus off the ball and the basket and turned around. Then, he understood. Every basketball player was also applauding, for there was a man in the middle of the pitch. He was at least twice Alaric's height, the same face, the same, chiselled jawline. Alaric remembered that face from the Land of the Dead too well, and now here he was again. It was his father.

'Dad, it's you!' Alaric said elatedly. Then, before he'd reached his father, he collapsed to the ground as he collided with something solid. And the emptiness in his head disappeared immediately. The fans were still applauding, but the players were not, for Rei hadn't really been there. It had been a hallucination. He'd been caught out by Naidos' Seela and then run into Jacob. Alaric felt his head go hot with embarrassment as the Naidos fans celebrated the score: Naidos: 32—Rei: 29.

'You actually thought your dad was there?' Franco taunted, guffawing. Alaric clenched his teeth and cast his eyes in the opposite direction, determined not to rise to the bait. 'You're such an idiot, Swift,' Franco went on. 'Your dad couldn't have been there. Do you know why that is? Do you know where your dad is, Swift?'

This time, Franco had gone too far. Alaric turned on his heel and charged towards him, not caring about the slippiness of the mud beneath his feet, his eyes locked on his target. He pounced forwards, toppling him to the ground. Franco did nothing in response. His eyes were wide in shock as Alaric knelt on top of him, grabbing his throat in one hand and punching his face over and over.

Alaric blocked out the noise surrounding him as the crowd shouted in protest, not caring about what they thought. The only thing on his mind now was hurting Franco.

'ALARIC! Stop!' Grace shrieked as she tried to pull him off Franco, Alaric desperately trying to hold on. Now, the referee had joined Grace as she prised Alaric's fingers from Franco's throat. Alaric could go on no longer; Hector and Grace were restraining him as he tried to break free and charge back towards Franco's bloodied face like a tied-up dog.

But the damage had already been done. Next, Dwayne and what looked like his older brother came at Alaric, Hector and Grace. They swung their fists, Alaric ducking and sensing Grace fall to the ground behind him from the impact. Then, Jacob and Laurence decided to get involved as they charged towards them, punching one player each. Before long, it was difficult to tell who was fighting with whom, the referee desperately blowing her whistle to bring an end to the mêlée.

And now there was a bigger problem. As Alaric looked into the stands, he saw exactly what he had feared at the start of the game. The black mass of Naidos supporters was charging towards the small purple section of the crowd, the security guards knocked over, their efforts to stop them to no avail. Some seemed to be heading towards the doors in an attempt to escape as others fruitlessly tried to fend them off.

Everything was out of control now. There were Naidos supporters on the pitch, trying to intervene in the brawl, and Alaric realised. They were outnumbered. He gave a start as someone grabbed him around the shoulders, marching him away from the field.

'Come on, son,' Alaric's muscular guard said to him gruffly. 'It's not safe here.'

Alaric—too dumbstruck to speak—followed him and the rest of the team out of the stadium, listening to what was going on. The rain was still lashing down as they exited the ground, the Rei players being helped into the back of a van. Each of them sat in silence, their teeth chattering, covered in mud, bruises and cuts.

'We'll drive you back to Oakwood. It won't be long,'

the guard driving the van said, starting up the vehicle. Alaric nodded absentmindedly, still trying to process what had just happened.

'What'll happen about the game?' Jacob said.

Hector sighed and shook his head. 'Naidos were ahead, and we'd played more than half the game before it was abandoned. The rules state we lose.'

Alaric's body tightened at those words. They'd lost, and it had been his fault. He said nothing for the duration of the drive, unable to find the strength even to apologise. He'd never lost a basketball match before, and losing to Naidos all because of him made it feel yet more bitter.

'So, with the semi-finals, we just wait?' Grace asked.

'I guess so,' Hector said. 'I'm assuming they'll allow us to compete after that; I hope so, at least. If they do, we only lost by three points, so there's every chance we could make the playoff.'

'Playoff?' Alaric asked.

Hector nodded. 'The structure of the tournament means there are only six teams in the quarters. So, the two best losers have a game to decide who takes the fourth spot in the semis. As we only lost by three points, that could be us.' Alaric felt a tiny bit of relief, even if Hector's tone was just as deflated as before. At least it wasn't all over yet.

The van slowed to a halt as they reached the Oakwood car park. Alaric, arms aching with bruises, undid his seatbelt and went to open the door. However, before he could do so, it had been opened from the other side by the very person he least wanted to see. Madame Sang stood there, smiling her most wicked smile. And Alaric felt sick as he remembered what he and Lucy had done to her classroom the previous day, how Lucy had flat-out lied to her. And it seemed that she'd got to them before they'd got to Master Ogden.

'Alaric,' she said with an almost victorious smile, her tone coldly soft. 'Could you come with me, please? You too, Laurence for that matter, wouldn't want you to miss out on this.' And her smile developed into the coldest laugh she could muster.

CHAPTER 14

ALARIC AND LAURENCE climbed out of the van and followed Madame Sang, unable to find the strength to say anything. Their clothes still sodden, they traipsed across campus, Sang remaining silent until out of earshot of the other Rei team members.

'Master Ogden will see you two and Miss Ray now,' Sang said. Even with her back to Alaric and Laurence, the smile surfacing on her face was obvious from her ears moving.

'Why?' Alaric asked, trying to sound innocent, though he was sure he already knew the answer.

'Why do you think?' Sang said, most of the amusement now banished from her tone. 'Having Lucy lie to me; leaving detention without my permission; rummaging through my personal, *private* belongings. You do realise the number of rules you've broken, don't you?'

Alaric didn't answer, taking a breath to compose himself. He thought everything through carefully. As frustrating as it was that Sang had got there first, he knew he could explain everything to Master Ogden, and he'd understand. Sang was just trying to cover herself up now.

'What have I got to do with anything?' Laurence asked.

'Everyone knows how much time the three of you spend together,' Madame Sang snarled. 'If Alaric and Lucy were both involved, there's no doubting you were too. Besides anything else, I'm sure he'd love to speak to you about that humiliating display in the basketball match.'

Alaric and Laurence kept their mouths shut, knowing anything they said could only make matters worse. Sang didn't say anything more either, which Alaric thought was for the best. By the time they reached the staircase down to Master Ogden's office, Alaric's legs were starting to feel heavy once again. A nagging thought surfaced in his mind: what if this interaction with Ogden didn't go as planned? What if they *did* end up in trouble with him? He tried to dismiss these thoughts, keeping a cool head as Sang knocked on the door, and the headmaster invited them into his office.

'Alaric, Laurence, take a seat, please,' Master Ogden said, none of the usual joviality in his tone, his face sunken with disappointment. Alaric and Laurence sat down opposite Ogden, staring hard at their feet. The only other time Alaric remembered the headmaster looking this serious was when Iglehart had accused them of stealing the Golden Pearl.

'I'll go and find Lucy for you, Quentin,' Sang said, sounding happier than Alaric had ever heard her.

Master Ogden nodded as Alaric heard her leave through the door and shut it gently behind her.

'Right, Alaric, Laurence,' Master Ogden began, 'this is really not good business at all, I'm afraid. We'll get to the second half once Lucy arrives but what I just saw from you two and the whole basketball team was utterly unacceptable. I trust you both know that?'

Alaric hesitated, debating whether or not to tell Ogden that Franco had provoked him. Then, he just resigned himself to nodding, Laurence doing the same.

'So, tell me, why did you do it, Alaric?' Ogden said, his eyebrows raised as he stared hard into Alaric's pupils.

'Franco made fun of the fact my dad's dead,' Alaric forced himself to say.

Master Ogden sighed, rubbing his eyes before speaking. 'I understand, Alaric, that's an emotional subject for you. However, reacting that way in front of the whole of Harramore gives the House of Rei and the school a very bad image. Are you aware of how fragile the situation is here at the moment?'

Alaric said nothing. Ogden was so calm with disappointment as he continued talking, it would have been more bearable to be shouted at by Madame Sang.

'The clashes in the streets tell you all you need to know. Rei and Naidos supporters have not been this divided since The Peace began. When you project that image of Rei to the world, what does it tell those on the fence? It's going to push them towards Naidos. Do you understand?' Master Ogden's tone was now extremely grave, forcing Alaric to nod. 'Unfortunately, I have no choice therefore but to take action. Now, Laurence, I can let you and the rest of the team off with a warning as everyone on the pitch was fighting by the time you got involved. However, Alaric, you started the entire brawl. So, I'm afraid I'm going to have to ban you from playing basketball for Rei's next two matches.'

'What?' Alaric and Laurence both shouted at once.

'I'm sorry,' Master Ogden said, 'I really don't want to, but you left me little choice.'

'But no one can replace Alaric,' Laurence groaned.

'You have Lucy,' Ogden said in a tone that would countenance no further response.

Alaric slumped in his chair. The day just kept getting worse, and he was already dreading to think how Hector would react to this news. Lucy had never played basketball before, so that was surely two more guaranteed losses.

'Now, speaking of Lucy, when she arrives, there is something else I need to talk to you three about,' Master Ogden said.

Alaric and Laurence sat in silence, Master Ogden also saying nothing as they waited for Lucy. When she finally came through the door, accompanied by Madame Sang, the medicine teacher gave one last gleeful smile before exiting the office. Then, Ogden started speaking once more.

'Madame Sang came to see me earlier,' he said sternly, 'and understandably, she wasn't impressed. She tells me yesterday evening, she had Alaric in detention. Lucy then came to tell her that I wished to see her in my office. In other words, you lied to her face. When she found my office was empty, she was unamused. She then returned to find her classroom in a state. The drawers had been pulled open, paper everywhere. In fact, she said it was rather appalling and suspects you three were behind it. Tell me, is this all true?'

'Yes, it is,' Lucy said without hesitation. 'And these students who are ill, it turns out Madame Sang's been poisoning them.'

Master Ogden raised his eyebrows and let out a sigh. 'Excuse me?' he said.

'It's true,' Alaric said, realising the truth was out there now. 'We'd been suspecting something was going on. Every person who's sick has some sort of trait that'd make people want to attack them. Then, a similar illness was going around in the Main World. We heard Sang and the nurse talking the other day, and we think they're working together. We raided Sang's desk to check, and it turns out they're using rumis. All the symptoms, everything matches.'

Master Ogden, who'd been listening to what Alaric was saying attentively, threw his head forward. There was a painful-sounding thud as it landed on the solid wooden desk. He kept his head there for a few seconds like he'd fallen asleep before he looked back up, and his lips thinned for the first time Alaric could remember.

'How did you not learn from last year that meddling in these sorts of things doesn't end well?' Ogden groaned. 'As laudable as I'm sure your intentions were, I am well aware of the situation and have known about the rumis for weeks. Madame Sang and Madame Bork are working together to find the best way to treat those who are poisoned and establish how it got into the school.'

'Well, that's obvious, isn't it?' Lucy said with a hint of smugness.

Master Ogden rolled his eyes, folding his arms. 'Is it?'

'They pretend it's medicine,' Lucy said. 'If Beatrice and Sang are in this together, then—'

'*Madame* Sang, Lucy,' Ogden sighed. 'Carry on.'

'Well, Madame Sang and Beatrice both work with medicines. So, the obvious way would be to slip a pill and say it's a cold remedy when it's actually this rumis poison,' Lucy said with certainty.

Master Ogden sighed again and shook his head. 'I told you, they're not behind this. They're trying to work out how it got into the school. Please leave it to us this time.'

'Honestly, please just trust us,' Lucy pleaded.

'The situation is under control,' Ogden said simply. 'I'll be writing to your families. Now go.'

'But—' Lucy protested.

'Go!' Ogden said, raising his voice.

Having never heard the headmaster shout before, Alaric, Lucy and Laurence rose from their seats without further question. Then, they jumped through the ceiling, leaving the gloominess of the office behind.

CHAPTER 15

Lancliff, England

ONLY ONE MAN in Lancliff ever went near the Hangman's Bridge. Although it had only been fourteen years since the incident, it displayed the cracks of a bridge that hadn't been used in centuries. Somehow, the whole town beyond it always felt colder, darker. Even on a warm summer's day, the sky would always be the same stormy grey, and the few who dared venture there never chose to return.

None of this bothered the man the locals called Neville. Quite on the contrary, it was the perfect reason to dwell under the bridge, for no one ever disturbed him there. And that was the way he liked it. He'd been sleeping in that same spot for the last ten years, ever since he'd been evicted from his one-room flat. He'd only aged a decade in that time, but he had the appearance of a man over a hundred, his thinning, greasy hair always the same colour as the sky, his beard just as matted.

For so long, his life had been nothing but mechanical: each day, he'd sleep, eat and sit, before drinking the night away with the cheapest alcohol he could find. In fact, bar the occasional visit from the local social services, he hadn't spoken to anyone in ten years on the night *they* turned up.

The weather was starting to warm up, probably early March. There was still a certain chill in the air as the nights came in, and Neville was climbing into the same moth-eaten sleeping bag he'd had all these years when he noticed them from afar. At first glance, he thought he'd been hallucinating. No one ever came near his bridge, let alone at this time of night. However, as he squinted, he realised they were indeed there, both approaching him with a hurried stride. He rummaged through his backpack, breathing a sigh of relief as he found his Swiss army knife. He clutched it so hard that his knuckles' whiteness was visible even in the night's darkness as he flicked out the blade.

'Remember, you leave it to me, Vido, okay?' Neville heard the slimmer of the two people say. It was difficult to make out either of the two people's faces in the blackness of the night. Both wore such dark clothes, it was hard to see them at all, but from the speaker's high voice and slightly curvy figure, Neville guessed she was a woman.

'Whatever you say, Beatrice,' the one called Vido said coldly. They were approaching him very quickly now, and Neville tightened his grip on his knife, staring intently as they stopped a few yards away from him.

'It's okay. We're not here to hurt you,' the one called Beatrice said, eyeing Neville's knife. She crouched down to look him in the eye. 'It's Neville, isn't it?'

Neville, still keeping a firm hold on his knife, nodded. 'That's what I believe they call me,' he said. He spoke in a voice that had become so raspy from lack of use, it was barely intelligible.

'What they call you?' Beatrice asked gently. 'Is it not your real name?'

Neville mused for a few moments and relaxed his grip on his knife. He couldn't remember the last time someone had asked his name. 'It's Keith,' he said, and for the first time in many years, a smile actually formed on his face.

Beatrice smiled back at him, placing a soft, gentle hand on his shoulder. 'Okay, Keith. I'm Beatrice, and this is Vido.' She indicated towards her friend, who nodded and gave a small wave. 'So, tell me, do you live here?'

Keith nodded, sitting up straight. For some reason, he was feeling something that had become so unfamiliar to him by now, he almost didn't recognise it: hope.

'Well then, Keith, what if I told you this night could be your last under this bridge?' Beatrice said with a smile revealing her teeth, which were white enough to gleam even in this light. 'We have a spare room…with heating *and* a bed,' she added when Keith said nothing, her sweet smile widening.

'I-I'd like that very much,' Keith said weakly, feeling his eyes well with tears, which he fought back.

'We can do that for you,' Beatrice said gently. 'We just need your help with something.'

'O-of course. I-I'll do anything,' Keith replied, fighting harder to hold back his tears.

Beatrice smiled even more widely, a look of endearment in her eyes. 'Excellent. Can you tell us why no one else ever comes here?' she said, almost in a whisper.

Keith's eyes widened. He hadn't been expecting a simple question; it seemed too easy. 'Well, a while ago, they found the body of one of the nurses from the hospital that used to be down there,' he said, indicating towards the dark side of the town. 'She was hanging from this very bridge. Suicide, they think. The locals reckon this part of town is cursed.'

'And has anyone been to the hospital since?' Beatrice asked.

Keith shook his head. 'It closed the same day.'

Beatrice looked upwards at the bottom of the bridge, raising her eyebrows interestedly. 'Is that so? Tell me, Keith, do you know where the hospital is?'

Keith nodded, shuffling on the floor, his hope now replaced with apprehension.

'Could you take us there?' Beatrice asked.

Keith gasped, his body frozen for several seconds. Go to the hospital? Even he wasn't that mad. 'I-I can't do that. Please, anything else.'

'That's no worry,' Vido piped up, his deep voice cold and emotionless. 'If he wants to carry on sleeping here, we can leave him, Beatrice.'

'No, please, I'll do it,' Keith said straight away. 'We'll go now.'

'Excellent,' Beatrice said gently. 'After you.'

Keith's heart racing, he stood up and started towards the dark side of the town. He tried to clear his mind as he led Beatrice and Vido to the hospital, forcing himself to ignore the sharp pain in his dodgy hip. Even though it had been so long since he'd been there, he'd visited the hospital so many times when it was open that he could still walk the way blindfolded if he had to.

But every single one of his instincts was telling him

not to go. This whole part of town was already giving him that familiar coldness people always felt when they ventured there. It was a coldness that seemed to emanate from the hospital, the epicentre of this energy. He fought his instincts with each step, forcing himself to pay no attention to the rows of abandoned houses on either side of the street. He cast a glance at Vido and Beatrice. Somehow, each of them seemed entirely unfazed by this journey, Beatrice still smiling serenely as Vido wore the same, steely expression he always had.

The hospital was in sight now, barely recognisable from the last time Keith had been there. The NHS logo was hanging askew, the windows opaque with thick dust. And the lifelessness inside Keith grew stronger with every step he forced himself to make towards the building.

'H-here, here it is,' he said to Beatrice and Vido, his voice shaking. He wanted to turn back now more than ever, settle down under the familiar comfort of his bridge, but he knew he couldn't. He needed that bedroom more than anything he'd ever had in his life.

'Go on in, then,' Beatrice said, almost laughing. 'We'll wait out here. Tell us what you find.'

'W-why?' Keith said, almost pleading. He wanted to run away, but he knew his hip wouldn't let him, especially not at this temperature.

'Do you want the room or not?' Vido snapped, picking up a fallen brick and hurling it at the glass doors, which shattered in an instant.

Keith shuddered and took a deep breath. He kept his mind as clear as possible and started towards the now empty doorway, treading gingerly on the broken glass. *Just think of the bedroom*, he thought to himself over and over again. And the moment he stepped through those doors, he wished he never had.

As soon as he got inside the hospital, darkness surrounded him. A darkness like no other. It was nothingness. No light, no heat, no sound. And now, hot tears did come. He panted, his breathing irregular as finally, an ambient sound filled his ears.

His whole body shook as he heard it: the whirring of the engines, the ear-splitting sound of the explosions. He remembered these sounds. It was that battle in Iraq, the one where he'd lost his hip.

He collapsed in a heap on the ground, his whole body convulsing uncontrollably. A cold, sticky sweat drenched his sickly white face, washing off the layers of dirt that had accumulated there over the last few weeks. Then, he actually screamed at what he saw next.

A woman, her face so pale, she could've been a

ghost, came gliding towards him. In fact, he would've thought she *was* a ghost if the rest of her hadn't looked so solid, so real. Her long, black dress, her dark hair—it was all truly there. She drifted ever closer, a serene, almost murderous smile etched onto her face.

'Have you come to help me?' She spoke in a child-like, girlish voice, which had a kind of spookiness that chilled Keith even more. And now, he did find the strength to stand up and run, in a blind panic towards where he hoped the door was. He looked over his shoulder, speeding up as fast as his hip would allow him to as he saw the woman gaining ground on him. Then, he was out. Vido and Beatrice stood there as before, and he fell to the ground as his legs lost all their strength.

'It's true!' Vido exclaimed. 'It's really true, Beatrice. We've found Cria. We'll be honoured over all other followers of Naidos!'

Keith looked again over his shoulder, scurrying towards Beatrice's feet as he saw the woman drifting towards him once more.

'Yes, indeed,' Beatrice said to Vido. 'Now bind her. We don't want her getting away.'

Keith watched on in a heap on the ground. He was still struggling to catch his breath as Vido pulled a rope from around his waist, strode towards the woman and bound her arms and legs. She didn't give off so much as a scream. Her face was just as relaxed as always, which unsettled Keith yet even more.

'Thank you, Keith. You've been most useful,' Beatrice said softly.

Keith took a few breaths, trying to refocus his mind. 'W-what about the room?' he stammered, his whole body perspiring profusely.

'Ah yes, don't worry about that,' Beatrice said, helping him to his feet. She was wearing the same, kind smile as when she arrived at the bridge. 'Naidos has plenty in his kingdom,' she whispered.

'Naidos?' Keith asked weakly.

Beatrice nodded, maintaining her smile. 'Our leader. You'll meet him soon, and he'll reward you. Don't worry.'

Keith didn't have the strength to reply. Instead, he looked up to the stars and realised how beautiful they were for the first time in years. Then, he smiled the same smile as Beatrice. And it was a good job he was still in shock, still somewhat unaware of his surroundings.

For it was because of this that he did not see the glint of silver in Beatrice's hand, nor did he even feel it as she slashed it across his throat. Then, his hip finally gave as he collapsed once more into a heap on the ground. And his last smile was etched onto his face forever, his lifeless eyes staring up at the stars they'd never see again.

CHAPTER 16

'YOU'RE BANNED FOR the next two games?' Hector said indignantly.

Alaric sighed and nodded, taking a seat on the edge of the sofa and laying his head in his hands. 'I'm sorry,' he said.

Even after reflecting on this as he journeyed to his lodgings, it still hadn't sunk in. They'd not only lost the match against Naidos because of him but looked sure to lose the next two as well.

'Right, well on the bright side, if we qualify for this playoff—which I think we will—then you'll be back for the final if we get that far,' Hector said, running his fingers through his still sweaty man bun. 'The trouble is it's a big ask. We're going to have to shuffle the team, probably make Jacob the forward. Lucy, would you be able to help Grace out in midfield?'

'I mean, I can try,' Lucy laughed. 'Might not be helpful, though; sport isn't exactly my forte.'

'Well, you're our only option. You'll have to do,'

Hector grumbled, then storming off to his room for a shower. Alaric eyed Lucy, who, to his surprise, didn't look in the slightest offended.

'This could be fun,' she said, her tone far more upbeat than Alaric was feeling. Neither he nor Laurence responded, still trying to come to terms with the fact they'd lost to Naidos.

Alaric stood up and forced the slightest of smiles at Lucy, then started towards the shower himself. He didn't bother going back into the lounge area that evening, instead heading straight to bed without even touching his homework. He lay there replaying the events of the evening in his head: the build-up to the basketball game; the match itself; the aftermath; the meeting in Master Ogden's office. Master Ogden's office.

Ogden had seemed so adamant that Madame Sang and the nurse were not behind this sickness...but he had admitted it was a poison, that rumis was in the school. And what Lucy had said: *they pretend it's medicine*. What if?

It seemed so plausible, such a simple way to target specific people, so easy for Beatrice and Sang to do. But why had Master Ogden denied it? Who did he think was behind it? And the thought seemed wild, but what if Ogden was in on it himself? No, surely not. He wasn't that type of person. But what if?

After all, was it not *his* brother Madame Cassandra had a crush on? And he'd just stood up for Sang and Beatrice as Goblinsfoe had stood up for Alaric last year. And he remembered how that had ended.

No, it was utterly ridiculous. What reason did Ogden have to attack random students? Plus, he'd been far too supportive of Rei in the basketball tournament before he'd suspended Alaric. He laughed to himself as he realised how absurd the idea actually was, and he'd honestly believed it for a second. Then, at last, he fell away into a deep sleep.

ALARIC AWOKE THE following morning to the coldest day he could remember on Harramore. As normal as it was for there to be a biting breeze in the winter months, he'd not once seen the grass of Oakwood blanketed with a layer of frost.

He, Lucy and Laurence all arrived in the canteen to find every head turning in their direction. He started feeling unwelcome as a few people jeered, some descendants of Naidos smirking, occasionally applauding sarcastically.

'Just ignore them,' Lucy said in response to Alaric's clenching jaw.

'What d'you reckon this is about?' Laurence mumbled.

'The basketball for sure,' Alaric said bitterly. 'I threw the game away against Naidos.'

'Don't beat yourself up, Al, it was one of the best things I'd ever seen,' a voice said from behind the three of them. Alaric turned to see Carlos standing there with Jorge and Rodrigo, all three of them grinning.

'Honestly, you should see Franco now,' Jorge said, his grin widening as he spoke. 'Whenever someone mentions you, he properly tenses up; he's scared of you.'

Alaric froze for a moment, unsure how to react before bursting into laughter. Franco was frightened of him. Hopefully, he and Dwayne wouldn't bother him again!

'Only thing is,' Rodrigo said, 'I think a few others are a bit shifty now as well. No one will be messing with you anytime soon.'

'Well, yeah. There's that, and a few are annoyed 'cus they feel it's your fault Naidos are still in the cup,' Carlos added.

The grin faded from Alaric's face immediately.

'Thanks, Carlos. That makes me feel loads better,' he said sarcastically before striding off to help himself to breakfast.

'Steady on, mate,' Laurence said as they browsed the morning's sausages. 'It was only Carlos.'

Alaric didn't respond verbally, just casting Laurence an exasperated glare.

'Laurence is right,' Lucy said gently. 'You don't want everyone being scared of you, and acting like that around people isn't going to help.'

'Yeah, well, I've got a lot going on in my life at the moment, if you hadn't noticed. I don't even know whose house I'm staying at this weekend yet,' Alaric said. Those words almost got stuck in his throat as he said them. He'd been trying not to think about that issue too much over the last few days, but now it was the middle of the week, he couldn't afford to put it off much longer.

'I understand that, Alaric,' Lucy said, 'but you know we all understand, whatever you decide to do.'

'Same here,' Laurence said. 'I love having you around, of course, but what you do is up to you. Plus, look on the bright side; we haven't got Madame Sang today.'

Alaric produced a faint smile as they sat down and

started eating their breakfast. For what it was worth, Wednesday was always one of the better days on his timetable. The afternoon was reserved for basketball training, but Hector had given them the day off. Madame Cassandra's absence also meant her lesson was free most of the time. This left them with just Master Idoss and Madame Moyglot to sit through that day, neither of whose classes were ever particularly challenging. In fact, he rather enjoyed Master Idoss' lesson as he announced they'd be starting a new unit when they began the class.

'Right, everyone, new topic, new hair colour, in case you hadn't noticed,' he announced; he was now sporting a bottle-green hair-and-beard ensemble. 'Today, we'll be talking about the post-war events on Harramore, specifically the trials of Naidos' most loyal supporters. Now to start off, kindly read page four-hundred-and-sixty-one.'

The usual rustling of paper filled the air as the class turned to the relevant page of the textbook. Then, everyone looked slightly taken aback at what they saw. On the right was the usual page of dense text, but on the left was a full-page image that was enough to startle even the calmest person. A dark-haired man with cold, empty eyes stood on a high stool, his hands and feet tightly bound, a noose around his neck. But he was grinning a grin that showed all his teeth right back to his molars, his eyes wide with joy as if relishing his forthcoming death. Alaric tried to brush off the sight and read on, these horrible eyes staring up at him.

As soon as Naidos fell, the Governor of Harramore, Hal Iglehart, ordered every war officer who had supported Naidos to be arrested and tried by his court. It is widely presumed that Iglehart had envisaged a quick process, but in fact, he could scarcely have been more mistaken.

Many of Naidos' most loyal supporters fled to live in the Main World. Most of these were never captured, including Eden Sang, the very woman Naidos praised for leading him to Rei.

'Sir!' Lucy called immediately. Alaric looked up from his textbook, knowing she'd have the same question as him. In fact, he'd be surprised if most of the class didn't.

'Yes, Lucy?' Master Idoss said.

'Is Eden Sang related to Madame Sang?' Lucy asked.

'It's not my place to comment on other teacher's family lives,' Master Idoss said firmly. 'Carry on reading, please.'

'Well, that's a yes then,' Alaric mumbled.

He looked back down at the textbook page, his mind drifting. So, Madame Sang was married to Master Ogden's brother, and her sister was right in Naidos' inner circle. He tried to dismiss the thoughts from his head for the time being, and he continued to read the textbook.

Later on, came the question of which criminals to actually convict. Defending parties in the trials repeatedly emphasised that too many convictions would harm prospects of unity on Harramore. Ultimately, after five years of legal proceedings, just fourteen of the three-hundred-and-fifty-six arrests Iglehart ordered resulted in an execution.

Such a result could have been a significant blow to the Governor's reputation. However, the successful conviction and hanging of Naidos' only son, Arimon Crow (pictured opposite), live on national television, substantially mitigated the impact.

'Sir, does this mean the other supporters of Naidos are still out there?' Alaric asked Master Idoss.

Idoss sighed and gave Alaric a wry smile before answering. 'It does indeed, Alaric, yes. The trouble was, Iglehart could only sentence the ones he could prove had committed crimes against civilians. Simply being on the other side wasn't enough to get you arrested, let alone executed.'

'So, if, say, there was another war,' Alaric began.

'Then, yes, many of Naidos' old high-ranking officials could return from the Main World,' Idoss said. 'But I'm a history teacher; my job is to tell you about the past. The future—that's Madame Cassandra's job. Back to work, please.'

The rest of the lesson went slowly. While interested in what Idoss said about the trials, Alaric was too eager to talk to Lucy and Laurence to focus properly. By the time they got outside to head to their next lesson in Madame Cassandra's classroom, the layer of ice on the grass had melted, the bright sun now shining down onto the grounds. Depending on which teacher was covering the lesson, Alaric thought he could try to talk to Lucy and Laurence then. And he pumped his fist under his desk when the swordsmanship teacher, Master McGraths, arrived. He didn't even enter the room, merely poking his head around the door.

'Unfortunately, I've got a lot of marking to do, and I can't be disturbed,' he announced. 'Can I trust you all to get on with your work if I go and get that done?'

There was an affirmative murmur around the room, and a few people grinned with delight at the idea.

'Great, thank you. If anyone asks, I was here all this

time,' McGraths said with a wink, then leaving for his office.

'That helps,' Alaric said to Lucy and Laurence. 'We need to talk about this whole Sang-Ogden thing.'

'I think we do,' Lucy agreed. 'If Madame Sang's sister was so close to Naidos, why is she allowed to teach at this school?'

'It's definitely her poisoning everyone. There is literally no other teacher in the school who'd do this,' Laurence declared.

'Actually,' Alaric said. He lowered his voice to be absolutely sure no one else could hear them. 'I was thinking last night, what if there is?'

'What do you mean?' Lucy asked, furrowing her brow.

Alaric took a deep breath. 'Well, I was thinking about this last night, and at first, I thought it seemed stupid, but now, I'm not so sure. Ogden wouldn't listen when we tried to tell him Sang and Beatrice were behind this. Sang's sister was right inside Naidos' most trusted circle, and we already know she's married to Ogden's brother.'

'You're not seriously suggesting this, are you?' Laurence asked.

'I know it sounds crazy. It's just looking at what we

know; it seems the Sang and Ogden families are much closer than we realised. Plus, we all thought Goblinsfoe seemed so nice last year,' Alaric said.

'So, you really think Ogden's in on this as well?' Laurence asked.

'It does seem plausible, now you mention it,' Lucy mused. 'Just why'd he want to poison these people?'

'Cassandra trying to marry his brother,' Alaric guessed. 'He may not be closely involved, but he could at least be turning a blind eye.'

'Great,' Laurence said sarcastically. 'And my parents don't want us getting involved in this kind of stuff either. That leaves us no one to talk to about this.'

Then, as if Laurence had made it happen, Alaric gave a start as he felt his phone buzz in his pocket. He pulled it out immediately; no Nephilim had phones with the capacity to text, meaning the only person who ever messaged him was Lucy. Then, as he saw the message on his phone, a smile surfaced on his face, and he looked up at the ceiling in relief.

Hi Alaric, Mr Trolley here. Sorry for reaching you this way. I've been in the Main World all week and Ogden's having the post searched because of the sickness stuff. He called me yesterday and told me what you'd said about these illnesses at Oakwood. I have to admit, it seems fishy. Since Ogden doesn't believe you, I'll use my position in government to look into it. Give me a few weeks, and I'll let you know what I find out. Anyway, I suggest you stay with Lucy and your mum for the next couple of weekends. We don't want people to suspect we're collaborating on this. Tell the others for me and let me know when you get this.

Alaric showed Lucy and Laurence the message, and each looked as delighted as him. Finally, they had a lead.

CHAPTER 17

THINGS STARTED TO look up again over the next few weeks. The House of Paz thrashed the House of Marfin's basketball team, meaning Rei qualified for the playoff the following Saturday. Alaric, not allowed to attend, received regular updates by text from Mr Trolley, who said Lucy performed surprisingly strongly as Rei edged the victory.

This gave Alaric and the rest of the team some hope that they'd be able to win their semi-final against the House of Orm, the Guardian of Snakes. While Lucy's level of play was nothing on the regular starters, she was never awful either.

Then came the return of the students and staff who'd been admitted to hospital the previous term. Peter Barrett visited the school once more to announce that there was no longer a cause for concern, his nervous stutter miraculously gone.

'After months in hospital, I am pleased to have been able to return your teachers and friends to this school,' he said to the cryptozoology class that Monday. 'It took a while, I know, but we have developed a treatment that can cure you within days. And, we're gifting unlimited stocks to your school for free. So, should anyone else fall ill with this sickness, there's no longer a need to worry. Just go and see the nurse, and she'll have you fixed up.'

'Seems pretty sudden that he's come up with a cure, don't you think?' Lucy asked after the lesson.

Alaric nodded. 'And how could he have found out it was rumis unless Ogden or someone at the school told him?'

'I guess this whole network idea. You said yourself, Alaric, last term that Barrett could be in on this somewhere,' Lucy mused.

Alaric sighed. 'I get that. Why'd they want to cure this, though? It just seems so odd that they'd make these people sick but make sure they live. What did anyone gain? It's not like Barrett is even making any money.'

'Of course, there's no reason to assume Barrett and Ogden should be in on it at all,' Lucy said. 'Ogden could simply have just told Barrett, and then he developed the cure.'

'Then gave it away for free as a publicity stunt,' Laurence suggested.

'It seems possible,' Alaric murmured. 'It just doesn't make sense.'

'Nothing does,' Laurence said glumly.

As the week continued, five more students were sent to the nurse with symptoms of rumis. All returned within a couple of days, having been treated with Peter Barrett's medicine. Clearly, Beatrice had no objection to curing the sick students either. This was frustrating Alaric, Lucy and Laurence even more as they tried to work out to no avail what was going on. Ultimately, they could do nothing but wait as Beatrice and Sang seemed to be planning their next move.

Then came the semi-final weekend, and Alaric started to feel low again as he thought about not playing in the big game. The only positive was that he'd be staying with the Trolleys, so he could at least watch the match on TV with Mr Trolley. Alaric forced a smile when he wished the siblings good luck as they set off for Orm's stadium. Then, his stomach sank at the sight of a lonely bottle of cola and packet of crisps on the living room table.

'We'll have a good time here, Alaric. Don't worry,' Mr Trolley said. He gave a reassuring smile as they sat down on the squashy settee and switched on the TV. Already, coverage of the match had started as Norman

McNulty sat in a studio in the stadium, discussing the game with two pundits.

'So, tell me, Ava,' he said to the one on his left, a young, angelic woman with dark, shiny hair, 'what do you make of Orm's chances in this game?'

'Well, what I know from my time playing for Orm is that they are a team who rely on their agility a lot,' Ava said haughtily. 'It'll be interesting to see how the game takes shape today. Normally, I wouldn't expect a physical encounter, but the history between Orm and Rei may well make it so. It'll be tough for them, but I think without Alaric Swift and the home advantage on Orm's side, we're just about the favourites.'

'It'll be an ugly game, for sure,' Mr Trolley grumbled. 'I trust you know about Orm and Naidos? Pretty big thing in the war.'

Alaric nodded. 'You mean that Orm has always been his closest ally?'

Mr Trolley bowed his head. 'We don't have to watch this game if you don't want to. I get if it'll be too painful for you.'

'I don't mind; if you want to watch it, we can,' Alaric said, trying to sound polite. In all honesty, as nerve-racking as he was sure it would be, he thought not being able to see what was going on would be even worse.

'I've got something more important to show you while my wife isn't here,' Mr Trolley said. 'It's about this whole poison affair.'

Alaric rotated his body towards Mr Trolley, giving him his full attention.

'Let me get my laptop,' Mr Trolley said, heading upstairs at a jog. Alaric waited in anticipation, one eye still on the TV as the two pundits debated how Orm should approach the match. Mr Trolley returned within a minute, holding his bulky, heavy-looking laptop with both hands.

'I have to say, Alaric, I was suspicious before,' Mr Trolley said seriously. 'Everything that's been going on, you know? Chandyo's assassination; all that stuff at the start of the year with you and Rei; Naidos' supporters getting more vocal; and of course, this sickness. Now that we know it's a poison, I'm certain something is up. Needless to say, there has to be someone inside Oakwood behind this, and my gut feeling is that it's not Madame Sang. As horrible as she may seem to you, she was—as I've said—always lovely when I was at the school. I think on this one, we need to give her the benefit of the doubt. You can't judge a person by their siblings. This does, however, bring me to the other person you brought up—'

'Beatrice Bork, the nurse?' Alaric said excitedly.

Mr Trolley nodded. 'Indeed. Now, I'm about to show you something that's strictly against the law, highly confidential. So, you mustn't tell a soul that you've seen this. Do you hear me?' He emphasised every syllable of his last sentence, and Alaric nodded without hesitation.

'What about Lucy and Laurence?' Alaric asked.

'You're in on this together, so if you can all keep a secret, fine. Just be extremely careful where you discuss this,' Mr Trolley said in a way that would countenance only one response. Alaric nodded again.

He watched on as Mr Trolley typed in more passwords than he could count, the camera on his laptop scanning his face. Then, he was at last onto some sort of complex search page with several boxes to fill in.

'This database has the birth records, medical history, place of work, anything you may want to know about every Nephilim to have existed since records began. Its access is strictly limited to people in government. If I get caught sharing this with you, I will end up with a lengthy prison sentence,' Mr Trolley said.

'We're going to look up Beatrice Bork?' Alaric asked, his skin tingling as he wondered what was about to happen.

'You bet we are,' Mr Trolley replied. He typed the nurse's name into the search fields, then walloped the return key with a triumphant grin on his face. 'Now, look here. Everything seems in order at first glance—you can see Beatrice's photo, that she works at Oakwood, employed about a year and a half ago; date of birth is there, all fine. Then, you delve deeper.'

Alaric watched on with wide eyes as Mr Trolley clicked on her employment history. Just one record was listed: her time at Oakwood.

'So, she's only ever worked as a nurse at Oakwood. Her date of birth makes her what, thirty-one? We therefore know she got her first job at about thirty and most people finish Oakwood at seventeen or eighteen,' Mr Trolley explained.

'What was she doing in-between times then?' Alaric asked. Although, he felt this alone was fairly weak evidence.

'Exactly. Now, it's not unusual for people to go off the radar for a few years after school. Some Nephilim like to spend a few years living out in the Main World, perhaps start up a family or something. But there's no record of her ever leaving Harramore…none at all. So, what was she doing?' Mr Trolley kept his focus on Alaric. He was unsure whether or not he was supposed to answer before Mr Trolley continued speaking. 'Well, I looked up the school registers from the time she would've been at Oakwood and guess what.'

Alaric thought for a few seconds as a strange iciness overcame him. 'You don't mean to say…she never was at Oakwood?'

'That's precisely what I'm saying, and in fact, that's just the cusp of it. I looked at the birth records for the day she was born, and there was again no Beatrice Bork. She does not exist. This identity is nothing but an alias, so how she even got into this school is beyond me. I always knew Ogden was unscrupulous, but employing this woman…he's clearly not bothered with a thorough background check—'

'Or he's turning a blind eye,' Alaric said.

Mr Trolley looked at Alaric as if he'd slipped popping candy into his food. 'What do you mean?'

'I know it seems far-fetched,' Alaric said quickly. 'It's just that Goblinsfoe seemed all innocent last year, and how do we know Ogden and Sang aren't closer to Naidos' supporters than we realised?'

'I understand where you're coming from, I really do,' Mr Trolley said gently, 'but as for Madame Sang, she was never like her sister. She had a lot of sympathy with some of Naidos' views, but she always called for a peaceful resolution to the conflict. This was why they wanted to make her a Guardian; she had ideas that united the two sides, a potential peacemaker. I never understood why they appointed Ogden.'

Alaric shook his head. 'I don't know. It did seem stupid, but people can be hard to judge.'

'Never has a truer word been spoken,' Mr Trolley chortled. 'Anyway, this Beatrice Bork…I took her photo from these records and did some searching out in the Main World. In the end, it wasn't difficult to find a record that matched the picture.'

Alaric shuffled in his seat, leaning in even closer to Mr Trolley, watching his lips intently.

'Annabelle Macauley,' Mr Trolley said. Alaric stared at him blankly; was this name supposed to sound familiar to him? 'She's a British woman. She worked in a shop, had a few kids, lived a normal life in the Main World. She's listed as a missing person now out there. She's not been seen since about two weeks before Beatrice Bork was appointed.'

'Now we know where she is,' Alaric said with a smile.

'There's more to it than that,' Mr Trolley replied. 'Some Nephilim do settle in the Main World, raise their children and even send them to school there. It's not unheard of for them to just choose to live as Ordinaries. Yet, no one in Annabelle's entire ancestry appears on Harramore's register of Nephilim.'

'So, Beatrice isn't even a Nephilim?' Alaric said weakly.

Mr Trolley shook his head. 'I'm afraid not. So, now we have several more unanswered questions. How did she, an Ordinary, get into Harramore, and for what reason? Then, why, of all the places she could've gone, did she take the job as a school nurse? It's just so random, so mundane on paper.'

Alaric stared at the ceiling, his mouth hanging open. Somehow, this whole issue made even less sense now than it did before. He glanced at the TV for a moment, pleased to see Rei were in the lead before returning his focus to the conversation.

'D'you think there's some secret society in the Main World? Say, a group of people who know about us, who want to destroy us before we destroy them?' he suggested.

Mr Trolley sighed. He massaged his forehead, thinking hard. 'I have no idea at this point, but I guess it would be possible. If that's the case, there could well be another war and one even worse than the first. However, it's not what I was thinking.'

Alaric stared fixedly at Mr Trolley as he took a mouthful of drink, his own palms beginning to perspire.

'I mentioned a while back Peter Barrett's friendship with Hal Iglehart, thought he could be behind Ali Chandyo's murder. Well, as it turns out, Iglehart paid Barrett three million nuggets to invent the cure for this sickness. I think he's in on this somewhere for some money, but as you've said, the targets can't exactly be mere coincidence: Madame Ettoga was one of the only cyclops to oppose Naidos in the war; some of the students had Ordinary heritage and so on. The point is each target had a reason to be attacked by a Naidos supporter, which seems logical until you realise Beatrice is behind them. An Ordinary would have no reason to support Naidos at all. None of this adds up.'

Alaric took a deep breath before rising from his seat and strolling over to the window. He leaned hard on the sill as he stared at the view of Dromkoping, sloping down towards the sea. He watched intently as a crow built its nest, thinking hard, searching for the link, the missing piece of the puzzle. He thought back to the beginning of the year, all the strange happenings, but anything he could think of to connect it all seemed too contrived, too unlikely.

'I guess if we expose this, we can get Iglehart out of office,' he said at last.

'And let Vido Sadaarm, the notorious Naidos supporter in? No thanks, better the devil you know in this case,' Mr Trolley said. 'One thing that is for certain, though, is that we need to see Master Ogden on Monday, make sure something is done about Beatrice. It's one thing when you, Lucy and Laurence go and tell him all this, but when it's me, a government official, he'll take it seriously. Trust me.'

'And what if nothing gets done?' Alaric asked.

'Then we'll have to sort it out ourselves,' Mr Trolley replied. 'I know I told you not to get into trouble this year, but if no one else is willing to act, it'll have to be us. Plus, you've all shown yourselves to be perfectly capable in the past.'

Alaric grinned and cast another look at the TV. The game had reached its third quarter now, Rei still leading Orm by thirty-four points to twenty-seven. As they watched the next few minutes of the match unfold, a part of Alaric was almost glad he didn't have to play. The Orm crowd's boos were echoing around the stadium every time Rei touched the ball. While Grace, Jacob and Hector all seemed unperturbed by this, it was clearly unnerving Lucy and Laurence somewhat. A few times, they fumbled a pass, dropped the ball, or were dispossessed, and it was no surprise when they reached the end of the quarter with the difference at just one point.

'There was one other thing I wanted to show you,' Mr Trolley said as the referee blew his whistle.

'What is it?' Alaric asked, his stomach aching because of both the match and everything Mr Trolley had said. He watched his adoptive father flick through a small pile of newspapers on the coffee table. He pulled out a crumpled one towards the bottom, a few small tears at the top of the front page. Alaric read the newspaper's title and realised instantly that it was from the Main World: The Lancliff Post.

'This is a few weeks old,' Mr Trolley said, 'but it's just as disturbing all the same. I'm assuming you know about Lancliff?'

Alaric scratched the back of his mind, searching for a time the name of that town had come up in his life. He could vaguely remember a sign pointing in that direction near one of his first houses but had never questioned its significance. Slowly, he shook his head.

'It's the town where you were born. A homeless man was found murdered outside the very hospital a few weeks ago, in fact,' Mr Trolley said darkly. 'Now, even in the local press, it didn't make the front page. No one cared about the poor man, but they found no suspects, no obvious motive and the police soon closed the case. However, I think there's something more to it. With all that's going on, a strange murder right outside your birth hospital could be connected.'

Alaric looked down at the floor. Somehow, everything that was going on meant he wasn't even upset that he hadn't known where he was born.

'So, what do we do? Does the hospital matter anymore?' he said.

'I did some research, and it turns out the locals view Lancliff as a strange town,' Mr Trolley replied. 'Shortly after you were born, one of the nurses was found to have killed herself. The hospital closed soon after. Then, those who could afford to move away did so; the place is a ghost town now. It's just there are a lot of strange occurrences going on and not much we can do about it. We must stay alert.'

Alaric forced himself to swallow his saliva, his throat sore as he poured himself another drink. None of this was pleasant to think about in the slightest, and having so much more knowledge made him feel less at ease than before.

Trying to take his mind off it, he and Mr Trolley

focussed on the TV, watching as the game approached its end. There were still five minutes remaining, Rei having extended their lead to four points. But as Alaric knew too well, one score in Orm's favour would change the result.

Please just slow the game down, Alaric thought to himself. Hector seemed to be thinking the same way as he, Laurence and the girls in midfield started a slow passing routine, running the clock down further. Jacob, however, looked incensed, frantically waving his arms, calling for a pass, a chance to score.

'They've got to be careful,' Mr Trolley muttered. 'If they lose it, they're in trouble and still plenty of time left.'

Alaric nodded as he leant in towards the TV, wringing his sweaty hands. Four minutes, three and a half, three minutes remaining. Still, the score was Orm: 35—Rei: 39. They watched in silence as the clock continued to count down, Rei not slipping up still.

Now, the ball was with Jacob up-front for the first time in several minutes. Alaric shuffled even closer to the edge of his seat as he beat the keeper. Shot. Missed. And then, he was outrun as the keeper beat him in chasing the ball. Alaric's breathing seemed to stop as he launched it straight up to the Orm attacker, who twirled past Hector, breathing a sigh of relief as he was wrestled to the ground. Rei still led.

'Don't want to be giving away too many chances like that,' Mr Trolley sighed. Alaric once again nodded, unable to find the energy to respond verbally. They were in the last two minutes now, three points up, and memories of last year's late drama against Ceus were springing to mind.

Once more, Rei had the ball, continuing to slow down the match, not slipping up as it moved between the team members. Final minute now, and they were still holding on, Alaric praying they wouldn't slip up again as the ball arrived in Jacob's hands once more. He grabbed the cushion tightly in his fist as Jacob shot. What on earth was he doing? What if Orm got the ball again?

But there was no need to worry as it landed straight in the basket, Alaric and Mr Trolley leaping up and hugging in joy. All of a sudden, Alaric's worries had been purged from him. Rei were eighteen points up with just seconds left. They'd won the game now. Alaric felt not even slightly nervous as Orm desperately pushed forward in the closing seconds to no avail. Rei were into the final. And more importantly, Alaric was out of gaol for his actions against Naidos.

CHAPTER 18

THERE WAS A positive mood in the Trolleys' house for the rest of the weekend, which spread to Alaric. As the Trolley children and Lucy came home for dinner on Saturday night, Alaric had no trouble keeping his concerns at the back of his mind. He nodded along as they discussed their favourite plays of the game, unable to bring himself to tell them they hadn't been watching very closely.

Even on the Sunday after Lucy had gone home, the positivity in the house didn't die down as they cracked on with their weekend's homework. By Monday morning, Alaric and Mr Trolley still hadn't found an opportunity to talk to Laurence about their findings. All the same, they set off for Oakwood earlier than usual to speak to Master Ogden, disgruntling the Trolley children. Their car was, unsurprisingly, the only one in the car park when they arrived, the early morning air still crisp as Mr Trolley helped them carry their bags to the House of Rei's lodgings. To Alaric's surprise, Master

Ogden was already there, sitting spread-out on the settee, perusing the newspaper.

'Aha!' he exclaimed as they all arrived. 'Alaric, Laurence, I need to see you before lessons start. You're not in trouble, but I must warn you that it may be rather difficult to take.'

Alaric started to feel sick, memories of their accusation of stealing the Golden Pearl coming to mind.

'I'd like a word as well, please, Quentin,' Mr Trolley said.

'Of course,' Master Ogden said sombrely, 'it may not be a bad thing if you come along as well anyway. Have a good day, the rest of you.' He tossed the newspaper onto the coffee table, stood up, and marched towards the door out of the room. Alaric, Laurence, and Mr Trolley all followed. Alaric was at a loss as to what to say, if anything. His stomach twisted, his legs almost numb as they headed across the grounds of Oakwood, the crispness of the air no longer pleasant.

'Is this related to the poisonings, Master Ogden?' Laurence said feebly.

'Yes, I suppose you could say that,' Master Ogden answered with a small, solemn sigh.

'What's happened?' Alaric asked, his voice panicked.

'I'll let you be seated before I tell you,' Master Ogden said, forcing a smile.

Alaric felt now even emptier as they descended the familiar staircase down to Ogden's office door. When he thought about it, it seemed strange that Lucy wasn't with them as well. Then, he shuddered at the idea, but what if Lucy had been poisoned? He tried to dismiss the thought from his mind, thinking that maybe she was already in the office waiting for them. But as Master Ogden opened the door and invited them inside, his heart sank to the region of his stomach.

The office was empty, and now it was clear what Ogden was going to say as they all sat down, and the headmaster took a deep breath before speaking.

'I've had a call from Lucy's mother. I'm afraid she's unwell, been admitted to hospital in the Main World. We're not a hundred per cent sure, but it seems to be the same thing that's been going around at Oakwood,' he said.

Alaric's heart sank even further as he looked down at his feet. It felt more real now Master Ogden had said it, confirming his worst fears.

'And the medicine?' Mr Trolley said. 'I thought Peter Barrett had found a cure? Is it no longer available?'

'It is Edward, yes. However, Lucy is sick in the Main World, where this cure isn't available. They've only just acquired the treatment all the patients were on beforehand,' Master Ogden said, Alaric feeling a little relief.

'That must mean she's stable, at least?' he asked. 'It helped the others. She can't be getting worse, can she?' He said his last sentence with more hopefulness than expectation, Master Ogden's sinking posture telling him the answer before he'd even said it.

'The thing is, Alaric, Nephilim are stronger, more resistant to these sorts of poisons than Ordinaries. As Lucy is not like other Nephilim—that's to say she was born to Ordinary parents—we don't yet quite know how this will affect her.'

'Sh-she won't,' Laurence said with a hint of a whimper, then almost mouthing the rest of his sentence, 'die, will she?'

'I hope not,' Master Ogden said, 'but I really need to level with you. We have to prepare for the worst, and that's why, if you wish, I'm happy to give you two the next few days off school. I thought you might like to go and see Lucy in hospital. I know how close you both are with her, so you have my permission.'

Alaric felt sick. Before the weekend, he'd have given anything for the information Mr Trolley had told him.

Now, he'd trade that to get Lucy out of hospital any day. He'd even give up Rei's place in the basketball final.

'I'm going out into the Main World again this week,' Mr Trolley told Master Ogden. 'My boat leaves towards noon. I'll take Alaric and Laurence with me if they want to come.' He glanced at the pair of them, both of whom nodded, too depressed to speak. 'And I needed to talk to you about all these poisonings as well,' he added.

Alaric sat watching Master Ogden as Mr Trolley told him everything that he'd told Alaric. His reactions were just as Alaric would have expected. He raised his eyebrows when hearing about Beatrice Bork and Annabelle Macauley; he concentrated intensely as Mr Trolley talked of Iglehart's payments to Peter Barrett. Then, he sat up straight as the monologue came to a close.

'Very concerning, indeed,' he said in a monotonous, low pitch. 'Certainly, a lot has been going on in the past months. And I'm afraid, I think I know why.'

He paused as if for dramatic silence before continuing to speak.

'When, last year, Alaric came so close to death but survived, when Rei escaped momentarily, the barrier between the Lands of the Living and Dead was weakened. This weakening was not temporary,' Ogden explained, the three people opposite him listening attentively. 'In fact, what we call "The Raven's Veil" was torn. The very fabric of what separates life and death was damaged. That's why Alaric could hear his father's voice, why so many people had visions of their deceased loved ones. And like with any tear, it doesn't heal by itself.'

'What does that mean?' Alaric asked, now feeling somehow even worse.

'Well, were the Veil completely destroyed, there'd be freedom of movement between the two worlds. All the laws of who belongs in which world as we know them would be void,' Master Ogden said.

'So, if that happened, could Naidos return?' Alaric said weakly. Even saying it was a challenge, sending chills down his spine.

'That's not clear,' Master Ogden said. 'The reason you and Naidos cannot exist in the same world involves all sorts of reasons other than the laws of life and death. However, these rules state this Veil could not be destroyed by itself. The tear could become forever larger, but still, it would not be shattered. That can only be done by the Raven.'

'The Raven?' Alaric queried.

'A family line,' Master Ogden said simply.

'Which family?' Alaric said, almost demanded.

Master Ogden shrugged. 'Nothing's been heard of them for millennia, I'm afraid. The stories state there was always one member of the family who had the power to destroy the Veil. However, to this day, no one knows exactly which family, not a single person. Most people think the line's died out. I'm not so convinced. Even most of the Guardians don't know; Ceus, Solo and Marfin tell us a lot less than I think they ought to. Anyway, I've already said too much. You three best go and catch your boat.'

There was a finality in Master Ogden's tone with which not even Mr Trolley was willing to argue, and the three of them headed towards the office door. Then, as they reached it, an idea came to Alaric's mind.

'Can we not take some of the medicine with us to Lucy?' he asked hopefully.

'The nurse doesn't have it anymore,' Ogden replied with a shake of the head. 'Peter Barrett wasn't happy with the way it was being administered, so it'll have to be given in hospitals.'

'But it was working!' Alaric exclaimed.

Master Ogden sighed and shrugged. 'I don't make these decisions, but to be honest, based on what we've heard about Beatrice, it may be for the best if she's not trusted with this. It'll be difficult to prove, but I'll try to suspend her. Now, please, don't miss your boat.'

THE JOURNEY INTO the Main World was nowhere near as exciting as it had been at Christmas. Not feeling the energy to visit any of the places on the boat, they sat quietly in the café with coffee and croissants. There was a melancholy atmosphere for the rest of the morning. Alaric and Laurence were both too depressed, too concerned about Lucy to say anything. Alaric had never visited anyone in a hospital before and had visions of Lucy unconscious, with tubes up her nose and breathing support, the machinery beeping ominously in the background. However, when they arrived at the hospital, it was nothing like Alaric expected.

As soon as they reached the reception desk and told the plump, rosy-cheeked receptionist they were there to see Lucy, they were hurriedly whisked away to a changing room. One of the nurses threw a gown over each of them, which Alaric thought felt like a bin bag. They were then given masks, goggles and latex gloves, none of which felt comfortable to Alaric, his goggles fogging up, digging into his skin.

'I expect they still think it's a contagious disease out here,' Mr Trolley muttered to Alaric and Laurence as they marched up to Lucy's ward.

Contrary to Alaric's visions, Lucy, in her own room, didn't have any breathing support or tubes up her nose. However, she did have two tubes connected to her wrist from an IV stand. She was sitting up in her bed, her cryptozoology textbook splayed over her lap. She looked up as the three of them entered, bursting into laughter as she saw their outfits.

'It is *not* funny,' snapped the bony, sharp-faced nurse accompanying them. 'We don't want you to infect them as well.'

Lucy shut her mouth, though Alaric could tell she was still giggling silently behind her hand and could understand why. There really was no reason for them to be so heavily protected.

'Okay,' Mr Trolley said, 'I'll give you three some time, I think. I'm going to head down to the café. I need a word with Lucy's parents.'

'Why didn't you say you weren't coming in?' the nurse sighed. 'Waste of a gown, now come on out.'

Alaric, Lucy and Laurence shared a laugh as the nurse marched Mr Trolley out of the room and down the corridor. Then, Alaric and Laurence removed their goggles and masks once they were sure the nurse wasn't coming back.

'How are you both?' Lucy said, gesturing towards the pair of them to come and hug her.

'I'm fine,' Alaric said as he bent down to give Lucy an awkward, one-armed hug. 'It's you we're worried about.'

'Oh, I'm fine,' Lucy said dismissively. 'Honestly, this is just like a bad cold. I'm more bored than anything else.'

Alaric took a seat next to Lucy, now feeling much better. Even though they'd only been there a few moments, Alaric could tell she was her normal self.

'We've got a lot to tell you,' he said. 'Laurence's dad and I were discussing it over the weekend, and I found out a lot of stuff about the sickness, Beatrice…everything.'

Lucy shuffled on her bed, and Alaric recounted everything Mr Trolley had told him. Even though it was the second time he and Laurence had had this conversation that day, the story felt no less interesting for it. Lucy listened attentively, concentrating hard as Alaric spoke.

'Hmm, well, it does all make sense,' she said as Alaric stopped talking. 'I can't say I heard anything of

Annabelle Macauley, though. It can't have been a big story at the time.'

'I suppose there was probably someone keeping it low-key,' Alaric said. 'If it were a major story with her face planted everywhere in the Main World, it would've got into Harramore eventually.'

Lucy bowed her head in agreement, Alaric noticing a couple of small, green spots on her neck as her hair moved sideways. 'I've been thinking about this as well, actually,' she said. 'I don't think this poison is rumis. The thing is, I felt ill yesterday, had a bit of a cold and took a couple of tablets. However, I was reading about rumis, and it's not actually that potent. Even if these pills were made entirely out of the stuff, it wouldn't hospitalise people.'

'So, what is it then?' Laurence asked. 'All the symptoms match: the cold, the spots…everything.'

'But I already had a cold before I took the medicine,' Lucy pointed out. 'That didn't come from the poison. The first thing I checked was the ingredients list for the pills I took. It turned out to be a waste of time. Though, I was thinking how strange it was that Beatrice was caring for that woppanine by Ettoga's classroom. Then, I remembered something Ettoga had said. They're the only creature resistant to farafig.'

Alaric and Laurence both scratched their heads pensively. When Alaric thought hard, he did vaguely remember Ettoga saying this.

'Farafig? As in the poison?' he said.

Lucy nodded. 'I just looked it up, and the symptoms match exactly. Though, normally it'd cause a quick death unless in small quantities. I think there must be traces of this stuff in the medicine, strong enough to kill the gnomes but small enough that we can survive with treatment. It'd explain why Beatrice was always there; she needed woppanine extract to create the cure.'

'Why'd she want to cure this, though?' Laurence said. 'It's hardly in her best interests to keep these people alive.'

'Peter Barrett's profits,' Alaric said instantly, and Lucy nodded with enthusiasm. 'We know how much money he's made out of this, and maybe Beatrice gets a cut.'

Lucy shuffled again to make herself comfortable, a smile so wide surfacing on her face, one wouldn't think she were ill were she not in a hospital bed.

'Well then,' she said, 'once I'm out of hospital, it sounds like we have a task on our hands.'

There were a few moments of silence as Laurence stared at her blankly, thoughts flooding Alaric's mind as to how they'd even achieve what he knew Lucy was thinking.

'We need to invade the factory, find the farafig and prove Barrett's guilt to the world. He'll be locked up immediately,' she said.

'That would be exceedingly difficult.' Alaric, Lucy and Laurence all jumped as they heard the voice speaking from the doorway, sighing with relief to see Mr Trolley standing there. He chuckled before speaking again. 'It's been on my mind as well, though, and, you know, I think we can do it. And you three will come in particularly useful.'

CHAPTER 19

ALARIC AND LAURENCE had regained their appetites in time for lunch. Seeing Lucy in good spirits had alleviated their own worries. They headed to a restaurant with Lucy's parents, who also seemed upbeat as Alaric and Laurence tucked into large knickerbocker glories.

'We were on the phone to Master Ogden,' Mrs Ray said. 'Lucy will be in hospital for a few weeks but should stay stable. They have a cure for this on Harramore, and once distribution to the Main World is approved, Lucy could recover in a few days.'

Any worries Alaric had felt upon travelling to England had disappeared by now. He still couldn't understand why Lucy couldn't just be treated on Harramore. When he asked, Mr and Mrs Ray merely stated that the hospital she was in wouldn't discharge her. So, Alaric and Laurence went to the Main World on each of the next few weekends to see Lucy. She remained positive, even if increasingly bored, having not left the hospital.

As much as Alaric enjoyed spending time with her, time to work became ever more limited. Hector—having lost the weekends as a time to train—was now scheduling several evening practices in the week, the basketball final approaching as quickly as the end-of-year assessments. What was more was that Naidos had also won their semi-final, meaning that they'd have another chance to get the better of them. Alaric knew how sweet a victory would be, but at the same time, how brutal another defeat could be to stomach.

The weekend before the assessments, Mr and Mrs Trolley agreed with Alaric and Laurence that it would be best not to visit Lucy, so they could focus on revising. However, in practice, this didn't happen. Instead, Mr Trolley spent most of Saturday speaking to Alaric and Laurence privately about their plans to catch Mr Barrett, seeming just as excited as they were.

'Now, I've been thinking,' he said as the three of them sat down in the garden with a pot of tea, 'how are we going to get Peter Barrett gaoled?'

Alaric and Laurence sat in silence for a few moments, waiting for Mr Trolley to continue speaking. Then, Alaric realised this hadn't been meant as a rhetorical question and tried to produce an answer on the spot.

'Well, I guess we just need something he could've written to Beatrice,' he said, realising how vague this sounded.

'Precisely,' Mr Trolley said as he spooned some cream onto a scone. 'So, we need to get into his factory; we need to trespass.' He grinned a wide, mischievous grin that was almost scary as it displayed all his teeth. 'And guess what. The security is impeccable; no way someone could just stroll in through the front door.'

'What do we do then?' Laurence said, his face sinking.

'Well, we got to the Land of the Dead past all that security. This can't be any tougher than that,' Alaric said.

'I admire your confidence, Alaric,' Mr Trolley said. 'We mustn't get complacent, though. We do need a plan as to how we're going to achieve it. Essentially, we have three options: number one, we charge in through the front door, hunt down the evidence and flee before the police come.'

Alaric scoffed at the idea. 'No way are we doing that. Four of us versus however many of them...we wouldn't stand a chance.'

'Yes, I agree that's far too high-risk,' Mr Trolley said with a nod. 'Another option is we do the opposite and try to sneak in undetected, bypass all the security. The trouble is this factory is littered with cameras on every corridor.'

'Couldn't Alaric just make a tunnel into the factory?' Laurence asked.

Mr Trolley gave Laurence a slow, frustrated blink. 'No. Very few places are that insecure. All private property has some level of anti-Seela enchantments around the border. I'm astounded you don't know that, to be honest.'

Laurence blushed furiously, Alaric thinking it best not to say he didn't know that either, and Mr Trolley carried on talking.

'So, that leaves us with a third option, which is to take the middle path,' he said.

'So, we'll need disguises,' Alaric said instantly. Mr Trolley looked taken aback but impressed as Laurence seemed perplexed.

'Indeed, we need to hide in plain sight,' Mr Trolley said. 'This is where I think Laurence and Lucy could be quite useful, you probably less so, Alaric.'

Alaric squinted at Mr Trolley, unsure whether or not to be offended.

'Relax, Alaric, it's not personal,' Mr Trolley chortled as he took a mouthful of scone and chewed it. 'It's just I need them disguised as workers, and most of Barrett's so-called staff are children…slaves. You'd be far too tall to pass as one of them. I know you're not even fifteen yet, but I'd think you could easily be seventeen if I didn't know you.'

Alaric shuffled uncomfortably in his seat. 'Is Barrett allowed to use children?'

Mr Trolley sighed and grimaced. 'Let's just say it's accepted. He's good friends with Iglehart, who turns a blind eye. Then, so many people use his company's products that they choose to ignore the matter. You see, those most unaffected by injustice, those who can make the most difference, are often the people who remain silent. But anyway, I have a different task for you.'

Alaric gulped. As much as part of him was relishing this adventure, he really didn't fancy being separated from Lucy and Laurence. They always stuck together if they could. That was how it had always been.

'You'll be coming with me,' Mr Trolley continued. 'I've been thinking of potential disguises, and the best one would be pest exterminators. That way, we can be split into two teams as well, cover the factory more quickly.'

Alaric stared at Mr Trolley blankly, seeing so many flaws in this plan. Neither of them had any experience in dealing with pests to start with. Nor did they have disguises, and above all, would there even be an infestation when they arrived?

'Now, I know what you're thinking,' Mr Trolley said. 'The plan seems crazy, I know, but I can get good disguises fairly easily. Then, on the day, we just need to make sure that Mr Barrett's expecting pest control.'

'So, we have to cause an infestation. How do we even do that?' Alaric asked, scratching his head thoughtfully.

'I have some connections,' Mr Trolley said. 'Pike Channing, a good friend of mine at Harramore's environment agency, has agreed to help out. He can pass by one night, drop a flying spider nest in the drain by the office. They breed like mad; the whole factory will be overrun with the things within a week. Then, the agency gets the call, he lends us his van and sends us into the factory to deal with the problem.'

'What are flying spiders?' Alaric asked.

'Ah, nasty things. Imagine a spider crossed with a mosquito. They hide in drains and bite like mad. Any responsible boss would evacuate the factory after an infestation of the things, but Barrett wouldn't. He had a fire at one of his sword workshops once and did nothing,' Mr Trolley said bitterly. 'There's no doubt this plan will work. Don't worry.'

'That's brilliant,' Alaric beamed, hiding his squeamishness. 'Is this already in place? When are we going to do it?'

'One step ahead of you,' Mr Trolley said with a proud grin. 'Pike will be down there to drop the nest in the next few days. Then, after your exams, we'll get the call. The word is that the cure should be approved in the Main World at some point this week, so Lucy should be back by then.'

Alaric and Laurence both said nothing as they sat grinning. This all seemed so perfect, and while Alaric tried not to think of it, it felt like there was so much potential for something to go wrong. As the week progressed, he hadn't felt so nervous since they'd agreed to head to the Land of the Dead, the prospect of this challenge distracting him throughout his assessments. He even felt that his history exam had gone far from swimmingly. His medicine exam turned out to be the most disastrous of all, Madame Sang grinning with pleasure as he struggled to answer her questions. For the first time in his life, he thought he may have actually failed a test. By the time the weekend arrived, and the assessments were over, Alaric felt yet more restless, the prospects of both Sunday's basketball final and invading

Peter Barrett's factory looming large.

The fact that Lucy was still not out of hospital made him feel even worse, the cup final preventing him from seeing her for the second weekend running. Even though Lucy's presence alone at the match didn't make much of a difference to the crowd volume, there was always something comforting about knowing she was there. It didn't help his nerves either that the match would be played in Harramore's national arena. The stadium was so large that Alaric didn't think those at the back would see the pitch. Nevertheless—and Alaric grinned at the thought—it'd be a great audience to thrash Naidos in front of. He knew cup finals had a history of being tight games and imagined how good it would feel to beat Naidos by a record margin.

When, early on Sunday morning, Alaric and the team set off for the stadium, the same familiar nervousness had filled Alaric that always did before matches like this. The sight of the ground gave him a peculiar numbness, as though he felt every emotion and no emotion at once. Already, when they arrived, warm rays of sunshine shone down onto the pitch, which had become the driest Alaric had ever seen.

He was starting to dread the prospect of the midday kick-off, his shirt already drenched with sweat, the team's faces scarlet as they warmed up before the match. Alaric watched on as the stadium filled up, and even with the sizeable security gap of empty seats between the Rei and Naidos supporters, the ground felt packed, energizingly daunting.

As the start of the match approached, a coldness then overcame Alaric. Both sets of fans were doing their own vocal warm-ups, which echoed around the stadium more than ever and before long, it had seemingly become a competition. The two sides battled to be heard over each other as the teams headed back down the tunnel for their final team talk before the game. The Rei team all sat in the same way on the bench: so close to the edges they looked about to fall off as Hector began to speak.

'Okay, we look good,' he said, a slight tremor in his voice. The fans' singing almost felt louder in the changing rooms, the walls seeming to vibrate. 'It turns out Naidos have shuffled their line-up since we last played them. Franco Sprott has moved into defence, and Dwayne McGlompher is the keeper.'

'Probably wanted a go at me,' Alaric grumbled, a part of him relishing the challenge even more now.

'Perhaps,' Hector said. 'Though that doesn't seem like a bad thing. After all, they're the two least experienced players on the team, and if they're not used to playing in those positions, that can only help us. So, I think there's something more to it. Their replacement forward is huge, and I don't think I'll be able to tackle him easily. Anyway, they may be focussing on us, but I know we're good enough that we don't need to adjust our tactics. And remember, most of Harramore is supporting us today. Good luck, guys.'

Alaric took a few deep breaths to compose himself as the team wandered back out into the tunnel, his chest feeling heavy. They stood beside the Naidos team, not even looking at each other, no customary handshaking. Even the feeling of their presence was firing Alaric up, and he was raring to go. Then, the referee gestured them out of the tunnel. And the whole stadium shook with the cries of one-hundred thousand supporters, so deafening that Alaric would be amazed if the players could hear each other.

They jogged out, Alaric's heart gaining pace already. Franco squared up to him as if to intimidate him. Still, he didn't succeed, as the top of his head barely scraped Alaric's chin. Then, the referee blew his whistle, and they were off.

Naidos started with possession, the ball with Dwayne. Alaric watched as he dribbled towards him, kept his eye on Franco, following him around the pitch, anticipating Dwayne's pass. Then, it came. It was the worst throw Alaric could ever have imagined, so wayward that it landed not in Franco's hands but Alaric's. This was the moment to seize the lead as the Rei crowd behind him roared expectantly. He sprinted away from Franco, right in front of the basket, no one around him. He had to score.

He bent his knees to shoot, almost wheeled away in celebration as soon as the ball left his hands. Then, he stamped the ground as he saw he'd put it wide, stunned silence in all corners of the stadium. He sunk to the floor, his head in his hands, struggling to fathom how he hadn't hit the target.

'Thanks, Alaric, nice shot,' Franco said derisively. Alaric forced himself not to rise to it, now realising the logic in having Franco and Dwayne mark him. Naidos wanted to provoke a reaction from him like the last time they'd played each other.

Alaric took a deep breath and stood back up. He wouldn't let them get to his head. They were still in the first minute of the game, and he'd have plenty more opportunities to score. This was just the start.

As the first quarter went on, the pressure of the occasion seemed to be getting to both teams. Just two minutes later, the Naidos forward found himself in just as much space as Alaric had been, only to sky his shot straight into a laughing Rei crowd. In fact, the two teams were both so error-prone that they kept throwing the ball to each other, neither side able to string two passes together. The standard of play was so poor, it wasn't until halfway through the quarter that Alaric got the ball again, only for Dwayne to close down his shot.

In a way, Naidos playing so poorly made it more annoying that Rei were also subpar. Ten minutes in, the score was still nil-nil. Even when Alaric tried to use his Seela, Dwayne was always on his back, blocking each attempt. He was now resorting to watching the clock tick down to the end of the quarter, hoping Hector's briefing would rejuvenate them on some level. But the clock seemed to drag on.

Five minutes to go, four minutes forty-five, four and a half minutes. Alaric took his focus off the clock, becoming more invested in the game, jogging closer to the halfway line with the rest of the action. If Grace could just get the ball out to him…

Now she had it, looked up, saw Alaric, and tossed him the ball. At last, he had a chance.

He took two steps forward, one to the side and shot. Then, there was a sarcastic cheer from the Naidos crowd as Alaric looked up. He hadn't even looked to see where the basket was and had aimed so low, the ball had gone straight to Dwayne.

Alaric clenched his fist as he saw him giggle, throwing the ball to Franco, who then hurled it to the Naidos forward. He watched on, holding his breath as the forward charged towards the basket. And Jacob tripped him up, leading to a thunderous cheer from the Naidos supporters. First point of the game on the board.

'Jacob, there was no need to do that!' Hector roared so he could be faintly heard over the crowd. 'Don't give away unnecessary points.'

Jacob waved his hand apologetically as play resumed, the next couple of minutes passing as the rest of the game had. Jacob passed to Grace, who then gave the ball away to Naidos, who then threw it back to Jacob, who returned it to Dwayne.

And at last, Alaric had the opportunity. Dwayne was off guard, and Alaric leapt up in the air as the ground swallowed him up, the ball loose on the field: Rei: 5—Naidos: 1. End of first quarter.

'Okay, team, we may have the lead, but that was poor,' Hector said as they all took a drink. 'We need to get a passing rhythm going, get the ball to Alaric for some shots. If we were against any other team on any other day, then we'd be losing heavily by now.'

The game opened up in the second quarter. Within the first few minutes, Alaric and the Naidos forward got their first shots of the period off, both putting the ball a few inches wide. Then, Naidos thoroughly outplayed Rei for the rest of the quarter. They dominated possession and created far more chances than Alaric got, and it was a good job their forward was so poor.

He was in with a clear sight of the basket three times, only to put his shots way off the mark. Then, moments later, he'd escaped Hector to receive the ball in open space, this time dropping the pass onto his foot, and the ball rolled away to safety. It was of little surprise when Rei's luck finally ran out halfway through the period. Titus McGlompher in midfield used his Seela to dispossess Laurence as he lost his sight, throwing the ball straight back to Naidos. Alaric breathed a sigh of relief when the midfielder's pass went straight out of play, keeping Naidos' newfound lead down to one point.

Now, Rei were revitalised. Alaric had the ball again within a minute, only for Dwayne to wrestle him to the ground to level the scores again. Alaric stood up, his whole side feeling bruised as Dwayne grinned down at him, apparently proud of having conceded a point.

Twice more before the end of the quarter, Alaric had another opportunity, each time managing to shoot. But on both occasions, he stamped the ground in frustration as the ball bounced off the ring of the basket and back into play. It just wasn't a forward's day. Still, as the halfway point in the game approached, the score remained Rei: 6—Naidos: 6. And now the game was slowing down again. It was as if both teams were happy to go into halftime with the scores tied. Last minute now. Alaric's head was feeling hot.

'Just give me the ball,' he said to Grace through gritted teeth. She glanced towards Alaric, then to Jacob and back again. At last, she decided to throw it to Alaric, narrowly avoiding Titus' tackle as he clattered into her.

Alaric suppressed a smile as Rei had regained the lead, jogging up the field with just seconds left on the clock. Franco was closing him down now, no easy way past as he dribbled towards the sideline, fifty thousand Rei fans screaming at him to shoot. He looked up at the scoreboard, seeing he only had ten seconds. Then, he glanced up at the basket. It was too distant, the angle too tight. Shrugging, he launched the ball into the air and hoped.

Then came the loudest cheer Alaric had ever heard.

It must have been the best basket he'd scored in his life. He'd been so far out, and still, he'd managed it, unable not to grin as the ref blew for halftime.

'That was amazing, Alaric,' Laurence said, beaming as the team gathered for a halftime briefing. All five team members grinned as the Naidos players sat subdued in stunned silence. Although Alaric knew barely one basket separated them, the scoreboard still gave him a confidence boost: Rei: 22—Naidos: 6.

'We mustn't get complacent, guys,' Hector said very seriously. 'It'll only take them to score once, and then it's game back on. Stay focussed, and Alaric, as many baskets as you can score will massively help. The job is only half-done.'

The message didn't seem to have got to them all as the third quarter started. While Grace seemed assured in midfield, Alaric had never seen Jacob and Laurence so rickety in defence. Three times within the first five minutes, the Naidos forward had a clear sight of the basket, thankfully missing on each occasion.

The next time, they were not so fortunate, however. As the forward charged through Rei's defence chasing the ball, Hector—too slow to keep up—was forced to trip him with a trailing leg, giving Naidos another point.

And the siege only continued. The Naidos fans, sensing the comeback, were now belting out songs like they'd won; the Rei supporters, meanwhile, remained nervously silent. The Rei defence became only more fragile, and as the Naidos forward continued to miss chances, it seemed like only a matter of time before they'd score. And before long, they had a basket.

'Timeout!' Hector shouted with a sigh.

The referee nodded, and the two teams gathered in their halves of the pitch. Alaric looked at each expression, the gleeful grins that had been there at halftime now gone.

'Okay, guys, we need to slow down the tempo for the last few minutes of this quarter, regroup. Please, we do not want to throw this game away now. Stay focussed,' Hector said pleadingly.

The message hadn't got through. Straight from the restart, Laurence was once again dispossessed as Titus made him temporarily blind, and Naidos had the lead. Now, they were in the final few seconds of the quarter, Rei set to go into the final stretch of the game behind. Then, the Naidos forward shot from range. An expectant roar came from the crowd. The ball's trajectory was clear; it was heading straight for the basket.

But Hector had an idea. He'd taken a leaf out of

Forto's book; he scurried to the basket pole and gave it a nudge to tilt it. And the ball ricocheted off its ring and back onto the ground. The referee blew to award five more points to Rei, and it was the end of the third quarter. Rei: 27—Naidos: 27. Alaric's heart was now beating as fast as it had all match, even though he'd had almost nothing to do. Everything, the whole tournament came down to these last fifteen minutes.

'Sorry to tilt the basket, Alaric,' Hector said. 'I only nudged it, so you should still be able to get the ball in.'

Alaric glanced at the basket and nodded, seeing it was only slightly askew.

'I had no choice,' Hector went on. 'We couldn't go into this final fifteen twenty points behind, but we're level. It all comes down to this, and we cannot approach it with a fear of losing. We need the courage to take risks, get the ball to Alaric. Only then will we have a chance of winning. Concentrate. Everything could come down to one key moment, one critical mistake. This is it: the biggest fifteen minutes of our last two seasons. Good luck, everyone.'

Alaric jogged into position as the referee blew his whistle, his legs feeling boneless. The Rei and Naidos crowds roared as one, the next few minutes some of the most open, most equal Alaric had ever played.

Within seconds, the Naidos forward was through once again, only to be fouled by Hector. And once again, the lead was short-lived as Alaric had a chance straight from the restart, only to fall to the ground as Franco pulled his shirt back.

Now, Rei and Naidos were trading like for like, the match resembling a game of Ordinary basketball as Naidos shot, then Rei shot, neither side quite scoring. And the crowd had become so raucous, the players couldn't hear each other at all.

Three minutes gone. The Naidos forward was advancing towards Hector. Tackled. Alaric readied himself as Hector launched the ball up towards him. Now, he had it again. Another chance. He was already in so much space. He'd shoot from range; he bent his knees, poised to score. But he stumbled to the ground as Franco and Titus both came diving into him at once, giving him the most painful fall of the match so far.

He punched the ground exasperatedly. Today really did not seem like the day for baskets. Alaric didn't even bother to celebrate Rei's regained lead. He knew that one point wouldn't suffice, and sure enough, Naidos levelled the scores almost instantly.

Then, as Hector gained the ball and resumed play, Alaric bounced on the balls of his feet. They were barely four minutes into the quarter, and already, both teams had added two points each. He knew the next chance was on the way as Hector threw the ball to Jacob, to Laurence, to Grace.

Now was the moment, Grace making a run down the wing, past the Naidos midfield. It was two against two now. Dwayne and Franco looked at each other, an expression of panic on each of their faces as they both scurried towards Grace. And now Alaric was completely unmarked.

Without a second thought, he moved towards the basket, point-blank range. Then, Grace lobbed the ball over the top of Dwayne and Franco straight to Alaric. Just like the chance right at the start of the game, he couldn't miss. And this time, he made sure he didn't, the roar from the Rei crowd enough to tell him he'd scored.

'FRANCO! DWAYNE! YOU IDIOTS!' came a thundering shout from the halfway line. Titus was storming towards the pair of them as Grace froze mid-hug with Alaric, too shocked to move. 'You both went to her, didn't even look at Alaric. You NEVER EVER leave a forward unmarked!'

Grace pulled away from Alaric, raising an eyebrow at him as Titus stomped back to the centre of the pitch.

Franco's face was even more colourless than usual as Dwayne flushed with embarrassment. Alaric almost burst into laughter at the very sight. Much of the Naidos crowd seemed to be feeling the same way as Titus. They shook their heads with thin lips and folded arms, a select few still applauding and cheering them on encouragingly.

Alaric forced the smile off his face as play restarted, knowing it would only take one basket for Naidos to get back level. But that moment didn't seem to be coming as Titus chucked his first pass from the restart out of play.

In fact, Titus seemed so furious that he'd lost all concentration. Grace managed to use her Seela without him even noticing, the ball transforming into a large ginger cat and bounding straight to Alaric. Then came the familiar sight of the fur turning back to leather, and Alaric scooped the ball up and shot. He looked up to the sky in frustration as the ball went marginally wide. Still, that was five more points for Rei.

They were twenty points up now, more than a single basket. The Rei fans were now in full voice, any half-hearted Naidos chants easily drowned out. Alaric forced himself to keep his expression neutral, refusing to celebrate prematurely.

Now, Hector seemed content to slow the game down as the minutes ticked away. Ten, nine, eight minutes remained in the match. Still, Rei: 49—Naidos: 29. Jacob had the ball now, straight to Grace, to Alaric. But he was camped on the halfway line, the basket too distant to shoot.

Then, he didn't know how it happened, but it did. He was in the air, gliding towards the basket, a feeling in his stomach like he was descending a steep drop on a roller coaster. He didn't dare look down as he reached the basket and stopped, hovering in mid-air. And he placed the ball into the net, the roar from the Rei crowd somehow even louder than the last one as he gently drifted downward. He could not process what had just happened.

Then, he looked up at the scoreboard and understood. Rei: 69—Naidos: 29. He'd been awarded twenty points. He'd used Ceus' Seela. And now, all five of the Naidos players were swarming the referee, his face expressionless as he waved off each complaint.

'That's not his registered Seela!' Titus protested.

'No rules say you don't get points for it,' the ref said uninterestedly.

The boos of the Naidos fans started to ring around the ground, some making rude hand gestures at the ref.

Titus picked up the ball and kicked it at the Rei crowd in frustration.

'Titus, calm the heck down, man,' said the other Naidos midfielder. 'We probably need three baskets now, and that's not going to help.'

Titus glowered at the midfielder and swore loudly, Alaric now feeling far more relaxed. Seven and a half minutes remained for Naidos to get forty points. And never had he seen a team so disunited. Each time one of them made a mistake, Titus would rage at them, and he was now so hot in the head, he was the most error-prone of the lot. There was almost no need to worry for Rei now when Naidos had the ball. They were too frustrated to do anything useful with it, the clock ticking down. Five minutes, four and a half.

And now Rei had possession again. Jacob passed to Grace, Alaric turning, ready to make a run as the ball bounced in front of him. But the pass was too heavy, and Alaric no chance of beating Dwayne or Franco to it, and they were comfortably there first. Dwayne scooped the ball up, Alaric watching as he passed it forward.

But it was the worst pass Alaric had ever seen as it bounced off Franco back towards the basket. Alaric chased it, and he couldn't miss as he scooped the ball up and lobbed it into the net. Then came the loudest cheer yet from the Rei crowd as the Naidos fans sat in disbelief, some storming out of the stadium in protest. Rei: 84—Naidos: 29.

It was turning into a rout, and Alaric was starting to wonder if they could record Rei's widest ever margin of victory.

'What on earth was that?' Titus screamed. He stomped again towards Franco and Dwayne, who both lay on the floor, hands over their faces. 'This is your fault.'

The next time Alaric received the ball, Franco bundled him over immediately. Titus was also now fouling Grace every time she had it, giving away three points in the next minute. It was as if Naidos had given up, Alaric soon finding himself unmarked again. And as he caught the ball and started towards the basket, there wasn't even an attempt from either Franco or Dwayne to stop him. He put the ball into the net with ease.

Two minutes remained now, Alaric ready to celebrate as he saw the score: Rei: 103—Naidos: 29. They were seventy-four points ahead, and since Rei's biggest ever win was by seventy-six points, they needed just three more to break the record. That was less than a basket; a Seela would do it, three fouls even. He glanced at the Rei following in the crowd, who seemed to have already started a party.

Then, he looked at the other section of the crowd and guffawed. Almost all the Naidos seats were now empty, the exit doors a bottleneck as the fans swarmed towards them.

Alaric was raring to go. He fancied Rei's chances of breaking the record, and with just a minute and a half remaining, they'd scored again.

As Titus picked the ball up in midfield, Grace managed to turn it into a cat, which gave a high-pitched shriek. It then scratched Titus' hands and drew blood, escaping his grasp and bounding towards Alaric.

Now, Alaric laughed hard as Titus clutched his hand in agony, Rei's record on track to be broken. They just needed to avoid conceding before the end of the match. Alaric, realising this, scooped up the ball and passed it back to Grace, an almost sardonic groan from the crowd greeting this decision.

'Come on, they want another basket,' Grace said with a grin. She tossed it back to Alaric, who smiled wryly as he dodged two half-hearted tackles. Then, he glanced up at the basket. Just one more score to round off the game. Missed.

The crowd gave another ironic sigh as Alaric jogged to collect the ball, not a care in the world if he missed this next attempt by miles.

'Again!' the Rei crowd cried as one when Alaric reached the ball.

And somehow, he missed once more as the ball went out of play. But he didn't care, merely laughing it off as the clock continued to tick down to zero. In a way, as the final minute came, he just wanted the referee to blow his final whistle. He'd had enough fun now, humiliated Naidos enough. More points would almost seem too cruel, too harsh on them. But only almost.

Thirty seconds remained now as again, Alaric received a pass from Grace. He didn't even need to dodge any tackles as he approached the basket one last time. And he scored. The match was decided now.

Rei: 123—Naidos: 29. The House of Rei were the basketball champions.

Alaric couldn't remember ever feeling better as the team gathered for a celebratory hug. They'd won the cup *and* humiliated the House of Naidos. He turned and watched in amusement as Franco and Dwayne sat sobbing on the ground, Titus screaming at them and storming off the pitch.

Grace and Hector followed suit in turning their attention to Franco and Dwayne. Then, they left the team's celebrations and hurried over to them. Alaric,

Laurence and Jacob watched on, all equally perplexed as Hector and Grace helped Franco and Dwayne to their feet, each with their arm around one of them.

'What are they doing?' Laurence grumbled.

Alaric shook his head dismissively and strolled over to the scene. Hector and Grace were muttering about how many shots the Naidos forward had missed, assuring them the loss wasn't their fault. However, before Alaric could get any closer, Franco and Dwayne glowered at him, broke free from Hector and Grace, and traipsed down the tunnel.

'Look out for them next week at school,' Hector said seriously.

'What? They're a pair of goblins!' Laurence exclaimed.

'You don't know what goes on at home with them,' Grace said defensively. 'You saw how Titus treated them. If this had happened to us, we'd have stuck together as a team.'

'Too right, we would,' Hector said earnestly. 'Please, just be the bigger people. I know it's hard.'

Alaric rolled his eyes as Hal Iglehart sauntered onto the pitch. He was carrying a magnificent golden trophy almost as large as his torso, making even his cufflinks look cheap.

'Congratulations,' he said with a smile, which irked Alaric intensely. He still wanted to punch the Governor whenever he saw him but thought better of it. 'Here's the cup. Normally, we have an awards ceremony at the end, present runner-up medals and all, but let's just say that the Naidos players have left. It seems more fitting you go and parade this around the field.'

Hector forced a smile as he accepted the trophy from Iglehart, the crowd letting out another earth-shaking roar of approval. This was every child's dream as they completed their lap of honour, the Rei fans applauding tumultuously. Then, after what could have been any amount of time, they headed to the car park. Mr and Mrs Trolley were waiting by their vehicle, which was now one of the few remaining.

'Congratulations,' Mr Trolley said with a smile under his goatee.

'Yes, you played very well,' Mrs Trolley agreed. 'We're both proud, as is much of the island.'

Alaric grinned once more as they climbed into the car, the trophy sitting awkwardly on Hector's lap.

'Now, I'm sorry to put a dampener on the day,' Mr Trolley said as his wife started the car. 'But I have some bad news. Iglehart and Barrett have banned exports of medicines into the Main World. Lucy's on her last batch now.'

It was as if a vacuum had sucked all the happiness out of Alaric. 'What does that mean?' he asked weakly.

'Well, we shouldn't give up hope,' Mr Trolley said, 'but unless things change, it may only be a matter of days before she passes away.'

CHAPTER 20

ALARIC WOULD'VE GIVEN anything at that moment, even reversed the score-line for it all to be false. It couldn't be happening.

'We thought Alaric and Laurence could go and see Lucy tomorrow,' Mrs Trolley said.

'Can we not go as well?' Grace asked. 'We knew her too. We shared the accommodation with her.'

'I understand,' Mrs Trolley said. 'However, the state she's in, the hospital will only let in close friends and family. Only Alaric and Laurence can visit, as difficult as it is.'

Alaric gulped, refusing to believe this was true. It was all a horrible dream, and he'd wake up any second. But as he stared aimlessly out the window, seeing all the road signs pass, he realised he could read. This was real.

Maybe, he thought to himself, this was all a trick, some sort of cruel joke. Then, he realised the Trolleys would never do such a thing. But there had to be some sort of mistake; it just couldn't be true. Lucy was the same age as him, a year younger in fact, and people his age didn't die.

They drove in silence, no one able to speak from the shock of the news. Alaric looked away from the others. He couldn't bring himself to see their faces. He didn't want to be seen either as he pressed his face against the window, watching the countryside fly by. Whereas just moments ago, the sky had been clear, it was now a gloomy grey as it spat down raindrops, which, just like the tears running down Alaric's cheeks, had come so suddenly. He couldn't look at anyone else now. He didn't want them to see him like this.

Maybe he wasn't supposed to have any real family. It had always been this way. At the thought, he started to feel genuinely sick. He hadn't eaten in hours but was now holding back vomit as he thought of Mr and Mrs Ray. Lucy's mother, his mother, all she'd been through and now this. The one child she'd been allowed to raise was about to die.

And now Alaric actually did throw up. Those words—Lucy about to die—even saying them in his head made it feel truer. He glanced at Grace apologetically, the jeans she'd just changed into now covered in his sick, but he had too little strength to say sorry. Grace looked back into his red, puffy eyes and pulled him into a tight hug, completely ignoring the fact her trousers were now ruined.

'Is everything all right?' Mr Trolley asked.

Alaric was silent, still lacking the strength to respond.

'Alaric's been sick,' Grace said. 'I wouldn't mind stopping if we can.'

'Right, don't worry about it,' Mrs Trolley said sympathetically, and they pulled over into a lay-by.

They all climbed out of the car, Mrs Trolley handing Grace some wipes to clean her trousers. Jacob and Hector stood together, watching the empty road forlornly as Mr Trolley approached Alaric and Laurence.

'Alaric, Laurence,' Mr Trolley said. 'Let's take a walk.'

Alaric didn't protest as the three of them strolled down the country road, leaving behind the others. As heavy as Alaric's legs felt after the match, a walk to clear his head still sounded appealing, even if a part of him would rather take it alone. However, as soon as he chanced a look at Laurence, he felt better, less embarrassed, seeing he was just as puffy-eyed as himself.

'Neither of you has to go back to school at all this week if you don't want to,' Mr Trolley said.

Neither Alaric nor Laurence responded, both preferring to continue on in silence.

'I have something else to say,' Mr Trolley went on. 'I can't make any promises about this, but we may still be able to save Lucy.'

At those words, both Alaric and Laurence stopped dead in their tracks, turning and staring at Mr Trolley expectantly.

'Now, we mustn't tell your mum, Laurence, because there's no way she'll approve of this. Do I have your word?' Mr Trolley asked very seriously.

Alaric and Laurence nodded. If there was any way they could save Lucy, even the slightest possibility, Alaric knew they had to do it.

'I have the disguises to get into the factory, and the good news is, the flying spiders are spreading like wildfire. Pike Channing said that Barrett wants someone there first thing tomorrow. It's short notice, I know, but if we go in the morning and execute the plan, we could steal some of the medicine. We're then all booked onto a boat tomorrow evening to England. Lucy has enough of the old medicine to last until then,' Mr Trolley said.

'Let's do it,' Alaric said without hesitation, but as he thought about it, it all seemed more and more difficult.

First, they needed to avoid getting caught, and Alaric had hardly any experience in acting. Then, without Lucy, Laurence would be on his own posing as a labourer, which seemed like a disaster waiting to happen. It would only take one slip-up, and the plan would come unstuck. But it was all they had.

'Perfect,' Mr Trolley said. 'Now, Laurence's mum will leave for work first thing tomorrow morning. I've told her we're leaving to get on a boat after that.'

Alaric and Laurence nodded, the tears having cleared from both their faces. All the sadness Alaric had felt was now replaced with a nervousness like no other. As he reflected on this over the rest of the day, nothing about his feelings made sense. Even journeying to the Land of the Dead hadn't felt this tense.

Back then, the whole world and their lives had been at stake. This time, the worst that could happen would be getting caught stealing and possibly a prison sentence. And this time, only one person's life was on the line. But that person was Lucy.

The very thought made him shudder as he climbed into bed that night. If anything went wrong, if they failed, he'd lose one of the only two close friends he'd ever had. And it seemed to him that every time they'd intervened, something had gone wrong. It had happened with the Pearl, the Land of the Dead, even this year. Now, there was no margin for error, the stakes the highest they'd ever been. They had to succeed, and they would succeed.

Alaric closed his eyes and repeated those words to himself in his head: *we will succeed, we will succeed.* The more he said it to himself, the calmer he felt, his mindset changing as he blocked out logic. Then, at long last, he fell asleep.

EVEN WITH HIS newfound calmness, the night was one of the familiar, restless ones Alaric had started to grow used to. A couple of hours after falling asleep, he woke up, thinking and hoping he'd slept the night away, only to see it was still pitch-black outside. He then closed his eyes again, waking up each hour, expecting to see sunlight, only to go back to sleep several times. When dawn finally came, he had an acute headache, even if he felt as awake as ever.

He and Laurence went through their morning ritual in silence, breakfasting with the rest of the family. Any attempts at starting a conversation fizzled out after a few sentences. The news about Lucy still hadn't fully sunk in, and the meal felt even longer for it. Alaric,

Laurence, and Mr Trolley were forced to sit on their secret until the others finally headed off to Oakwood. Then, Mr Trolley perked up.

'Finally,' he said with a relieved sigh. 'We can go through today's plan in peace. Either of you want any more coffee?'

Laurence shook his head, Alaric giving a slight, indifferent nod. Mr Trolley rose from his chair, heading over to the work surface and grinding some beans.

'Can't function without coffee,' he said brightly, then humming a strange tune that was so off-key, it could barely be called a tune at all. Alaric couldn't decide whether his positivity was uplifting or annoying as he returned to the kitchen table, a mug of black coffee in each hand. 'Probably not a bad thing if you can't function, mind you, Laurence. I don't think Mr Barrett's workers are exactly the sharpest.'

Laurence looked at his father, bemused. 'I never drink coffee anyway,' he said.

'Well, you should. Maybe then you'd be more awake in class,' Mr Trolley replied. Laurence rolled his eyes in response. 'Anyway, Pike should be here in about half an hour with the pest control van. We will then drop him off back at work and drive to Peter Barrett's factory. Alaric, you and I are expected there, so we can just drive straight up. With Laurence, we need to be cleverer.'

'What do you mean?' Laurence asked doubtfully.

'I mean,' Mr Trolley replied, 'that if we just turn up with one of the workers in the van, that'll raise a few eyebrows. So, we'll drop you off a few hundred yards down the road in a secluded spot. All the kids who work there will then turn up at the same time; you won't miss the crowd. Follow them in.'

Laurence's face went white at these words, Alaric starting to feel nervous again. The thought of them being separated made him uneasy, and it would be reassuring to know where Laurence was at all times.

'Once inside, Alaric and I have it easiest,' Mr Trolley went on. Laurence gulped nervously. 'We simply listen to what they say about the infestation, then pretend to be looking for it, act as if we know what we're doing. Laurence, you need to make out that you're going to the loo or something and sneak off. If anyone catches you out of bounds, questions will be asked, so stay hidden. We'll keep in touch with these.' He pulled two cheap-looking flip phones from his pocket. 'Text us updates, Laurence.'

'I…I don't know how to use Ordinary phones like those,' Laurence said hesitantly.

'Ah, right, well, that's a bit of a problem,' Mr Trolley said.

'Are you sure it wouldn't be best if Laurence and I switched roles?' Alaric suggested. 'I know these phones well; I can even use my own.'

Mr Trolley slurped his coffee pensively. He tilted his head as though concentrating, visibly weighing up the risks. 'I suppose so,' he said. 'If you blend in among the crowd, it shouldn't be too much of an issue. I'm just concerned you're a lot taller than most of these children who work for him.'

'But that's better than losing contact with Laurence,' Alaric countered, his stomach aching, almost shouting in protest at what he'd said. Going at this alone wasn't even slightly desirable, but he knew it was better him than Laurence.

'No, I agree,' Mr Trolley sighed, 'just stay inconspicuous. Once you're on your own, it'll be harder, but do your best.'

Alaric nodded, now feeling much worse, the only consolation being that some colour had returned to Laurence's face. The next half hour dragged on as they changed into their disguises and waited downstairs for Pike Channing to arrive. Alaric started to pace the rooms of the house, his legs feeling weaker with each individual step. He had no idea as to whether or not he'd get into the factory, or worse if he'd get out before the end of the day. He was so deep in thought that when Pike Channing finally arrived, he almost collapsed, the knock on the front door startled him so much.

'Everything's in place, Edward,' Pike said in his deep, soothing voice when Mr Trolley opened the door. 'Ah, these must be the boys. Alaric and Laurence, is it?'

He stepped through the door, having to stoop to do so. He approached Alaric first, who was made slightly uneasy by Pike's size. He was several inches taller than Alaric and could easily have been thrice as broad, his shirt somehow appearing both baggy and tight-fitting at once.

'Pike Channing,' he said with a warm smile, extending his hand for a shake.

'I'm Alaric.'

'I know who you are, matey. I was at the game yesterday. Bet it felt good to get one over Naidos after last time, eh?' Pike laughed an infectious belly laugh, which made even Alaric and Laurence chuckle.

'Thanks for agreeing to help out, Pike. I know this wasn't exactly risk-free for you either,' Mr Trolley said.

'Ah, it's my pleasure,' Pike said offhandedly. 'I've wanted to do something like this for years, truth be told. Plus, I hate that Peter Barrett guy, thinks he's above the rules I set. The final straw was when I banned the hunting of the Honduran horn-headed dragon a few years ago. He killed almost all of them for his clothing brand. No chance of ever getting those dragons back into the wild now.'

'Why'd you want to put them into the wild?' Alaric asked, puzzled as they headed to Pike's van. To him, the idea of fire-breathing monsters running loose didn't exactly sound appealing.

'Same reason you want any creature in the wild,' Pike said. 'It's diversity.'

'Diversity?' Alaric said doubtfully as they climbed inside.

'That's right, matey.' Pike let out another laugh, which, while small, still seemed to come right from his belly. 'You probably think like most people in the Main World do, eh? Dragons, out in the wild, what a crazy idea. Almost as dangerous as a lion, am I right?'

Alaric sat there, looking perplexed, as Mr Trolley started up the van and pulled out of the driveway. 'Lions are different,' he said, then wishing he never had.

'How so?' Pike responded, Alaric relieved when he carried on speaking as he didn't have an answer. 'When you think about it, they're pretty similar. Because they're big and scary, you see, stories say they're these horrible beasts; killing the poor things is seen as heroic.

You come from England, right, Alaric?'

'Well, yeah, I do,' Alaric said, struggling to see what that had to do with anything.

'Talk about Saint George out there, don't you?' Pike asked. 'Hero for killing the dragon, same way as people think they're all tough when they murder a lion or a bear. I'll tell you now, humans are the real beasts, not them. Dragons—as with most animals—don't bother them, and they won't bother you.'

'I wouldn't exactly go near them, though,' Mr Trolley mumbled. 'They're still not the tamest of creatures.'

'Oh no, of course not,' Pike agreed. 'Not likely to be a problem 'round here, though.' He let out another one of his belly laughs.

'What d'you mean?' Alaric asked. 'Where are the dragons?'

'Asked like a true Ordinary,' Pike laughed. 'Where are the dragons? They're hidden, matey and for good reason. Of course, you have a few in the Harramore wilderness, but no visitors ever go there. They're not allowed without permits. Then there are some out in the Main World, not that any Ordinaries see them anymore. They're in reserves.'

Alaric screwed up his face in concentration, trying to understand. Surely even in reserves, something as large as dragons couldn't go unnoticed?

'You know about other beings in the Main World, don't you, Alaric?' Mr Trolley said. 'Gnomes and sphinxes hide as statues, or sometimes sphinxes hide as lions. Woppanines, well, they can't ever be photographed. Then, there are some creatures like yetis or the Loch Ness monster where Ordinaries speculate, but they're hidden well enough that they can't prove their existence. Dragons, their reserves work in the same way as the island of Harramore. Only a few people know the exact location because as soon as a plane or boat gets nearby, it sends the signals haywire. Even if you got near there on foot, you'd decide to change direction.'

'But what if the dragons got out?' Alaric asked.

'They can't do that, matey,' said Pike with a grin and wry shake of the head. 'They're too big.'

Alaric stared hard at Pike, expecting him to say more, but he remained silent as Mr Trolley slowed the van down. They were in a town now, and it was the first place Alaric had been in Harramore that didn't have a view of the sea. Rather, they were surrounded by ragged-looking terraced buildings, the roofs of which varied in height like half a jigsaw, the colours just as random. It was—if there ever were such a thing—a coastal city without the coast.

'Well, it was nice meeting you,' Pike said as he climbed out of the van. 'Good luck today.'

'We're here? This is where the government works?' Alaric asked. He'd expected the Harramore Government to be based in a grand building, of which there was none in sight.

'Ah yes,' Mr Trolley said. 'There are so many departments and staff, we just have a whole town.' He started up the van again and drove. 'This whole street deals with the environmental side of things. Cryptozoological creatures, pests.'

He turned a corner, and now they were on a street identical to the one before, only this one was crowded with people. Except they weren't people. Or not like normal people anyway. There were some who, while the same size as humans, had only one eye, which Alaric recognised immediately as cyclops. Then, others barely came above the cyclops' knees, looking precisely as Alaric had seen them in fairy tales. Their long beards and hair almost brushed the floor, they were so small.

'Are they dwarves?' he asked.

'Yes, they are,' Mr Trolley said bitterly. 'Poor things. I'm not surprised you've never seen them, Alaric. They're even worse off than cyclops; they have hardly any rights at all.'

'What d'you mean?' Alaric said.

'This street is the department for sub-humans and near-humans. That's cyclops, dwarves, and you see the ones with shrivelled skin and pointed teeth? They're goblins,' Mr Trolley said.

Alaric scanned the crowd, expecting the goblins to be among the shortest beings there, but they were actually about the same height as the cyclops. In fact, they could have been mistaken for humans from a distance. But they were different. It was the pointedness of all their facial features and the shrivelled, slightly yellowed skin like old parchment.

'What are they doing here?' Laurence asked with a repulsed grimace. 'You always said they weren't allowed near us.'

'They're not normally,' Mr Trolley said. 'But they have to present themselves to the government every few months for monitoring purposes. They like to keep count of how many there are.'

'Why are they not allowed near us?' Alaric asked. 'Are they dangerous?' A lump formed in his throat at the thought. Being surrounded by so many of these beings made him uneasy, feeling out of place.

'Not at all,' Mr Trolley said assertively. 'It's because they're not seen as being like us. Dwarves and goblins are confined to their own towns on the edge of the wilderness, not allowed to leave without good reason. Iglehart likes to pretend they don't exist. Cyclops were the same until recently. It's just there have always been more of them to put up a fight. Still, most people won't employ them. Madame Ettoga's lucky Ogden's in charge at Oakwood.'

Alaric's skin began to crawl. He thought it was too horrible to be true as the van left the town and started down another country lane. Were the people of Harramore aware of this? Were they okay with it? He felt too sick, too sorry for them to open his mouth and ask Mr Trolley as he turned his focus to the task ahead. This year, Harramore had seemed like less and less of the paradise picture he'd painted when he first arrived, a feeling that the sight of Peter Barrett's factory compounded.

He could see it a mile off. There were no other buildings nearby. This enormous steel eyesore did not fit in with the surrounding landscape in the slightest, the barbed wire fence making it look somehow even less inviting. Mr Trolley braked a few hundred yards away from the front gate, out of sight of anyone there. Alaric climbed out, his heart gaining speed again and his lips going dry.

Then, as Mr Trolley started the van again and drove off towards the building, it dawned on him that he was on his own from this point on. He took a deep breath, determined not to panic as he thought again of Lucy, and the stakes in this quest. It was time.

CHAPTER 21

THE JOURNEY INTO the factory felt like one of the longest Alaric had ever taken. He gained enough speed to see Mr Trolley and Laurence waved through the gate from a distance, then wondered if he'd be so fortunate.

He started up the dusty path alone, his face sweating, incredibly hot under his mask. His throat began to feel as dry as his lips and mouth. Mr Trolley had said there'd be a crowd of children heading to work, but as the factory got closer, such a crowd never appeared. Alaric's stomach moaned ominously as he approached the building, scanning the fence perimeter. There didn't seem to be an obvious way in, and climbing over the fence wasn't an option either; he'd end up impaled on barbed wire. He did his best not to panic as his breathing sped up. He continued to pace the perimeter of the barrier, the only sign of a way in being a small gate, which was padlocked and chained shut. He sighed and approached it, then noticed right behind the fence, a wooden, battered-looking door. It certainly wasn't the main staff entrance but seemed like a better option than the heavily guarded route the others had taken.

He rattled the gate, and as he did so, he wished more than ever he had Lucy with him. She often had good ideas, and the comfort of her company would've helped him massively. Then, he gave a start as the door on the other side opened, and a rotund, rosy-cheeked man with a mop of grey hair waddled out.

'What on earth are you doing?' he snapped, his cheeks darkening to a deep shade of crimson. 'You're twenty minutes late. Come on!'

Alaric felt his stomach tighten as the man bared his teeth, pulled out a key from his pocket, and unlocked the gate. He raised his hand, and for a moment, Alaric thought he would strike him, but instead, he waved him through.

'Come!' he ordered as if Alaric were a misbehaving dog. Alaric followed him inside without hesitation, feeling slightly less nervous now. The first step was done.

He didn't dare speak as the man led him down a dark, narrow corridor. There were full-length windows on either side through which he could see the children working. He felt sick at what he saw, looking away instantly before something inside him made him stare at them once again. He didn't want to see it but, at the same time, couldn't take his eyes off the sight.

What must have been hundreds of children, some of which could've been half Alaric's age, were crammed inside each room, not one of them smiling. Their faces were dirty and sweating as some put lids on bottles, others sticking on labels at a remarkable rate. Even seeing it made Alaric exhausted as a suited man paced the length of the production line. He'd occasionally smack one of the children on the head with his cane when they stopped for a few seconds, growling like a dog. Alaric winced every time he did so, amazed they never reacted with anything more than a rub of the head. It was as if they were so used to it by now that they didn't notice. Alaric cleared his mind and didn't dare speak as they continued walking, thinking it best to avoid any conversation. As much as a part of him wanted to barge into the rooms and attack the suited men, to free the children, there was another task at hand. He had to stay focused.

'What's your name, boy?' the rotund man asked.

'Al…Alistair,' Alaric said, clenching his fists nervously.

'Surname?'

'McGlompher.' Alaric didn't know why, but it was the first name that came to his head other than his own.

'Well, Alistair McGlompher, I'll be reporting you to Peter Barrett. If you're this late again, you'll lose your job. Now, what department do you work in, boy?'

Alaric let out a few incoherent babbles. He had no idea what any of the departments were called, and surely any answer he gave would be seen right through.

'Crikey, you're not with it at all, are you?' the man sighed. 'I could do with some help in my department anyway. Follow me.'

Alaric obeyed, and they reached a double door at the end of the corridor. The man continued through it, holding it open for Alaric without a trace of a smile. He momentarily considered darting away as the hallway split off in three directions. However, he thought better of it and followed the man up the stairs. There was no way he'd go unnoticed now, and the last thing he needed to do was incense this man even more. There was a horrible, acrid smell in the air as they reached the next floor and started along an identical corridor, the source of which soon became apparent.

Hundreds of blood-red spiders, no larger than the freckles on Alaric's hand, were drifting around like crane flies. The scent tickled the back of Alaric's throat as they marched through the swarm, making him cough. A few spiders landed on his face to bite, which he swatted away impetuously.

'Stupid bugs!' the man roared, his own shirt covered with them. 'They're everywhere!'

Alaric coughed again to suppress a giggle, earning himself a glower from the man. They continued down the corridor, getting further away from the flying spiders until the man stopped at the last door on the left. He whisked Alaric inside the room, looking somehow even less happy now.

The lights came on automatically. The room was ever so dank as Alaric began to sweat, an unpleasant damp smell in the air. Most of the floor was covered with cardboard boxes, in places stacked three or four high, the material creased in parts, looking worn away by the air's moisture.

'Mr Barrett wants these boxes incinerated,' the man said gruffly. 'Downstairs and to the right. Just toss them in.'

'Why?' Alaric asked, and the man gave him a hard slap on the back of his head.

'That's none of your business. You are a weird kid, aren't you?' he snarled. 'Now, your name was Alistair McGlompher, was it?'

Alaric nodded, unsure he could keep up a convincing lie if he responded verbally.

'Right, Alistair, I'm going to speak to Mr Barrett about you. When I come back, there better have been good progress made on these boxes. Do you hear me?' the man barked.

Alaric nodded again, and the man growled and backhanded him on the cheek before storming off. Alaric exhaled deeply once the sound of his footsteps had faded into silence. He was completely alone now, precisely what he needed. He poked his head out of the door, checking there was no one coming down the corridor and headed back into the room. There was no doubt in his mind that he wasn't supposed to search through the contents of the boxes, something which spurred him on to do so even more.

He took a deep breath to compose himself and ripped the tape off one of the boxes, his heart seeming to skip a beat at the noise it made. Every sound as he opened the box seemed to be amplified a hundred times. Then, he punched the air in celebration. The container was full of small packets of pills, all identical to each other.

Anti-poison tablets for treating farafig. Contains woppanine extract.

Alaric glanced towards the door again, listening hard. Then, when he sensed no one coming, he took one of the boxes and scanned the instructions on the back.

Take two tablets every four hours for three days. All signs of sickness should disappear.

And now, Alaric grinned from ear to ear. He'd hit the jackpot. He grabbed a handful of the boxes, stuffing as many into his pockets as would possibly fit, then withdrew his phone and unlocked it. The only sounds he could hear now were his own breathing and his taps on the phone screen. They seemed to echo off the walls, making his heart beat hard enough to be heard as he texted Mr Trolley.

I have the medicine. Now just need to raid Barrett's office. Where are you? He wrote. Sent.

Mr Trolley's reply came within seconds. The buzz his phone made startled him so much, it slipped out of his sweaty hands and onto the floor. He picked it back up hastily; there was a small chip in the screen now, but that was the least of his concerns as he read Mr Trolley's message.

Great. Come and find us. We're in the middle of the factory. Walk confidently, like you know what you're doing. If anyone asks, say you've been told to see Mr Barrett.

Alaric locked his phone and pocketed it, a strange sensation in his legs, almost like pins and needles except with feeling. He forced himself to keep his face expressionless as he went through the door at the end of the corridor, not daring to look at anyone in case he broke cover.

He concentrated on his breathing to distract himself, desperate to see Mr Trolley and Laurence. He knew once they were together, he'd feel so much better. Then, they could just search Peter Barrett's office and get out. And Lucy would be safe. He continued walking, following the signs pointing to Barrett's office. Surely, that would be central.

He turned a corner, then another, winding down this maze of a building. After about ten minutes of walking, he was there, his legs feeling heavier than ever. He peered through the office door's window. It seemed empty as far as he could tell, the chair tucked in behind the mahogany desk.

Tentatively, he turned the doorknob. He froze as he heard it click before pushing it open slowly. He stopped once it was ajar enough that he could fit through the gap to scan his surroundings. Then, seeing he was alone, he entered Peter Barrett's office.

'ALARIC, NO!' came a voice from somewhere in

the room, surprising Alaric so much, he audibly gasped.

He took two steps towards the desk and could now see Laurence and Mr Trolley sitting against the back wall, sweat visibly dripping off both of their foreheads. Laurence's face was completely colourless. And Alaric's heart stopped as he saw Mr Trolley. Several cuts scattered his face, his eye so badly bruised he could no longer open it.

'W-w-what happened?' Alaric said. He felt sick, rooted to the spot. Then, as he looked down, a horrible realisation dawned on him. Both Laurence and Mr Trolley's wrists had been tied together with rope, so tightly their hands had whitened.

'Jackpot!' said a triumphant voice from behind Alaric. He gave a start and turned quickly on the spot to see Peter Barrett standing there. He was smiling a smile that showed every one of his perfect, white teeth.

Everything clicked into place in Alaric's mind at once. He'd walked right into a trap. Without a second thought, he sprinted towards the doorway. But he fell to the ground after just a few steps when he collided with something solid. He tried to clamber to his feet, but as he looked up, he saw the rotund man he'd met earlier swing his foot at his head. He didn't have the time to dodge it, and he felt the sting, the blood filling his nose, as he fell back to the ground.

This time, Alaric couldn't even lift his chest up as the man pressed his foot down on his body, and he could barely breathe. Then, two more men came marching through the doorway, both of them broad-shouldered and muscular. And now, the truth dawned on Alaric. He was trapped.

'Tie him up, boys,' Peter Barrett said. 'And make it quick. The van's waiting outside.'

CHAPTER 22

ALARIC DIDN'T PUT up a fight as the muscular men bound his hands and feet. There was no point, no real chance of success. The door was completely blocked off as four more burly men arrived and stood cracking their knuckles menacingly.

Within seconds, Alaric's wrists and ankles were tied together as tightly as Laurence's and Mr Trolley's, the rope digging into his skin painfully. The men then picked the three of them up, carrying them along the corridor like coffins, and Alaric felt empty once more.

They were outside now, Alaric staring up at the cloudless sky, squinting at the shock of the bright light. He tried to devise an escape plan in his head, but it was no use. He had no experience in escapology at all, and even if he did, running away would seem futile; they were too heavily outnumbered to have a real chance. He tried to use Solo's Seela, imagining a hole in the ground for them to fall into, but even that failed as if Alaric had lost all his power.

'Seelastry won't work against us,' one of the men carrying him snarled.

Then, they stopped moving, and Alaric heard the sound of a car door being opened. He looked around hopefully, in case this was help arriving. But all the hope drained from him when he saw the two men in front of him toss Mr Trolley into the back of a van.

The men carrying Alaric then took two steps towards the vehicle, Alaric bracing himself for what was about to come. He felt himself fly through the air before landing on the floor with a thud, feeling his body bruise. Then came another crash as Laurence was thrown inside, the doors were shut, and all was black.

'Oof, there's not a lot of room in here, is there?' Mr Trolley said, his tone remarkably upbeat given the circumstances.

'There was plenty of space till they threw you in,' said a friendly, familiar voice before laughing his infectious belly laugh.

'Pike?' Mr Trolley gasped as Alaric felt the van jolt and start to move. 'What are you doing here? What happened?'

'We were betrayed, my friend,' Pike replied. 'I'm sorry.'

'No one blames you, Pike,' Alaric said, his mouth

dry and sticky. Not only was the inside of the van pitch black, but it was also incredibly hot, exacerbated by the tightness of its space.

'That's kind of you to say, my man, but it probably was my fault. We should've known Barrett's friends are everywhere in the government. One o' them probably heard us talking about this, right, Ed?' Pike said.

'We share the responsibility, Pike,' Mr Trolley said. 'We should've been quieter. I'm sorry I couldn't warn you, Alaric. They'd been expecting us. They took my phone and lured you in. Anyway, we are where we are now and what we need is a plan to get out of here.'

'Well, if they're taking us to the police, can't we just tell them what Barrett's been doing? Explain what's gone on,' Laurence said, his voice shaking.

'I wish it were that simple,' Mr Trolley muttered. 'But no, the police are as corrupt as Iglehart himself; they'd turn a blind eye to all of this.'

'A blind eye, eh?' Pike said. 'That reminds me, we could do with some light in here, could we not?'

There was a rummaging sound for a few moments as they sat waiting. Then, there was light, Alaric able to see each of the three other people in the van. While covered in more cuts and bruises than Mr Trolley, Pike was not tied up. Rather, his hands were free as he held what looked like a turquoise caterpillar in one fist.

'I should've known, Pike, I should've known,' Mr Trolley said with a wry smile.

'Was that your Seela?' Alaric asked in awe.

Pike chuckled. 'No, no, matey. You see this here?' he pointed towards the turquoise caterpillar. 'This is a lunef. I was keeping it in my pocket, marvellous creatures. No matter how dark a room is, they'll light the whole place clear as day as soon as they enter it. We get a few complaints about them at the environmental office. It's a real problem when people are sleeping, and they slither into the bedroom under the door. Whole place lights up, and more often than not, you're no longer sleeping.'

Alaric gave a small laugh at the idea, but neither Mr Trolley nor Laurence did the same, Laurence's face still colourless in shock.

'I love them too,' Pike chortled. 'I actually breed them at home. They can be handy if there's a power cut. Mustn't forget to put the lid on the tank, though. One night, I hadn't put it on properly, and they all got out. My wife and I were up till dawn roundin' them up. She was angry at me all week.' He let out another belly laugh, which made even Laurence smile slightly. 'Anyway, I expect you'd probably all be more comfortable if I untied you?'

'Please do,' Mr Trolley said with a relieved sigh. Pike shuffled over to him and started undoing the knots binding his wrists and ankles. Then, he did the same to Laurence and Alaric, who could still feel the burns after the rope came loose.

'Wawet's Seela is useful at times like this,' Pike said. He lifted one of his hands, and then claws that must have been several inches long, as sharp as daggers sprouted from his fingers.

'Guardian of Wolves?' Alaric asked.

Pike nodded. 'Used these claws to cut myself free.'

Alaric grinned. He was liking Pike more and more and, when he thought about it, he was unsure where they'd be without him. While they were captured now, they did at least have the medicine Lucy needed, and if they could escape, there was still hope of saving her.

'Is it worth trying our Seelas again at some point?' Alaric asked.

Mr Trolley and Pike both shrugged.

'We need to find the right moment,' Mr Trolley said. 'We may only get one chance, but now that we're untied, we might get one. Just wait until either Pike or I say so.'

Alaric nodded and sighed. Even with the light and

his hands untied, the back of this van was still far from comfortable, and the solid floor made his back and buttocks ache. It was also still sweltering and stuffy, making the four of them cough frequently, Alaric's tongue almost completely dried out. He'd lost all track of time and had no idea how long it was before he felt the van come to a halt, nor any clue where they were. But something inside him told him this wasn't the police station.

'Where are we?' Laurence said weakly.

Mr Trolley shushed Laurence and pressed his ear against the van's wall. Pike and Alaric followed suit, but it was no good. The soundproofing was too strong for them to hear anything of use, any talking reduced to indecipherable murmurs.

'Get ready,' Mr Trolley whispered.

Pike nodded in agreement, and Alaric stared fixedly at the doors. He was now so parched that his head was aching, his vision fuzzy. He blinked slowly, trying to get everything to come into focus, but still, the blurriness stayed.

Then came the sound of the bolt on the door sliding sideways. Alaric jumped as Pike and Mr Trolley shuffled slightly towards the door, ready to pounce. Alaric saw Pike tense his hands up and sprout the wolf claws he had earlier. He winked at him and Laurence as the door swung open.

'Don't. Try. Anything.'

The man standing on the other side was holding the longest sword Alaric had ever seen. He raised it, forcing Mr Trolley and Pike to retreat to the back wall. Alaric stared hard into the man's empty eyes, seeing behind him what looked like a vacant car park and, in the background, the sea. Then, they started to move once again. Not the van, but the whole car park. They were on a ferry.

'Where are we going?' Alaric asked hopefully.

'You'll find out when we get there,' the man said unkindly. Alaric didn't react. He hadn't been expecting an answer but thought it was worth a try. 'I brought you water,' the man went on, tossing a pack of bottles into the van. 'Make it last. It's all we've got, and we need you alive...for the time being.' He smiled malevolently, making Laurence whimper. Then, keeping his eyes locked on them, he crouched down to pick something up. Next, he threw an empty, wooden bucket into the van and backed away slightly. 'That's your toilet. Bon voyage.' He gave them another malign grin and shut the door once again, and Alaric's heart sank as he heard him bolt it shut.

'What do we do, Dad?' Laurence whined.

'I'll think of something, don't worry,' Mr Trolley said. Alaric wasn't convinced but forced a smile to keep Laurence calm.

'Of course we will,' Pike said, taking a bottle of water and unscrewing the lid. 'This'll be a story to tell our kids when we get out, eh, Ed?' He downed the bottle of water in one go. Alaric, Laurence and Mr Trolley followed his lead, chugging their drinks so quickly that Alaric felt even worse.

'It will indeed,' Mr Trolley said brightly, 'and you'll be able to tell Lucy and all your friends about this. Last year was the whole Golden Pearl thing, and now this adventure—you'll be the most popular kids in school. All the girls will come flooding, Laurence.' He winked and gave a reassuring smile, which Laurence managed to reciprocate weakly.

'How do you know we'll get out, though?' Laurence said.

'Because, Laurence, we're descendants of Rei. We have most of the Guardians on our side, and most importantly, we believe. We have more to fight for than these men,' Mr Trolley replied.

'And think about it, matey, when have things ever *not* turned out all right?' Pike said.

Alaric and Laurence smiled thinly, though Alaric was feeling neither optimistic nor reassured. As true as Pike's words were, he'd rarely been in a situation this severe before. He'd got lucky when Solo saved him from John and Sue and when Rei had stopped Goblinsfoe. But this time, he couldn't exactly see any help or good fortune on the way.

The time in the van dragged on. The four of them rarely spoke, Pike and Mr Trolley losing the energy to keep spirits up. It somehow seemed to get even hotter and stuffier, making Alaric feel yet more nauseated, and he lost the power to speak. He was on the brink of passing out from exhaustion. His head was hurting so much, and he was so parched that he'd forgotten what was going on. And now, he was beyond caring where they were going or how long it would be. He was too weak, too tired, and having forgotten the discomfort of the van, he fell asleep.

Now, Alaric was dreaming. He recognised the sensation immediately, that strange feeling of being both present and absent at the same time. He felt as hot and parched as he had in reality, and as he scanned his surroundings, it seemed logical. All around him was black, volcanic rock. Red, hot lava seeped through the cracks, and he coughed from the acrid smell overwhelming him. He had no idea where he was, his first thought being Hawaii. He knew they had volcanoes there, but why had he suddenly dreamt it?

He looked upwards, all the pain in his body rushing to his head like a stream as he saw the sky. Or was it a ceiling? There was no light coming from it, no stars, not even clouds. Just blackness. His gut feeling told him this wasn't Hawaii.

Now, he was drifting through the air. He didn't fight it as he usually would. He felt too weak to do so, and something in his subconscious mind told him he needed to see this, that he was meant to have this dream. Like a feather in the wind, he floated on past the volcanic rock.

Then, he was flying over grass plains, a herd of wildebeest grazing nonchalantly, a jeep full of people on the adjacent dirt road. Was this Africa? It would make sense since Alaric had always wanted to go there, but something was off. There was a family of kangaroos, which he knew didn't exist in the African wilderness. Something about the sight made Alaric shudder. Sure, there were often minor inconsistencies in dreams, but not one as major as that. At least, not in Alaric's dreams.

He continued drifting over the plains, waiting to see where his mind would take him. He was nearing a mountain now, the peak of which was only just visible below the sky. And on top of it was a castle. A magnificent castle. It was even grander than he remembered the Guardians' Palace. Several of its towers were too high-rising for the tops to be seen, and it had more gold-framed windows than Alaric cared to count. He carried on, floating towards its giant double doors. And when he reached them, they swung open for him as if they'd been expecting him.

Then, as often happens in dreams, Alaric didn't see the building's entrance hall nor the staircases and corridors leading to the room. Instead, he arrived at his destination immediately, like he'd teleported.

It was one of the most extravagant rooms that Alaric had ever seen. There was a fireplace against one wall, at least twice as tall as Alaric himself. Every inch of the wall was painted delicately with plants, people and patterns, exactly like a room out of a typical palace.

There were three other men there, two of whom Alaric recognised instantly. The other one, he could not see as he was stationed behind a marble pillar, but he could hear his voice.

'The moment is coming,' Goblinsfoe said, bowing slightly at the man behind the column. 'They're on their way as I speak.'

'Excellent,' said the man behind the pillar in his deep, amiable voice. 'And I trust all is well with Alaric?'

'Everything is in place as I understand it,' Goblinsfoe said with a nod. 'We'll be free soon. You know, I've really missed the coffee out there.'

Now, Alaric understood. He was in the Land of the Dead. Naidos was the man behind the pillar, this was his palace, and he was plotting his escape. Did this mean Alaric was dead, that he wasn't dreaming after all? It certainly seemed like a strange thing to be imagining, and when he thought back to that van, he wouldn't have been surprised if the heat had killed him.

'I think we all miss a lot of stuff out there,' Naidos said with a chuckle. 'For me, it's the Turkish delight, but we'll worry about that once we're out.'

'What about Alaric?' the third man in the room said, speaking for the first time. Rei was lying on the floor, his hands and feet tied. 'You promised me my son would be safe.'

Goblinsfoe struck Rei over the face with his cane, producing a crack that echoed off the walls.

'You may have been the King Guardian in your lifetime,' Goblinsfoe snarled, 'but in the Land of the Dead, there is only one king, and that's Naidos.'

'Now, now, calm down, Walkul,' Naidos said gently. 'He has every right to be concerned about his son;

everyone would be in such a situation. Rei, I've assured you Alaric has no reason to worry as long as he listens to me.'

'You monster,' Rei said through gritted teeth, earning himself another strike from Goblinsfoe's cane.

'*You* are not in a position to lecture on such topics,' Naidos said coldly.

Then, Naidos' palace was gone as Alaric jerked awake. He could see Mr Trolley and Pike shuffling towards the van doors, Laurence looking faint as if about to doze off. The vehicle had stopped, and Alaric was still alive. He had to be. But that must've meant he'd been dreaming, which he knew he hadn't. It had been too far beyond his mind. Then, as he heard the lock on the van door slide, he thought back to what Goblinsfoe had said.

They're on their way as I speak.

Alaric's heart sped up as he realised what was going on, feeling now as alert as when he'd woken up that morning. Then, his worst fears were confirmed as the van door swung open, and he saw what was outside.

He recognised the setting immediately. Behind the muscular man were the thousands of irregular rock columns lit up by the full moon, the sea violently crashing against them. They were at Giant's Causeway. This was the entrance to the Land of the Dead.

CHAPTER 23

'PIKE! MR TROLLEY! We have to do something! Now!' Alaric shouted. His tone was panicked, his heart racing. They'd walked into another trap.

'You try nothing,' the muscular man outside the van snarled, his sword raised once again. 'Now come.'

They all crawled towards the doorway except Alaric, not daring to disobey. Laurence paused as he was the first to reach the door, hesitant about what to do. After a few seconds, another one of the muscular men arrived, took his shirt in his fist, and pulled him outside. This seemed to have persuaded Mr Trolley and Pike to jump straight out of the van, each assigned two muscular men to restrain them.

'Who tied you all up?' one of the men growled. 'Didn't do a very good job, did they?'

'Never mind that,' Peter Barrett said, appearing from around the corner of the vehicle. 'We need to get on with this. Now, get the boy.'

At those words, the two men who still had free

hands poked their heads inside the van, Alaric still against the back wall. As he looked ahead and assessed his chances, he could see no obvious way out. The escape route was blocked, and once restrained, he didn't fancy his odds of outdoing these men for strength.

'Come!' one of the men barked.

Alaric did not do so. Instead, he took a deep breath and stood up as much as the height of the ceiling would allow him to. Then, as the man crawled inside the van, Alaric swung his foot at his head. He had no idea what he was planning, driven entirely by instinct. He didn't look back as his foot made clean contact with the man's head, hitting it so hard that the man recoiled, stopping for a moment. There was no cry of pain, but the shock of being kicked was enough to buy Alaric the second he needed.

Without thinking about anything, he darted out of the van, squeezing past the other man and sprinted. He had no idea where he was going, but he knew he had to get away from there as he hurried up the road as fast as he could. He must've run at least a hundred metres now, the cliff's green grass coming into sight.

He chanced a look over his shoulder, slowing almost to a halt as he saw there was no one in pursuit. Rather, Peter Barrett and his men simply stood on

Giant's Causeway, Alaric able to make out Barrett's laughing face. The balloon of hope that had formed inside him popped in an instant. But he kept on sprinting up the slope, his stamina apparently limitless. Then, as he reached the top, he actually did grind to a halt.

Six of Peter Barrett's men were waiting there, standing nonchalantly as if they'd been expecting him. They each leered at Alaric and started strolling slowly towards him. He had no idea what to do. He turned on his heel, thought about running sideways. But he was surrounded as more men appeared out of nowhere. The only direction to flee was behind him, straight back down to Peter Barrett.

'It's no good running,' said one of the men. 'There are hundreds of us stationed around here. It'll be much easier for you if you do as we say.'

Alaric, realising there was no way out, stood still as the men closed in on him, handcuffed him and marched him back down to Giant's Causeway. He could only hope that Mr Trolley or Pike could muster up a great escape. If what he'd seen in his dream had been real—and his horrible gut feeling was telling him it was—he'd been lured into a trap, and Naidos was about to return. He tried not to think about that, hoping against hope that he was wrong about something, that this wasn't what he thought.

They were all standing on Giant's Causeway now. Peter Barrett's face lit up as one of the men threw Alaric onto the ground, bruising his body even more.

'Open!' Peter Barrett called, a gleeful, malevolent smile surfacing on his face.

And just as Alaric had remembered from last year, the sound of rock grinding against rock filled the air as several basalt columns slid back from one point. He started to tremble as Peter Barrett approached the newly formed hole among the columns and peered down into it. Then came the strong suction as Alaric and the others fell through the air, the falling slowing until they gently touched ground.

Everything was exactly as Alaric had remembered it under Giant's Causeway. He'd never felt so helpless as Barrett led them down the stalactite and stalagmite-filled tunnel, right up to the entrance to the first chamber. As Barrett pushed it open, Alaric shut his eyes instantly, unsure if the gorgons would still be turned to stone. But as it happened, he needn't have bothered.

'We're here on business for Naidos,' he heard Barrett say.

'Ah yes,' the five gorgons said as one. There was no

coldness in their voice this time; rather, they almost spoke like hotel concierges. 'Just this way, sir.'

Still, Alaric kept his eyes tightly shut as he felt himself being dragged through the gorgons' chamber. He wasn't willing to take any risks, no matter how small. He would not squander any tiny glimmer of hope he had left.

The next door creaked open, Alaric still feeling himself being marched onwards, not putting up a fight. He opened his eyes a crack, now sure they were beyond the gorgons' room and saw the familiar lake of treacle. Only this time, it had parted in two as if it had also been expecting them. A part of Alaric would have liked the lake to merge back into one as they were dragged across it, to take Peter Barrett and his men down with them if they had to die here.

However, such a thing did not happen. Everything seemed to go exactly as Barrett was intending. Even the door where they'd had to complete the puzzles last year swung open before they'd reached it. They were there now, right at the entrance to the Land of the Dead, the knife still placed on top of the stone table like a sacrificial altar. Everything was the same as last year, only the back wall was now scattered with several cracks.

Now, they were even more outnumbered as three people stood waiting by the table, the first of whom Alaric recognised. Smiling a falsely sweet smile, her spiked-up hair matching the colour of the blood on the wall, was Beatrice Bork. To her left was a man whose photo Alaric remembered seeing on the news from time to time but whose name he couldn't recall. His broad frame and steely eyes were enough to make him look intimidating even without his stiff, bald face.

'Vido Sadaarm?' Mr Trolley gasped, and the bald man nodded expressionlessly. Alaric's stomach tightened. This was the Naidos supporter running for Governor.

Alaric didn't recognise the remaining person at all. She, like Beatrice and Sadaarm, was dressed entirely in black. Her long hair was the same colour, contrasting her glowing, pearly white face. Despite this, she didn't seem to fit in with the others at all, her expression suggesting she was hardly aware of where she was, staring dreamily at the ceiling.

'Excellent, we're all here. Now, are we all comfortable?' Beatrice said as if about to do storytime at a nursery. When no one responded, she said, 'then let's begin.'

Peter Barrett, his expression neutral, paced softly

towards the dreamy-faced woman and stared hard into her eyes. Alaric felt it in the air, the familiar tingle when a Seela was about to be used, but he was too weak to block it. Then, the woman's mouth started to move. Only, something in her voice told Alaric that it wasn't her speaking, but her mouth as if the two were separate, like she was possessed.

'Only the Raven can destroy the Veil,' the mouth said, the words bouncing off the walls.

Peter Barrett slapped the woman on the cheek and spat in her face. 'Yes, Cria, I know that. But how does the Raven destroy the Veil?'

Alaric's mouth hung open as the facts clicked into place. How they'd found her, he had no idea, but he was staring at the Guardian of Creation; Peter Barrett was reading her mind, and she knew all the laws there were to know in the world. And now, her mouth was moving again.

'When the Darkest of the Guardians destroyed the King, he cursed himself and was trapped in his kingdom by his nephew. One cannot walk in the Land of the Living while there, the other thrives. One cannot thrive in the Land of the Dead while there, the other walks.'

'So, the nephew must die?' Barrett asked indifferently. At those words, Alaric's heart seemed to swell to the size of a boulder. Then, he tried to clamber to his feet, only to be knocked down by the man behind him.

'No! Don't you dare touch the boy!' Pike ordered. Suddenly, he managed to break free from the two men restraining him and charged towards Peter Barrett. But he'd barely taken two steps when he fell over his own legs and hit the ground with a thud. 'My eyes! I can't see!' he screamed, and the two men assigned to him held him once more.

Beatrice snorted before giggling malevolently. Alaric shot her a contemptuous yet inquisitive glare. She'd used her Seela to blind Pike. So, she *wasn't* an Ordinary.

'Be quiet please,' she said in the same falsely sweet voice she'd been using, 'or things will get worse for you.'

Alaric started to panic as Peter Barrett paced slowly towards the knife on the table. He frantically looked around him, but Mr Trolley and Laurence both looked just as clueless, just as panicked as himself. There was no way out. If help was coming, it needed to arrive now.

'All is void if the nephew exists on both sides,' Cria said. 'Only one drop of blood need be shed, and the curse shall be lifted.'

'Hmm, very interesting,' Peter Barrett said. 'Only the Raven can destroy the Veil, and Alaric need not die. We just need his blood.'

'I said don't touch the boy!' Pike commanded.

Then, everything seemed to happen at once. Beatrice stared at Pike with raised eyebrows before giggling the same malevolent giggle. Next, she paced softly towards him. She snatched the sword from Pike's guard and, in one swift movement, thrust it into Pike's chest. And Alaric felt as faint as ever as he watched the life leave his eyes. Even in death, Pike's expression was defiant.

'You murderer!' Mr Trolley screamed once he'd found the energy. 'He was a good man! He had a wife and kids!'

'I told him to be quiet!' Beatrice shrieked. 'So, you shut up, or your son will be next!'

Alaric heard Laurence whimper like an injured puppy. He couldn't look at him but didn't want to point his eyes towards Pike either, struggling to process what had just happened. Beatrice had killed a man right in front of him.

'Let's all just calm down,' Barrett said softly. 'There need not be any more death tonight. We've heard it from Cria herself that Alaric doesn't have to die, and there is no reason to kill the others either.'

'Of course, that doesn't mean that we *can't* kill Alaric,' Beatrice said with a hopeful smile.

'No, Beatrice,' Barrett said firmly as she took a step towards Alaric. 'My father wants him alive, so he shall live.'

Alaric felt a small amount of relief as Beatrice threw her sword to the ground in a strop. Then, he clocked what Barrett had said.

'What do you mean "your father"?' Alaric blurted out, earning him a malicious glare from Beatrice.

Barrett crouched down to Alaric's eye level, then spoke so softly, he was almost mouthing. 'Naidos.'

'W-what?' Alaric stammered. 'Naidos' last son was Arimon Crow, and he was executed years ago.'

Barrett sniggered. 'No, dear boy. Arimon Crow was never executed. The government official responsible for the task made sure of it, faked my death on national television and hid me in his house.'

Alaric stared at Barrett, gaping. He'd said, "faked *my* death"?

'That's right, Alaric. I am Arimon Crow, son of Naidos,' Barrett said. 'So many years, Walkul Goblinsfoe had to hide me for. He'd stopped people being fed to the Kraken alive *precisely* so he could stage my execution. Then, once he'd stolen the Golden Pearl, he could lend it to me, and I could take over Peter Barrett's body.' He started towards the table and picked up the knife, panic surging through Alaric as he began to understand. He was about to open the Veil.

'You're the Raven?' Alaric said weakly.

'Oh, for goodness' sake, is the clue not in the name?' Arimon shouted. 'Arimon CROW. Of course, the story was translated from Greek, which uses the same word for both, but yes, I am the Raven.'

And before Alaric could process this, Arimon had picked up the knife from the stone table and strode towards him. Alaric wanted to run away right then, but he couldn't move. His hands were still cuffed together, two guards holding him firmly in place. He took a deep breath, braced himself for what was coming, but nothing could prepare him for what happened next.

Arimon raised the knife and pressed it hard against Alaric's bicep. Then, a seething pain ran right down his arm as if his blood had turned to lava, the sleeve of his shirt drenched within a second. He cried out in pain, eyed Mr Trolley, who was determinedly keeping his mouth shut, and watched. Alaric tried to focus on his breathing as Arimon, grasping the bloodied knife, marched over to the cracked back wall.

But the next thing that happened ensured the pain in Alaric's arm was the least of his worries. Arimon raised the knife once again and slashed the wall. Then, as if it were a curtain, it became torn from corner to corner. For a moment, there was but a gaping crack running the length of the wall. Then, there was no longer a wall there but a pile of rubble. And behind that pile of rubble was nothing, an empty dark hole from which thick black smoke emanated.

Then came the footsteps. The loudest, most stomping steps Alaric had ever heard, drawing nearer and nearer. Now, the outline of the man was in sight, his features becoming clearer as he entered the room.

And Alaric didn't need an introduction to know who this was. He shared his same chiselled jawline. Only, it was covered with a shaggy, jet-black beard. His gaunt and pallid face looked as though it had once been handsome before it had been deprived of sunlight for so long. Naidos was back.

CHAPTER 24

THERE WOULD HAVE been no need for Alaric's guards to hold him in place now; he wouldn't have been able to move anyway, petrified in shock.

'Father,' Arimon breathed, falling to his knees and hugging Naidos' legs. 'It's been so long.'

'Indeed, it has,' Naidos said with a smile. His voice, while deep, sounded worn out from lack of use. 'Fourteen years, more than that, in fact.'

'Can't we do the family reunions later?' Vido Sadaarm said coldly.

'Yes, can we please get on with this?' Beatrice asked.

'You don't understand, Beatrice. Just because you never got on with your family, it doesn't mean others can't have their moments,' Arimon snarled. He let go of Naidos' legs and climbed to his feet.

'No, my boy, they're right; there is much to be done first,' Naidos said. He turned his head towards Alaric, looking into his eyes with his own. There was almost a kindness in them, which unnerved Alaric even more than if they'd been lifeless.

'Alaric, my nephew,' he said, a hint of a cry in his voice. Alaric flinched as he raised his arms and approached him as if about to hug him. Naidos recoiled, affronted.

'How dare you speak to Alaric! How dare you try to hug him like that!' Mr Trolley screamed, his face as livid as Pike's had been. Then, Alaric closed his eyes impulsively as Beatrice picked the sword up off the floor, raised it above her shoulders and strode towards Laurence.

Not Laurence as well, please not Laurence, Alaric thought to himself pleadingly.

'Stop!' Naidos ordered, and Beatrice threw the sword back onto the floor, letting out a frustrated, almost agonised scream. 'There need be no more death tonight!'

Alaric stared at Naidos with a screwed-up face, utterly perplexed. In all honesty, he was amazed he was still alive. As soon as he'd seen Naidos, he'd been expecting him to kill him straight away and certainly not anticipating him saving Laurence's life. Still, Alaric dared not reciprocate the way Naidos looked at him, staring determinedly at the ground.

'Alaric,' Naidos said softly. 'I can't begin to tell you

how pleased I am to meet you. Like a mini-Rei, you are. The face, everything is the same.'

Then, as if the mention of Alaric's father had ignited a flame inside him, he tore himself away from the guards, pulled his wrists apart and snapped the handcuffs around them in one movement. He pounced at Naidos' neck like a leopard going for its prey, knocked him over, and squeezed his throat with both hands as hard as he could. Hot rage coursed through Alaric's body, only one thing on his mind: he was going to kill Naidos, the man who'd murdered his father.

At first, Naidos' face went wide-eyed with shock. Then, he twisted his mouth into a smile, letting out a laugh that was stifled but no less genuine as a result. Still, Alaric tightened his grip, wanting nothing more at that moment than to watch the life drain out of this man, this monster, to hear his last gasp for breath. He ignored the sound of approaching footsteps behind him, still strengthening his grasp, fighting the two men pulling him away from Naidos.

For a moment, he thought he might succeed as he used his newfound strength to keep his grip on Naidos' neck. But even then, he was no match for the power of four of Arimon Crow's men. They wrenched him away from Naidos' body, all restraining him as he desperately tried to charge back towards his uncle.

'My word, I knew Walkul said you were feisty, but I did not expect that,' Naidos said as he clambered to his feet. 'What was all that about, eh?'

'You murdered my father!' Alaric seethed, breathing heavily through gritted teeth. 'It's your fault I never knew my parents! You sent Goblinsfoe to kill me last year!'

'Hmm, that's one out of three correct,' Naidos replied as if he were discussing the weather. 'Maybe one and a half, being generous. I suppose that's fifty per cent, not bad, would probably get you a C-grade. However, from what I understand, you're much better than that…top student, apparently.' He smiled at Alaric like a particularly proud father, which enraged him even more, and his breathing became heavier still.

'I think, Naidos, that we all have some explaining to do,' said a familiar voice from among the black smoke. Walkul Goblinsfoe emerged into view, making even more fury swell up inside Alaric. He was still using a walking stick and looked even frailer than when Alaric had last seen him. His face was paler, sicklier, his baggy clothes giving off the impression that he'd lost weight as well.

Then, the room seemed to tremble as a sound like

thunder came from above, startling everyone as they looked to the ceiling.

'Crikey, stormy night,' Naidos remarked. 'But yes, I think you're right, Walkul. Alaric has a right to understand what's gone on, and first thing's first, we're not here to hurt you.' Naidos gave another smile, which would have been reassuring if it had come from anyone else, but the very fact it came from the man who'd killed his father made Alaric's blood boil even more.

'I don't believe you,' Alaric said as coldly as he could.

Naidos sighed, smiling wryly. 'I didn't think you would. After all, your understanding of events has been extremely warped by those who have told them.'

'You killed my father!' Alaric snapped.

'Yes, I will concede that I did do that,' Naidos sighed. 'Am I especially proud of it? No. Why did I do it? Because it was necessary.'

Alaric scoffed, struggling to no avail to break free from the guards holding him. 'Killing is never necessary,' he shouted so hard, he could see the spit flying from his mouth.

'It was, Alaric, the lesser of two evils. You see, I tried for so long to get your father and the other Guardians to listen to me, but they never did. The world was and will be doomed if it stays under their rule,' Naidos said. His tone was so calm and composed, one could have been forgiven for thinking he was discussing this over tea with a friend.

'What are you on about?' Alaric snapped. 'You're the one who wants to wipe out the human race.'

'Too right he does,' Vido Sadaarm chimed in. 'A whole lot of good it'd do the world too. I'll tell you; humans are the vilest creatures on this planet.'

'Thank you, Vido,' Naidos said, raising a hand to halt his speech. 'Yes, Alaric, I do want a world without humans or, rather, *Ordinaries* because Earth would be better off without them. You spent so long in the Main World. You were raised by so many Ordinary families; you've seen what they're really like.

'Tell me, have you not seen what they've done to the planet? I've been looking in on you from the Land of the Dead all these years; you loved meeting dodo birds, didn't you? Ordinaries, they hunted the poor things to extinction in the Main World. How many other creatures have suffered the same fate?'

'Don't listen to him, Alaric!' Laurence shouted. Alaric turned his focus towards him, astounded he'd found the energy, that he'd had the nerve to speak.

'BE QUIET!' Beatrice shrieked, and this time, she

did use her sword, swiping it across Laurence's shin and drawing blood. Laurence gasped in pain but kept his face determinedly neutral.

'Enough, Beatrice,' Naidos said firmly. 'Drop your weapon, now.'

Beatrice gave Naidos a resentful glare and let go of the sword in her hand.

'Perhaps it's best if I speak with Alaric privately. Take Mr Trolley and his son out of here, please and *don't* hurt them. No more blood will be unnecessarily spilt tonight,' Naidos said, casting an almost pitiful look at Pike's corpse. 'No, Beatrice, Walkul, Vido, Peter; you four best stay and help me fill in the gaps. Keep Cria here as well,' he added as everyone headed towards the door.

For a moment, Alaric saw an opportunity to escape as his security guards released him. However, before he'd even taken his first step, the room vanished before him, all was black, and he fell to the ground in a heap.

'Not so fast, Alaric,' Naidos said. 'I need to talk to you, and you have no reason to fear. This is just a chat, uncle to nephew, nothing to be afraid of.'

The blackness cleared, and once again, the room was in sight, only now Mr Trolley, Laurence and the guards were gone. He turned towards the door again hopefully, but now Beatrice, Vido and Arimon Crow all stood there guarding it. The only way out of this room now was through the smoke, which Alaric knew led to the Land of the Dead—surely even worse than this room.

'Now that we're alone, we can chat more openly,' Naidos said with another irritating smile.

Alaric, now free from restraint, climbed to his feet and charged towards Naidos, but once again, it was to no avail. He'd barely taken one step when Naidos clapped his hands, and the smoke behind him turned to rope. It launched itself at Alaric like a chameleon's tongue, coiled itself around him, and his whole body was bound as if mummified from his shoulders down.

'I gave you a chance to be trusted, and you blew it,' Naidos said.

Alaric struggled to break free from the coils, but they were stronger than anacondas, and he couldn't even move his arms a millimetre, let alone break free.

'Relax, Alaric, I'm still not going to hurt you,' Naidos sighed. 'You just need to understand.'

Alaric thinned his lips. This was ridiculous. There was nothing more to understand.

'You see, Alaric, I've not always been against Ordinaries. In fact, I, like the rest of the Guardians, was born an Ordinary so many million years ago,' Naidos went on. 'But as time progressed, as I saw what humans did to each other and to the world, I realised something had to change. Have you not noticed how Ordinaries treat this planet as their own, make everything about their own personal gain? You've seen how they kill other animals, even each other, for nothing more than pleasure. You know how the world is, how many creatures have been hunted to extinction by Ordinaries, the way they burn forests, the state of the seas. This planet cannot survive like this forever. At first, I tried to be diplomatic. I tried to explain to my brothers that we needed a solution, a control on the population. But they never liked me. I was the youngest sibling; the others never listened to me.'

Alaric opened his mouth to protest, unsure exactly what he would say, but he knew something had to be said. Yet, before he could make a noise, one of Naidos' ropes stuffed itself inside his mouth, gagging him.

'You will have your chance to speak when I'm finished, Alaric,' Naidos said gently.

Each time he spoke kindly was annoying Alaric more and more; it would've been better if he'd just screamed at him.

'Anyway, eventually, it became clear that to get my

Beatrice Bork had been Madame Sang's sister. It couldn't be true, just couldn't be. But everything did fit; it explained exactly why Annabelle Macauley, an Ordinary, was working for Naidos. She wasn't an Ordinary at all.

'Of course, we still needed to know how to tear the Veil,' Arimon said. 'I knew I was the Raven, but only Cria knew how to do it. My father told me of a place called Nun, an abyss between worlds, where he believed Cria had been trapped. He told me how your birth let off so much power, this place could've opened up. I looked up the hospital where you were born and hit the jackpot. That part of the town had been abandoned since your birth. So, I sent Beatrice and Vido there to investigate.'

'Yep, and there was Nun,' Vido said proudly.

'Of course, we weren't going into that place ourselves, so we sent in some tramp who'd been living under a bridge there,' Beatrice said. 'He found Cria, I disposed of him, and then, everything we needed was in place. We just had to extract the information from you, didn't we, Cria?' Her tone had become falsely sweet again as she gave Cria a horrible smile.

'Indeed, and then my son read Cria's mind and did what she said: cut the Veil using a knife impregnated with your blood. Your mark is on both sides of the Veil, so I can exist freely in this world now,' Naidos said.

'And once the news of his freedom gets out, those on the fence will flood to support him, and I will beat that Iglehart oaf. I will be the next Governor of Harramore, and we shall have our new world order,' Vido Sadaarm said.

Naidos nodded with a smile, seemingly now satisfied with what had been said. 'Indeed, we will, Vido. You see, Alaric, I don't want you dead at all. I want to recruit you. I want you on my side. You'd be a precious addition to my team. Just picture it. We could have a new world free from war and suffering, in which all peoples would be equal; a world free from pollution, with clean oceans and lush forests that would never be destroyed. We'd have a world where humans, cyclops, goblins, dwarves, and all other races could live in harmony. That's all I want, Alaric. I want a new world, a world worth living in.'

He paced softly towards Alaric and removed the rope from his mouth so that he could speak, smiling down at him warmly. Alaric had no idea what to say. He couldn't deny that the world he spoke of sounded tempting. He'd seen the way humans treated animals, heard what Mr Trolley said about the goblins and dwarves in Harramore. Everything could be better. But still, something wasn't right.

'My mother is an Ordinary,' he said hotly.

'We could spare her, and we could still rescue your sister. You have the medicine, don't you?' Naidos said. 'Trust me, you don't want to follow Solo and Ceus and their vision. You know what they're like, how they tore you away from your mother. It's them who are the evil ones.'

Alaric mused for a few moments. Such a world sounded so good, and if he helped create it, he'd be remembered throughout history. He grinned at the thought of the glory; he'd be the true saviour of the Earth. But still, something was off. Nothing changed the fact that the man smiling down at him had deprived him of ever knowing his father. And he couldn't trust him.

'You're lying,' Alaric said defiantly.

Naidos sighed deeply, a true sense of regret in his voice as he said his next words. 'Such a shame. In that case, you leave me no choice but to kill you.'

CHAPTER 25

EVERYTHING BECAME A blur. As soon as Alaric saw Naidos reach for the sword on the floor, the strongest flame yet ignited inside him. In one movement, he tore the ropes around him in two, and he was free. He instinctively rolled across the ground, Naidos' sword colliding with the floor behind him.

Nothing in Alaric's mind made sense anymore; not a single one of his actions was thought through. The room was too confined, and he was too outnumbered to take everyone on. He needed now more than ever for help to come. If the Veil had been lifted, maybe now Rei could come and save him again.

'It's no good, Alaric,' Naidos said coldly as though he'd read his mind. 'Your father is chained up, and the dead answer only to me.'

Then came another thunder strike, stronger this time, shaking the room so much, the table almost tipped over. But that was just a foreshock. The next noise was even louder, and also sharper, ear-splitting.

The closest thing Alaric had ever heard to it was the Kraken scream on that boat journey, but this was amplified hundreds of times.

From the smoke, what could've been thousands of people and animals, ranging in size from beetles to bulls, emerged. Only they weren't solid, but outlines made from the smoke. They were ghosts, the souls of the dead, and their opaqueness was nothing like Alaric had expected. If anything, they were only more frightening because of it.

Still, the ear-splitting noise became louder as more of the spirits emerged, shrieking as though in pain, hurting Alaric's head so much, it could tear in two at any moment. But he didn't care about that as once again, Naidos' sword came swinging down. Alaric dived aside, bouncing along the floor as the weapon crashed to the ground.

'Seize the boy!' Naidos roared, and Goblinsfoe, Arimon, Beatrice and Sadaarm all took a step inward. 'No, not the living, you keep guard. I meant the spirits!'

Alaric gave no thought to those words as he fled, not just from Naidos but the spirits as well. He knew it was pointless, that there were too many of them not to catch him, but he charged towards Arimon Crow. He still had a knife in his hand; Alaric could snatch it from him. He knew it'd be no match for a sword, but it was his only hope.

His body was now in overdrive, and Alaric leapt at Arimon, squeezing his shoulder so hard with his newfound strength that he heard the bones crack. Arimon's eyes widened, he let out a whimper, and the knife clattered to the ground. Alaric picked it up without hesitation, making Naidos cackle. Then, Alaric stopped and turned on the spot, realising he was no longer being chased.

'You really think that will work against spirits, against those already dead?' Naidos said mockingly.

Before Alaric could even process this, he could see nothing, engulfed in the spirits' smokiness. His legs gave as if he'd been hit by a bus, and he was spread-eagled on the ground. Then, Naidos' face came slowly into sight among the mist, his sword still in hand, poised for the task about to be performed.

'I give you one final chance, Alaric,' Naidos said softly, pressing the point of his blade to Alaric's throat. 'Join me or die.'

Alaric winced and said nothing. In a way, death didn't seem too bad at that moment. He could join his father, and soon Lucy would be with him in that world too. And he'd never have the extinction of the Ordinary race to his name. Slowly, he closed his eyes and readied himself.

'So be it then,' Naidos said, and he slashed the blade across Alaric's throat.

For a moment, Alaric felt nothing. Then came a slight, almost pleasant, tingling sensation around his neck. Surely this wasn't what death felt like? He'd always imagined it being a painful, fruitless struggle. Slowly, he opened his eyes and didn't believe what he saw.

Naidos was staring at his sword, as disbelieving as Alaric. The blade was on fire, melting away like ice until it was no more than a handle. For a moment, no one moved; even the smoke seemed to retreat in astonishment. Alaric ran his hand gently along the line Naidos had tried to cut. He was completely unscathed, not a drop of blood on his fingers at all.

'What the devil is this?' Naidos screamed.

Alaric couldn't explain it. It made no sense whatsoever, but it had given him belief. He jumped to his feet and pounced at Naidos with the dagger still in his hand. He was going to kill him, to escape; he could taste it now. But as he cut Naidos' throat with his own blade, the same thing happened: the whole knife melted away until he too was holding a mere handle. It was impossible.

Then, Naidos swung a fist at Alaric's gaping face, knocking him backwards onto the ground. Alaric saw Naidos come leaping towards him, hands outstretched as if about to strangle him.

There was a third thunder strike, again even louder, and this time, the table did topple. The smokiness of the spirits retreated back into the Land of the Dead, and Naidos was suspended in mid-air, the malice frozen into his face.

Two more men had entered the room. Only, they were more than men. They were Guardians whom Alaric recognised instantly. On the right was a man with a wonky, battered nose, easily eight feet tall with a brown, bushy beard. Alaric had seen his photo before. It was Ceus, and there he was, standing by the door with Solo. And Arimon, Vido, Goblinsfoe and Beatrice were now all wrapped from shoulder to toe in some sort of silvery-white string. They couldn't move, Alaric struggling to comprehend how this had all happened so quickly. He watched on, frozen to the spot as Solo waved his hand. Then, the same string that was binding the others wrapped itself around Naidos in an instant.

'You're an idiot, Naidos!' Ceus boomed. 'Ripping open the Veil like that, do you have any idea what the consequences will be? You hear that thunder? You've merged the Lands of the Living and Dead, the two worlds that must never ever be joined! The Earth is ending.'

Naidos sniggered. 'You two are such dramatists. A new world is beginning.'

'No, it isn't!' Solo snapped. 'The whole planet, the Lands of the Living and Dead are ending, ceasing to exist.'

A fourth strike came, the whole room quaking visibly. Dust fell from the ceiling and walls as if about to cave in.

Now, Alaric was even more panicked as he climbed to his feet, forgetting all the hatred he had for Ceus and Solo.

'What do we do?' he said.

'We have to restore the Veil and fast, Alaric,' Ceus said, his tone no less troubled than Alaric's. If anything, he sounded more concerned.

'How?'

Ceus sighed. 'Normally, only Cria could do such a thing. However, she's too weak.'

Alaric's breathing got heavier. 'What do we do then?'

'There is still a way, and we need you, Alaric,' Ceus said, panting.

'Alaric, I have to level with you,' Solo said, looking kindly into his eyes. 'You may not survive this; even Ceus and I might not, but if we don't do it, everyone dies.'

'Whatever it takes,' Alaric said immediately.

Thunder struck again, and small bits of rubble fell from the ceiling.

'Your bravery is admirable,' Solo said, tears visibly shining in his eyes. Alaric smiled at him, something he never thought he'd do again.

'Okay, Alaric, you're the son of Rei, a prince,' Ceus said urgently. 'This means at the right moment, you're the most powerful Nephilim there is, stronger than even some Guardians. So, the power we three have combined should be enough to do this, but there's no guarantee. Stare at the Veil. Use every ounce of your mind to picture it restored. For it to work, it'll require so much strength, I expect it'll drain us of our lives, but it's all we have.'

Alaric nodded, not even thinking about death now. He felt no fear. His life didn't matter to him anymore.

'Okay,' Ceus said, 'on three. One, two, three.'

At that moment, Alaric did as Ceus had instructed, all three of them staring hard at the Veil. Alaric screwed up his face and focussed with all his might on the wall of smoke. He pictured the physical barrier that had been there before. Then, the strongest wind he had ever felt blew at him from every single direction. His face started to burn, a pain that spread to his whole body, feeling as if every inch of his skin was being torn from his skeleton.

Alaric screamed cathartically; Ceus and Solo each did the same, louder than even the thunder had been. He could've sworn his body was on fire now, and as he concentrated even harder, the pain became only more intense. He could see a few bricks piling up by the wall, but it was still not enough. It wasn't working.

Now, two more people were in the room, Alaric not even turning to see who they were, still focussing on the Veil.

'Here, take these swords,' Mr Trolley's voice said, and he gave Ceus and Solo a weapon each.

Laurence approached Alaric, giving him a sword as well and now all five of them were staring hard at the Veil, more of the wall rebuilding itself.

Alaric, Ceus and Solo drove their blades into the ground, squeezing them as if to channel all their pain into those swords. Alaric's grip was so tight he could feel the handle bend and crush. Then, the room was filled with more people than Alaric cared to count, and they formed a crescent around the now-toppled table. As he glanced sideways, he saw Master Ogden's scarred face, Luna's dreamy expression, and several other Guardians he'd seen in Master Idoss' textbook. Sort was there but didn't look so happy, and Forto seemed to be losing his strength. Every face was sweating, screaming as the wall rebuilt itself, Alaric unsure how much more pain he could take.

They were nearly there now. Just two more feet of wall to go. But even with the pain lessening, Alaric's body was weakening.

One corner left, and it'd be done. The exhaustion was almost too much now as the last piece of wall slotted itself into place. The Raven's Veil was restored, and they'd all survived.

Alaric could've collapsed at that very instant, his legs and whole body had been weakened so much by what he'd just experienced. But there was no time for that now as an earth-shaking crash filled the room. This time, the ceiling really was caving in.

'We need to get out of here,' Ceus said urgently. 'Now!'

Alaric looked straight to the door and sprinted towards it, but as soon as he peered through it, he realised it was no good. Already, the whole ceiling in the adjacent chamber had caved in, rocks blocking the exit.

'I guess there's only one way out,' Master Ogden said. 'My favourite way! Through the ceiling!'

'What?' Alaric exclaimed. 'It's not like your office ceiling.'

'The mind, Alaric. You use that. It's how my office responds to everything I do,' Ogden said.

The crashing continued as more of the ceiling came tumbling down.

'Just trust me, Alaric,' Ogden said. 'You're one of the cleverest, most powerful boys I've ever known. You can do this.'

Alaric closed his eyes, realising he had no other choice. He grabbed Mr Trolley and Laurence each by the arm, bent his knees and jumped, fully expecting to collide with what was left of the ceiling.

But it didn't happen. Instead, Alaric felt the same strong suction he always felt when he jumped through Ogden's roof. Then, he opened his eyes, feeling the incredibly uneven rock beneath his feet. And there they were, once again, standing safely on top of Giant's Causeway.

CHAPTER 26

THE NEXT FEW moments could've lasted forever, but Alaric didn't care. He sat down on the rock for several minutes, catching his breath and staring at the rising sun. In many respects, it was a good job that Giant's Causeway was free from tourists at that hour; if any Ordinary had passed by, they would've seen the most peculiar combination of people. With a pop, each of the Guardians came sliding up through the rocks, and it was fair to say that none of them looked like normal people.

It was only standing next to other Guardians that Alaric could appreciate just how large Ceus was, Master Ogden barely reaching his elbows. Then, there was, of course, Solo, whose head was no higher than most of the other's navels. And even the regular-sized Guardians had their peculiarities.

There was one man covered from head to toe in thick, grizzly hair. It grew even from the palms of his hands and soles of his feet, and Alaric instantly recognised him as Wawet. By his side was a woman dressed in leopard print with pointed ears, who would've seemed perfectly normal were she not purring like a cat. Alaric guessed this was Jeeline.

They all waited silently and formed a circle as if about to summon a spirit as each Guardian appeared. Then came Naidos and his supporters, all still wrapped tightly in the same thin, silver string.

'Spider silk,' Solo said once the assembly was complete, smiling proudly, 'strongest stuff on the planet. They won't escape from that anytime soon.'

'That they won't,' Ceus agreed. 'We'll take them all to the Guardians' Palace. I think the events of tonight call for an emergency summit...and send out pictures of Naidos, call a televised press conference. We can't give that Iglehart an excuse to act as if Naidos isn't back. Speaking of which, could you inform the press please, Quentin?'

Master Ogden nodded. 'I'll give Norman McNulty a call now. We might even make this morning's news if we're quick.'

'Perfect,' Ceus said. 'I shall extend the invitation to Governor Iglehart to attend the summit. Alaric, Laurence, Edward, I'd be honoured if you all joined as well.'

The excitement of the invitation made Alaric and Laurence grin for the first time in hours. *Them* at a Guardians' Summit? On the same level as the Guardians and Governor of Harramore?

'I think their good friend, Lucy Ray, ought to join too,' Master Ogden said. A smile formed on his face as he turned to Alaric. 'I trust you still have the medicine?'

Alaric's heart jumped to the region of his throat as he put his hand in his pocket, relieved to feel the medicine was still there. He looked at Master Ogden and nodded, then when Ceus and Solo entered his eye line, he felt a mix of emotions. On the one hand, there was the excited urgency of saving Lucy. At the same time, his resentment towards the pair of them had come back as he thought of her, how it was their fault they'd grown up apart, how he'd been away from his mother for over fourteen years.

'Excellent,' Master Ogden said. 'Lucy used up the final batch of the old medicine last night. She should have a couple of days to live, but the sooner you get the cure to her, the better. Solo, might I suggest it'd be best if you take Alaric?'

Solo nodded, grinning gleefully. 'Of course, I'll disguise myself as a doctor. Awfully good at disguises, I am, as you'll remember, eh, Alaric? All that time, you believed I was your social worker.'

Solo chuckled, but Alaric didn't laugh back, keeping his face determinedly straight. There was an awkward silence as Solo became quiet, a sense of realisation appearing on his face.

'I see,' he said. 'You're upset with me and Ceus about your mother, aren't you?'

'You should never have separated them,' Naidos piped up.

'Zip it!' Ceus snapped.

Naidos opened his mouth to retort, but before any sound could escape, Solo clapped his hands. Then, everyone tied up had their mouths gagged with soil, Alaric unable to suppress a laugh this time.

'Perhaps it'd best if Solo and Alaric go to the hospital alone, so they can discuss all this in private?' Master Ogden suggested.

Alaric looked at Master Ogden as if he were crazy. The last thing he wanted to do right now was spend several hours alone with Solo. Laurence, however, seemed even more outraged at the idea.

'What about me?' he complained. 'Lucy's my best friend too, and I was supposed to go with Alaric before.'

'This is a private family matter,' Master Ogden said firmly. 'Now more than ever, it's important that quarrels between us are settled. If Solo doesn't discuss this with Alaric and his family, that may never happen.'

Alaric huffed. 'I want Laurence to come.' He looked at his friend and winked at him, and Laurence smiled thinly in gratitude.

'If I may say so with the greatest respect,' Mr Trolley said as if he were the chief Guardian, 'Laurence has been through as much this evening as Alaric. The pair of them came with me to infiltrate Mr Barrett's factory at great personal risk. They did this just so there was a chance they could save their friend. All three of us were kidnapped, very nearly died, even watched a man be killed. Do you not think, Quentin, that the least we can do is let Laurence visit Lucy? Let him see his friend and be a part of saving her life?'

Master Ogden sighed, musing for a few moments before responding. 'I guess so. Alaric, Laurence, you two go with Solo to the hospital. We'll have the summit when you return, if that's okay, Ceus?'

Ceus nodded. 'Everyone else, come with me to the palace. I think we could all do with a big breakfast and some nice, strong coffee.'

Alaric and Laurence watched as Mr Trolley and all the Guardians except Solo strolled along the columns. Ceus had enchanted the tied-up captives to float along behind them. Alaric had no idea how they planned to return to Harramore but had no doubt Ceus had planned a way.

'You'll want to see this, trust me,' Solo said, smiling slightly.

Alaric and Laurence followed Solo along the causeway and down a short path until they'd caught up with the others. They were all huddled around a giant rock, which Alaric thought looked like a shoe. Then, he remembered. He'd learnt about this place at school in the Main World.

'It's the Giant's Boot,' he said.

'It is indeed,' Solo said with a nod. 'And it's Northern Ireland's passage to Harramore. There's one in every country in the Main World.'

Alaric watched on as Ceus crouched and lifted the rock from the ground. He rolled it across the surface just enough for a gaping hole to appear, large enough for a man to jump into, and each one of them did so. Then, the boot slid back into place and Alaric, Laurence and Solo were alone on the shore.

'That's your father's boot,' Solo said after a few seconds of silence.

Alaric stared at Solo, unsure whether or not he was serious. 'What do you mean?' he asked.

'You know the story about Giant's Causeway. I deliberately timed one of your school moves so you'd learn about it,' Solo replied.

Alaric thought back to the lesson. It'd been five years since then, but he remembered the day as well as any other. 'A Scottish giant challenged an Irish one to a fight. So, the Irish built this Causeway, so he could get across, and they could meet. You don't mean to say that's true?'

Solo nodded, chuckling. 'Who do you think the Irish giant was?'

Alaric shook his head in disbelief. 'It can't be…but then, who was the Scottish giant?'

'Marfin,' Solo answered. 'Of course, in Irish legend, the two of them go by different names these days, and the story's evolved. It's not just Naidos who was jealous of your father's power at some point, Alaric. There was a time—a long time ago now—when Marfin wanted to usurp Rei. Marfin challenged Rei to fight for his power; he accepted and built this causeway. I don't think Rei had realised his little brother had outgrown him; as soon as he saw Marfin, he fled and destroyed the path across the sea. Marfin came round to our side about a thousand years after. He's on good terms with Ceus and myself now.'

'Did anyone else try to boot out Rei?' Laurence asked.

Solo shook his head. 'Ceus and I were slightly bitter when Rei was first chosen. We got over it pretty quickly, though. In a way, I'm glad I never had that much responsibility. If Naidos teaches me anything, it's that power may just be the most dangerous drug there is to mankind.'

He raised his hand as if waving at something in the sea. Then, a huge mast like that of a pirate ship emerged from the water's surface, approached the shore and stopped several metres from the edge.

'Here's our ride,' Solo said, and they waded over to the boat.

'Could I see your tickets please?' said the guard as they climbed on board.

'Excuse me,' Solo said with authority. 'Aren't you forgetting who I am? I'm on serious Guardian business with these boys.'

'Oh, of course, sorry,' said the guard, looking mildly embarrassed.

'Being a Guardian has its advantages,' Solo said as the three of them descended the stairs into the passenger cabin.

'I can tell,' Alaric grumbled. He deliberately kept his

tone a tad aggressive to show his bitterness towards Solo. 'Why was Marfin not here tonight?' he asked.

'He's always a dolphin these days,' Solo said. 'Moving between bodies is very tiresome. Anyway, what we all need, as Ceus said, is strong coffee and a big breakfast.'

Neither Alaric nor Laurence said anything back as they headed to the café. Everything that had happened in the last few hours was replaying in Alaric's head: how hopeful, how nervous he'd been going into the factory, oblivious to what was about to come; the kidnapping, how he'd nearly suffocated in that van, and the dream.

The dream.

The moment that he'd realised it hadn't been a dream at all but a genuine vision. Then, everything that had happened at the entrance to the Land of the Dead. He lost his appetite as the image of Pike's dead body rushed back to his mind. That poor man. He felt a twang of guilt in his stomach as he remembered how he'd been dragged into it by Mr Trolley, by them. He bit his lips to fight back the tears at the thought of it, not daring to cry in front of Solo. The last thing he wanted at that moment was questions from him.

Alaric dismissed all images of Pike from his head. The more he seemed to comfort himself, the worse he seemed to feel. But then came an even worse thought: Naidos was back. And it had been *their* fault. For the second year running, they'd strolled straight into a trap.

He glanced across the table at Laurence, who had large bags under his eyes as he ate a sausage dejectedly. He was chewing remarkably slowly by his standards, his mouthfuls much smaller like he'd lost his love of food. Alaric couldn't help but feel the same way. Really, what he needed at that moment was not a big breakfast but to sleep.

'You need to stay awake, Alaric,' Solo said as he saw him starting to doze off. 'England's really not far; you'll only feel worse after a short nap.'

Alaric grunted; knowing Solo was right made him feel even worse. Laurence didn't seem to be paying any attention, though, as he swallowed his last mouthful of food and closed his eyes.

'The same goes for you, Laurence,' Solo said firmly.

Laurence jerked awake again and let out a few unintelligible babbles. Solo ordered a round of double espressos, Alaric downing his with a wince. He felt no more awake due to having done so but found himself in a tired state of insomnia as the boat pulled up by the English shore.

'Right, the plan,' Solo said as they reached a car

park. 'I pretend to be a doctor and give Lucy the medicine. You two should be allowed in anyway; they're expecting visitors, but they won't like it if you give her unauthorised medicines since you're not qualified.'

Alaric and Laurence nodded. Adrenaline started to pump through Alaric again as he thought about saving Lucy. Straight after, he felt his heart drop to his stomach as a dreadful thought crossed his mind: what if they were too late?

When they arrived, Alaric's legs felt leaden once more, fearing what he was about to see as he and Laurence kitted up and hurried to Lucy's bedside.

Alaric sighed with relief when they got there; she didn't seem anywhere near as well as she had the last time they'd seen her, but her chest was still moving up and down as she breathed. Her face had drained of all colour, covered in a cold-looking sweat as she slept. Mrs Ray was by her bedside, looking tired and anxious, a nurse standing guard by the door.

'Where have you been?' Mrs Ray said weakly. 'I was expecting you yesterday evening.'

'It's a long story,' Alaric replied dismissively. He broke into a whisper to avoid being heard by the nurse. 'Solo—Mr Solomon—is on the way. We've got the cure for Lucy.'

Mrs Ray placed her hand on her chest, looking from Alaric to Laurence and then back again, her jaw dropping several inches. 'Are you sure?' she asked.

Alaric nodded. 'It's what they used to cure everyone on Harramore. We had to steal some from the factory. Then, well, it didn't all go to plan, but we have the medicine.'

'Good grief,' Mrs Ray said, her breathing audibly speeding up. 'Well, I'm glad you're both all right. You should've told me. My husband and I have been worried sick.'

Alaric and Laurence smiled slightly as Solo came into sight, dressed for the first time Alaric had ever seen, in a suit. The trousers concealed his shoes completely, the sleeves of the jacket over his fingertips. Yet, even wearing such attire, he still sported his usual red, cone-shaped hat.

'Thank you, madame, I'll take care of Miss Ray now,' he said to the nurse in the room, barging past her. She stared at him in wide-eyed indignance, as if expecting an apology, but then her expression changed to one of alarm.

'Who might you be?' she demanded.

'Doctor Solomon,' Solo said. 'Specialist in rare diseases. They sent me here urgently from Dromkoping

Hospital in Sweden to check on Miss Ray. I have a new medicine they'd like me to try. I thought they'd have told you?'

Alaric couldn't explain what it was, but something about the way Solo had said all of this was so convincing. In fact, he almost forgot he'd been lying as the nurse looked mildly embarrassed.

'Oh, so sorry,' she said. 'I'll leave you to it then.'

She turned on her heel and strode off down the corridor, the remaining people in the room waiting until she was definitely out of earshot before Solo broke the silence.

'We best wake her up and give her this before they realise there's no Dromkoping in Sweden,' he said.

Alaric nodded as he and Laurence stood at either side of Lucy's bed, each shaking a shoulder to wake her up. Alaric's heart skipped a beat as she stirred, gave a feeble groan, and slowly opened her eyes.

'Oh, hi guys,' she murmured. She flailed her arm at Laurence flimsily as if trying to hug him, but she missed and ended up slapping him around the face.

'We have the cure,' Alaric said.

Lucy sat up in her bed at these words, a new liveliness seeming to have overcome her. Mrs Ray strode over to the bathroom to get a glass of water as she saw

Alaric pull a box of pills from his pocket. He read the instructions and popped two out of the packet, which he gave to Lucy, her hand feeling as sweaty as her face.

'Okay, darling?' Mrs Ray said as she returned.

Lucy nodded, putting the pills into her mouth. Mrs Ray tilted the glass for her to sip, and she swallowed them with a mouthful of water.

'She could probably do with some rest,' Mrs Ray said to Alaric and Laurence, 'and you two look like you could too. Lucy's dad will be here to swap with me shortly, and you can come home and get some sleep.'

Alaric nodded as Lucy put her head back on the pillow and closed her eyes again. Mrs Ray's offer was most welcome. It felt like days since they'd last slept properly. Even with thoughts about Lucy circling their heads, they dozed the whole day away, waking up in the evening to hear she'd taken a turn for the better.

When they visited her after supper, she was sitting up in her bed, some colour in her cheeks now. In fact, she didn't look far from her usual self at all. She was so much better that Alaric, Lucy and Laurence were allowed some time alone together, and Alaric and Laurence recounted the events since the basketball final.

'You did all that for me?' Lucy sobbed as they finished their story, tears running down her cheeks. She pulled both of them into the tightest hug she ever had, Alaric almost relieved when she let go, so he could breathe again. 'I love you guys,' she said.

Laurence blushed as Alaric smiled back at her, and now, everything they'd been through seemed worth it to save Lucy. Pike's death, Naidos' return—it almost no longer mattered to Alaric as the three of them sat in silent reflection.

'They're having a Guardians' Summit when we get back,' Alaric said. 'We're all invited to be there. It's about Naidos' return.'

'Why are we invited, do you think?' Lucy sniffled.

'I dunno,' Alaric said, shrugging. 'Laurence's dad will be there too. I guess they want us to give a witness account or something.'

'Nah, I reckon it's bigger than that, mate,' Laurence said with a shake of the head. 'I think there's gonna be a plan to fight Naidos, and we're part of it.'

Alaric shuddered. He'd had enough trouble in his life as it was, and the last thing he wanted to think about was leading a war.

'I think Laurence may be right,' Lucy said. 'If your birth stopped Naidos, I expect there might be something more to it. Maybe it has to be you to stop him, and whatever that means, we'll stand by your side.'

'Sure we will,' Laurence agreed.

Alaric looked down at the ground in silence. It felt like too much to swallow.

'If it means putting yourselves in danger, I don't want that,' he said. 'Pike already died because of me. I don't want more.'

Laurence shook his head. 'If you think Pike dying was your fault, you're wrong. My dad and I came with you, planned that whole thing and agreed to get involved. It's not anyone's fault except Beatrice's.'

'And I mean, it was all to save me in the end,' Lucy said. 'It was so brave of both of you. If anything, all this is my fault. If you'd let me die, none of this would've happened.'

'Are you saying we shouldn't've saved you?' Laurence asked, almost shouting. 'Because if you think we'd just sit back and let you die like that, our best friend, what do you even take us for?'

'Boys!' said a voice from behind Alaric. He turned to see the sharp-faced nurse standing there, her lips thin. Laurence had inadvertently raised his voice too much and attracted her attention. 'The patient needs rest. I think it's best if you two leave now.'

'No, I don't mind them staying, honestly,' Lucy said quickly.

'No, you need rest, dear girl. Now out, you two. Go. Quick,' the nurse said.

The way she spoke told Alaric there'd be no point in arguing with her. So, he and Laurence sighed, gave Lucy another hug and left her behind for the night.

CHAPTER 27

LUCY WAS DISCHARGED from hospital the next morning. She, Alaric, and Laurence had lunch with her parents, the mood more upbeat than it had been for weeks as they ploughed their way through mountains of pizza and cake. Even with only five of them there, it felt more like a party than if there'd been hundreds of guests, none of them wanting the meal to end.

They chatted throughout the day, even all huddling around Lucy's bed as she packed her bag for the last few days of term. This continued right up until teatime, when there was a knock on the front door, startling them so much that Mr Ray spilt tea down his shirt.

'Who could it be at this time?' Mrs Ray said. She rose from her chair and started towards the front door.

Mr Ray, Alaric, Lucy and Laurence turned their heads towards Mrs Ray, watching as she pulled the door open. Her shoulders slumped in disappointment as she saw Solo standing on the other side, dressed once again like a garden gnome.

'Oh, it's you,' she mumbled. 'What d'you want?'

'I think if I could have a word with you, Lucy and Alaric, that'd be a good idea,' Solo replied.

Mrs Ray sighed. 'Well, we're just having tea, so this really isn't the best time,' she said bitterly.

'I don't mind, Mum,' Lucy called.

Mrs Ray sighed again. 'Well, how does Alaric feel? Is it okay with him?'

Alaric shrugged. 'I guess so,' he said.

Deep down, he knew the conversation was needed but, just like Lucy and Mrs Ray, was disappointed to be pulled away from the kitchen. He was still bitter towards Solo, even if he had helped save Lucy's life. Together, they headed into the living room, leaving Mr Ray alone with Laurence, trying to explain the rules of rugby.

'How can the ball be shaped like an egg?' Laurence asked. 'Balls are meant to be round.'

Alaric chuckled as they sat down on the squashy sofas in the living room with their drinks. Mrs Ray seemed to have decided not to offer Solo one.

'Now, I know a lot happened over the winter when Alaric came here,' Solo began, 'and I think we need to chat about everything.'

The silence that followed seemed to last forever, all of them too lost for words to know what to say.

'Just why?' Alaric said weakly with a shake of the head.

'We wanted to keep you safe for the good of the world, Alaric,' Solo said, sighing. 'Really, I didn't want you to have the childhood you did, but it was necessary. Harramore was too unstable for you to live safely there, and with more of Naidos' supporters fleeing to the Main World, there was always a chance they'd find you. So, we felt we had to move you around until it was safe for you to come here.'

Alaric didn't respond, just staring rigidly at Solo. Even if a small part of him understood, none of him was ever going to completely forgive Solo and Ceus for this. He couldn't not resent the childhood he never had.

'Were you going to tell us we were brother and sister?' Lucy said, her tone more disappointed than angry.

Solo let out another sigh. 'I don't know. We always knew we'd have to tell you at some point, that you had the right to know, but I have no idea when. I suppose there was always going to be a moment.'

'Is that it? Did you think we'd never find out? Were you that stupid?' Alaric said, sensing his tone become more aggressive.

Solo shook his head, shuffling uncomfortably in his seat. 'I don't know what we thought…I'm sorry.'

'Just get out,' Mrs Ray snarled.

Solo's face twitched as he leant forward, wringing his hands. 'Unfortunately, there's something else I needed to discuss with Alaric alone first. He can feedback to Lucy and Laurence if he wishes, and in fact, I suggest he does so.'

'Are we ever going to be able to just finish our tea in peace?' Mrs Ray said, rolling her eyes.

'We'll see how long this takes,' Solo answered calmly, and Lucy and Mrs Ray rose from the sofa and traipsed out of the living room.

Alaric remained seated, crossing his arms impatiently as Solo shut the door.

'I'm guessing you've been wondering why you're invited to the Guardians' Summit?' Solo asked.

Alaric shrugged. 'I'd just assumed it was because I saw Naidos come back, but Lucy and Laurence think it's something bigger.'

Solo smiled, retaking a seat. 'Lucy and Laurence are right,' he said. 'Ceus and I saw some of what unfolded between you and Naidos. Tell me, what happened when he tried to cut you with that sword?'

Alaric's eyes widened as he remembered that moment. So much had happened over the last couple of days that it had seemed like a small detail among everything, as clearly as he could recall it. Yet, when he gave it some thought, it was the strangest thing to happen all night.

'The sword, it just…melted. It sounds crazy, I know, but—'

'Don't worry, Alaric,' Solo interrupted. 'We saw, and really, we weren't surprised. It actually confirmed what we thought we already knew.'

'W-what do you mean?' Alaric asked.

Solo stared hard into Alaric's eyes. 'You know what they call you, Alaric, don't you? The name they give you because you're the son of the King Guardian, what your birth did?'

Alaric looked back at Solo blankly. 'You mean that I'm a prince?' he said, struggling to see how this was all connected.

Solo nodded. 'The Miracle Prince. And when you're a prince, Alaric, that often means that you're so much more than just a king or queen's son. You, Alaric, are Rei's last immediate child; that would normally make you the heir to the throne.'

Alaric opened his mouth, freezing as he sat motionless, trying to take this in. 'Does this mean then, that I'm a Guardian?'

Solo screwed up his face as if trying to work out exactly how to respond. 'Not quite,' he said. Alaric felt somewhat relieved, unsure he wanted such a level of responsibility. 'The trouble is, there are two ways traditionally that people become a king or queen: the first is being a natural heir to the throne, like you; the second is that they usurp the incumbent, by which I mean, kill the current king or queen, like Naidos did.'

Alaric shuddered, an iciness running down his whole body as he took this in, not wanting to say the next thing on his mind, not wanting it to be true. But he had to, knowing if he didn't ask Solo, he'd regret not having the certainty.

'Does this mean that Naidos is the King Guardian then? I mean, he killed my dad before I was born?'

Solo sucked in some air through his front teeth, making Alaric dread whatever he was about to say even more. 'This is where it gets tricky, but the short answer is no.' Alaric breathed a sigh of relief, but his uneasiness was restored as soon as Solo started speaking again. 'When Naidos killed Rei, you weren't yet born, but you still existed inside your mother. Your presence in this world then was strong enough to block Naidos from a clear path to power. As it stands, the throne is empty. That is until one of you two kills the other or accepts their claim to the throne. That, Naidos knows.'

Alaric gulped, these words having lodged themselves sharply in his throat. It almost didn't feel real. That was it. His whole purpose was to kill a Guardian, a being far more powerful than him, or to let him wipe out the human race. He didn't know what to say but had no intention of breaking down in front of Solo, keeping his expression determinedly neutral. However, one thought wouldn't leave his mind.

'He tried to get me to join forces with him. You know, before he tried to kill me,' he said. 'Does that mean he would've accepted me as king?'

Solo squinted, his glabella narrowing like he didn't believe what Alaric had said. 'I doubt it,' he replied. 'He probably would've had it the other way round, knowing him. You'd be an asset to his cause, though. If the son of Rei came and told the whole of Harramore to support Naidos, undoubtedly most would; even a lot of the Guardians would listen to you, I think.'

Alaric took a deep breath, struggling to take this all in. 'I couldn't ever accept him in power,' he said, 'but why did the blades melt when we tried to kill each other?'

'I'm glad to hear it,' Solo said with a smile. 'And the weapons, well, that comes down to two laws. The first one, Naidos knows and better than any other Guardian. We're all immortal, so you can't defeat us through regular means. I'm afraid there is only one way to kill a Guardian. Rei created a weapon and, to keep it a secret, didn't even tell any of us. So, to this day, no one knows what or where it is.'

'So, how did Naidos find out how to kill my dad?' Alaric asked.

Solo shrugged. 'It's a mystery. That's the issue we have, you see. If Rei knew all this time how to kill Naidos, why he never told anyone, I don't understand. He must've had a reason. All we know is that the only one who can kill Naidos is you.'

'But why couldn't he kill me?' Alaric asked. 'I mean, you said I'm not a Guardian.'

Solo smiled. 'That's the other law. Naidos doesn't understand this one quite so well, and he was fooled for the second time. You see, as your uncle, Naidos has a duty of care to you until you come of age when you're sixteen. Until that point, you are protected from him by this law.'

Alaric felt only slightly relieved. That gave him just over a year before he lost his protection from Naidos. It'd been longer since he first came to Harramore.

'So, when I reach sixteen, I'm no longer protected. I

should get Naidos before then?' he asked.

'Yes and no,' Solo replied. 'You will lose the protection, but no, I wouldn't expect you to defeat Naidos before then. In fact, it could take so long to prepare yourself to do so, I'd be amazed if you did. It's likely to be so difficult, you'll need Laurence and Lucy to help you, hence why they're invited to the Summit.'

Alaric nodded. It was too much information to take in at once. He had no idea what to say, nor did he particularly want to speak at that moment. Apparently sensing this, Solo stood up and started towards the living room door.

'I trust all is well for your return to Harramore tomorrow? We'll have the Summit then?' he asked just before he stepped out of the room.

Alaric nodded, and with that, Solo disappeared out of sight. Then, Alaric heard the front door open and shut again, telling him he'd left the house.

CHAPTER 28

Alaric, Lucy and Laurence returned to Harramore in the morning. Mr Trolley was already waiting to meet them, dressed in his best suit and tie, standing by his car. He still appeared slightly off-colour from the events of Monday. His face was paler than usual, and the swelling under his eye still partially there, but he wore a smile as he greeted the three of them.

'We're going straight to the Guardians' Palace,' he said. 'The Summit can't wait any longer; Iglehart's already there.'

Alaric thinned his lips as they climbed into the car. Even the sound of Iglehart's name made him feel bitter.

'We'll sort this Governor out, don't worry,' Mr Trolley said reassuringly. 'He does not know what's about to come his way.'

Alaric smiled thinly as Mr Trolley started to drive. The palace was just half an hour away, Ceus and Solo already waiting outside its magnificent, jewelled doors. They invited them inside, escorting them down the marble hallway and through a doorway on the left-hand side.

Then, as they entered the room on the other side of the arch, the sound of tumultuous applause filled Alaric's ears. Around a dozen people, all of whom Alaric recognised as Guardians, stood in a horseshoe, clapping them as they entered this room, this chamber. Several rows of high-rise leather seats extended to the back wall, circling the round, marble floor. Alaric thought it looked like a stage, this room some sort of indoor colosseum, almost a courtroom.

His skin started to tingle, his legs seeming to have turned to trifle. Although only a dozen people were applauding him, the fact they were Guardians made him more emotionally charged than ahead of basketball games.

'Thank you, thank you,' Ceus called, silencing the applause. 'If you four would like to take a seat, we'll get started.'

Alaric, Lucy and Laurence, feeling rather out of place, followed Mr Trolley to the nearest empty spot on the front benches. All four of them shuffled nervously in their seats, Alaric wincing as he glimpsed Hal Iglehart among the crowd. His arms and legs were folded as if he didn't want to be there, like something could be more important than this meeting.

'Good morning, Honourable Guardians of the Chamber, Governor of Harramore, our honoured guests,' Ceus boomed from the stage. 'We meet here today to discuss the return of Naidos and our path to peace.'

'Please, Guardian Ceus, might I raise a point of order?' said a small voice to Alaric's right. He turned his head to see a frizzy-haired woman with square glasses and protruding front teeth had risen from her seat. He recognised her instantly as Seeba.

'Please, do go ahead,' Ceus said, waving his hand towards Seeba and taking a seat.

'How can we have a proper discussion about this matter without Naidos here? To have an open negotiation, should all sides not be welcome to put forth their point of view, even Naidos and his supporters? How can we really hope to avoid a war if we don't invite them to speak?' Seeba asked, taking a seat once she'd finished speaking.

Ceus rose from his chair and strode to the centre of the stage to respond. 'Thank you, Seeba, for asking this. As you know, we did, on many occasions during the first war, try to make peace with Naidos, and he showed no interest in such a proposition.'

'But to have an exclusive meeting like this,' the dreamy-faced Luna said from the back row, 'it makes it look like we're making the first move towards war.'

There was a collective murmur of agreement from a few of the Guardians as Ceus scowled, staring at the source of disruption intimidatingly.

'Only speak if called to speak,' he shouted so loudly, the room seemed to shake. Alaric shuddered.

'To be fair, Ceus, not even everyone on our side is here. Neutrals like Paz could've been invited, as could've Guerris for that matter,' Solo chimed in.

Ceus blinked slowly, breathing heavily as if to suppress another outburst of anger. 'They refused the invitation, Solo,' he said.

'Only because you didn't invite Naidos and Orm,' Seeba muttered.

'SILENCE!' Ceus thundered, Alaric shuddering again. Already, he wanted to leave; he couldn't recall a place ever making him more uncomfortable than Madame Sang's classroom. 'This is a Summit. We discuss matters in an orderly fashion.'

This time, no one dared question Ceus and talk over him, his authority in the room unwavering as he spoke again. 'We are joined here today by Rei's son himself, Mr Alaric Swift.' There was a small mutter of approval, no one daring to cheer or applaud this time. 'As many of you know,' Ceus went on, 'it is Alaric, and only Alaric, who can defeat Naidos. He is, if you like, our one true hope, our leader.'

Alaric felt his cheeks go hot as Ceus said this, all eyes in the room turning their attention to him. For a moment, he sat awkwardly until Ceus continued talking, the focus of the room returning to him.

'But Alaric cannot do this alone. If we are to win this war, we need an army. We need as many of the people of Harramore on our side as possible. Over the coming months, we must rally our descendants, build a following, and Mr Iglehart, your support on the matter will be pivotal.'

'I'm sorry, Ceus,' Seeba interrupted, 'but I highly doubt the people of Harramore will want another war, not after all those years of conflict.'

'No one ever wants a war, Seeba,' Ceus said coldly.

'Guardians, if I may,' Mr Trolley called out. He rose from his seat, startling Alaric, Lucy and Laurence. They hadn't expected any of the regular Nephilim to have the audacity to speak over the Guardians. 'I agree that war is looking highly likely, if not inevitable. Supporters of Naidos have over the last year been increasingly vocal, which I must say, you never exactly helped, Mr Iglehart.'

The Governor's cheeks flushed a deep pink as he scowled at Mr Trolley, not saying anything. Clearly, something about the atmosphere of this room was making him just as uneasy as Alaric felt.

'However, if there is any chance of us avoiding a war, I believe it is our duty to at the very least try,' Mr Trolley continued. 'To do so, we must convince Naidos and his supporters that a palatable compromise is possible. We need to create unity on Harramore, and this is where you come in, Mr Iglehart, your chance to be viewed as a hero. We must look to those who supported Naidos in the first war and seek peace with them. Mr Iglehart, the first thing you must do is win the next election, then reach out to the goblins and dwarves.'

'That's preposterous!' Iglehart snapped. He was so outraged at the idea, he'd risen out of his seat and taken a step across the stage. 'If I'm seen to be associating with these sub-humans, imagine what that'll do for my reputation.'

'I agree with Mr Trolley,' Master Ogden said from among the crowd.

Ceus tightened his face again but didn't snap at anyone this time. It was as if he knew his authority had dwindled, and the meeting had become a free-for-all as

Ogden continued speaking.

'And please, Hal, do not use the term "sub-humans". It implies inferiority, and trust me when I say they are not lesser than us. We must reach out to them as soon as we can, make peace before it's too late.'

'I have to say, Hal, that the more support we have, the better. It's time to put our differences aside,' Ceus agreed, his tone much calmer than Alaric would've expected.

'Absolutely!' Solo called out. 'If people with a clean history were to head over to meet the goblins and the dwarves, I think that'd be best. Perhaps this summer, Alaric, Lucy, Laurence, you could all go over and speak with them. Quentin, it'd be good for you to go with them; of all the Guardians, you have the best record when it comes to the rights of, excuse the term, sub-humans.'

'Indeed,' Master Ogden said, looking slightly miffed by Solo's use of the term. 'We'll make a strong delegation, I think. But, Mr Trolley, it'd be good to have someone from the government; you should come too.' Ogden turned to the four of them and winked with a friendly smile.

'Of course,' Mr Trolley said.

Alaric felt a weighty pressure drop onto his shoulders. He'd never expected to carry so much responsibility in his life. He turned to look at Lucy and Laurence, Lucy sitting up straight, her expression like iron as Laurence grinned.

'We should reach out to Marfin too,' Solo said very seriously. 'Naidos will want to capitalise on the state of the seas at the moment to recruit him, especially since he was the least invested of our supporters last time.'

'Absolutely,' Ceus agreed, 'you and I should get on that straight away.'

'Excuse me!' Iglehart said indignantly. 'Are you not forgetting who's in charge of Harramore at the moment? I refuse to associate with those savages! In fact, I forbid you from going as a delegation.'

Alaric shuddered, not daring to speak. To him, it seemed best if Mr Trolley and Master Ogden did all the talking.

'You don't have the power to do that, Hal. You are not the police like you seem to think you are,' Mr Trolley said firmly. 'And I think that if you actually took some time to get to know the dwarves and goblins, you'd realise they're actually rather like us.'

Iglehart scoffed, spraying spit in all directions. 'We do not associate with these creatures, and my word on that is final.'

Mr Trolley sighed, and to the astonishment of the room, started towards the exit. 'Very well then,' he said. 'Quentin, you and I shall go with Alaric, Lucy and Laurence to greet the goblins and dwarves this summer. I trust you three are okay with that?' he asked, turning towards the teenagers.

Alaric bowed his head as Lucy and Laurence nodded with more enthusiasm. As nervously sick as the responsibility made Alaric feel, there was undeniably something exciting about the idea. Besides, after the last two years, he could hardly meet anything more dangerous than he already had.

'As for you not associating with the, I quote, "savages", you have left me no choice,' Mr Trolley went on. 'This is something I never once in my life thought I would do, but Harramore needs it. If you are allowed to govern, the island faces another long, deadly war. On the other hand, if Vido Sadaarm wins, supporters of Naidos will control Harramore completely. I must, therefore, offer a third option, a chance for unity. Ceus, Solo, I wish to stand in the election. I want to be the next Governor of Harramore.'

There was a stunned murmur around the room, Iglehart looking livid with Mr Trolley, his whole face scarlet. A few of the Guardians were grinning, not daring to applaud.

'Very well then,' Ceus said. 'Your name shall be added to the ballot papers. Unless anyone else has something particularly pressing to say, I think we can conclude this meeting.'

Silence greeted these words, and after several seconds, there was a shuffling as everyone in the room stood up and started towards the exit.

'May the best man win, Hal,' Mr Trolley said without a hint of a smile. 'I best get these three to Oakwood for the end of term.'

'ARE YOU REALLY going to do this, Dad?' Laurence asked excitedly. 'Are you actually going to be the Governor of Harramore?'

'I certainly hope so,' Mr Trolley said with the widest grin Alaric had ever seen on his face. 'With Iglehart unpopular and Sadaarm so openly supportive of Naidos, I'd say my chances are pretty strong. It'll give supporters of Ali Chandyo a viable option, I hope.'

There was a tremendous buzz in the car as they drove back to Oakwood for the end of the school year. None of them could quite believe that Mr Trolley was really going to take on Iglehart.

'You won't end up like Chandyo, will you?' Lucy

asked concernedly.

Mr Trolley shook his head. 'No, don't worry about that. Chandyo was an old man, much frailer than me. All will be fine.'

Alaric bit his lip. As exciting as this seemed to him, now Lucy had said it, he couldn't dismiss the danger Mr Trolley had put himself in from his mind. It had been tough enough going through the last few weeks with Lucy in hospital.

Indeed, the announcement of Mr Trolley's campaign was officially announced later that day and had spread around Oakwood before the next. This, combined with the news of Naidos' return and what had happened at the Land of the Dead, meant that Alaric, Lucy and Laurence were the celebrities they'd been the previous year. Naturally, everyone—staff and students—was eager to hear their account of recent events.

Nevertheless, there was not the same excitement there had been last year. In fact, when, over lunch, Alaric recounted what had happened, no one seemed to know how to respond, remaining silent.

'Naidos is really back?' Trevor asked weakly.

Alaric nodded, unable to say more. A lump formed in his throat each time he told the story, feeling larger with each retelling. As the closing moments of term had gone on, he'd felt worse and worse; the only way to comfort himself was thinking of how he'd saved Lucy. He looked up at the faces surrounding him, all of them as glum as each other. The only smiles in sight were those of Franco and Dwayne, who'd been listening in from a distance. Alaric forced himself to ignore them as he sensed Madame Ettoga and Master Idoss approaching.

'Well, I'm glad my woppanine came in useful,' Ettoga said with a small smile. 'It's lovely to see you all back again, especially Lucy. We really didn't think you'd make it.'

'Indeed,' Idoss said. 'The worst bit, Lucy, is you missed the basketball final. You'd have loved to have been there, seen how well they all played.'

Alaric grinned, grateful Idoss had changed the subject. So much had happened since the match, the memory had been brushed under the carpet in the grand scheme of things. He'd not had a proper chance to enjoy the win, and now it felt even better with Franco and Dwayne in earshot.

'They won by ninety-four points,' Carlos told Lucy enthusiastically. 'You should've seen it; some of Alaric's baskets were out of this world. Franco and Dwayne, though…I don't know what they were doing.'

Alaric chuckled shallowly. Carlos had spoken so loudly that Franco and Dwayne had heard, the smiles now wiped from their faces. They discussed the match for the rest of the lunch hour. By the end of it, Alaric felt as carefree as he had in weeks, momentarily forgetting everything that had happened. However, as all the students filed off to their final lessons of the year, a strange sadness overcame him once more. He looked up at Lucy and Laurence as they prepared to follow the other students to class and forced a small smile.

'Something's bothering you, isn't it?' Lucy said, seeming as uneasy as him.

Alaric nodded. 'You heard what Ceus said? About how only I can defeat Naidos?'

'It's exactly what we thought,' Lucy stated.

'We'll help you,' Laurence said.

'Too right, we will,' Lucy agreed.

Alaric shook his head. 'I don't know what's going to happen. I have no idea how dangerous it'll be, but what I have to do this summer will just be the start. I don't want you risking your lives for me.'

Lucy snorted a laugh. 'You really think you could do this alone? After the last two years, none of us would be alive if we hadn't all been in it together.'

'Lucy's right, mate,' Laurence said. 'You need us.'

Alaric smiled slightly. Deep down, he knew they were right, and he appreciated their support. But, as memories of Pike came to his mind, how close they'd all come to death, he shuddered, feeling sick.

'Look, Alaric,' Lucy said, 'you risked your lives to save me this year. So, of course, I'll do the same for you.'

'We're doing this together, mate, like it or not,' Laurence agreed.

Alaric shook his head wryly and said no more. He knew there was no persuading them otherwise, and in truth, he'd welcome their company. The swordsmanship area was in sight now, and their conversation came to a close. As usual for the last day of term, the lessons were reduced to nothing more than chatter. When the day finally ended, Alaric was unsure how he felt ahead of what awaited them in the summer. As he saw the other Trolleys, a ball of sadness formed inside him. With their quest to meet the goblins and dwarves coming up, Alaric was unsure just how much time he'd have left to properly enjoy with them for a while. There was, however, one thing that was for sure: he was determined to make the most of the moments he did have.

Thank you for reading

First of all, thank you very much for purchasing and reading this book. I know you could have picked any novel to read, but you chose this one. For that, I am extremely grateful.

If you enjoyed reading, it would be really nice if you could share it with friends and family. I'd also love to hear from you, and it would be great if you could take some time to post a review on Amazon. Any feedback will encourage other readers to buy the books and help me develop my writing for the future.

And finally, if you would like to know more about me and my books or the series, don't forget to visit my website at williamedmonds.com and join the Readers Club!

Once again, I hope you enjoyed reading, and thank you for your support!
William Edmonds

If you'd like to know more about William Edmonds and 'The Miracle Prince' series, please visit his website at williamedmonds.com. And if you'd like to receive exclusive content and updates on future releases, join the William Edmonds Readers Club!

Printed in Great Britain
by Amazon